More praise for *Blind Run*

"The nerve-shattering beginning draws the reader immediately into this book. What follows is a thriller lover's dream of white-knuckle action. It is also the story of a man's redemption, a love re-kindled, and a chance for vengeance. Ms. Lewin is an author whose star is on the rise."

—*Rendezvous*

"Lewin's taut thriller is filled with hair-raising car chases and complex double crosses . . . spunky children and fast-paced action."

—*Booklist*

"[A] fast pace [and] abundant action."

—*Publishers Weekly*

BLIND RUN

Patricia Lewin

BALLANTINE BOOKS • NEW YORK

In memory of my mother,
Eileen Broeker Van Wie,
who always loved a good book and
would have gotten a kick out of showing
this one off to her friends.
We all love you and miss you, Mom.

A Ballantine Book
Published by The Random House Publishing Group

This book contains an excerpt from *Out of Reach* by Patricia Lewin, published by Ballantine Books.

www.ballantinebooks.com

ISBN 0-345-44323-3

Manufactured in the United States of America

First Hardcover Edition: April 2003
First Mass Market Edition: January 2004

OPM 10 9 8 7 6 5 4 3 2 1

ACKNOWLEDGMENTS

This book has been a voyage of discovery about the craft, about publishing, and about myself as a working author. I could not have completed the journey, or even begun, without the help and support of so many people.

Thanks to Sandra Chastain and Deborah Smith, for grabbing onto my kernel of an idea and making me run with it; Jill Jones, who worked with me (reading and rereading) through the process; Gin Ellis, Illona Haus, Karen Hawkins, Ann Howard White, Pam Mantovani, Jim Paulson, Robert Schwaninger, Donna Sterling, and Rachelle Wadsworth, who read the early draft(s).

And to those who gave of their technical expertise, answering my endless email queries and telephone calls. Sharon Reishus, for her insight into the CIA, which included telling me when I was making stuff up. Jonathon M. Sullivan, M.D., Ph.D., and Edward R. White, M.D., J.D., for reading my medical scenarios and answering my numerous questions. And Laurie Miller, R.N., for educating me on the workings of an emergency room. Tom Peace, Garrison Atkisson, and Paul Golick for their ideas on computer hacking. Berta Platas, who acted as my Spanish dictionary.

And to those who helped with my various locales: Marian May (Texas), Mimi Moore (New Mexico), and Pat McLaughlin (Chicago).

All mistakes (or literary license) are mine.

Thanks also to my husband, Jeff, for his endless patience; my daughter, Andrea, for being my biggest fan; my agent, Meg Ruley, for never giving up; and Shauna Summers, for taking my story and making it into a book.

CHAPTER ONE

Ethan Decker welcomed the pain.

It rolled through him like waves of heat rippling across the desert floor. With eyes closed and head propped against the door behind him, he sat on the trailer's flimsy aluminum steps and waited for the desolate landscape to stop spinning. Given time, the desert would succeed where his enemies had failed. It *would* kill him.

But not, unfortunately, today.

Last night had been a mistake, an attempt to blot out the date and its memories with a bottle of Jack Daniel's. It hadn't worked. The throbbing within his skull had become a dark angel crouched upon his shoulder, prodding and laughing, reminding him he was still alive.

The heat pressed in, and he longed for the feel of a crisp ocean breeze against his face, or the pungent scent of pines in the mountain air. Instead, beneath the tattered green-and-white awning that stretched from the tin can he called home, he felt the dry, hot hand of the New Mexico desert. If the pain had become his angel, then the desert heat had become his unwelcome lover, wrapping herself around him with tight, searing arms.

And he deserved no better. Three years ago yesterday, his five-year-old son had died. Murdered. And nothing, not the Jack Daniel's, nor the desert could change Ethan's role in that senseless death.

He opened his eyes and squinted at the sun. It sat

hours above the western horizon, a flat white disk piercing a dusty sky. With shaky hands he lifted a cup of lukewarm coffee to his lips and forced the bitter liquid down his throat. He should eat something, too, but he couldn't bring himself to go back inside the stifling trailer. Just the thought brought a fresh wave of nausea. He'd get something later, before heading out into the desert.

Or maybe he wouldn't go tonight. How hard could it be, just this once? He'd stretch out on the desert floor, beneath a million pinpricks of heavenly light and sleep.

Ethan shuddered and downed more coffee.

He wasn't fooling himself. He couldn't escape into sleep, any more than he could hide in a bottle of Jack Daniel's. Sleep brought the faces. They haunted his dreams with painful accusations in their small, frightened eyes. Children's eyes. They stared at him, asking their unanswerable questions, condemning him without speaking a word. No, he couldn't stay here tonight and sleep like normal men. He'd given up that right with Nicky's death.

As usual, he'd seek oblivion through the ritual that had ruled his nights for the past three years. From sunset until dawn he'd perform the moving meditation of tai chi. The practice promised balance where none existed and peace where none reigned.

So far he'd found neither. The intense regimen brought only fatigue, a physical exhaustion so complete he'd fall into a heavy dreamless slumber.

In the distance, a ribbon of dust rose from the direction of the road, drawing his thoughts from the nightmare of his life. He was about to have company. The approaching vehicle was still three or four miles away, but Ethan had no doubt about its destination. The poor excuse for a road led one place. Here.

The question of who would seek him out only vaguely interested him. None of the locals would come looking for him. He rarely went into town except to get supplies, and then he kept to himself. But there were hours last night he couldn't account for, time when the Jack Daniel's had ruled his actions.

He tried remembering what he'd done, or if he'd spoken to anyone. He'd gotten into town about nine and ordered something to eat, washing down the food with a couple or three beers. Then it had been straight Jack, and his memory blurred. The next thing he knew, he'd awakened in his own bed with the full force of the New Mexico sun beating on his face.

The dust cloud grew as the vehicle got closer.

If someone had gone to the effort of driving out here, it meant trouble. He thought of the Glock, buried under three years of pictures and regrets within an old metal box beneath his bed. In a few minutes it would be too late, but he made no move to retrieve the weapon. If the Agency had finally found him, then so be it.

He'd been dead for a long time anyway.

Dr. Paul Turner was a dead man.

The thought struck him with icy certainty as he watched the approaching helicopter through sheets of rain. They wouldn't kill him right away, not while they still needed him, but it was just a matter of time. Then they'd make it look like an accident. He'd be on the mainland conducting Haven business, and his car would miss a turn and hurtle over a cliff. Or his heart would give out due to some rare and untraceable drug delivered via a hypodermic in the middle of the night. Possibly he'd be working in the lab and discover a tear in his bio-containment suit.

However they chose to end his life, no one would ask any questions or investigate the death of the once prominent Dr. Paul Turner. He'd disappeared from the scientific community nearly fifteen years ago, and as far as any of his peers knew, he'd been dead ever since.

Paul shivered and steered himself away from such morbid thoughts. He needed to concentrate on the next couple of hours and the upcoming meeting. Then, if he was smart and very careful, maybe he could come out of this alive.

Meanwhile, the rain and wind battered the aircraft as it hovered over the landing pad. The pilot fought for control, but the storm seemed determined to keep the helicopter from landing. A crash would solve his problem, Paul thought with a grim smile. Unfortunately, he had no doubt the vehicle would set down safely. The man on board, Avery Cox, wouldn't be stopped by anything as minor as inclement weather.

For the past ten years, as director and lead scientist at the Haven, Paul had answered to Cox. The facility, located on a remote, private island at the northern edge of Puget Sound, was home to a staff of doctors, nurses, teachers, and a variety of very special children. It included dormitories, classrooms, laboratories, a hospital, and the finest equipment and scientific minds money could buy.

Except for his yearly trips to Langley to deliver his annual report, Paul had very little contact with Cox. Generally he left Paul alone to run things, while supplying everything he needed: money, equipment, and the most important thing of all, anonymity. In return, Cox expected Paul to deliver results, which he'd done, consistently and without fail since taking over the Haven Project.

Now this.

Paul had done the unforgivable, committed the one act Cox wouldn't overlook. He'd lost two of the island's children.

If he'd been given time, a couple of days, a week at the most, he would have set things right without anyone knowing the difference. His people would have found the runaways, and things would have returned to normal. Unfortunately, it was too late for that. Someone had made a call, and it had taken Cox fewer than eight hours to arrive.

As Paul watched the helicopter descend, whipping the wet air into a frenzy, he realized anyone could have made that call. Cox had eyes and ears everywhere.

For a moment, Paul considered running.

It wasn't the first time the thought had crossed his mind. He had more than enough money stashed in off-shore banks. If he could get off the island and disappear into one of the backwater countries of Central or South America, he could live like a king for the rest of his life. Except it was a fool's dream. There was no place to hide, nowhere on earth where the Agency couldn't find him.

Finally the helicopter set down, and Paul hurried forward to greet the two passengers. "Mr. Cox." Paul shifted his umbrella to shield the other man. "This is an unexpected surprise."

"Is it?"

Paul stammered something unintelligible, but Cox and his companion had already started toward the shelter of the Haven's main building. Disgusted with himself, Paul scrambled to keep up.

Inside, he forced a smile and tried to regain his composure. "You know we're always happy to show you our facility."

"The Agency's facility, Dr. Turner." Cox removed his damp overcoat, shaking the moisture from its surface, and scrutinized the utilitarian lobby. "I suggest you remember that."

Embarrassed by the reprimand, Paul caught the amusement on the second man's face. A rush of loathing tightened his stomach, and he quickly looked away. "There's never been any doubt of that, Mr. Cox."

Cox arched a skeptical eyebrow and gestured to the man on his right. "You remember Morrow."

Paul nodded. "Of course."

Morrow wasn't someone you forgot. He was physically intimidating—even if the reason wasn't immediately apparent. At first glance, he appeared average enough at just under six feet, with medium brown hair and nondescript eyes. He was neither handsome nor homely, with the kind of face one might easily ignore on another man. But something about him, something in the way he held himself, like a cobra bracing for a strike, made you look twice. Then it took but a cursory second glance at those deceptively plain, brown eyes to realize that behind them lived a killer.

Despite Morrow's deadly presence, however, it was Cox who truly frightened Paul. Cox, with his receding hairline and steel-framed glasses. Cox, who stood barely five and a half feet tall and wore expensive ill-fitting suits. Cox, who would give the final order.

"I know you're concerned about the missing children," Paul said. "But I assure you we're doing everything possible to locate them."

"It's a little late for your assurances," Cox said. "Now, where can we talk?"

The rebuke churned Paul's fear, and he again resisted the urge to make a run for it. He wouldn't get ten feet before a bullet exploded into his back. "I've prepared a conference room where we won't be disturbed."

"Then, let's get to it."

Paul led the way to the facility's main conference room. When they entered, Morrow took control of the computer, while Cox moved to the counter where the kitchen staff had set up coffee and sandwiches.

As he helped himself to a cup, he asked, "Why these two particular children, Dr. Turner?"

Surprised, Paul had no answer. "I'm not sure." The question hadn't occurred to him, but he realized it should have. "Danny's one of our older boys and a bit rebellious, perhaps. But—"

"What about the girl?" Cox moved to the table and took the chair at the head.

Paul considered the coffee but decided against it. He was already too jumpy. Following Cox's lead, he sat across from Morrow, who seemed entirely focused on the computer. Paul turned back to Cox. "I don't know why Callie went with him."

"Did they know each other?" Cox sipped at his coffee, but his eyes never left Paul. "Were they friends?"

"All the children know each other." Paul glanced at Morrow uneasily. He seemed totally immersed in his task, tapping at the keyboard and sending commands scrolling across the wall screen.

"But do these two understand who they are?" Cox asked, reclaiming Paul's attention. "Or their relationship?"

"No, absolutely not." But if they did, that would explain a lot. "That would be disastrous."

"Then, I repeat." Cox's voice was patient but firm. "Why did these two particular children run?"

Paul spread his hands, palms up. "Coincidence?"

"There's no such thing, Dr. Turner."

Morrow's tapping ceased as an image leapt onto the screen.

"I believe you know this woman," Cox said, his eyes fixed on Paul.

Unsettled by the sudden shift in subject, Paul didn't recognize her at first. Once he did, he barely suppressed his surprise. "That's Anna Kent."

But the woman on the screen looked nothing like the quiet woman he knew. Instead of her usual demure suits and hair carefully twisted into a neat chignon, she wore a black leather jacket and jeans that hugged long, lean legs. The camera had caught her looking over her shoulder, her straight, black hair whipping around her head. There was a wildness about her, and a hardness not unlike the man asking the question.

"She's one of our teachers."

"Where is she?" Cox asked.

Dazed, Paul considered lying, then caught himself. If Cox was inquiring about the whereabouts of Anna Kent, it was because he already knew she was missing. "I don't know."

Cox frowned, but Paul knew he'd made the right choice by telling the truth. He didn't understand all the moves in Cox's game, but if he caught Paul lying, it would be all over.

"Ms. Kent lives in the staff quarters here on the island," Paul hurried to explain. "But when the children turned up missing this morning, and we assembled the entire staff, she wasn't among them. It's her day off, and we assumed she'd gone to the mainland."

"And it didn't occur to you she might have had something to do with the kids' disappearance?" Morrow said.

"It crossed my mind," Paul admitted, trying and failing to keep the fear from his voice. "Only I decided it was unlikely."

Morrow laughed abruptly.

Paul glanced from Morrow to Cox and back. "Ms. Kent came highly recommended. Her credentials are impeccable, and . . ." He forced himself to look directly at Morrow. "*Your* office placed her here."

Morrow's eyes chilled. "What are you suggesting, Doctor?"

Paul flinched as if struck. "I was just—"

"Enough," Cox said. "Arguing among ourselves will accomplish nothing." He glared at Paul, then turned back to Morrow. "Go on, tell Dr. Turner the rest."

Morrow's nod of acquiescence was barely visible, but

he turned back to the wall screen, tapped a few more keys, and a list of vital statistics appeared next to Anna Kent's picture. "Her real name is Anna Kelsey."

Paul scanned the text, words leaping out at him, pricking his spine with sharp needles of terror. Words like mercenary and terrorist, espionage and kidnapping.

"As you can see," Morrow added with a bit of amusement in his usually dull voice, "she's no schoolteacher."

Ethan tried to see beyond the tinted windows as the white late-model Ford drove into the yard and stopped, raising a cloud of sand and reflected light. In most places, the vehicle would have been nondescript. But here in the New Mexico wasteland, it stood out like a lone desert lily among the spindly creosote. If he wanted to blend in, the driver would have done better to find himself a rusted-out pickup.

Again, the Glock flickered across Ethan's thoughts. He should make them pay to take him. After all, the Agency had created him, bought and paid for him since the time he'd been old enough to hold a gun. He could at least give them their money's worth.

Who was he kidding?

He had no one but himself to blame for the things he'd done, the man he'd become.

The car door opened and the driver stepped out, surprising him in a way he no longer thought possible. She was a tall woman, tightly built, with features hinting at blended Asian and European ancestry. Ethan had always thought she'd inherited the best of both races, with straight, even features, thick dark hair, and skin the color of cream. Where she'd gotten the hardness, the angry edge most men lacked, he couldn't say.

Anna Kelsey.

They'd never been friends, but they'd been colleagues

once and soldiers together in an unnamed war. Now he understood how the Agency had found him. Only six people knew about this place, his team's last-ditch rendezvous spot if all else failed, and Anna was one of the six. Only he'd thought she was dead along with the others.

"So, it's true." She closed the door and walked toward him, stopping a few feet away. "You're alive."

Ethan tightened his hold on the cup. "Disappointed?"

"The rest are gone." She leveled cold eyes on him. "Lee, Mike, Jenkins, even T.J."

"What about you? You're still breathing." He had to wonder about that, how she'd escaped the Spaniard's wrath. Although, he supposed he shouldn't be surprised. Survival had been Anna's special skill, a talent he'd once used without conscience. But Ramirez had found the rest of them, one by one, and made them pay. Even Ethan. Especially Ethan. "Someone might question how *you* managed to stay alive."

She ignored the implied question and said, "You look like hell. I'd heard you'd given up, but I didn't believe it."

"Now you do." He frowned and dumped the last of his coffee into the sand. "So let's cut the bullshit, shall we? Do what you've come for and be done with it."

"You think I'm here to kill you." She cocked her head and smiled slightly. "Under different circumstances, the idea holds some appeal. But that's not why I'm here. Not this time."

He didn't believe her. Anna thrived on the hunt, and at one time he'd been the best. She would have wholeheartedly embraced the task of bringing him down, if for no other reason than to prove she could. But he wasn't playing by the rules, and it would eat at her.

"Let me guess," he said. "You just happened to be in the neighborhood and thought you'd stop by for a chat." Surprisingly, he felt no fear, and even the guilt had fled. He felt only relief that it might finally end.

"I need your help," she said.

He must have missed something. "You want to run that by me one more time?"

"You heard me. I need your help."

He didn't respond right away, then he laughed, the irony of it too much. "Sorry, but you asking me for help, it's a bit funny."

"This is important."

"It's always important." An edge of anger touched his voice. "Isn't that what we told ourselves, Anna? How we justified the things we did, the people we killed?"

She flinched. "That was an accident. We didn't know Ramirez had a kid in his cabin. How could we? We didn't even know she existed."

"No?" It was a question Ethan had turned over in his mind a million times in the last three years. Had it been an accident? Or had he and his team unknowingly accomplished what they'd been sent for? "Maybe you're right. Then again . . ." He let his voice trail off. Accident or not, the end result was the same, and he couldn't hide from the responsibility of it.

"Look, Decker, I don't have a lot of time."

"Then you best be moving on." Ethan pushed himself to his feet, swaying a bit as the pain in his head reasserted itself. "You had it right to begin with. I'm finished. I'm no good to you or anyone else. Go find yourself another gun."

"I don't need a gun. I just want you to—"

The back car door opened, cutting her off, and a boy of about twelve stepped out. Behind him a small blonde girl edged out as well, clinging to his arm.

"Callie needs a drink of water," the boy said to Anna.

"Get back in the car," she said, without looking at him.

"Not until you get Callie some water."

Before Anna could respond, the girl said, "Please, Anna, I'm not feeling very well."

Anna turned to the girl, a softness creeping across her features that Ethan had never seen before. Then the momentary gentleness vanished as she swung back to face him.

"*They* need your help."

"We're here to help, Dr. Turner." Cox's voice was warm, solicitous. "Those children are the heart of this project, and they must be brought home safely and quickly."

Paul wasn't fooled. Cox didn't care about the children. It was the project and its outcome that interested him. But Paul had found his way out, his scapegoat.

"Are you telling me this woman," Paul inserted just a trace of indignance in his voice, "this professional killer, kidnapped two of my children?"

"Your children?" Morrow mocked.

Paul bristled. "I think of all the children here as mine."

"Yes," Cox replied. "I'm sure you do. And yes, we believe Anna took the children. The real issue is why, or more specifically, for whom?" He nodded to Morrow, who worked the keyboard until another image replaced Anna's on the screen. This time it was a tall man with dark blond hair, strong features, and blue eyes that seemed to leap off the screen. "Do you know this man?"

"No."

"Are you sure?" Morrow asked.

"I'm sure." Paul shot Morrow an irritated glance. "Who is he?"

Without answering, Morrow tapped the keys and another image materialized next to the first. "What about him?"

The second man had classic Latin features: dark eyes, hair, and skin. He stared down from the screen with an intensity and quality of danger not even the grainy computer image could hide. Paul thanked the powers-that-be it was only a picture.

"I've never seen either of them. Who are they?"

"The first is Ethan Decker," Cox said. "The Latino is Marco Ramirez." He paused, as if gauging Paul's reaction. "We believe Ms. Kelsey is working with one or both of them."

"For what purpose?"

"Come now, Dr. Turner," Cox said. "The children here are not without value. Certainly you understand there are people, governments even, who would pay dearly to possess them."

Of course Paul knew that, but he was playing for his life and needed to act the part of the outraged father. "And you believe these men," Paul motioned toward the screen, "plan to sell Danny and Callie? Why that's . . . inhumane."

Cox eyed Paul with amusement. "So it is."

"But do they have the connections to arrange such a sale?" Paul asked, ignoring Cox's obvious sarcasm.

"Decker was an Agency officer with international contacts," Morrow answered. "His specialty was search and retrieval. He's good at finding . . . things."

People.

Though Morrow hadn't said the word, Paul understood what he'd meant. Ethan Decker hunted other men.

"And," Morrow added, "Decker and his team got in and out of places conventional service personnel couldn't reach."

Committing acts of horror those same conventional soldiers would not, Paul thought but dared not say. "It sounds like you admire him."

Morrow shrugged. "He was good at his job."

"He was an exceptional officer," Cox said. "With a

high mission success rate. And, yes, he had the contacts to arrange a sale."

Paul realized they'd been speaking of Decker in the past tense. "I take it he's no longer in the government's employ."

"He dropped out of the intelligence community several years ago," Cox said. "After a particularly nasty business which resulted in a failed mission and the death of an innocent bystander. A child."

"My God."

"I doubt God had anything to do with it." Cox took his time folding his hands on top of the table. "More likely, Decker simply became overzealous in his determination to carry out his mission."

Paul shuddered at the thought of two of his most valuable children in the hands of a man like Ethan Decker, a man who specialized in hunting other men. "And the other?" he asked, knowing the information about the Latino would be worse. "This Marco Ramirez?"

"Now that's a man I can admire." Morrow's smile sent another sliver of unease down Paul's spine. "Ramirez's talents run along a different vein than Decker's. In fact, you might say Ramirez's skills make Decker look like an altar boy."

Paul didn't want to know more, but he had no choice. He needed to know the kind of men he was dealing with if he had any chance of surviving. "What skill is that, Mr. Morrow?"

"He's a shooter. There are maybe five, six men in the world who can handle a rifle like he can. And now that he's no longer on the government payroll, he works for the highest bidder."

"What exactly does that mean? What does he do?"

"Isn't it obvious?" Morrow grinned. "He's an assassin."

* * *

Ethan knew Anna Kelsey was capable of assassination, all of them had been. What he found hard to accept was her traveling with two children. Or asking for help.

"What's going on here, Anna?"

She stepped to the girl's side and placed a hand on her thin shoulder. "This is Callie and her brother Danny."

"That's not what I asked you."

"What's bothering you, Decker?" She crossed her arms and eyed him with equal parts annoyance and curiosity. "That I'm alive? Or that I invaded your self-imposed exile?"

"Both."

"They need your help."

"Cut the crap." He'd worked with Anna for too long to be fooled. She wasn't exactly the maternal type. Nor was she into humane gestures. Anna Kelsey cared about one thing: her own skin. "We both know you're not here for some altruistic reason."

"You think you know me so well." Her eyes sparked with anger. "Did it ever occur to you there are some lines even I won't cross?"

"You forget who you're talking to."

"Seems you're the one who's forgotten who and what he is."

If only that were true. "Did the Agency send you?"

"They know nothing about this."

He studied her, trying to gauge the truth of her words. It was impossible. Anna lied as easily as most people breathed.

"Look," she said. "I just need to leave the kids here for a couple of days, three at the most. There's something I need to take care of, then I'll be back for them." She hesitated, as if deciding how much to say. "I need you to protect them for me."

"From who?" The question escaped before he could

stop it, before he could remind himself it wasn't his concern.

"I'll tell you." Her voice held a sudden note of fatigue. "Just . . . Would you get Callie a glass of water first?"

Ethan looked at the girl, then at the boy standing at her side. They were as unalike as any two kids he'd ever seen. Anna had said they were brother and sister, but Ethan didn't see it. The boy, Danny, was dark complected with hair and eyes to match, while Callie was blonde and blue-eyed with an angel's face. She stared at Ethan with open, sweet curiosity, while the boy oozed with hostility.

"We're hungry, too," he said, daring Ethan to refuse.

"Please, Decker," Anna said. "We've been on the road for nearly forty-eight hours. Let us catch our breath, then I'll explain everything."

Ethan didn't believe her. Anna would tell him exactly what she thought he needed to know—just enough to get him to go along with the game. What she didn't realize was that she couldn't change his mind, he wanted no part of her or these kids. He was out of it. Finished.

But he couldn't refuse a glass of water to a little girl or her angry big brother. Not even he had sunk that low. "Okay, I'll get your water, but afterward, you're on your own."

Anna nodded and urged the girl toward an old lawn chair beneath the awning. "Come on, Callie, you need to get out of the sun."

Feeling dismissed, Ethan went inside.

It took a few minutes of rummaging through cabinets to come up with a couple of clean glasses. As for food, he didn't have much. He found a box of crackers and a half-empty jar of peanut butter. It would have to do.

He'd just started filling the glasses with water when an engine kicked over outside. For half a second he froze, caught by his own gullibility. And by the time he made it through the door, Anna was gone, the white Ford leaving a whirlwind of dust and the kids in its wake.

"Damn it!" Ethan gritted his teeth, feeling like a fool. He'd known better than to trust that lying—

The boy claimed the glass of water. "She said to tell you she'd be back."

"Yeah, right."

"I don't believe her, either." The kid shrugged, not looking any happier about the situation than Ethan, and returned to his sister's side. "Looks like you're stuck with us."

"Like hell." Ethan hurried back inside.

He found his keys beneath the rumpled sheets where he'd dropped them the night before. As he passed back through the narrow kitchen, he grabbed the box of crackers. Outside, he tossed the package to the boy. "Come on, we're going after her."

"Callie's too sick."

"I don't care. You're going with me."

"You want her to heave all over your truck?" The boy let out a snort of disgust and nodded toward Ethan's pickup. "Not that it would make much difference in that heap."

The kid needed a lesson in manners, but Ethan didn't have time to argue with him. Besides, the girl did look pitiful. "What's wrong with her?"

The boy gave his sister a couple of crackers and looked like he'd refuse to answer. Then he said, "She gets carsick, okay?"

Just his luck, stuck with a couple of kids and one of them got carsick. Ethan couldn't wait to get his hands on Anna. "Okay, stay here. I'll be back." As he climbed into his truck, he added, "Don't touch anything."

"Don't worry." The kid glanced around the shabby yard. "I wouldn't want to catch something."

"Smart-ass," Ethan muttered, threw the truck in gear, and headed after the Ford.

A part of him knew he'd never catch her. Anna's car had looked relatively new, while his truck had been on its last leg for some time. He'd managed to keep the vehicle running, but driving at breakneck speed in the desert heat wasn't the best way to prolong its life.

At this point, he didn't care.

Anna had dropped those kids in his lap, and he wasn't about to let her get away with it. Hell, he could hardly take care of himself. He certainly couldn't be responsible for someone else. Not anymore. The last time a child's life had been in his hands, he'd blown it.

He kept the gas pedal pressed to the floor, swerving to avoid the potholes dotting the ragged road. He seemed to find more than he missed, and with each jarring hit, his head pounded in protest. It didn't slow him, and he managed to make the two-lane blacktop that passed for a highway in record time.

Skidding to a halt on the shoulder of the road, he searched for the white Ford.

"Shit." He slammed his fist against the steering wheel.

What the hell had he expected? That she'd be waiting for him, giving him a chance to catch up to her? Not Anna. The woman was a pro and knew exactly what she was doing.

He pulled out onto the highway, turning east and away from town. Anna wouldn't head for a speck-in-the-desert place like Draco. She'd want the nearest big city where she could blend in and disappear. Again, he jammed the gas pedal to the floor, despite the ominous clanking from the already overheated engine.

As usual, the highway was mostly deserted. He saw only one other car, which passed him going in the opposite direction. It seemed odd. A dark import. Expensive.

The likes of which one seldom saw way out here. It teased his thoughts, as did the image of the driver, flashing across his vision as he passed. Then ahead, the glint of sun on metal chased all other considerations from his mind.

Anna?

He lifted his foot from the accelerator. Even before he made out the shape of her vehicle on the wrong side of the road, or noticed the odd angle of the car with its flat, left front tire in the ditch and the driver's door wide open, he knew something was wrong. Stopping several yards behind the car, he sat motionless, wishing now he'd taken time to dig out the Glock.

Everything was too quiet.

Cautiously, he climbed out of the truck, using the door as a shield, and scanned the surrounding area. Because of the car's angle, he could see into the empty front seat, but what hid behind those tinted rear windows was anyone's guess. With no other vehicles around, however, the chances of someone hiding in the backseat were pretty slim. Dismissing the car for now, he searched the desert for any signs of life or activity. It, too, seemed preternaturally still.

Then he spotted the body.

About a hundred yards from the car, beneath a prickly yucca, it lay long and slender, with a fall of dark hair. Ethan felt himself go cold. Once more he checked out the surroundings and saw nothing—no lurking madman, no other vehicles, and nowhere for a killer to hide in the flat, nearly featureless desert.

Whatever had happened here, it was over.

He kept up his guard as he made his way to Anna's side. Her body lay facedown, a single gunshot wound in the back of the head, a .38 automatic caught in her lifeless grip. She'd been killed execution style.

Ethan dropped down beside her. "Damn it, Anna." It surprised him how much it hurt to see her like this. It was one more death on his conscience, another life he'd been unable to save.

Picking up her gun, he checked the clip. Empty. As he'd expected. As was a second clip, dropped to the sand when she'd loaded her spare. Also near the body was her leather pouch, looking enough like a woman's handbag to pass but filled with the tools of Anna's trade. He searched it, quickly, and found nothing unexpected. Several sets of false ID. Cash. A cell phone. And a third empty clip.

She'd obviously held off her attacker until she'd run out of ammunition. Then she'd had nowhere to run, no place to hide, nothing left to do but accept her fate.

"Why couldn't you have just stayed underground?"

She alone of his team had escaped the Spaniard's wrath. Why had she surfaced now? And why show up on his doorstep with two kids? What had she said? Something about a line she wouldn't cross?

Standing, he ran a shaky hand through his sweat-dampened hair. He couldn't afford to be questioned by the authorities, but he couldn't just leave her body out here, either. She'd been a member of his team, and he owed her. Then he realized he was avoiding the most pressing question of all.

Who had killed her?

Who could have gotten the better of a woman like Anna Kelsey, a professional who'd managed for years to evade one of the deadliest assassins in the world?

The answer sent a shard of ice through his veins.

Kneeling again, he carefully turned over Anna's body. Without looking into her lifeless eyes, he opened her mouth, feeling for what he already knew he'd find. Beneath her tongue was an antique Spanish coin.

Despite the desert heat, the chill settled into his bones.

He'd hoped he was wrong, but there was no mistake. The coin was the Spaniard's signature. Marco Ramirez had killed Anna.

Without warning, the old nightmare rose up to blind him in the full light of day. He saw the faces of children, watching him with accusing eyes. No, not accusing. It would be so much easier if they did blame him. But all he ever saw in those small questioning faces was fear.

Ethan struggled to calm his chaotic thoughts.

It was no coincidence that Ramirez had found Anna here after all this time. He hadn't known Ethan's location any more than anyone else. Only Ethan's team had known about the desert canyon. So he must have followed Anna.

And what about those kids?

Anna had said they needed his help. Could Ramirez even now be . . . The memory of an expensive import flashed across his thoughts.

"Jesus."

He grabbed Anna's weapon and bag, surged to his feet and sprinted toward the truck, leaving her body to the desert. The Spaniard had no qualms about crossing forbidden lines. To him, one life was like any other—dead or alive.

For the first time in years Ethan prayed. He had to reach those kids before Ramirez got to them.

CHAPTER TWO

Avery Cox stared through the rain-streaked windows of Turner's office. Outside, the storm ranted, churning the troubled waters of the outer Sound and slapping wind against the small island. Inside, watery light spilled into the dim room and cavorted with shadows on the thick carpet. From where he stood, Avery couldn't tell whether it was morning or evening, winter or summer. It was always like that here. Storm or no storm, the weather remained constant: wet and dreary.

God how he hated this place.

He'd seen suicide statistics claiming more people took their own lives in the Pacific Northwest than in any other part of the country. The experts blamed the lack of sun, claimed it decreased the levels of serotonin in the brain. He believed it. The place was damn depressing.

Turning away from the dismal seascape, he studied Turner's office. It was large, spacious, and expensively furnished with sleek rosewood and burgundy leather, glass-fronted bookcases, original—and questionably obtained—art, and a well-stocked bar. Turner had spared no cost in surrounding himself with comfort.

Avery smiled at the irony.

Things could have turned out quite differently for Dr. Paul Turner. Ten years ago the scientific community had ostracized him for his illegal and morally questionable experiments. He'd been one step away from criminal charges and a prison cell.

Then Avery had stepped in.

He'd offered Turner an escape route, along with this facility and the funds to run it. It had meant he'd had to disappear, become invisible, but it had been a small price to pay for his freedom. In exchange, Avery had expected loyalty.

Now he had to decide whether Turner had betrayed his end of the bargain, or was just incompetent.

The door opened, and Morrow stepped into the room. "The storm's letting up," he said. "We can leave within the hour."

"Where's Turner?" Not that Avery expected trouble from the mealymouthed scientist, but one could never be too careful. Turner was frightened, and frightened men were unpredictable. It would be a shame to have to kill him for something stupid. Like running.

"I have a man watching him while he's preparing to interview the boy," Morrow said. "He'll send for us when he's ready."

Avery snorted in disgust.

Turner's transparency had been almost painful to watch as he scrambled to save himself. Now he'd sworn one of the other boys, Danny's friend, knew where the runaways were headed. Even if Turner was right and succeeded in getting the information, Avery doubted it would help. He knew Anna Kelsey. She'd have her own agenda and wouldn't share it with a couple of kids. But at this point, Avery couldn't afford to ignore even the smallest lead.

They had to find those kids. Fast. Before someone else discovered them.

"So what do you think? Did Turner have a hand in all this?"

"Turner's a coward."

Leave it to Morrow to state the obvious. "Yes, but did he help Anna?"

"Not a chance."

"Anna Kelsey is a beautiful and resourceful woman. She can be very persuasive."

"I'm sure she could have gotten to Turner if she'd wanted, but why would she? She didn't need him to take those brats off the island."

Avery agreed, but it never hurt to hear your deductions reinforced by another. That way if things went wrong, there was someone else to take the fall. "So the question remains"—he settled into Turner's chair—"what's Anna up to?"

Morrow leaned against the desk, picked up a glass paperweight from the surface, and tested its weight. "She could be planning to sell them herself."

"Possible, but very risky with Ramirez still at large. She'd have to surface to find a buyer, and then she'd be vulnerable." Avery considered Anna's choices, not liking any of them. "No, our Anna is too fond of her own skin to take that route. Or else she wouldn't have let us bury her on this godforsaken island."

"So she got tired of the place and decided to take off. Can't say that I blame her." Morrow tossed the glass ball from one hand to the other and shrugged. "She's cocky and figures we'll never find her, but then, why take a couple of kids. They'd slow her down."

Morrow was right again. Anna Kelsey never did anything without a self-serving reason. Avery swivelled back to the windows, as if his answers could be found in the storm.

"She could have made a deal with Ramirez," Morrow suggested. "The kids for her life."

"Too risky. Ramirez doesn't care about the money. He wants Anna dead. Besides, if Ramirez knew anything, he'd have surfaced by now, and you'd have a much bigger problem than Anna Kelsey."

"Let him come. Or better yet, let me go after him."

Avery smiled, amused by Morrow's ego. They were all alike: Morrow, Ramirez, Decker. Like gunslingers from the Old West, they needed to prove who had the biggest gun. Over the years, Avery had carefully perpetuated that myth within all of them, nurtured and used it.

A knock on the door, and Avery swung back around as Turner's assistant entered the room.

"Dr. Turner is ready for you now," she said.

She was an interesting woman, young but not too young, attractive but not beautiful. Probably Ivy-League educated. Another perk Turner had awarded himself.

Avery dismissed her with a wave of his hand. "Give us a few minutes."

She looked ready to object. Avery suspected she wasn't used to taking orders. Then she caught herself and backed out of the room, and Avery added smart to his list of adjectives describing her. But as the door closed behind her, he leaned forward, elbows on the desk, the woman already forgotten.

"There's another option we haven't considered," he said. "If Anna made the connection between the attempted hit on Ramirez three years ago and the island, she could have taken the kids to either bargain with him or blackmail the Agency." It was the chance Cox had taken when placing Anna on the island. Only he'd counted on her fear of Ramirez to keep her in line. Evidently the years had dimmed her memory of the assassin's revenge on the rest of Decker's team. "Either way, she'll need help."

"Decker?"

"If anyone knows where he's hiding, it's Anna." And she had nowhere else to go, no one else she could trust. If she did, she never would have asked to be brought in when Ramirez started his rampage.

"Decker's not coming out of hiding to face Ramirez, not for the likes of Anna Kelsey."

Avery wasn't so sure. Decker had a weakness for the underdog. "Maybe not for her, but what about a couple of stray kids? And don't forget his son."

Revenge was a motive Morrow understood, and Avery could almost see the gears grinding in the other man's head. "We don't know Ramirez killed the boy."

"His death seems too coincidental otherwise." With a shrug, Avery leaned back in his chair. "Besides, it doesn't really matter what we know, just what Decker believes. He'll come out of hiding to help those kids, and in the process he'll have to deal with Ramirez." He smiled, for himself as much as Morrow. "Which means we can turn this situation to our advantage." Three problems solved in one carefully orchestrated stroke: the runaways, Ramirez, and Ethan Decker.

Morrow didn't look convinced. He had a blind spot when it came to Decker and Ramirez. They'd been Avery's first string when Morrow was still ripping off old ladies' social security checks, and it gnawed at him.

Decker had been Avery's best officer. He'd found Decker during Desert Storm, recognized his potential, and recruited him for the Agency. At the time, Avery had just taken control of SCTC, the Strategic Counter-Terrorism Center, and was on the lookout for talented officers. Two years later, after the traditional year of career training and another of proving himself on solitary assignments, Avery had given Decker control of the best retrieval unit in the Agency.

Avery had considered Decker his special project, training him and mentoring him. Then his team had killed a kid while attempting to bring in Ramirez, and Decker had resigned with nothing more than a handwritten note. No one had seen him since. It was as if he'd vanished from the face of the earth. Avery could have overlooked the mess with Ramirez, but no one walked away from Avery Cox. Not even Ethan Decker.

"Okay, so Anna heads for Decker," Morrow said. "What good is it? We don't know where he is."

"He'll surface." For the first time since hearing about the kids' disappearance, Avery felt that everything was going to work out. "He's got no choice, he's been on his own too long and will need money, transportation, and identification."

Morrow considered for a moment, then nodded. "Okay, I'll set a watch on his family, friends, Agency contacts, old Army buddies. And I'll put word out on the street that we want him."

"Use whatever resources you need, but find him."

"Don't worry, someone will get greedy."

"Pay particular attention to his ex-wife. There's a good chance he'll turn up there." Avery had known Decker too long, understood him. That woman was his weakness, his Achilles' heel, and Avery had no qualms about using her.

"You want him dead?"

"First I want Danny and Callie, then we'll let him finish Ramirez." That would be two problems solved. "Then he's all yours." Avery pushed to his feet. "Meanwhile, let's see what the good doctor has in store for us. If Decker ends up with those kids, the boy's information just might lead us somewhere after all."

Through a one-way mirror, Avery and Morrow had a clear view of the examination room where Paul Turner sat at a wall-mounted Formica counter, scribbling on a medical chart. Then the door opened and a good-looking boy entered the room. Avery, who'd studied all the children's records, mentally rattled off his vital statistics. Adam. Born August 1991. IQ 142. He was one of Turner's earliest successes, though not nearly as promising as some of the younger children.

"Good morning, Adam," Turner said without looking up from his notes. "Climb up on the examination table, will you."

The boy hesitated, then did as instructed.

Turner continued writing for several minutes, while Adam began to fidget. Finally Turner lay down his pen, took off his glasses, and faced the boy. "And how are we feeling today?"

Adam put on a bright smile, obviously forced. "Great."

"That's good." Turner stood and placed a hand on the boy's narrow shoulder. "Let's take a look, shall we?" He pulled a tongue depressor from his top pocket.

The boy swallowed, then opened his mouth.

"No sore throat?"

Adam shook his head, looking ready to gag.

"Hmm." Turner withdrew the tongue depressor and picked up an otoscope from a nearby instrument stand. "What about your ears?"

"No problems."

"Well, we'll see about that." Turner checked one ear, frowned, then shifted to the other. "You're a friend of Danny's, aren't you, Adam?"

The boy blinked. "We're in the same dormitory."

"Are you sure you're not having trouble with your ears?"

"Yes, sir. I mean, they don't hurt or anything."

"Really?" Turner arched an eyebrow and started on the boy's nostrils. "But you and Danny are special friends, aren't you? You hang out together, play ball, work on the computers?"

"I guess."

Turner dropped the instrument into his jacket pocket and probed the boy's neck with his fingers. "You know we're all worried about Danny, don't you, Adam?"

Next to Avery, Morrow laughed abruptly. "I didn't know Turner had it in him."

Avery agreed, the kid was growing more nervous with each question, each physical invasion. "Desperate men are capable of almost anything," he said. And Paul Turner was as desperate as they came. If the wrong people found those kids, he'd be the first casualty.

"I know it's all over the dormitories by now that Danny ran away," Turner was saying as he examined the boy's eyes with a bright light that had the boy blinking furiously. "What about headaches?"

"No, nothing like that, Dr. Turner. I feel fine."

Turner flicked off the light. "Did you know Danny took someone with him, a young girl named Callie?" Turner gave the boy a bit of space. "You know Callie, don't you?"

"Sure."

"Did you know that she's very sick?"

Adam nodded, warily.

"We need to find Callie, Adam. You understand that, don't you?"

Adam threw a quick, nervous glance toward the door.

Turner again placed a hand on the boy's shoulder. "Where did they go?"

The boy seemed to recoil from Turner's touch.

"If we don't find Callie, she might die." Turner's grip visibly tightened. "You don't want to be responsible for that, do you?"

Adam dropped his eyes to his fisted hands.

"Where did they go?" Turner repeated, sterner this time. "You have to tell me."

"But I don't know."

Avery shook his head. "Stubborn little bastard." Under different circumstances he might admire the kid.

"Let me have a crack at him," Morrow said.

"He'd be no good to us dead."

Turner's voice took on a edge of impatience. "But you

did know Danny was going to run away," he insisted, waiting a couple of seconds for a response before lifting the boy's chin and forcing him to look up. "Adam?"

"Danny told me, but I didn't believe him. Kids talk about running away all the time. That doesn't mean they're gonna do it."

"He asked you to go with him, didn't he?"

Adam's eyes widened. "No."

"You expect me to believe that?"

Morrow shifted impatiently. "He's losing it."

Avery didn't comment as Turner released the boy and gave him his back, peering straight at the window where Avery and Morrow watched, his anger and frustration a physical presence behind the glass. But by the time Turner turned back to the boy, he had his temper under control.

"Adam, I don't care whether Danny asked you to go with him or not." He was noticeably calmer, though the effort to maintain control showed around his eyes. "All I care about is Danny and Callie, and finding them before it's too late."

"He didn't tell me where they were going. Honest." The first tears leaked from the boy's eyes.

Turner stood unmoving for several long moments, then sighed and turned away. "Okay, I believe you."

Adam wiped at his eyes, his body sagging.

Morrow started as if struck. "What?"

"Wait," Avery said. "Let's see where Turner's going with this."

The boy's relief lasted only a few seconds, until Turner reached the counter and started doing something Avery couldn't see. "I don't need a shot, Dr. Turner." Panic cracked Adam's voice. "I'm not sick. Really."

Turner turned, needle in hand. "The dormitory monitor told me you were coughing in the middle of the night."

"It wasn't me."

"It seems you have a very faulty memory today." Turner returned to the boy's side. "Think very hard, Adam. Are you sure you don't know where we can find Danny and Callie?"

He shook his head, his eyes never leaving the needle in Turner's hand. "No."

"That's too bad."

Adam scooted sideways, slipped off the table, and backed toward the door. "I don't need a shot." He was sobbing now. "I'm not sick."

"Don't be foolish." Turner reached beneath the counter and pushed a button. "It's for your own good."

Two orderlies burst through the door and grabbed the boy.

"Hold him," Turner instructed the men.

It was over in a matter of seconds, the boy not standing a chance against the two burly men and the needle in Turner's hand.

"There now," Turner patted Adam on the head, "that wasn't so bad." And he nodded to the orderlies, who took the crying boy away.

Avery stepped into the examination room. "That was quite a show, Dr. Turner."

"And pointless," Morrow added.

Turner looked nervously at him, then focused on Avery. "I think he knows more than he's admitting."

"Maybe, but he doesn't seem ready to tell us anything."

"I still think I should have a go at him," Morrow said.

"That won't be necessary," Turner said quickly. "Adam's about to get very sick. If he knows anything, he'll talk."

"And if he doesn't?" Avery asked.

A glint of anger sparked in Turner's eyes. "Well then, he'll die."

CHAPTER THREE

The day had been long, and Dr. Sydney Decker felt the effects down to her bones. Unlocking the door to her condominium, she stepped inside and entered her security code on the keypad, shutting off the alarm and locking the door behind her.

She hated having to be so cautious. The alarm system had been Charles's idea after a neighbor's apartment had been broken into and robbed. She supposed she didn't have much choice; it was the price she paid for living in the city. Dallas, like most major metropolitan areas, had a high crime rate.

She dropped her mail on the hall table and kicked off her shoes. The cool tile felt good beneath her stockinged feet as she started for the living room, where she flipped on the stereo. Strains of Chopin filled the room, and she sighed, heading for the kitchen. She wanted a glass of wine, a long hot bath, and about twelve hours of uninterrupted sleep. Maybe then she'd start to feel human again.

Without bothering to turn on the lights, she went straight to the refrigerator and pulled out a chilled bottle of chardonnay. She set it on the counter, then opened a nearby cabinet. As she reached for a wine goblet, she heard heavy footsteps and spun around, sending the glass shattering to the floor.

"Jesus, Sydney, take it easy."

"Charles." She pressed her hand to her racing heart. "What are you doing sneaking up on me like that?"

He frowned. "I wasn't sneaking up on you. I was in the den watching the news when I heard you come in."

"But what are you doing here?"

He took a step toward her, noticed the broken glass at his feet, and stopped. "I told you this morning that I'd be here when you got home."

"Of course." She felt foolish and petulant, and it seemed like years since she'd spoken to Charles. Had it really only been this morning? "You're right, I forgot."

"And you forgot about our dinner plans as well."

Sydney glanced at the wall clock. It was after nine. "What time were the reservations?"

"Eight-thirty." His voice held a slight edge, and she knew she'd disappointed him. Unfortunately, it wasn't the first time.

"I'm sorry," she said. "I got tied up at the lab." *Again.* She didn't have to say it, the word hung just as heavily between them without having been spoken. "I know you've had those reservations for weeks."

For a moment she thought he'd let his anger show—she almost wished he would, just this once. Then he sighed. "Sit down and I'll get your wine."

"Charles, really, I—"

He raised a hand to stop her objection. "Just this once, Sydney, don't argue with me."

"Okay then, I'll get the broom and clean up my mess."

She saw another flash of annoyance in his eyes. "Just sit down. I'll do it. You're liable to cut your feet on all this broken glass."

She wanted to object but held back. Charles was accustomed to giving orders and having them followed, and though he tried to hide it, she knew it irritated him that she refused to jump at his every command. At times she contradicted him for the sole pleasure of being the only one who seemed to have the courage to do so.

However, this once, if it made him happy to take care of her, she'd let him. After all, she'd been the one who'd ruined their evening. With a nod of acquiescence she settled onto a counter stool and watched him retrieve a couple of glasses and pour the wine before going for the broom and dustpan.

"You're obviously beat." He started cleaning up the broken glass. "Rough day?"

She sipped her wine and nodded, letting the alcohol work on her frayed nerves.

"Dr. Mathews?"

"Who else?" She and Tom Mathews had an ongoing battle. The man was old-fashioned and considered women an unwelcome addition to the scientific community. Unfortunately, he was also her supervisor.

"Do you want to talk about it?" Charles asked. "You know I could—"

She cut him off. "No."

Technically, Charles was both her and Mathews's employer. He'd founded and now headed the board of Braydon Labs, one of the finest genetic research laboratories in the country. Although Charles liked telling people he acted only as an adviser, everyone knew nothing of consequence happened without his approval. All it would take was one phone call, and her troubles with Tom Mathews would vanish.

Charles had offered several times to make that call. He wanted to help, and it was a sweet thought. But it was her life and her career, and she wouldn't have anyone pulling rank to smooth her way.

"Charles, please," she said. "I can handle Tom."

She thought they might be in for another round on the topic, but Charles surprised her by changing the subject. "So, what would you like for dinner?"

Nothing, she thought, but knew he would never accept that. "I could throw together an omelet or something."

His frown was all the answer she needed. Sydney wasn't much of a cook, and they both knew it. "Well, we could still go out," she offered. "Not to La Belle's, but we could go over to Mario's. They're never busy during the week."

"With good reason."

She sighed. She didn't have the energy for this tonight.

Charles and food, or she should say, restaurants. He prided himself on his gourmet taste and frequented the best restaurants in the city where he could see and be seen. It was his one obsession, though looking at him you'd never know it. He was as lean and firmly muscled as any twenty-year-old athlete.

"What do you want to do, Charles?"

He considered, then said, "Why don't you relax for a bit, and I'll go out and pick up something."

She eyed him warily. Takeout wasn't Charles's favorite choice. He liked being served. "You wouldn't mind?"

"What I mind is that you're working yourself to death."

She tried to make light of the comment. "But think of all the money you're saving by not having to feed me as often."

He came over to her, wrapped an arm around her shoulders, and kissed the top of her head. "Don't joke. You work too hard."

"My work is important."

"I know, Sydney, but fourteen, sixteen hours a day." His disapproval was evident in his tone.

"We've been over this before, Charles." She slipped from beneath his arm, got up from the stool, and headed into the living room, where the Chopin sonata offered comfort.

Charles followed her. "All I'm saying—"

"I know what you're saying." Irritated, she stopped in front of the mantel, looking at the picture of a blond five-year-old with bright blue eyes and a smile that never failed to stop her heart. She closed her eyes and let the music flow over her, hoping it would soothe her.

Charles came up behind her and rubbed her upper arms. "It's because of your son, isn't it? That's why you're driving yourself like this."

She didn't answer. Three years ago yesterday she'd lost her Nicky. For everyone else, the date had come and gone without incident. But she'd remembered.

"Sydney, your son's death was a tragic accident." Charles gave her arms a gentle squeeze and lowered his forehead to rest against the back of her head. "But you need to get on with your life. We need to get on with our life together."

She pulled away and turned to face him. "This has nothing to do with Nicky." It took effort to keep her voice calm, when she wanted to scream at him. "I'm looking for candidate genes to prevent childhood leukemia. Not a remedy for little boys who fall from trees and break their necks."

Silence filled the room, except the Chopin, which wound its way between them, tantalizing and frenzied as the piece neared its finale.

Charles reached over and shut off the stereo. "I'm sorry. I shouldn't have said that about Nicky."

She lifted her chin, not yet ready to forgive him.

"It's just . . ." He backed away, straightening and smoothing his tie. "I understand what it is to lose someone you love, and I worry about you."

The anger left her in a rush. He always seemed to know just the right thing to say to make amends. Several years ago, he'd lost his brother. It had been before she'd met him, but she knew Charles had taken it hard. "I know you do," she said, feeling guilty for forgetting she wasn't the only one who'd lost someone they loved. "But please try to understand how important this project is to me. We're so close."

When he didn't respond, she closed the distance between them and pressed a light kiss to his lips. "Please, Charles. It won't be much longer. I promise." She saw the doubt in his eyes and maybe even a bit of jealousy.

"Marry me, Sydney, and I'll give you more children."

Surprised, she took an involuntary step back. It wasn't the first time he'd asked, nor the first time she'd put him off. It *was*, however, the first time he'd mentioned having children. "Charles—"

"Don't." He grabbed her hand before she could say more. "Don't answer me now. Just think about it. Please."

She blinked, then nodded, though there really was nothing to think about. She thought he knew that. There would be no more children. Not for her. Not ever. Her one and only child had died three years ago, and she'd never risk caring that much again.

"Okay then, you relax," he said, smiling a bit too brightly as he went into the den and came back out with his suit jacket. "By the way, I was expecting a call so I checked your phone messages for you."

She bit back another rush of annoyance. "And?"

"Just a couple of hang ups." He slipped on his jacket.

She nodded, exhausted and not wanting to argue further.

"Have a bath," he said, kissing her on the cheek before heading toward the door. "I'll be back with your dinner."

With arms wrapped tightly around her middle, she watched him go. He meant well, worrying about her long hours and handling things for her, like dinner and phone messages. It wasn't his fault she preferred doing things for herself. In time they'd reach an understanding, a compromise between his desire to take care of her and her need for independence.

What really concerned her, however, was his claim that she wasn't getting on with her life. Maybe she wasn't ready to jump into another marriage, nor would she ever be ready for another child, but hadn't she gotten on with her life? Hadn't that been what she'd been doing these last few years, learning to live without Nicky? Without Ethan?

She walked slowly to the bedroom, pulled off her jacket, and dropped it on the bed. It had been an uphill struggle, but she'd survived. At first she hadn't wanted to. It had been an effort just to get out of bed in the morning and face another day. She'd often wondered if it had been her anger at Ethan that had pulled her through, pushed her on until she'd begun to heal.

Giving up her pediatric practice had been the first step in the process. Unable to face the string of children who paraded through her office day after day, she'd taken a research job and discovered an affinity for the laboratory that she hadn't known she possessed. But mainly, working gave her a reason to get up in the morning, something to do. Then one night she'd realized she'd gone an entire day without once thinking about her son or ex-husband, and she knew she'd found a new reason for living.

Braydon Labs had saved her life.

Some time later she'd met Charles at a fund-raiser, and her life had taken another turn. Their relationship had developed gradually over months of charity functions, dinners in expensive restaurants, and evenings at the theater.

When he'd asked her to marry him the first time, it hadn't surprised her. He was everything Ethan wasn't: steady, considerate, responsible. And if their relationship lacked the intensity or passion she'd known with Ethan, that was all the better. She'd learned the hard way not to trust feelings based on anything other than common background and companionship. She and Charles were comfortable together, and she was content with that.

Still, something had stopped her from accepting his proposal. She'd told herself, and him, that she just wasn't ready. She needed more time, and to his credit, he'd been patient. Only tonight he'd accused her of not moving on with her life.

She unbuttoned her blouse and tossed it on the bed next to her jacket, wondering if Charles was right. Maybe she hadn't put the past behind her as well as she thought. From her walk-in closet, she retrieved the small step stool she kept for reaching the upper shelves. Climbing up, she pulled down a large box and carried it to the bed.

When she'd finally surfaced from the depths of her depression, she'd gotten rid of the daily reminders of all she'd lost. She'd sold her house, left her practice, and given away her son's clothes, furniture, and toys. She'd kept very little, only the single picture of Nicky in the living room and the contents of this container.

For several minutes, she couldn't bring herself to open it. Inside was all that remained of her child's life, and as long as she left it untouched, she could keep the pain at bay. Putting the past to rest, however, was what this was all about, why she'd taken this box from the shelf for the first time since she'd stashed it away. She had to go through it or continue letting the past rule her present.

With trembling hands, she finally lifted the lid, bracing herself for the rush of grief. Instead, as she gazed at the contents, a bittersweet melancholy filled her. Tentatively, she touched each item in turn: the soft-blue baby album, decorated with blocks and booties; the tiny plastic hospital beads, spelling Nicky's name; the first drawing he'd brought home from kindergarten, depicting a mom, dad, and little boy under a bright sun; a slim stack of progress reports from sweet, twenty-something teachers who doted on their young charges; and the single pale blond curl from his first haircut, held with a navy ribbon.

Tears slipped down Sydney's cheeks, and she brushed them aside.

God, how she missed him, how she hated that this box wasn't filled with more little-boy treasures. She wished there were report cards and school programs, or maybe a ticket stub from a baseball game. He might have given her homemade Mother's Day cards as he grew, or a favorite rock he'd found just for her. By now he'd be in fourth grade, and the keepsakes might include sports or school awards, or just more photographs, tracing a child's growth toward adolescence. But there was none of that, of course. Her son had died before experiencing any of those things.

The anguish rose up to choke her, closing around her throat with a strangled sob. He'd been so young, so full of life.

Why?

It was a question she'd asked a thousand times—a million—in the days following the accident. No one should have to suffer this, no parent should have to bury a child. But she had, and she needed to know why.

Clenching her fists, as if that action would somehow keep her from flying apart, she fought for control. There were no answers, she knew that. Her son was dead. She may never get over it, but she would have to live with it.

Again, she brushed at the tears, determined to get on with this, to move on with her life as Charles had suggested. Her hands trembled as she reached for a photo-shop envelope of pictures she'd always meant to put in an album. Now, she never would. She couldn't handle having them around where she could look at them, where they'd be a constant reminder of the child she'd lost.

As she lifted the envelope, something dropped to the bottom of the box. Stunned, she stared down at the heavy silver band. She'd forgotten it was here, that she'd saved it, storing it with her memories of Nicky. Slowly, she set down the pictures and picked up the ring.

Ethan's ring.

It, too, had the power to inflict pain. She remembered the first time he'd put it on her finger. It had been a beautiful April day, and they'd known each other less than a month. They'd taken a picnic lunch to the hill country west of Austin, and in a field of bluebonnets, they'd made love for the first time.

Later, on their way home, they'd stopped at an arts and crafts fair in Fredericksburg and held hands as they wandered among the booths. She didn't remember what had attracted them to the display of silver and turquoise trinkets. On a woven mat before an old man, the inexpensive items were no different from a dozen other similar collections. But as Ethan crouched down to look, the stranger had pulled a small leather pouch from inside his shirt and offered it to them. The bag contained two matching silver rings, beautifully and intricately carved. Ethan had bought them on the spot and slipped one on her finger.

The memory brought fresh tears to her eyes.

It had been a foolish and spontaneously wonderful gesture. And so like Ethan. He'd never been one for planning or scheduling, whereas she'd always lived by the rules.

Before she'd met him, her life had been predictable. She'd had her whole future mapped out. She'd been twenty-five and almost finished with medical school. Another few years and she'd set up her practice. Then Ethan had exploded into her life, changing everything.

He'd been unlike anyone she'd ever met, handsome

and charming on the surface, while possessing an underlying wildness that reminded her of leather jackets and motorcycles. She'd never stood a chance.

It was funny that a woman who'd grown up following the straight and narrow could fall so hard. But she had, and for the first time in her life she'd wanted something other than a career in medicine. She'd wanted Ethan Decker.

Holding the ring up in the light, she looked at the inscription.

Forever and Always. Ethan.

But it had been a lie. When she'd needed him most, Ethan had deserted her. They'd buried their son on a bright Texas morning, and by nightfall, Ethan was gone. The tears came hot and unbidden now, temporarily blinding her. But this time, it was anger that spurred them on.

Charles was right. She had to get on with her life. Their lives. She'd been holding on to the past just as she'd held on to this tiny circle of silver. No more. Clutching the ring, she headed for the front of the condo.

She'd loved Ethan unconditionally, but he'd betrayed her and their son's memory the day he walked out on her. Turning off the alarm, she left the apartment and walked down the hall to the utility room. Inside, with her hand on the trash chute handle, she hesitated.

Ethan's ring.

Then, before she could change her mind, she opened the lid and dropped the ring, hearing the ping of metal against metal as it fell twelve stories to the Dumpster in the basement.

By his own choice, Ethan had ceased to be a part of her life. It was time she accepted it.

CHAPTER FOUR

Danny watched the hawk soaring above the desert.

He'd seen lots of birds before; blue herons and osprey were common in the San Juans, and the bald eagles used the islands as a breeding ground. But something about the solitary hawk, searching for his next meal, made Danny realize just how far he was from home. For a moment, he wished he could take back the last three days and return to Haven Island. Then he remembered all the lies and betrayals and knew he could never go back.

Besides, he kind of liked it here.

In school they'd learned about deserts, but this was nothing like those boring lessons. And it was so different from the island, with its damp evergreen forest hemmed in by the Pacific. Here there were no boundaries. The sand seemed to stretch forever, and the colors were almost nonexistent. Except the sky. He didn't remember ever seeing anything so blue.

"Do you think he'll catch her?"

Danny glanced back at his sister. "In that old truck? No way." Walking over, he picked up his backpack and sat on the trailer steps. "How are you feeling?" Callie looked better, but he had to watch her. She got sick a lot and had been to see Dr. Turner the day they'd run away, which made Danny worry that she might be coming down with something.

"I'm okay." She took another cracker from the package and handed him the rest. "What did you think of him?"

"Who? Decker?"

Callie nodded. "He'll be back when he doesn't find Anna."

"Probably." Danny rummaged through his backpack for the Game Boy Anna had bought for him. "But it won't make any difference whether he comes back or not."

Though that wasn't entirely true. Anna had been bad enough. Danny knew he couldn't trust her, but he also knew she wouldn't send them back to the island. He wasn't sure about Decker. It was pretty obvious he didn't want anything to do with helping a couple of kids. What would he do if he didn't find Anna? Would he even care what Danny and Callie wanted?

"We'll be okay," he said, as much to reassure himself as Callie. "The Keepers don't know we're here. So we'll just rest up a bit, then walk out to the road. Someone will give us a ride."

Callie looked toward the horizon, where the sun hovered just above the western mountains. "It's gonna be night soon. Shouldn't we wait until morning?"

Danny didn't like the idea of being alone in the desert after dark, either, but he wasn't sure they had a choice. Not if they wanted to get away. "We can't stay here that long. If Decker returns and decides to hand us over to the police, they'll send us back to the Haven. We'll lose our only chance to find our parents."

"He won't do that. Anna said he'd help us."

Danny laughed abruptly. "Anna said a lot of things. That doesn't make them true." She'd lied to him from the beginning, pretending to be his friend and promising to hide him and Callie from the Keepers on Haven Island.

What a jerk he'd been.

He'd thought he was so smart, smarter than any of the teachers. Even Anna. But she'd fooled him so easily it was almost funny. Though he didn't feel much like laughing. He'd known the night they ran—even before they were off the island—that she had no intention of keeping her promise. Then before he could figure out what she *did* want with them, she'd dropped them off here, in the middle of nowhere, with a man who obviously wanted nothing to do with them. It didn't make any sense.

"The Keepers will come after us," Callie said.

Danny considered denying it. It would be easier than admitting the truth. But what was the point? If they were caught, there would be nothing he could do to protect her. Besides, Callie wasn't stupid.

"Yeah. They'll come after us."

She accepted that calmly, probably because she'd already known it. He'd discovered in the last couple of days that his little sister wasn't as fragile as she appeared.

"What will they do to us?" she asked.

"I don't know." That, too, was the truth, and something else he didn't want to dwell on. The Keepers had never physically hurt Danny, nor had he seen them harm any of the others, but kids had a way of getting sick and disappearing. And there was the time he'd seen Sean in the infirmary, after he'd supposedly been taken to a mainland hospital. Danny shuddered at the memory and vowed he and Callie wouldn't end up like that. "They have to find us first, and I'm not going to let that happen."

He wasn't sure how he would keep his promise, but he had to try. This was all his fault. He'd convinced Callie to run away and to trust Anna.

He searched the sky for the hawk and saw it gliding overhead. Then, flapping its wings in slow easy motions, it let out a screech, caught an updraft, and flew out of sight. Danny envied the big bird and its freedom. He wished he and Callie could just fly away as well.

"Danny." The fear in Callie's voice brought him back to earth. She'd deserted the chair and moved to the edge of the awning. "Someone's coming."

Danny looked toward the road, where a cloud of dust rose in the distance. Quickly, he moved to Callie's side, fear tightening his stomach.

"Can you make out what kind of car it is?" His sister's eyesight was better than his. "Is it Anna or Decker?"

Callie squinted, shading her eyes with her hand. "I can't tell, it's too far away. But I didn't expect them back this quick."

"Me, neither."

"Could it be the Keepers?"

Without answering, Danny turned from the trailer to scan the surrounding desert. He couldn't let them take him and Callie back. They needed to hide. Think, he ordered himself, desperate now, but he saw nothing but miles and miles of sand.

Callie slipped her hand into his, and she may as well have wrapped her small fingers around his heart. "I'm scared."

Danny sucked in a breath. "Me, too."

Ethan was too late.

He stared at the empty chair beneath the awning where he'd left the girl and her brother. Next to it, on a plastic table covered with dust, sat an empty glass and the clear plastic wrapper from the crackers. As earlier, when he'd found Anna's car, everything seemed entirely too quiet.

Without warning, another child's face leapt before his memory's eye, a laughing, blue-eyed boy. Ethan had been too late then as well. And too slow.

Though he fought it, the sudden upsurge of memories tore at him, making him look again at his failure. Nicky was what he saw, lying peacefully beneath a tree as if taking a nap. A little boy enjoying a hot summer day, while his father . . .

No.

Ethan shut down his thoughts, refusing to head down that road. It wouldn't do them any good. Not him, not Nicky, and certainly not those two kids Anna had left behind.

Gripping her .38, he climbed out of his truck. The empty gun was useless, except as a bluff, but it was all he had. He made a quick visual sweep of the trailer and surrounding desert. Then he scanned the boulders and crumbled-down cliff face a couple of hundred yards behind the trailer, watching for the glint of sunlight on steel that would mark him as a target.

Nothing.

Except the silent, hulking trailer and endless sand, dotted with its sparse desert vegetation.

He checked the ground. No extra tire tracks. No signs of a struggle. Plus his instincts told him Ramirez hadn't been here, and fourteen years of military and Agency work had taught him to trust those instincts.

Even if Ethan assumed the dark import on the highway belonged to Ramirez, he doubted whether the assassin would have had time to get to the trailer and back. It was at least a twenty-minute drive to the highway, forty minutes round-trip, not counting the time it would take to grab the kids and run. And Ethan was willing to bet the boy wouldn't have gone easily. So maybe it would have taken fifty minutes.

Had Ethan been on the highway chasing Anna that long?

He didn't think so. It definitely hadn't been that long since he'd passed the other car. Besides, if Marco Ramirez had come for those kids, they wouldn't be gone, they'd be lying facedown in the sand.

Like Anna.

Pushing the truck door closed behind him, Ethan moved to the trailer's open window and put his back against the metal frame.

"Danny?" he called over his shoulder, keeping his voice low and his eyes on the desert. "You in there?"

No answer.

Ethan sidestepped to the door, stopped, and swung it open while keeping his back pressed to the wall. He counted to three, took a deep breath, and swivelled on the balls of his feet, leading with the .38 through the open door.

Again, nothing. No kids. And no sign of a struggle.

He moved a little deeper into the cramped space, past the narrow galley to the head, and flicked open the door. Empty. Then he took the few extra steps to the bedroom at the end of the hall, which was no more than an unmade bunk, a couple of built-in drawers, and a small closet. It was the last possible hiding place in the tin trap of a trailer, and it was as quiet as he'd left it.

Unable to escape the inevitable any longer, he shoved Anna's unloaded gun into the waistband of his jeans, then reached beneath the bed and pulled out a metal box. Inside was the Glock he'd put away three years ago, telling himself he'd never take it out again.

He smiled grimly at his own naïveté.

He'd spent most of his life with a gun in his hand, and he'd most likely die that way. Picking up the weapon, he checked the clip and headed back outside.

Again he scanned the desert, the throbbing in his head taking on a life of its own. Could he do this? So far he'd been acting on reflex, pulling out rusted skills that had once been as much a part of him as breathing, but his head ached and his hands trembled. The kids were gone. He couldn't do a damn thing about it, and hadn't that been what he'd wanted?

Not like this.

Then he caught a flash of movement out of the corner of his eye and whirled around, again leading with the gun. A small, dark head rose from behind a clump of boulders at the edge of the cliff. The boy cautiously stepped from behind the rocks. His sister appeared beside him, and together they started forward.

Relief swept through Ethan, followed by a surge of anger. He met them halfway. "What the hell are you doing?"

Danny glared at him. "How were we supposed to know it was you? I figured it was safer to hide."

It had been a smart move, but Ethan wasn't about to tell the kid that. Besides, he wanted answers. "What's going on?" What could these two possibly know about the likes of Marco Ramirez? And what line had Anna been unwilling to cross? "Who's looking for you?"

"No one. Anna rescued us," Callie said quickly.

"From kidnappers," Danny added. "And she promised to find our parents."

"And then she got lost . . ." The girl threw a guilty look at her brother, realizing her mistake. Anna Kelsey lost?

The boy tried to cover for her. "And so she came looking for you. To help."

What a load of bunk, Ethan thought as he studied the two earnest faces. He had to give them points for creativity and spunk, though not for honesty.

"Come on," he said. His questions would have to wait. "We need to get out of here. You can tell me the truth later."

To their credit, neither kid argued as they followed

him toward the trailer. "Did you find Anna?" Callie asked in a quiet voice.

Ethan hesitated, looking into the child's impossibly blue eyes. He couldn't break her heart. "We have to hurry," he said, instead of answering her question. "We may not have a lot of time." He scanned the area for a flash of metal or other sign that Ramirez had found them.

"She's dead, isn't she." Behind him, Danny's voice was deadpan and certain.

Ethan glanced back at the boy, surprised at the slight quiver at the corner of his mouth. So he wasn't as brave as he wanted the world to believe. For a while Ethan had forgotten Danny was just a kid, holding himself and his sister together by a thread.

Just a kid. Eleven, twelve maybe, a few years older than Nicky would have been if he'd lived. "Yes," Ethan answered, steering his thoughts away from that particularly painful place. "She's dead."

"Did you—"

"No." Ethan shook his head. "Not me. But whoever did may come here next. So we need to get going."

The boy hesitated.

"I'm all you got, kid." Ethan steeled himself against the uncertainty in the boy's eyes and the long-buried instincts it awoke. "You come with me or . . ." He made a sweeping gesture at the dreary landscape. "Or you stay here."

"Danny." Callie tugged on her brother's sleeve. "It's okay. He'll help us."

Danny's expression softened. "But, Callie, he's—"

"It's okay," she said. "We have to go with him."

Ethan suspected the boy knew that as well, so he gave the kid a break and didn't force him to admit it. "I have something to take care of," he said. "Meanwhile, take your sister and gather stuff from the trailer. There's some bottled water, and get whatever nonperishable food you can find."

"Where are you going?" Danny challenged.

Ethan suppressed the urge to snap at the boy, reminding himself that despite his show of bravado, the kid was scared. "I'll be back in a couple of minutes. Just do as I told you."

Without looking back, Ethan headed out across the sand for the rock face behind the trailer. When he reached it, he stepped through a small hidden opening into the cool darkness of a cave.

Years ago, while still under the Agency's yoke, he'd recognized the need for a refuge, a place only his team would know about, a sanctuary and rendezvous point where they could meet in case things fell apart. He and the five people he'd led had pledged their lives to their country, but none of them totally trusted the men who gave the orders.

Together, they'd chosen this desert valley for its seclusion and the ridge behind the trailer. It provided both privacy and a wall at their backs. Plus, limited access. There was only one way in and one way out of the canyon, unless you were partial to a two-day hike across hot sand.

It was a good choice, but they'd never come back after selecting the site. They'd never needed to—until the end. Then none of them had made it. Except Ethan.

The memory of those first months when he'd waited, hoping against all odds that one of his team would escape the Spaniard's wrath, was bitter still. Eventually he'd resigned himself to being the only one left alive. But Anna had lived, and it gnawed at him, raising questions he couldn't ignore. Including why she'd waited all this time to seek him out.

Later, he promised himself, after he got those two kids to safety. Then he'd find out about Anna and how she'd managed to escape Ramirez. For now he used a flashlight he'd stored near the mouth of the cave and made his way deeper into the darkness.

The final advantage of this location was the warren of tunnels beneath the ragged bluff, tunnels where a desperate man could evade capture or hide whatever he didn't want found. When he'd first retreated here, Ethan had buried a duffel bag—an insurance policy against some future need. That had been before the nights had become his enemy and the desert isolation his only friend. He'd never touched the bag. Hell, most of the time he'd forgotten it was there, which was probably a good thing. He might have wasted the contents, and now he desperately needed the cash, identification, and weapons it contained.

Fifteen minutes later he returned to find Danny and Callie loading supplies into the truck. Besides his stash of bottled water, they'd found what passed for food on his nearly bare shelves. There was also an old first-aid kit Ethan had forgotten about, a flashlight, rope, and several blankets.

Ethan had to admit they were a couple of smart kids. Now, if only the boy could do something about his attitude. Tossing the duffel into the truck, he said, "Get in."

"Where are we going?" Danny asked.

"Away from here." Ethan started to climb behind the wheel but stopped, the sight of Anna's leather bag still on the seat giving him an idea. "Just a minute," he said, pulling out her cell phone and hitting the redial button. It was a long shot, but Anna's last call might tell him something. After five long rings an answering machine picked up, and a familiar feminine voice sent him reeling.

"I'm sorry," it said. "No one is available to take your call. Please leave your name and number, and we'll get back to you as soon as possible."

Sydney.

Anna had called his wife. Ex-wife. And just hearing her voice again stirred the guilt that had plagued him since Nicky's funeral, when Ethan had abandoned her.

An eye for an eye, one child's life for another.

The words, once whispered to Ethan in the dead of night, played in his mind with a sick, singsong quality.

One life for another.

Ramirez had lost a child and taken Ethan's in return. The debt had been paid. Except there was another promise Ramirez had made, another life he could claim.

Sydney's.

She was safe as long as Ethan kept his distance. That had been the rest of Ramirez's message. "Walk away, *amigo*," that voice in the night had whispered, "and we will end this."

Ethan had understood. He could go after Ramirez and find him. Neither of them doubted that. But an assassin's bullet could find its mark with frightening ease. The question was, could Ethan stop Ramirez before *his* bullet found Sydney?

It wasn't a risk Ethan was willing to take. So he'd left her and stayed away, knowing Ramirez would keep his word. Sydney would live. Now Anna had drawn Sydney into their twisted game with one call, and it changed everything.

"Mr. Decker?" Callie said, her voice small and frightened. "Are you okay?"

Ethan looked down at the child but couldn't speak. Why would Anna call Sydney? And what did it have to do with these children? He started to touch the child's cheek, but stopped himself.

It had all come full circle.

He'd been born with a talent for the hunt, a skill the Army Special Forces had trained, the Agency had honed, and practice had refined. Because of that ability, or because he'd chosen to use it, his son had died. And now, Sydney's life was in danger once again as well.

He'd been a fool to think he could outrun fate. There would be no easy out for a man like him, all he could do was try and save the innocents.

"Get in," he said to the kids. "We're going to Dallas."

CHAPTER FIVE

Marco Ramirez had always thought of Dallas as a sleek young woman, all clean, straight lines with just enough flash to make her interesting. For those with money, she was indeed stunning, a high-class whore, hustling by day and spreading her legs at night. For everyone else she was an impossible dream, a temptation just beyond reach.

Sydney Decker's building, a glass and steel high-rise at the heart of the business district, was no exception. It catered to those who put convenience first and didn't mind paying for it. Privacy would be their top priority, and Marco doubted whether the former Mrs. Decker knew any other residents of her new home.

The thought made him smile.

Living there would be a far cry from the sprawling suburban ranch house, with its gaggle of nosy neighbors, she'd once shared with her husband and young son. To Marco's way of thinking, she'd come up in the world.

Sipping a cup of steaming coffee, he shifted in the leather seat of his rented Mercedes and settled in for the duration. He'd been here an hour already, watching Dr. Decker's building from the cool shadows of a parking garage. He would stay as long as it took. Another hour. The whole night if necessary.

Until Ethan Decker showed up.

Following Decker from New Mexico to Dallas hadn't been necessary. Marco knew he would show up here sooner or later. The man had always been too much of a Boy Scout for his own good, and it made him predictable. Once Marco had taken care of the Kelsey woman, Decker would declare himself the kids' protector, which would put him back in the game and his ex-wife in danger. So he'd come to Dallas in an attempt to beat Marco to Sydney. The irony was that although Decker had lost the race, Marco wasn't interested in the woman just now.

It was the niños he wanted.

They were the missing link, the key to unlocking the questions which had plagued him for three long years.

Suddenly, out of the corner of his eye, he sensed movement and froze. Slowly, he slipped his hand to the Beretta beneath his arm and eased it from its holster. Then, hunkering down, he slid across the front seat and out the passenger door.

Decker?

Possible. Though Marco wasn't expecting him so soon.

He kept low and worked his way along the body of the car to the rear fender, his weapon ready. A half dozen parking spaces away, something scraped lightly against the cold concrete.

He frowned.

Not Decker. Kids maybe, stealing hubcaps. Hardly worth the effort. But Marco hadn't survived this long by guessing. With all his senses on alert, he worked his way along the cars to investigate.

The nearer he got, the odder it seemed. He couldn't identify the sound. Pausing, he listened closely. It wasn't metal against metal like someone popping hubcaps, or the slight thump of a petty thief punching holes next to door locks.

Nothing recognizable, just an occasional scraping.

Marco calmed himself, settling into the stillness. He counted slowly to three and swung around the bumper, the Beretta extended.

Suddenly, something brushed against his leg. Marco recoiled, his finger a hairsbreadth away from the trigger. Then stopped. "*Murrda!*"

A scrabbly yellow tom darted from beneath a nearby car.

Embarrassed, Marco laughed shortly and lowered his gun. "What a brave *hombre* you are." He returned the weapon to its holster. "Chasing down *señor gato*."

He stepped forward to see what the cat—hunched now against the concrete—had cornered. A ratlike creature cowered within the arms of a steel girder. At first Marco thought it was a field mouse from the empty lot behind the building. Then he realized it was some other type of rodent, the kind rich kids kept in cages. Not much different from the rats he'd once used as target practice in East L.A.

This one must have escaped and was as good as dead out here. If it managed to elude the cat, some other beast or vehicle would end its life.

Marco moved closer, the tom hissing in protest. With a nudge of his foot, he sent it scurrying off, although it didn't go far. He was about to deprive it of its prey, and the cat was not happy about it. Squatting down in front of the small animal, Marco recognized its fear in the wild-eyed stare and nervous twitching of its tiny paws. He'd looked into the eyes of death too often not to recognize it. It was no different here than in any of the men Marco had killed.

Fear was something Marco understood, as was honor in the hunt.

"*Chiquitin,* you are no match for *señor gato.*" Marco extended his hand. "He should be ashamed, hunting one such as you."

The creature sniffed Marco's fingers, obviously recognizing the familiar human scent.

"Come." Marco slipped his hand around the small body. "He must find more suitable prey."

He continued to croon as he carried the animal back to the car. A fast-food box from his dinner worked nicely as a cozy cage, bits of leftover lettuce and tomato a fine meal for a refugee. He'd find a willing pet store to take his new charge. Meanwhile, the tiny creature curled into himself and slept.

Forgetting the animal and returning to his vigil, Marco's thoughts wrapped around the past three years. During that time he'd lived for one purpose—to punish those who'd tried to kill him and murdered a child instead. *M'hija.* A girl-child of his heart. An innocent under his protection.

At first he'd been maddened by grief, and revenge had been his only comfort. He'd hunted down each member of the team who'd pulled the trigger and made them pay. Only Anna Kelsey had slipped through his grasp. But he was a patient man and knew he'd find her eventually. Yet, as he'd eased his rage with blood, he'd discovered revenge wasn't enough. He had sworn his life to the Agency, they'd been the only family he'd ever known, and they'd turned on him. Now, Marco needed to know *why*.

Like the elusive Anna Kelsey, however, answers weren't easily found. So Marco had gone underground, selling his services to the highest bidder in a world where anything could be gotten for a price. Especially information.

In this case all rumors, and the child he'd lost, led him to a private island in the northern reaches of Puget Sound, an island with children who never left its shores.

All except one. His. And she was dead.

He'd been hanging around the docks of Anacortes, gathering information and working on a plan to get out to the island, when he'd spotted Anna Kelsey. His first impulse had been to kill her, but at the last minute, he'd held back, deciding to use her instead. He had questions, and he figured Anna had the answers.

So for six months he'd waited and watched, and his patience had finally paid off. Three days ago Anna had fled Haven Island with two kids.

He'd considered taking them immediately, but again chose to bide his time. Without their cooperation, running with the kids would be risky. Besides, he wasn't sure yet what to do with them or how best to get the information they possessed. So he waited to see what Anna planned and where she'd take them.

It hadn't been easy trailing her.

She would have lost him more than once if not for the *niños*. They slowed her down and foiled her ability to fade into the surroundings. Despite them, though, she got away from him in the New Mexico desert, on a long stretch of empty highway where he couldn't risk following too closely.

Once he realized he'd lost her, he backtracked, cursing himself and her. He'd waited too long and was afraid he'd lost them for good. Spotting her a short time later was sheer luck, and he wouldn't make the same mistake twice. He wanted answers.

But he should have known it wouldn't be that easy. Nothing having to do with the Agency or Anna ever was. She'd gotten rid of the kids, and with a gun to her head she refused to give him anything. Not a hint at who they were, why she'd run with them, or where she'd taken them. So he'd had no further use for her. Nor the time to extract what she knew by force. Besides, they had an old score to settle.

She owed him, and he collected.

Afterward, he retraced her steps to look for the *niños*. He knew they had to be close. The question was where.

Decker's arrival on the scene a few miles later wasn't really a surprise. The desert seemed a fitting place for him to hide, and Anna would know where to find him. Plus, it made a sort of Boy-Scout sense that she'd run to him.

After that, it was a simple matter to figure he'd head for Dallas. Marco had left Anna's phone behind as bait, or an invitation, depending on your point of view. Decker had the kids, and if they and Anna's death weren't enough to bring him out of hiding, the call would be.

Now it was just the two of them, and they both needed answers. But first Decker would show up here at his ex-wife's condo to prevent Marco from carrying out his threat to end the woman's days.

Decker didn't disappoint him.

A little before daybreak he arrived in a broken-down pickup. Parking the truck on the street, he took his time getting out and scanning the area. His gaze lingered on the garage with its layers of concrete rising above the street, and Marco willed himself to fade into the darkness of the car's interior. For a moment he thought Decker had spotted him, that some sixth sense had honed in on this particular vehicle and its occupant.

Finally he turned away, and Marco breathed easier. Even now, years out of practice, Decker wasn't a man to toy with. If things had been different, it would be Decker doing the hunting. Fortunately Marco still possessed one piece of leverage, and he had every intention of using her.

As he watched, Decker grabbed a duffel bag from behind the driver's seat, circled the truck, and opened the passenger door. The kids climbed out.

Marco wondered how Decker planned to get past the building's security—not that there was a rent-a-cop alive who could stand against Ethan Decker if he chose to take him down.

As the three approached the front entrance, Decker leaned down and picked up the girl. She draped herself across his shoulders as if asleep, and all three disappeared into the building. With two sleepy children, Decker was going to charm his way past the night watchman.

It might just work. Decker had a talent for slipping into places where Marco would have needed firepower. And if Decker's plan didn't work this time? Well, Marco suspected, nothing would stop him from getting in to see his ex-wife and protecting her from the likes of the Spaniard.

Marco smiled and reached for the door handle. It was an illusion he'd enjoy destroying.

CHAPTER SIX

Sydney opened her eyes and lay very still, unsure what had awakened her. Then she heard it again, the same insistent buzzing that had pulled her from her dreams. Someone was at her front door. She sat up and checked the time. Five A.M.

The buzzer sounded once more, three quick stabs of an impatient finger.

Warily, she climbed out of bed, slipped on her robe, and started toward the front of her apartment. Who could be at her door this time of the morning? She considered dialing nine-one-one but quickly dismissed the idea. With the night watchman at the desk downstairs, it had to be one of her neighbors or Charles. Though it wasn't like him to show up unannounced in the middle of the night. Maybe there was a problem in the building, or someone with a medical emergency. She usually kept to herself, but several people on her floor knew she was a doctor.

As a precaution, she got her cell phone from her purse and slipped it into the pocket of her robe. At the door, she took a deep breath before saying, "Who is it?"

"Sydney, let me in."

Her stomach tightened. The voice was low, masculine, and hauntingly familiar, a voice she hadn't heard in three years. She must be imagining things.

"Who is it?" she repeated, pressing one hand to the wood frame while the other gripped the fabric at her waist.

A brief hesitation. "It's me. Ethan."

No. She wanted to say it aloud but simply shook her head and backed away. It couldn't be.

"Sydney." His voice was insistent, drawing her back to the door, though she wasn't about to open it. She wasn't even sure it was Ethan—or so she told herself. It had been three years, and voices could be faked, imitated. Couldn't they?

Reluctantly, she looked through the peephole. On the other side, she saw the shape of her ex-husband, strangely distorted through the tiny glass. She pulled back abruptly, her heart pounding in her chest. "What do you want?"

"Open up. We need to talk."

"I have nothing to say to you." She managed to sound more in control than she felt. He had a lot of nerve showing up here after what he'd done. Did he think she would welcome him with open arms?

"I'm not leaving." He pressed the buzzer again. "Now let me in before we wake the entire building."

"Go away." She pressed her hands against the door, hating him for doing this, for showing up on her doorstep after three years of silence.

"Sydney." He pounded on the door.

Damn him!

"Stop," she said, knowing he would keep on until he'd awakened everyone on her floor. "Give me a minute."

She hesitated, slipping a hand into her pocket and closing it around her cell phone. One brief call and she wouldn't have to deal with this, with him. It would serve him right to spend the night in jail after what he'd put her through. In the morning she'd visit him and find out what he wanted. Not that she cared. Hell, maybe she wouldn't go see him at all. He could rot in prison for all she cared. She pulled out the phone, pressed three numbers, and listened for the ringing. Then she quickly hit the disconnect button as a sob caught in her throat.

She couldn't do it.

Damn him, she thought again as she fought back her tears. She wouldn't cry over him, not now. Not ever again. But she couldn't have him arrested, either, and she hated herself for that weakness.

She shut off the alarm, released the dead bolt, and barely had time to back out of the way before he pushed inside and turned to relock the door behind him. He wasn't alone. Two children, a girl and a boy, had hurried into the room ahead of him. But they barely registered in the wake of the man whose presence filled her foyer.

He looked a little wild, with his hair too long and at least two days' worth of stubble on his chin. He wore dusty jeans, scuffed boots, and a faded denim shirt. Although he'd always leaned toward casual clothing, he'd been meticulously neat. Now, like his clothes, he appeared rumpled and well worn. His eyes, however, hadn't changed. They were the same intense blue that he'd passed on to their son.

Nicky's memory fueled her anger. "What are you doing here? Do you know what time it is?" Her questions sounded absurd considering their history, but she didn't know what else to say to him. "Who are these children?"

Without answering, he crossed to the sliding glass doors to her balcony and checked the locks. "Is there a back entrance?"

"Yes, but . . ." She followed him as he headed toward the kitchen and the back stairway. "Ethan, stop this and tell me what's going on."

"There's no time." His voice was brusque and commanding. "Get dressed. We have to get out of here."

"Get out of here?" They'd returned to the living room, where the children had collapsed on her couch. "What are you talking about?"

"You're in danger, Sydney."

"That's ridiculous." She crossed her arms, tossing a quick glance at the children before turning back to him. "I think you need to leave."

"We don't have time to argue, just get some clothes on."

It infuriated her, *he* infuriated her, storming in here like some kind of madman and issuing commands. "I don't know what game you're playing, Ethan,"—she turned her back on him—"but I'm calling the police."

He grabbed her arm, the contact disturbing her in a way she hadn't expected. "This isn't a game, Sydney, and I'm not playing. Now, you have two choices. You can come with me, or you can wait here to die."

A sliver of fear slipped down her spine, but as she met his gaze, icy anger rose up to banish it and her troublesome reaction to his touch. He had no right to be here, to put his hands on her. He'd relinquished that privilege three years ago, the day he'd walked out on her.

"Let go of me." Very purposely, she looked at his hand on her arm. And saw the gun.

Sydney froze.

As if shocked, Ethan released her and backed up. "I'm sorry." He shoved the weapon behind him, into the waistband of his jeans. "It's been a long night." His hands visibly shook as he ran them through his hair, pushing it away from his face. "Look, Syd, I'm sorry if I frightened you, but this is real. You're in danger."

She tried a safe question, a rational question. "Who are these children?"

"I'm Danny," the boy said. "And this is my sister Callie."

Sydney forced a smile. "I'm Sydney."

"We know," the girl said with one of those beautiful smiles only the very young can produce. "Ethan was in a hurry to get here. He was worried about you."

Sydney didn't know how to respond to that. Why would Ethan be worried about her? It was a question she didn't even want to think about, so she concentrated on the children. The girl was lovely, angelic even, with soft, sweet features. The boy was her counterpart, as dark as she was light, but just as beautiful in his own way. Who were they? And what were they doing with Ethan?

"Syd?" She turned back to Ethan. "We don't have time for this." He was calmer now, almost deliberately so. "I'll explain everything later, but for now you have to trust me. There's a man, a very dangerous man, on his way here. So please, get some clothes on, and let's get out of here."

Sydney realized she'd been wrong, not even his eyes were the same. There was something frightening about them, about him, an edge of danger she'd never seen before.

Deciding it was best, safest, to humor him, she nodded. "Okay, if you think that's best."

Doubt flickered in his eyes, and she worried that she'd acquiesced too easily. Of all people, Ethan knew she wouldn't willingly go along with this insanity.

"Give me a couple of minutes to get dressed," she said quickly, "and throw some things in a bag."

Ethan nodded, although he didn't seem convinced. "Hurry."

Sydney walked to her bedroom, but when she went to close the door, Ethan grabbed it. "Leave it open."

She glared at him, forcing down a sharp retort. Then, turning away, she moved about her bedroom gathering clothing. At the entrance to her bathroom, she looked back at him. "Do I have to leave this open as well? Or would you rather come in and make sure I don't climb out the window or something?"

"Just make it quick, Sydney." He retreated to the living room, his voice a low muffle as he spoke to the children.

Sydney shut the bathroom door and closed her eyes, conscious of her rapidly beating pulse and angry at herself as much as at him. He wasn't the man she'd known, he was different, sick maybe, and definitely dangerous. Her response to him was insane. He was unstable, and the sooner she could get away from him, the better.

After turning on the faucet full force, she took out her cell phone. It took less than a minute to place her call, and her only regret was that she hadn't done it before letting Ethan into her apartment. Once she hung up, she let the minutes stretch out as she cleaned up and dressed, pulling on a pair of jeans and a knit top. She had to give the police time to arrive. Back in the bedroom, she slipped the cell phone into her purse, then took down her overnight bag and started filling it with toiletries.

Ethan appeared in the doorway. "Come on, Sydney, you've had enough time."

"Just give me a few more—"

Two quick strides and he was beside her, one hand taking her arm, while the other grabbed her jacket, purse, and half-filled bag. "We have to go. Now."

He'd hustled her into the living room before she could stop him. "Take your hands off me." She pulled free, her resolve to remain calm shattered. "I told you I'd come, you don't have to manhandle me."

"You're stalling." He shoved her jacket into her hands.

She slipped it on, the supple leather reminding her that he'd given it to her for their third wedding anniversary. Paper, cotton, leather, fruit, wood, and candy: the traditional gifts for the first six years of a marriage, and he hadn't missed one. A true romantic, or so she'd thought until he'd walked out on her.

"I was just getting my things together." She had a hard time keeping the anger out of her voice.

He eyed her the way he did when trying to see past her words, then motioned to the children. "Come on, we're getting out of here, with or without Dr. Decker."

A knock on the door stopped them.

He looked at her, a spark of anger in his eyes. "Who'd you call?"

She backed away from him, her hands raised. "It's okay, Ethan, they're here to help. You're not well."

"Shit." He rubbed a hand over his face. "Danny, take your sister down the back stairs and wait there for as long as you can. If things start going bad, get out. Head for the *Dallas Morning News* and tell them your story. Understand?"

Danny nodded, took Callie's hand, and headed for the kitchen.

"No, wait." Sydney blocked their way. "You can't just go off by yourselves."

"Dr. Decker." The booming voice came from outside her apartment. "Police. Open up."

The children slipped past her.

"Wait," she said, but they didn't even slow down.

"Dr. Decker, are you in there?"

Unable to stop the children, she started for the front door, but Ethan caught her hand. "They can't protect you, Sydney."

She looked into his eyes, and it was as if time itself stopped breathing. Once she would have followed this man to hell and back without question. Now she wasn't sure. Yet an eerie sensation crept up her spine, a certainty that he spoke the truth. "Can you, Ethan? Can you protect me?"

He didn't answer immediately. "Maybe."

She frowned, tugged her hand free, and backed away.

The door burst open, and two uniformed officers scrambled into her apartment, guns extended, finding and aiming at Ethan. "Hands where we can see them."

He obeyed, slowly. "You're making a mistake, officers."

"Are you okay, Dr. Decker?" One of the men stepped to her side.

Sydney kept her eyes on Ethan, who seemed remarkably calm considering the circumstances. And dangerous. "Yes, I—"

"Tell them you made a mistake, Sydney," Ethan warned. "Explain that I'm your husband and have been out of town. I surprised you this morning and that's why you called."

The officers appeared uneasy. "What's going on here, Dr. Decker?"

Sydney hesitated, torn. Part of her wanted to trust him, to put her faith in the man who'd been her husband, the man she'd promised to love, honor, and cherish. Another part, the rational part, balked. Three years ago he'd abandoned that oath, and now he'd all but broken into her apartment, brandishing a gun and talking about someone coming to kill her. How could she trust him?

"I'm fine," she said to the uniformed man at her side. "But this man isn't my husband. Not anymore."

Ethan went very still, the shift subtle but frightening. With her denial of their relationship, he'd grown calmer and more alert, ready. Had the others sensed it? She glanced at the police officers, realizing they hadn't noticed, and felt a chill ripple through her. Ethan had no intention of allowing these officers to arrest him.

Then she remembered the gun. "Watch out, he has—"

Behind her a muffled creak, and Ethan spun toward the sound, a weapon already in his hand. "Get down!"

His words had barely reached her when she heard a soft thud, and a bright crimson rose blossomed on the chest of the officer at her side. Sydney jerked backward, a scream caught in her throat. The young man tumbled to the floor, eyes wide.

Gunshots exploded and glass shattered as Ethan shoved her to the floor, the impact forcing the scream from her throat. The second officer went down, his gun hand jerking upward without pulling the trigger, a grunt of surprise escaping his open lips.

Reflexively, she moved toward him, but Ethan had her pinned, covering her as he fired toward the balcony. One shot. Two. And the panel erupted outward, showering glass fragments on a dark figure as it disappeared over the railing.

Then Ethan was off her, moving to first one officer then the other, checking for life. Sydney scrambled to help, going to the young man who seconds earlier had stood by her side. Before she could do more than press trembling fingers to the pulse point in his neck, Ethan grabbed her arm and dragged her to her feet.

"We have to get out of here," he said.

"No, wait." She tried to break free. "Let me go—"

He tightened his hold on her arm. "There's nothing you can do for them."

"No, I—"

"They're dead, Sydney." His voice was cold, hard. A stranger's voice. "Come on, or we'll be next."

Ethan urged her toward the kitchen and the back door.

In shock, she let him lead her into the stairwell. "How did that man—we're twelve floors up."

"Climbing gear," Ethan answered without slowing. "He either rappelled down from the roof or another balcony."

"But . . ." They'd descended several flights, and suddenly she noticed the blood. "You've been hit." She tried to stop their headlong flight and get a look at Ethan's arm.

"It's nothing." He kept her moving.

"You could be seriously hurt."

"Later." They'd almost reached the bottom, where Danny and Callie waited. "In the truck," Ethan commanded.

The boy pushed through the door, setting off alarms that would soon bring more of the city's finest.

Ethan kept going, hurrying her through the door and across the parking lot as the sky began to lighten. The children scrambled into an old truck, and then she was sliding in as well, with Ethan pushing in beside her and starting the engine. As he put the vehicle in gear and screeched away from the curb, she heard the sirens in the distance and wondered when she was going to awake.

CHAPTER SEVEN

Ethan drove with his left hand, his right gripping the Glock in his lap. Sydney sat wedged against him, her tension palpable and expectant, while the kids huddled together between her and the passenger door, their fear seeping into the silence.

What the hell had he done?

By barging into Sydney's condo with no other plan than to get her out, he'd nearly gotten her killed and himself shot in the process. And with his adrenaline levels returning to something resembling normal, he was only too aware of the ragged hole in his arm. The bullet had ripped through the outer portion of his right bicep, searing his flesh like a white-hot flame. Warm blood soaked his sleeve and plastered the wet fabric to his skin. Already, the limb had stiffened. Before he lost any more mobility, he needed to get Sydney and the kids to safety.

Damn. He wished it were later. In an hour the Dallas roads would be choked with early morning traffic, making it easier to blend in and disappear. As it was now, the few vehicles on the streets didn't provide much cover.

He checked the rearview mirror, noted the cars behind them, then turned his attention to his three passengers. "Is everyone all right?"

"I'm okay," Callie said.

"Danny?"

"Just great."

Ethan bit back his annoyance at the boy's attitude. After all, he couldn't blame the kid for being angry. Danny was fiercely protective of his younger sister, and Ethan had put both kids in danger by bringing them to Dallas.

"What about you, Sydney?" He glanced at the woman beside him, not daring to let his eyes linger more than a second or two. When she didn't answer, he risked another glimpse.

She met his gaze briefly, then frowned at his arm, avoiding his eyes as studiously as he had hers. "You should be in a hospital."

He focused on the road, annoyed that he'd allowed himself to be distracted by her for even a moment. It could get them both killed. "It's not that bad."

"You've been shot." She enunciated each word, as if telling him something he didn't know. "And you're bleeding."

"There's a medicine kit," Callie said, scooting forward to open the backpack at their feet and pull out a white, tin container with a bold red cross on the lid.

"It's just a scratch," Ethan said as Sydney dug through the limited medical supplies. "We have more important things to worry about." He scanned the street signs, watching for the highway access. It had been years since he'd been in Dallas, and things had changed. "We've got to get out of the city."

"It's a bullet wound, Ethan, not a scratch." Sydney found and ripped open a package of sterile pads. "Callie, tear off about a foot of that gauze and cut it into strips."

"Let it go," he said. They didn't have time for this. "You can take care of it later."

She peeled the fabric from his arm, ripping his sleeve in one quick motion from elbow to shoulder. Then she pressed the pad to his torn flesh, and pain bolted up his arm.

"Jesus, Sydney . . ." He sucked in a breath, wondering if she'd turned into a closet sadist. "Take it easy."

"As usual, you're not listening to me," she said. "There won't be a later, not for me. Callie, give me one of those gauze strips."

The girl obeyed, and Sydney secured the makeshift dressing, her quick, competent hands tying first one then the other piece of gauze to his throbbing arm. "That will slow the bleeding until you get to a hospital." She placed the supplies back in the box and shut the lid with a snap. "Luckily, the bullet passed through, but you still need to have it cleaned and properly dressed. I'd suggest a hospital, but that's entirely up to you. Now, stop and let me out."

Ethan snorted in disbelief. She still didn't get it; her life was in danger. No way he'd just drop her off somewhere to take her chances. "Forget it."

"You can't keep me in this truck, Ethan."

"Look, I know you're upset—"

"Upset? We've been shot at, we saw two policemen—" She stopped speaking abruptly. Then, with what seemed a great deal of effort, she lowered her voice. "This is insane."

Yeah, he thought, insane was as good a word as any. "Look. I'll explain what I can later. Just let me get the three of you out of the—"

"Who was that man?"

Ethan glanced in the rearview mirror again and didn't like what he saw. "Does it matter?"

"Of course it matters," she snapped. "You say I'm in danger, someone shot at us. I want to know who."

She'd always had a hell of a temper beneath that mon-eyed veneer of hers. Usually she kept it tightly reined. That is, until faced with some injustice. Then she'd become a tigress: fierce, fearless, and breathtaking. He'd once loved that about her, admiring the clarity anger brought to her thoughts and the sharpness it brought to her tongue. Right now, however, he'd have preferred someone a bit easier to handle.

"I'm not sure," he said. It wasn't exactly a lie.

"Take a guess."

Okay, so he could do more than guess, he knew who'd shot at them. Marco Ramirez. The only surprises were his timing and that he'd missed. He was one of the best, but with three guns in the room—Ethan's and the two cops'—the chances of even Ramirez succeeding without getting shot had been slim. So why had he picked that moment to carry out his threat against Sydney?

"Ethan?"

Before he could answer her, something else caught his eye. It seemed they had another, more pressing problem. Maybe two. "Not now. We're being followed."

"What?"

"Don't," he said, as both Sydney and Callie turned to look out the back window. "Danny, check your side mirror. Can you see the Mercedes? It's dark gray, about five or six cars back."

Danny straightened. "Yeah, I see it."

"Watch him, and let me know if he follows us."

"What are you going to do?" Sydney said, more anxious now than angry.

"Nothing much." Ethan took the next side street, keeping his speed steady and unhurried. "We're just taking a little detour to see whether this joker is really on our tail, or if I'm imagining things. Danny?"

"He pulled into a parking lot."

"Give him a block or two to pick us up again. If I'm right, he'll flow with the traffic while keeping his distance."

The car Ethan had passed in the desert before finding Anna's body had been a high-priced import, just like the one he suspected of following them now. Ramirez, probably. In both cases. He would want to keep Sydney in his sights, and the Mercedes fit his self-image. But what about the second car, a sedan, flitting at the traffic edges a block or so back? Was the vehicle following them, or was Ethan letting his paranoia get the best of him?

The Mercedes reappeared, closer than before, surprising him with the driver's incompetence. Or boldness.

On the one hand, Ramirez had never been worth jack at running a tail. A high-powered rifle from a rooftop or a lethal encounter in a crowd were more to his liking. Which was probably how Anna had managed to evade him for so long. His methods weren't meant for a target in hiding—especially one as good at it as Anna Kelsey. But even Ramirez could do a better job of keeping out of sight than the driver of the Mercedes.

Ethan looked for the second car, but this time saw nothing unusual. Except Ramirez, making himself plainly visible. Could the assassin be a decoy, a distraction for other, less obvious pursuers? Ethan considered it but quickly dismissed the idea. He'd known Marco Ramirez since their earliest days with the Agency, and although a lot could change in three years, not this. Ramirez worked alone.

So what was he up to?

Ethan watched the Mercedes as a long-suppressed rage stirred within him. After Nicky's death, Ethan had bowed to Ramirez's threats. He'd left Sydney and the Agency to hole up in the desert, where each new day had reeked of his failures.

"Goddamn you, Ramirez." All Ethan needed, all he'd ever needed, was one shot at the bastard. "It's time we finish this."

"Ethan?"

Sydney's unspoken question momentarily cut through his anger, but he shoved his hesitation aside. He'd waited too long for this chance, he wasn't about to lose it now. He would make Ramirez pay for Nicky's death.

"Hold on," he said and made several quick turns, heading away from the downtown area. The awakening city fell away to the trendy Deep Ellum district, where residents still slept behind their shuttered windows. At the end of a quiet block, Ethan spun the truck around, bringing them full circle, and stopped.

"Okay," he said. "Come and get me."

"Ethan, stop this. Please."

He ignored Sydney's fear, shut his heart to the panic in her voice. She didn't understand, couldn't, without knowing the truth about their son's death. It hadn't been an accident. Nicky had been murdered, and the man responsible now had his sights set on Sydney.

The Mercedes materialized, a dusky wraith in the early morning light. It stopped a block away, spotting them and gauging its next move. Then it started up again, creeping toward them.

"That's right, you coward." Ethan checked the Glock's clip and ignored the flash of fire in his arm. "Just a little closer, and we'll settle this once and for all."

As the Mercedes approached, the shapeless driver emerged from the shadows and took on Ramirez's familiar features. Ethan had expected no one else, but the shock of it, of seeing the face of his son's killer after all this time, froze him in place. The vehicle stopped, and for a moment they stared at each other, the distance between them collapsing in a crush of bitter memories. Ethan saw the hatred in Ramirez's eyes, the madness, and he expected his own face screamed the same.

They would end this. Now.

Ethan grabbed the door handle, but Sydney's fingers bit into his forearm, stopping him, begging him without words to stay. Her silent plea shredded his resolve. The last time she'd needed him, he'd walked away. Could he do that again and live with himself?

"Let's get out of here," she said. "Please."

But could he turn his back on Ramirez? Just take Sydney and these kids and run, and never look back?

A flicker of movement caught his eye. A blue sedan rounded the far corner, slowed, then picked up speed as it switched lanes to come straight at them.

A trap. The son of a bitch set us up.

"Hang on." Ethan punched the accelerator and twisted the steering wheel hard to the right. Tires squealed and bumped as they struck the curb. The truck careened onto the sidewalk, colliding with a trash can and sideswiping the metal collar around a sapling.

"Get down." He shoved Sydney's head below the dashboard, half expecting a bullet to shatter his window. "All of you."

The kids ducked, and Ethan laid on the horn as a warning to pedestrians. Glass-fronted shops whipped by on his right and parked cars on his left. Behind them, Ramirez took off in the opposite direction. But the sedan slammed into reverse, matching Ethan's speed and blocking his escape back to the road, its tinted windows frustrating his attempt to identify the driver.

Near the end of the block, Ethan saw his chance and aimed for a gap between two parked cars. The truck hurtled off the curb. The sedan screeched to a stop, but not quick enough to avoid the scream of metal and burst of sparks as Ethan skimmed its bumper. With a clear road ahead, Ethan used the sedan's turnaround time to put some distance between them.

He sped back toward downtown, taking a circuitous route and keeping one eye on the rearview mirror. The trick was to lose the tail without picking up a cop. Meanwhile his passengers sat up, bracing themselves against the truck's erratic maneuvers.

"Are they still after us?" Callie asked.

Ethan glanced at her, then her brother and Sydney. All three were noticeably shaken but okay. "We'll lose them."

They ended up back on Commerce, a main thoroughfare through the center of Dallas. He hadn't seen the sedan for several blocks, but he had no illusions about having lost it. Not yet anyway. And where the hell was Ramirez? Had he set them up and taken off? Or had he been surprised by the sedan as well?

"Danny, watch for the Mercedes while I ditch the other car."

The early morning rush hour was at full force now, which gave Ethan the advantage. He threaded the truck across three lanes of bumper-to-bumper traffic, waiting for the right moment. A few blocks back, the sedan entered the fray and Ethan took his shot. Just as the next light turned red, he made a quick left in front of a line of oncoming vehicles. Horns blared and brakes shrieked, but Ethan skidded around their outrage and headed down a secondary road, the sedan stuck in gridlock behind them.

No one said a word, though Sydney had braced an arm across the front of both kids, holding them against the seat. Ethan expected the three of them were too stunned or frightened to do more. He couldn't help that now.

He continued to snake his way through Dallas as even the side streets filled with commuters. Unless Ramirez reappeared, they had a clear shot to the highway, but Ethan wasn't about to let down his guard. He'd misjudged the assassin once today and wasn't going to make the same mistake again. "See anything, Danny?"

The boy took a moment to answer, his voice shaky. "No, I think we lost them."

"Me, too."

"That's a good thing," said Sydney. "Right?"

"I'll feel better when we've put some miles between us and Dallas." Not to mention knowing what the hell was going on. "What's the quickest way to the highway?"

She hesitated, then gave him directions that put them on the entrance ramp to U.S. 75, heading north.

For several miles the silence continued. Then Sydney spoke up. "Ethan, we need to go to the police."

"They can't help us." Ethan released the Glock and flexed his fingers. "You saw what happened at your place."

"But they were taken by surprise. If we warn them—"

"It won't matter. The man driving that Mercedes was on your balcony this morning." Ethan hesitated, wondering just how much to tell her. "His name is Marco Ramirez, and the authorities can't touch him."

"But why?"

"He's an assassin, Sydney, government trained and owned. Even if the cops manage to arrest him, which is unlikely, they won't hold him."

"That doesn't make sense. The government doesn't use assassins, it's illegal."

He didn't respond, letting her work it out for herself. Legal or not, the Agency had their secrets, and she was smart enough to see that.

"Okay," she said. "Say I believe you. What does he want? Why did he kill those policemen?"

"They weren't the target, they were just in the way."

"Who then?"

He hesitated, though he could no longer shield her from the truth. It was the only thing that might save her. "You."

She flinched as if struck, then sat straighter, instinctually defensive. "I don't believe it."

"I caught this bullet pushing you to the floor."

He felt a shudder tremble through her. "That doesn't prove anything." But doubt had crept into her voice.

"Do you really want to take a chance on that?"

For what seemed a long while, she didn't answer. "What about that other car?" she asked finally.

"I'm not sure." His thoughts jumped to the kids, no doubt listening intently. "I don't know who they were or what they're after." Though he had a pretty good idea. What he didn't know was why. "I was hoping *you* could tell me."

"Me? I don't know anything about any of this."

"Do you remember Anna Kelsey?" He pulled the cell phone from his pocket. "She worked with me at the Agency."

"Of course I remember her."

"This"—he handed over the phone—"was hers. Push the redial button." When Sydney hesitated, he said, "Go on, listen."

She obeyed with obvious reluctance, her eyes widening as the recorded message reached her ears. "I don't understand."

"Neither do I." He took back the phone, snapped it closed, and slipped it into his pocket. "Did you talk to her? Or get a message from her?"

"No, I hardly knew her. Why would she call me? Have you asked her?"

"I would have . . ." He paused. "Except Anna's dead, Sydney. Murdered. And that call to you was the last she ever made."

CHAPTER EIGHT

Murdered?

For a moment, Sydney couldn't speak. She'd met Anna Kelsey only once, years ago, although she couldn't say exactly when or where. The only reason she remembered Anna at all was that a woman that beautiful was hard to forget, especially when she worked with your husband. Now, according to Ethan, Anna was dead, murdered, and she'd called Sydney before dying.

It must be a mistake.

Or was it? Something nipped at Sydney's thoughts, a hazy memory or bit of information she was forgetting. What? She almost caught it, but it slipped out of reach.

"Ethan, what's going on?"

He shifted on the cracked vinyl and tightened his grip on the steering wheel. "I hoped you could tell me, or at least shed some light on the subject."

She couldn't, not about Anna or anything else that had happened in the last few hours.

"You might know more than you think," he said. "But let's get somewhere safe, then we'll talk."

Somewhere safe.

Just a few hours ago, she'd taken safety for granted. Now it had become something to seek, a goal to reach. Or die trying.

Then the memory snapped into place. Charles had listened to her phone messages last night. "There were a couple of hang ups on my answering machine yesterday."

Ethan looked at her. "Is that unusual?"

She shrugged. "No, but if Anna called me, why didn't she leave a message?" In truth, Sydney couldn't have sworn the other woman hadn't left a message. Although she couldn't imagine why Charles would lie about it.

"Too dangerous. Anna wouldn't have exposed herself like that." For a moment, Ethan let the silence rest. Then he said, "Do your parents still own the cabin on Lake Texoma?"

The question seemed out of place, and it took her a moment to understand what he meant. "Yes, why? Is that where we're going?"

"Not exactly." He checked the rearview mirror, as he'd done a dozen times or more since getting into the truck. "It's too obvious and will be one of the first places Ramirez and company look."

"How would they even know about it?"

Ethan shot her a quick glance, eyebrows raised.

"Never mind," she said. It had been a stupid question. This was the information age. Any kid with a computer and a talent for snooping could get into state or county tax files and find a record of all property owned by her or her family.

"I was thinking of Laurel Lodge," Ethan said.

The statement surprised her as much as anything else he'd done since storming into her apartment. "Are you serious?"

"It's off the beaten track and won't open for another month or so." He flexed the fingers of his right hand, balling his fist then reopening it. "Unless—"

She lost his words as he worked his arm, straightening and bending, demanding its mobility despite the pain shadowing his features. She checked the makeshift bandage for signs of fresh blood but saw none. Not yet anyway. But if he continued pushing himself, it was only a matter of time.

"Sydney?"

She met his gaze, fear and something stronger clenching her chest. With a bullet hole in his arm and Dallas falling farther behind, he remained vigilant and determined to protect them no matter the cost. In some ways, he hadn't changed at all.

"Has something changed?" he asked.

Again he'd thrown her, as if he'd been reading her mind. "What?"

"Laurel Lodge, have they altered their season?"

"I don't know." She forced herself to forget the man and consider his question.

Laurel Lodge was a small, exclusive resort perched on the rocky bluffs above Lake Texoma. For thirty years it had opened on Memorial Day and closed the day after Labor Day weekend, catering to wealthy Dallasites wanting to get away from the heat. The owner had been a friend and patient of her father's, and she and Ethan had . . .

"I haven't been to the lake since . . ." *since Nicky.* "For a long time." And she didn't want to return with Ethan now. Or ever.

"Will anyone look for us there?"

"I doubt it." Laurel Lodge had been their secret, one she'd kept safe amid the rubble of her marriage. She hated admitting it and letting him know how much the memory meant to her. "But someone may already be there, a cleaning or setup crew."

He considered that, then shook his head. "We'll have to chance it."

Everything inside her rebelled at the idea, but she didn't argue. It wouldn't have done any good. Once Ethan had made up his mind about something, nothing could change it. Besides, objecting too strongly would only draw more attention to her discomfort at returning to the lodge.

So the quiet stretched out, punctuated by the rhythmic thump of hard rubber against asphalt and the grumble of an old engine. Miles of spring green grassland flowed past them, watched by the endless blue of a Texas sky. With the silence came an acute awareness of the close quarters: the truck, ripe with the copper of dried blood and the scent of overheated children; Callie, her head lolling in sleep against Sydney's arm; Danny, his eyes fixed on some unknown point past the windows. And Ethan, mute and tense beside her, his muscular thigh pressed against hers, electric and unsettling.

A sense of unreality swept through her. If she thought too hard about the last couple of hours or how she came to be here beside Ethan, she might start screaming. Yet she felt more alive than she had in years.

An hour and a half later, they pulled off the highway and headed toward the lake. As far as she knew, Ethan had never driven to the lodge, but he found the entrance, an unmarked dirt track like a dozen others in the area. A mile or so down a shaded road, Laurel Lodge emerged from the woods.

On the outside, it looked the same.

Sitting amid a smattering of oak, elm, and bois d'arc, the two-story structure rose atop a limestone bluff. Clustered beneath the trees and edging the base of the building, spring wildflowers—anemone, blue-eyed grass, and purple verbena—flourished. Beyond the clearing, the woods closed in, a dense growth shielding the lodge from the bustling tourism of the lake community.

Off to one side of the cliff, a path led down to a ragged beach, boathouse, and dock. From there, if you followed the shore another mile, climbing over rocks and wading through slippery pools, you'd come to a secluded inlet with sandy beaches and a cluster of vacation homes. Her parents owned the largest of these.

Shortly after their marriage, she and Ethan had spent a long weekend there. Her parents hadn't approved of her husband, but she'd believed if they got to know him, they'd change their minds. By the second night, however, she acknowledged her mistake. All they'd seen was the Army brat raised in a dozen different military towns and educated in the public school system. They'd closed their eyes to the man, to everything that made Ethan special, his strength and kindness, his intelligence and warmth, his integrity and devotion to his country.

It had made her angry, but Ethan had agreed with them, claiming he wasn't good enough for her. She'd known better, and later that night had talked him into sneaking out in search of privacy so she could prove it to him. With a full moon reflecting off the lake, they'd followed the nonexistent path along the shore to Laurel Lodge, silent and deserted, as it was now.

"Callie, wake up." Danny nudged his sister and reached for the door handle.

"Wait—" Sydney and Ethan said at once.

Sydney glanced back at him, awkwardly aware they'd fallen into an old pattern. How often had they spoken to Nicky at the same moment, to issue a warning or give an instruction?

"Stay out of sight," Ethan said, seemingly unaware of her discomfort. "And away from the cliff."

The boy nodded, and both children scrambled from the truck.

Their enthusiasm made Sydney smile, reminding her of how much Nicky had loved the lake. Every summer she had brought him to spend a week or two at her parents' cabin. Sometimes Ethan joined them, but mostly they'd come alone or with her folks, who adored their only grandchild.

Neither she nor Ethan had ever brought Nicky here though, to Laurel Lodge. "How are we going to get in?"

Ethan smiled, a ghost of his old self peeking through, and another unwanted shiver of awareness caressed her. "The same way as before."

He climbed from the truck, using his good hand to slip the gun into the waistband of his jeans. Then he grabbed his duffel bag from behind the seat and started toward the rear entrance. Sydney hurried after him, and by the time she caught up, he'd started on the back door, working the lock with two slender metal picks.

Once before, she'd watched him do this and had half-jokingly asked, "Does the Agency train all their analysts to pick locks?"

"Sure, they taught us all kinds of nefarious skills."

She'd laughed, unsure whether he was kidding, though it hadn't really mattered at the time. Their adventure held little peril that night. If caught, she and Ethan risked little more than embarrassment. Now, however, the stakes were higher, and she shuddered at the thought of the men from Dallas finding them here.

Isolation could work for or against them.

Ethan finished with the lock, retrieved the gun from his waistband, and opened the door. "Wait here while I make sure it's clear."

She nodded, her eyes drawn to the weapon, no longer taking anything for granted. "I'll check on Danny and Callie."

Back out front, she spotted the children at the edge of the woods, facing the lake. Danny was talking and pointing toward a large turkey vulture perched on a scraggly ash at the cliff's edge. She couldn't hear him, but he seemed to be explaining something to Callie, who listened with rapt attention.

The resiliency of children never ceased to amaze Sydney. No one watching them would guess what these two had been through in the last few hours. They seemed so normal, so unaffected by the morning's harrowing events.

"The kid's got a thing for birds," Ethan said from behind her.

Sydney started and spun around.

"Sorry," he said, taking a step back. "Bad habit."

And not a new one. His ability to approach without making a sound had startled her more than once. In the past she'd have scolded him for sneaking up on her, and he'd have laughed and swept her into his arms. The memory warmed her, and she squelched it as quickly as it surfaced.

"Forget it," she said, turning away. They were better off avoiding such precarious terrain. "How long have those children been with you?"

"They showed up on my doorstep yesterday afternoon."

She glanced back at him. "Alone?"

"With Anna, who dropped them off and split. I went after her, but by the time I found her, she was dead."

Sydney wrapped her arms around her waist. She hadn't liked Anna. She'd been too much of everything: beautiful, intelligent, intense. Still, to die so young was a waste. "What kind of trouble are they in?" she asked, nodding toward the children.

"Not sure. Anna didn't tell me squat, just that she wanted to leave them with me for a few days. Then, *adiós*."

"But Danny and Callie must have told you something."

"Oh, yeah." Ethan laughed abruptly. "On the way to Dallas, the boy gave me his version of the facts." He crossed his arms and leaned his good shoulder against the building. "Danny claims they were kidnapped. Anna helped them escape and was trying to reunite them with their family."

"And you don't believe him."

"Anna wasn't the kind of woman to go out of her way to help someone, not even a couple of kids."

It fit Sydney's impression of the woman and raised more questions than answers.

"All I know for sure," Ethan said, "is that those two kids are running from something, and Anna was killed delivering them to me."

Sydney turned back to watch the children, as if somehow their actions would reveal their secrets. Danny had taken Callie's hand as they explored the edge of the trees, letting go only as the small girl squatted to pick wildflowers.

"They obviously adore each other," Sydney said.

"He reminds me of . . ." Ethan left the sentence unfinished, and Sydney turned to him.

"You can say it," she said. "I won't fall apart. Danny reminds you of Nicky."

Ethan kept his eyes on the children. "Silly, isn't it? They don't look anything alike, and Nicky was half Danny's age, but the kid's got spunk."

"Like our son." Who'd never been afraid of anything, including climbing a tree to return a baby bird to its nest. In the process he'd fallen and broken his neck. And his parents' hearts.

Grief creased Ethan's features. "Nicky would have grown up like that, you know, like Danny, watching out for the little guy."

Which was exactly what Ethan was doing, she realized with a flash of guilt. Okay, so she'd been furious at him for barging back into her life and dragging her from her home. Who could blame her? He'd taken her by surprise. But she knew Ethan, and if he believed she was in mortal danger, he'd do whatever was necessary to protect her. It was simply the way he was made. He possessed a streak of gallantry she'd always found endearing, if somewhat old-fashioned. She couldn't fault him for it now.

"Come inside," she said. "Let me tend your arm and you can tell me the rest."

"You go on." He backed away, the gun no longer visible. "I need to move the truck out of sight and check around."

She started to object, then thought better of it. After all, facing the past alone might be easier. At least initially. "Are Danny and Callie okay out here?"

"I'll bring them with me when I come."

She nodded and watched him head toward the front, waiting until he disappeared around the building. Then, with a sigh of resignation, she entered the lodge. She passed through the kitchen and dining room into the reception area but stopped at the entrance to the two-story great room, the building's heart.

It looked different in the daylight, but familiar, too. As before, the oversized leather furniture had been covered for the winter, the chunky wood tables and bookshelves cleared, and the rugs rolled and stored.

She crossed to the windows, the pungent scent of the log walls reaching beneath her defenses. She fought it, trying to ignore the room's whispered memories. Beyond the glass, an empty deck clung to the side of the building, and the lake shimmered with late morning sunlight. A lone sailboat skidded across its surface.

The last time she'd stood in this spot, everything in her life had been different. She'd been young, in love, and full of dreams for their future. Ethan had been her world, and together in this room, they'd needed nothing and no one else.

The memory dissolved her resistance, and she saw again the room lit by moonlight, felt the crisp night air caressing her bare skin, and heard Ethan's voice, gentle, trembling, as he lowered her onto the couch.

"Let's not wait," he'd said. "I want a family. With you."

His words had slipped into her heart and sidestepped their decision to put off having children. She'd pulled him to her, and one sensation melded into another. His strong hands, caressing, arousing. His mouth, coaxing, demanding. The hardness of his body, above her, on her, inside her. And the certainty as she called his name into the cool darkness of the deserted lodge that they'd created a life. Their child.

That night she'd believed nothing could ever come between them. They would be together always.

A shiver skated down her spine. She'd been a fool.

"Sydney, are you okay?"

She turned from the windows. Ethan stood across the room, concern and caution shadowing his face. She considered lying, the polite kind of lie that left everyone feeling better. But the enormity of all they'd lost demanded truth.

"No," she said. "I'm not okay. I haven't been for a long time."

He took a step toward her, but she held up a hand to stop him. There was something she needed to know and it was about time he told her. "Why did you leave me, Ethan?"

CHAPTER NINE

Sydney's question immobilized him.

For the first time since barging into her apartment, Ethan absorbed the physical changes marking her. She was thinner. Time, or possibly grief, had carved hollows in her cheeks and etched fine lines around her eyes. She'd cut her long, dark hair to frame her face, and it suited her, as did the new thinness. She'd always been attractive, though not in a way that stopped men in their tracks. Her beauty had been more subtle, revealing itself in the warmth of her smile and the intelligence behind her eyes. Now she'd become striking in a way she'd never been before. She possessed an allure, a deep sadness and mystery that would draw attention.

It hurt Ethan to look at her.

The loss of their son had changed her, destroyed the innocence that had been her special gift. He had a sudden urge to answer her truthfully and confess everything, and maybe he would have, except for the sound of approaching feet.

"Is there anything to eat in this place?" Danny said, breaking the silence. "We're starving."

Sydney blinked, and a shutter fell across her features. "I'm not sure," she said without taking her eyes off Ethan. "There might be some canned goods in the pantry." She released him then, turning her attention to the children. "Go take a look. And, Callie, I need that first-aid kit."

"I'll get it out for you," she said, and both kids took off toward the kitchen.

Sydney closed the distance between them, her expression carefully blank. "Come on, I'll look at your arm."

He followed her into the dining room and lounge, where Callie had gotten out the first-aid kit before joining her brother's search for food.

"Take off your shirt," Sydney said, as she lined up their limited medical supplies on the table. "I hope you have another one with you."

"Yeah, I do." Ethan shrugged out of the garment, feeling a bit awkward and foolish because of it. Sydney had seen a lot more of him than a bare chest. Pushing the untimely thought aside, he carefully peeled the fabric away from his injured arm. Scratch or not, it hurt like a bitch.

He must not have done such a great job of concealing his discomfort, because Sydney went to the bar and returned with a glass of water. Then she took a bottle of aspirin from her purse, shook a couple into her hand, and offered them to him. "Here, these will help."

So much for macho stoicism; he never could fool her. "It's going to take more than two," he said, swallowing the pills dry. The whole damn bottle was more like it.

"And I expected an argument." Sydney tsked, retrieved two more of the painkillers, and handed them over. "Aren't you the one with a phobia about medication? Even aspirin?"

He let out a short laugh, and this time used the water to down the pills. That was him, all right, never met a drug he liked. At the moment, however, he needed the use of his arm. "There's a time and place for everything."

"Now I know you're hurting," she said. "Sit down and let me see how bad it is."

He did, and she gently removed the makeshift bandage. "Looks like more than a scratch to me."

He shrugged, liking the feel of her hands against his bare skin. "I've had worse."

Her gaze slid to his, an uncomfortable memory passing between them. Five years ago he'd almost died from a gunshot wound to the chest. A hunting accident, he'd told her. Only he'd never explained what he'd been hunting. Now he saw the questions in her eyes and wished he'd kept his mouth shut.

"It was almost worse this time," she said. "Six inches to the left and we wouldn't be having this conversation." She opened a bottle of hydrogen peroxide and started cleaning the hole in his arm. "Now, why don't you start from the beginning and tell me what's going on. Or at least what you know."

He did, repeating what he'd told her earlier about the kids, while ignoring her closeness and the memory of how once her touch had possessed the power to bring him to his knees. If he didn't know better, he'd have thought she wasn't listening. All her attention seemed focused on the damage caused by Ramirez's bullet, but when he got to the part about finding Anna's body in the desert, she tensed.

"Do you know who killed her?" she asked.

The old anger stirred, but he slapped it down. "Ramirez."

"And now you think he's after those children."

"Maybe." It's what he'd thought until that second car materialized in Dallas. Now he wasn't so sure. "It's possible."

Danny and Callie came in from the kitchen, carrying bowls of glossy fruit.

"I see you found something to eat," Sydney said, her smile forced.

Callie grinned. "Peaches."

"Yeah, that's all there is." Danny headed toward a

large screen TV by the bar. "Except for some dumb vegetables."

"There's more fruit," Callie said as she trailed after her brother. "If you want some."

Sydney watched them, her expression distant. She didn't speak again until they'd settled down. "Why you?" she asked without looking at Ethan. "Why did Anna bring them to you?"

It wasn't a question he could answer with complete honesty. He could guess why Anna had come to him, and might even come close to the truth, but he couldn't tell Sydney. Not all of it anyway. "We worked together for eight years. She trusted me."

"And knew where to find you."

"Yeah."

Sydney's face tightened. She probably suspected him and Anna of having an affair. Well, they *had* been involved, but not in the way Sydney imagined.

She let it go and again bent her concentration to his arm. Work had always been her panacea, and at the moment he expected she needed to focus on something concrete. Something she could control. As she applied the topical antibiotic and covered the bullet hole with a gauze pad, however, her hands trembled.

He couldn't stop himself, he took her hand. To his surprise she didn't resist, and it felt good to just touch her again. And familiar. "Sydney . . ." He searched for the words to reassure her, words he didn't have. "I'm sorry." It was all he had.

She slipped out of his grasp and, steadier now, finished wrapping his upper arm with gauze. "I'll give you a prescription for antibiotics to avoid infection." She secured the last piece of tape. "And you'll have to change the bandage every day. Do you want something for the pain?"

"Aspirin will be fine." Anything stronger would cloud his mind and dull his reflexes.

"No surprise there." She started storing the supplies.

Ethan examined the bandage and flexed his arm. "Thank you." He got his spare shirt from his duffel bag and slipped it on, suddenly aware of how studiously she avoided looking at him. The idea that he might still affect her pleased him, though he knew it shouldn't. Not after how he'd hurt her, and not now, when their lives depended on his ability to remain focused.

"You okay?" he asked.

"Sure." She sat on a chair across from him. "You know,"—she still didn't meet his gaze—"nothing you've said so far explains what any of this has to do with me."

Ethan glanced toward the kids in front of the television. Danny worked his ever-present Game Boy, while Callie seemed entranced by a group of preteens frolicking with full-size cartoon characters. "I'm not sure who's after them. Maybe Ramirez, maybe someone else. But what I do know is that Ramirez is a pro. He kills for a living." Anger nudged him again, but he rolled past it. "Now he's after you."

"Why, because he thinks Anna called me?"

Now, that was the tough question, but Ethan had to tell the truth. At least about this. "That's only part of it. He's out to get even with me for something that happened a long time ago."

"That still doesn't explain why he wants to hurt me."

"He wants to punish me." He hesitated, unsure how she would respond to his next statement, or if she'd even believe him. "He plans to get to me by hurting you."

She looked stunned, her lovely dark eyes widening with fear and confusion, and he couldn't blame her. Everything that had happened in the last few hours was outside her experience. Now this, a killer stalking her because of her ex-husband, a man who'd deserted her. Ethan wished he could comfort her, but even if she let him put his arms around her, he had nothing to offer.

"Hey," Danny said, turning up the volume on the television. "You've got to see this."

"What is it?" Ethan kept his eyes on Sydney, who seemed lost in his last revelation.

"You're on the news."

Sydney started and turned, as did Ethan, his attention leaping to the big screen.

A reporter in a vivid red suit stood on a Dallas street in front of a modern high-rise. "This is Joanna Farley, reporting live from downtown Dallas. Two police officers died here today in an early morning shootout at this upscale building."

Sydney lifted a shaky hand to her mouth, and Ethan moved to her side, slipping an arm around her shoulders.

"The shooting occurred at the home of Dr. Sydney Decker, a medical researcher at Braydon Labs," the reporter continued, her expression grave. "According to sources close to the police, Dr. Decker dialed nine-one-one around five A.M. this morning, claiming her ex-husband had broken into her home. Two officers were dispatched to the scene, and residents of the building heard gunshots coming from Dr. Decker's apartment a short time later. One witness claims to have seen a man fleeing from the scene holding Dr. Decker at gunpoint.

"Authorities are looking for Ethan Decker in connection with the shooting and possible kidnapping of his ex-wife."

A photograph of Ethan appeared on the screen.

"Damn," Ethan said.

The camera switched back to the reporter, and Ethan's picture slid to one corner. "Decker is described as six foot one, with dark blond hair and blue eyes. He is considered armed and dangerous and should not be approached."

"What the . . ." Remembering the kids, Ethan cut his sentence short.

There was no mention of Danny, Callie, Anna, or parents looking for lost children. No speculation about a shooter on the balcony or reports of abandoned climbing gear. No body found at the side of a desert highway. Only the dead cops in Sydney's apartment. And Ethan's name.

Someone was playing hardball.

In a couple of quick strides, Ethan crossed to the television and shut it off.

Whoever was after these kids was making damn sure Ethan didn't go to the police. They'd gotten into Sydney's condo and cleaned up the shooter's tracks, leaving Ethan as the only suspect. As for Anna, he could buy the authorities not connecting a murder in New Mexico to a shooting in Dallas, but Danny and Callie had been visible. The night security guard at Sydney's building, if no one else, had seen them with Ethan. The media should at least have a hint of them, and the police should be questioning their identity and relationship to Ethan.

Instead, it was as if they and the shooter didn't exist. Ramirez's work? No, not alone. He didn't have the resources to shut down witnesses, bury evidence, or sanitize Sydney's building. Someone with a lot more clout than Ramirez was behind this. It bore all the earmarks of an Agency operation, especially considering Anna's involvement.

Turning toward the others, he saw the guilt on Danny's face. The boy knew more than he'd admitted. "Okay, Danny, it's time you told me what's really going on."

Danny's cheeks reddened, his eyes focused on the floor.

"And this time," Ethan added, "I want the truth."

CHAPTER TEN

Paul had found the truth.

With shaking hands, he pushed back from the computer on his desk. For long moments he couldn't move, could hardly breathe. Once again, death had slid up behind him ready to make its claim. Only this time Paul saw no mercenary angel hovering in the wings, showing him the way out.

He knew where to find the missing children.

It had been nearly three days, seventy-two hours, since they'd disappeared. With each passing hour, it seemed less likely that Cox's people would find them. A frightening loss, but Paul had managed to keep his head. Literally and figuratively.

Thanks to Anna Kelsey.

Since the Agency had placed her on Haven Island, Cox couldn't hold Paul accountable for her actions. Such a woman was beyond Paul's experience or expertise. Even Morrow had admitted that much. But all that could change with one phone call.

Paul not only knew where Danny was headed, he knew why. The boy had hacked into the facility's computer system, accessing birth records and God only knew what else. It explained everything: why he'd run, why he'd taken Callie, and where he would go.

Paul closed his eyes, fear sweeping through him.

At first he'd prayed he was wrong, but after checking and rechecking his findings, he knew that wasn't the case. He'd spent the last eight hours going through the system. The evidence was irrefutable. Although Danny had been smart enough to hack his way in, he'd left trails.

Every time he'd accessed a restricted file, the system made a log entry containing time, date, and user ID. He'd known about the log and figured out how to alter it to hide his tracks, which was why his activities had escaped notice. What Danny obviously didn't know was that every time the system made a log entry, it also wrote a copy on a WORM (write-once-read-many) device for safe storage. So by the time he physically changed the online log, it was too late, his snooping had been recorded on a nonchangeable piece of hardware.

It took some time and effort, but Paul had been able to compare the online entry with the WORM version and find the discrepancies.

Paul knew he should be proud that the twelve-year-old had broken the facility's state-of-the-art security system. After all, he'd created the child, made him, so to speak. But pride was the last thing Paul felt. Cold, mind-numbing terror was closer to the mark.

He wanted to scream at the injustice of it. This wasn't his fault, he wasn't a goddamn teacher or psychologist. He'd never even particularly liked children and had as little day-to-day contact with those on the island as possible. Someone on his staff should have warned him, someone else should have known the boy's capabilities. Whether Danny was smarter than they knew or simply more motivated, one of *them* should have known.

But Cox would never see it that way.

Paul dropped his face to his hands and cursed the day he'd met the other man. No matter what course he chose,

Paul wouldn't escape unscathed. If he revealed what he knew, Cox would find the children, but Paul would have to admit that Danny had been hacking into the system for some time—maybe as long as a year. That would be disastrous. Cox's people would take over, turning the island upside down looking for security breaches. But if Paul kept the information to himself, and Cox found out in some other way, or they found Danny and he confessed . . .

The intercom buzzed.

Paul straightened, steeling his voice against the churn of fear in his gut, and pressed the receive button. "What is it, Sheila?"

"Dr. Bateman called from the infirmary," said his assistant. "He asked if you could come over right away."

"Did he say what it's about?"

"It's Adam." She paused. "He's sick."

Paul broke into a smile. Why hadn't he thought of this? He'd known Adam would exhibit symptoms quickly. All Paul had to do was claim that Adam had finally revealed the runaways' destination, and Cox would have no reason to send his people in here to check for security breaches.

"Tell Dr. Bateman I'll be over in a few minutes," he said, and severed the connection.

Paul was almost giddy as he made his way to the hospital wing, nodding at the staff he passed on the way. He'd injected Adam with a designer strain of Avian Influenza A (H5N1), which had surfaced in Hong Kong in 1997 and killed a third of those infected. The potency of the virus had been high in its original state, but the strain Paul had used on Adam had been altered to further increase its virulence.

In part, the injection had been a test to see if the boy's system would repel the deadly virus. However, when

Adam had refused to talk about Danny's plan, Paul had used it as a weapon, counting on it to make Adam more willing to talk as the illness took hold. Now it didn't matter whether Adam talked or not.

When Paul reached the hospital wing, he donned an expression of grave concern and pushed through to the isolation ward.

Bateman intercepted him before he made it to the boy's room. "Dr. Turner, thank you for coming so soon."

"How is he?"

"Not too bad yet,"—Bateman followed Paul to the observation window—"but in another twenty-four hours, he'll be one sick young man."

"Fever, cough, sore throat?"

Bateman nodded. "All the classic symptoms."

"I guess we shouldn't be surprised. Have you run tests yet to verify the strain hasn't shifted?" In its unaltered state, A (H5N1) showed no signs of human-to-human transmission, but the influenza virus was tricky and could alter itself in unexpected ways. The last thing Paul needed was a pandemic of influenza running through the island. Most of the children would survive, but he'd lose a high percentage of the staff.

"It's stable," Dr. Bateman said, suddenly edgy. "But since we know Adam has no immunity, what is the point of withholding treatment?"

"He's strong and may still fight off the infection without interference." Although Paul had no intention of letting the boy recover. "We need to monitor the progression of his illness."

"Yes, but—"

Paul turned on him. "Are you questioning my judgment?"

Bateman paled and looked away.

"I didn't think so." Paul smiled to himself, enjoying

the other man's discomfort. It felt good after bowing to Cox and his thugs these last few days. Paul was still in charge here; this was still his facility. "Now, I want to examine the boy, and I'm sure *you* have other matters to attend to."

Bateman backed off. "Yes, of course."

Paul watched him scuttle away, then entered the hospital room. Grabbing a stool, he pulled it over to the bed and sat. "How are you feeling, Adam?"

The boy glared at him and rolled onto his side, giving Paul his back.

"I suspected you were coming down with something yesterday," Paul said.

"I wasn't sick then." Adam's voice was muffled but angry.

Paul ignored the accusation. "You're lucky we discovered how sick you were before it was too late." He sighed for the boy's benefit. "But I'm afraid Callie's not going to be that lucky."

"I told you I don't know where—"

"Oh, I don't need you to tell me anything, Adam. I know where they went." He shifted on the hard metal stool, making the wheels squeak, and watched the boy. "And I've sent someone to bring them home. I only hope it's not too late for Callie. If you'd told me yesterday where they went . . ." He shook his head. "I might have been able to save her."

Adam turned around. "What's wrong with her?"

Paul smiled sympathetically. "I thought you understood. Callie came down with the same virus as you, right before she and Danny ran away." That much, at least, was true.

Tears filled the boy's eyes. "Will she die?"

"Not only her . . ." Paul felt a particular delight in tormenting this boy who'd given him so much trouble. "But

I'm sure she's infected others by now as well, including Danny."

Danny felt sick.

The TV reporter had lied just like the Keepers. Ethan hadn't killed anyone, there had been a man with a gun on the balcony.

Sydney touched his arm. "Danny?"

They expected him to explain, but he didn't know anything. Not about gunmen, anyway. All he knew was that he and Callie couldn't go back to the Haven. Not ever. But he was afraid to tell them even that much. He doubted they'd believe him, especially after he'd lied to Ethan earlier. Well, it hadn't been a complete lie. He'd just stretched the truth some.

"Tell them." Callie poked him in the arm. "They can help us."

Danny wasn't so sure about that, but he knew he had to do something. If he couldn't convince Ethan that he and Callie were telling the truth, Ethan would turn them over to the authorities in the time it took to dial nine-one-one. And who could blame him? The reporter had called him a murderer. What did Ethan care if the police sent a couple of kids back to a place where everyone lied and kids disappeared in the middle of the night?

"We ran away from a place called the Haven," Danny said. "It's on an island off the coast of Washington State."

"Is it a school?" Sydney asked.

Danny stole a glance at Ethan. "Well, sort of. I mean, I don't know exactly." He turned back to Sydney, who might be their only hope. "We live there and go to school with a bunch of other kids."

"How many children are there?"

"I'm not sure exactly, twenty-five maybe."

"There used to be more," Callie said, "but some of them went away."

Danny shot her a warning look. "The number changes." Six months ago there had been close to thirty of them. Now Danny wasn't sure, but he didn't want to talk about that. If he did, Ethan and Sydney would think he was lying for sure. "They told us our parents were dead, and that we had no other family."

"But they lied," Callie added. "Danny and I didn't even know we were brother and sister until he got into the computer."

"That's right." Danny felt like he was running out of time. "And that's when I found out that our father is alive."

"Whoa," said Ethan, speaking up for the first time since demanding an explanation. "Slow down a minute and back up. Who are *they*?"

"The Keepers. That's what I call the teachers and doctors and guardians. They don't like it, but I don't care. I hate them all."

"How long have you lived there?" Sydney asked.

Danny shrugged. "I don't remember living anywhere else. None of us do."

"Do you remember your parents?"

"No." Danny concentrated on Sydney now that Ethan had again retreated into silence. "I figure they brought us there when we were all really little."

Sydney frowned and glanced at Ethan. "But there *are* adults who take care of you, and teachers?"

"I know what you're thinking." Weren't they hearing him? "We're *not* orphans. Callie is my sister and our father is alive. They stole us from our parents."

For a moment no one spoke. Then Sydney said, "How can you be sure if you don't remember your parents or living anywhere else?"

He'd known they wouldn't believe him. Adults always

thought they knew more than kids. "What else could it be? Our mom and dad wouldn't just give us away."

"Take it easy," Ethan said. "Let's say for now that we believe you." Danny opened his mouth to protest, but Ethan cut him off. "Just bear with me a minute. I'm trying to understand all of this. Callie said you got into the computer system. How did you do that?"

Danny looked at his sister, who nodded. "I'm good with computers. . . ." He hesitated. Adults never liked it when kids were too smart. "Sometimes when Dr. Turner, the head Keeper, went to the mainland, I'd sneak into his office and use his computer to hack into the system."

"Wait a minute," Ethan said. "You expect me to believe you cracked their computer's security? How old are you? Eleven? Twelve?"

Danny rolled his eyes. Was this guy living in the dark ages or something? What difference did his age make? "Oh, yeah, I forgot, you've been living out in the middle of nowhere." Which is where Danny would like to be right about now. "You probably don't even have electricity, much less a computer."

"Look, kid—"

"It doesn't matter how he got into the system," Sydney said, interrupting Ethan.

"It does if he's lying."

"I'm not lying," Danny insisted, desperate to make them believe him.

"He's not," Callie said.

Ethan held up a hand in surrender. "Okay, forget about how you got into the computer. Assuming you did, that's how you found out about Callie and your father?"

"That's what I said." Wasn't he listening? "I was searching for my school records, just to see what some of the teachers had written about me." His cheeks heated at the confession. "That's when I found out all the other stuff."

"Like?" Ethan prodded.

"Birth records with times, dates, and places for all the kids. Also, parent and sibling names with hot links for more information. I found out about Callie and our father."

"What about your mother?" Sydney asked.

Danny stuttered to a halt, surprised that this bothered him. After all, he'd never known his mother. "I don't know," he said. "Callie and I have the same father but different mothers. All the records showed was a woman's first name." He hated admitting that he didn't have all the answers. "I tried to get more information about them but ran into a firewall that I didn't have time to break."

He could have sworn he saw tears in Sydney's eyes before she closed them briefly and looked away. "I'm sorry."

She and Ethan seemed to have run out of questions, and Danny had no idea if he'd convinced them. He thought about all the other kids, his friends, back at the Haven. Would they wonder what had happened to him and Callie? Adam knew the truth, but he wouldn't tell. So what would the Keepers say? Would everyone think he and Callie had disappeared like . . .

"Tell them about Sean," Callie said, as if she'd read his mind.

"Why? They won't believe me."

"They will." She turned back to the adults. "Sean's bunk was next to Danny's, and they were best friends, the two of them and Adam. Then one morning, Sean was gone."

Sydney leaned forward in her chair. "Gone?"

"Go on," Callie said to him. "Tell them."

He glowered at his sister but didn't have a choice now that she'd started this. He had to tell Ethan and Sydney the rest. "The Keepers said Sean got sick in the middle of the night, but there was nothing wrong with him when we went to bed. They did something to him."

Sydney looked uncomfortable, glanced at Ethan again, then said, "Danny, sometimes children get sick."

"No, he wasn't sick." Danny didn't know what he'd do if they didn't believe him. "And he wasn't the only one. Lots of others disappeared, too. Mostly the little ones, but sometimes one of the big kids."

The room got real quiet, and Danny could tell they thought he was making it up.

"Sean wasn't sick," Danny insisted. "None of them were sick before they went away, but every time the Keepers told us the same story. They said Sean was too sick to stay on the island, and they'd taken him to a hospital on the mainland."

Danny saw the doubt on Sydney's face, but couldn't tell what Ethan was thinking.

"Tell them the rest," Callie said.

Danny needed no prompting. "I know the Keepers were lying, at least about Sean." He stopped, looking from one unconvinced face to the other. "Because a few days after Sean disappeared, I saw him. I snuck into the infirmary and he was there." Danny had been terrified of what the Keepers would do if they caught him. Would he be the next one to disappear in the middle of the night? "They'd stuck all kinds of tubes and needles in him, and he'd looked . . ." right at Danny. For a second, Sean had opened his eyes, and Danny could have sworn his friend had seen him hiding. "He looked real scared." Something swelled in his throat as he remembered the look on Sean's face, and that he'd been too scared himself to help.

Silence hovered in the room.

"A nightmare?" Sydney said.

He'd had nightmares about it for weeks, but he'd been awake the first time. "It was daytime." And the last time he'd seen his friend. "Why did they lie and say they took all those kids to a mainland hospital? And why did none of them ever get well and come back?"

Again, no one spoke.

Finally, Ethan pulled out a barstool and sat. "Tell me how Anna fits into all this."

Danny took a deep breath. Maybe Ethan believed him. "Anna was one of our teachers."

Ethan looked doubtful.

"She was," Callie said.

Danny understood Ethan's doubts. Anna, the real Anna, the one who'd helped them run away from the island, wasn't like any of the other teachers. And he had a feeling Ethan knew all about the real Anna.

"She wasn't like that in the beginning," he said, speaking to Ethan now. "I mean, she was different from the other Keepers, but she was nice."

"She told us stories," Callie added.

"We weren't allowed off the island," Danny explained. "We studied geography and everything, but that's not the same. We didn't really know what it was like on the outside. Anna told us all kinds of stuff." She'd convinced Danny she was his friend, their friend, his and Callie's. But she had lied, too. "I told her about seeing Sean, and she offered to take Callie and me away from the Keepers. She promised to help us find our father."

"How was she going to do that?" Sydney asked quietly.

"That part is easy," Danny said. "I know where he lives."

CHAPTER ELEVEN

Where the hell was Morrow?

Avery Cox pressed the off button on the remote and tossed it onto his desk. He shouldn't have to get his news from a goddamn television report.

It had been twenty-four hours since they'd left Haven Island and gone their separate ways, Avery back to Langley, Morrow off to track Kelsey, Decker, and the runaways. At the very least, Avery had expected a progress report by now, but Morrow hadn't checked in. Now this mess in Dallas, two dead cops and Decker on the run, and it had Morrow's grimy prints all over it.

"Damn the man."

Avery pushed to his feet and crossed to the glass wall overlooking the SCTC bullpen, a hive of activity deep within the bowels of Langley. Dozens of computer workstations filled the room, and two walls of monitors displayed video feed from around the world. Directly across from his office, a massive electronic map tracked worldwide operations. Around it all, hustled a score of people, his people, the best and brightest analysts in the world.

Morrow was getting out of hand.

Unfortunately, Avery still needed him. Turner had called a little over an hour ago. Not only had Adam finally revealed Danny and Callie's destination, but the girl was sick. Real sick. With those two pieces of information, they had a rare, and narrow window of opportunity to retrieve them. If Morrow showed up.

Using traditional SCTC resources to find him was out of the question. It would raise too many eyebrows. Avery had also considered sending someone else after the kids, but that held its own risks. It was how they'd gotten into the current situation with Anna and Ramirez. The fewer people with contact to Haven Island, the better.

He'd built this place from scratch, fighting for funds from tightfisted politicians. He wasn't about to let it all fall apart because Anna Kelsey had helped a couple of kids run away from that damn island. Or because John Morrow was too damn arrogant to follow orders.

Avery had come too far.

Twenty-five years ago he'd arrived in Washington, a young man with no family connections and a law degree from a no-name school in rural Mississippi. He'd had to scramble for a position as a law clerk, which paid less, with longer and more grueling hours, than the bartending job that had gotten him through school. Add to that the subtle and not-so-subtle snobbery of Washington's elite, and he'd been little more than an overeducated gofer.

A lesser man would have given up and gone home. Avery had joined the CIA, where talent mattered more than family name, and a flair for navigating the underpinnings of a bureaucracy counted more than his alma mater. With an eye for talent and no desire to go into the field himself, he'd done well. Very well.

Now, if he wasn't very careful, he could lose it all.

John Morrow wasn't his only problem. That had become evident at the morning's quarterly budget review before the Senate Select Committee on Intelligence. A week ago, the meeting would have been a mere formality, but something had changed. The opposition had emerged unexpectedly. A junior senator from Montana or Idaho, or one of those god-awful backward states, had started poking his nose into Avery's business. The senator had questioned the money allocated to the SCTC and wanted a detailed accounting of operations. Others had picked up on the inquiry, and it had become a feeding frenzy as old rivals surfaced.

Avery had crushed the questions, presenting charts and graphs and dire warnings about the need for newer and better technologies, along with the SCTC's requirements to operate without interference. In the end the committee had approved his budget. For now.

The opposition's timing, however, was too coincidental. It had to be related to the situation on Haven Island. Someone had gotten word of, or at least suspected, the true nature of the project and its current problem.

Avery retreated to his desk, the idea a nasty prick at the base of his skull. Who could have found out about the Haven Project? And how? Could Anna have sold information instead of the kids, then taken them as proof?

The approach fit her personality. It held less risk, and the outcome would be much the same. She might still have to face Marco Ramirez, unless she'd sold out to someone powerful enough to protect her. It was a tall order.

Avery tented his fingers beneath his chin and considered the few men with enough power to accomplish it. There weren't many, and all of them had their own agendas, which Avery wouldn't hesitate to expose if they delved too deeply into his affairs. No one wanted that. After all, Washington was the ultimate old boys' club.

Could there be someone else, an unknown player Avery had overlooked? Someone behind the scenes of the Senate committee? A money man, pulling a few senators' strings? No one got to the U.S. Senate without backing, without owing a favor or two. And in Avery's experience those without a public political agenda posed a greater threat than those courting the voters' favor. The possibility that such a man or men knew about the Haven Project disturbed him. It would mean the situation had moved beyond his control, and today's battle had been a warning, the victory a memory if Danny or Callie surfaced in the wrong place.

Goddamn Morrow. If he'd blown their chance to retrieve those kids, Avery would have his head.

The intercom buzzed.

"Excuse me, Mr. Cox." His assistant's voice held a nervous edge. "John Morrow's on line three." She dealt with dangerous and powerful men on a daily basis, but Morrow disturbed her. She wasn't alone. He intimidated even the most stalwart of Avery's staff, and that was exactly the way Avery wanted it. Usually.

"Make sure I'm not disturbed." He disconnected his assistant, punched the speaker button, then the flashing line. "You better have good news for me."

After a single barb of silence, Morrow said, "Take me off the speaker."

Avery smiled tightly, allowing Morrow his petty victory, and picked up the receiver. "Tell me you have good news."

"You want me to lie."

"What the hell happened?"

"We didn't expect Decker's ex-wife to call the cops."

"And you let them get away." Avery barely contained his anger, reminding himself he needed Morrow for a little longer. "Killing two police officers in the process."

"It couldn't be avoided."

Avery doubted that. "Half the state of Texas is looking for them." Under different circumstances he might take some pleasure in the high-minded Decker wanted for murder, but at this point the police could only complicate matters. The stakes were too high to indulge in personal pleasures. He, at least, wouldn't risk the future of the Haven Project and control of the SCTC. "This better not come back at us."

"We sanitized the building." Morrow's words sounded forced. He didn't like justifying his actions. "Decker's their only suspect. If they pick him up—"

"They won't." Not unless they got very lucky, or Decker fucked up, and Avery wasn't about to count on either scenario. No, he wasn't worried about Decker turning up in a jail cell. "He's more likely to go so far underground we'll never find him." Until he surfaced to bring Avery and his organization tumbling down.

"He's got the woman with him," Morrow said.

"I heard the news," Avery snapped. Sydney Decker was yet another factor he couldn't predict. "And I don't give a damn about the woman."

"She's not going to give up her life and go into hiding. Sooner or later, she'll surface, and Decker won't be far behind."

"You don't know that."

"Call it an educated guess. We'll get Decker," Morrow said. "And the kids."

"Yes, let's not forget the kids." Morrow's priorities were screwed up. "*They* are what this is all about, not your personal vendetta against Decker."

Morrow didn't respond, a damn irritating habit which told Avery he'd hit on the truth. Morrow's hatred of Decker went back to the fiasco with Ramirez. Something had happened between them that night, something that had left Morrow hungry for the other man's blood. But Avery had no time for Morrow's petty agenda. They had one shot at salvaging the situation before all hell broke loose, and he wouldn't stand for another mistake.

"What about Anna?" he asked. "The media didn't mention her."

"No one's made the connection, but New Mexico Highway Patrol found her body in the desert this morning, and I sent someone to check it out. It was a single gunshot to the head. Looks like Ramirez's work."

Avery leaned back in his chair, uneasy with this latest development. It could be good or bad, depending on who she'd contacted before dying. "Go on."

"My men did a little digging and found a recently deserted trailer about ten miles from where the cops found the body. Someone had left in a hurry."

"Decker?"

"Anna could have dropped off the kids and split." He let out a short, humorless laugh. "Maybe she figured selling them was more trouble than it was worth. No surprise, with Ramirez on her tail."

No, no surprise. The twist was that Ramirez had found her so quickly. Though it no longer mattered what had happened to Anna Kelsey, except in the matter of who she'd been working for, but Avery would deal with that later. For now, Decker had the kids.

"Any further sign of Ramirez?"

"Other than the increased body count?" For the first time, Morrow sounded a bit uncomfortable. "He's out there, I can feel him." He paused. "And I can bring him in."

Morrow was entirely too eager, and he was hiding something. Avery considered calling him on it. Instead he decided to bring Morrow down a notch or two. "Maybe, maybe not. Ramirez just might find you first."

Silence echoed across a thousand miles of phone lines. Avery suspected he'd struck the nerve that was Morrow's ego. He would like nothing better than to wrap his hands around Avery's throat. No, that wasn't quite right. The gun was more to Morrow's taste. Like Ramirez. Morrow's fantasy would be to put a bullet between Avery's eyes.

A fantasy he'd never realize.

Morrow knew he couldn't survive without Avery's protection. No one in the intelligence community wanted officers like Morrow, men who liked to kill. And he *did* like to kill, entirely too much. Such men had their uses, if they could be controlled, but Morrow was quickly getting beyond even Avery's influence.

"This time, stick to the plan." Avery's tone allowed no argument. "First I want Danny and Callie, then Ramirez. After that, Decker's all yours."

"You're running the show."

"I suggest you remember that." Avery paused, letting his own anger carry across the line. Then he repeated Turner's information. "Decker and the kids are on their way to Illinois. Champaign-Urbana." He heard the surprise in Morrow's sudden stillness. "The boy's going after a Dr. Timothy Mulligan. He thinks the man's his father."

"Is he?"

Avery ignored the question. It had no relevance to what he wanted from Morrow. "Don't screw this up, John. And," he paused for emphasis, unable to resist taunting Morrow one more time, "don't underestimate Decker. If it comes down to it, he *will* kill you."

Silence again, cold, angry silence. "I'll be in touch."

"See that you are."

Avery hung up the phone, resisting the urge to slam it in place. Instead he pulled out a handkerchief, removed his glasses, and polished the lenses.

Just a couple more days. A week at the most.

Morrow was a lot of things, but he wasn't stupid. He'd deliver the kids, and Decker would take down Ramirez. Then the three-year-old nightmare surrounding the assassin would finally come to an end. As for Ethan Decker, his death would be a bonus.

Then, Avery would have time to consider the best way to rid himself of John Morrow.

CHAPTER TWELVE

A door closed, and Sydney opened her eyes.

The room was quiet and oddly empty, and she knew without looking that Ethan had gone out. It was a relief. Earlier, his intense presence had filled the room, making it difficult for her to breathe, much less think. He no longer behaved like the man she'd once married. Despite an undercurrent of defiance and recklessness that had always excited her, her husband had been easygoing, letting her set the pace of their lives. Now he possessed a fierce edge that was as unnerving as the situation was unreal.

She looked at her watch and saw she'd been sleeping for over three hours. Evidently she'd been more tired than she'd realized.

After the news about the shooting and Danny's story about the Haven, nothing had seemed clear-cut. They'd all been too exhausted to think straight, so she'd suggested they get some rest. The children had objected, but she'd dug out blankets and pillows and tucked them onto a couch, where they'd fallen asleep almost immediately. She'd claimed the recliner, planning to close her eyes for just a few minutes, and Ethan had stretched out on the second, now empty, sofa.

The children, on the other hand, slept on, entwined like a pair of kittens, Danny's arm curled protectively around his sister. The sight clenched at her heart, though she couldn't say exactly why their plight affected her so strongly. They seemed healthy, with no outward signs of physical abuse, but their story had contained a ring of frightening truth. And they were clearly afraid of returning home.

If nothing else, she wanted to find the man Danny claimed was their father: Dr. Timothy Mulligan. He held a Ph.D. in physics and was on the faculty at the University of Illinois in Urbana-Champaign. Danny even had the man's address and phone number. It wouldn't take more than a simple phone call to determine if Mulligan was indeed the children's father, but Sydney wanted to meet the man. She wanted to question him and make sure he wanted these children and would . . .

No.

She cut off that thought abruptly. *Forget it.* She wasn't traveling down that particular road. She'd gone to a support group a couple of times after Nicky's death and seen women like that—broken, grasping women—and she'd sworn she'd never be one of them. She wasn't looking for a child to replace the one she'd lost. All she wanted was to help Callie and Danny, and move on.

Straightening in the chair, she shoved down the footrest and thought of the cell phone tucked away in her purse. It would be so easy to contact the authorities and let them take over. Or at least call Charles, who must be frantic by now, to tell him she was okay and ask again about the hang ups on her machine. Plus he could help them. He had friends and influence at both the state and federal levels of government. Together they could find out the truth about Haven Island. She reached over, letting her hand rest on her bag for several seconds, or maybe minutes.

So easy.

She couldn't do it, not without talking to Ethan first. A

few hours ago, he'd saved her life. She couldn't go behind his back and bring someone else into this.

Deserting the chair, she crossed the room to the picture windows framing the main entrance. Outside, the afternoon light had faded, throwing long shadows across the day. Ethan's truck was nowhere in sight and she wondered if he'd gone or had just parked it out of sight.

Then she saw him near the edge of the clearing. At first she couldn't figure out what he was doing, it seemed so out of place considering his injured arm. Then she knew. She'd watched him and their son perform this same routine too many times not to recognize the precise movements; hands, arms, and feet flowing gracefully from one position to the next.

Tai chi.

Moving meditation, Ethan had called it. In China thousands gathered in parks and squares every sunrise and sunset to perform this ancient ritual, and although the movements seemed simple, they took years to perfect. So Ethan had taught Nicky as the Chinese taught their children. He'd promised to teach her as well, but she'd somehow never found the time. In truth, she hadn't wanted to learn. She'd gotten so much pleasure out of watching father and son together. The slow, practiced pace and the concentration on their faces had been too beautiful to miss.

Now she watched Ethan perform those same moves, but with an intensity he'd lacked with Nicky. She sensed the anger in every sweep of his hands and shift of his feet. And with a rush of shame, she felt his torment, an agony that had nothing to do with the bullet hole in his arm.

Not once since he'd walked out on her had she considered his grief, or the guilt he must live with. She'd blamed herself for not preventing Nicky's death, wishing she'd gone with her husband and her son that day. One small change, and everything might have been different. But if she'd tormented herself with what-ifs, how much harder must it have been for Ethan? He'd dedicated his life to protecting those weaker than himself, first as a soldier, then as an intelligence officer. Yet he'd been unable to protect his own son. Ethan had been with Nicky the day he'd died, while her only sin had been her absence.

A small hand slipped into hers.

Startled, Sydney almost jerked away before realizing Callie had come up beside her without a sound. "I thought you were asleep," Sydney said, keeping her voice low so as not to wake Danny.

Callie smiled shyly. "I woke up."

Sydney nodded, a bit unnerved by the girl's presence. "Me, too." She turned back to the window and the man beyond it, although now all her attention was on the child at her side.

With Callie's hand in hers, Sydney felt the tug of old emotions. It had been a long time since a child had touched her like this, simply and with trust. And Callie was nearly the same age as Nicky had been when he died.

"He's really good," Callie said, obviously referring to Ethan.

"Yes," Sydney replied, grateful for anything that diverted her from the direction her thoughts had taken. Even if that distraction was Ethan. "Do you know something about tai chi, Callie?"

"I used to watch the others."

Sydney glanced at the girl. "The others?"

"The other children at the Haven. They start their exercises every morning with tai chi. I watch them from my window." Her smile turned wistful.

"Why didn't you join them?"

Callie lifted her small shoulders in a resigned shrug. "I get sick a lot."

"Really?" Concerned, Sydney sat on the arm of the nearby chair and turned the girl to face her. With a physician's eye she examined the child. She was a little thin, but nothing serious. Her eyes were clear, her skin soft and healthy looking, though a little warm—which could have been from sleeping. Outwardly, Sydney could see nothing wrong with her. Although appearances could be deceptive, an illness serious enough to deprive her of participating in a relaxed form of exercise such as tai chi would most likely be visible in some way.

"Are you sick now?" Sydney asked, perplexed.

"I'm okay, just a little tired."

Which was hardly surprising after what she'd been through the last couple of days. Sydney considered letting the subject drop. Callie wasn't her responsibility, but the physician and mother in her couldn't ignore the possibility that the child was ill.

"Is there some reason you get sick, Callie? Do you have allergies, or some other condition I should know about?" She ran her hands down the girl's thin arms and took both her hands. "You do know I'm a doctor, don't you? I used to take care of children like you."

"Oh, yes." Callie nodded. "Ethan told us. He said you were the best kid doctor in all of Texas."

Sydney laughed softly. "Did he now?"

"Yes, he said—"

"Callie," Sydney interrupted, not wanting to get off the subject. Or into a discussion about her ex-husband. "Why do you get sick all the time?"

Callie shrugged. "My immune system is weak." It was a very adult statement, something the child had been told. Something she'd memorized and repeated verbatim. "That's why I have to stay away from the others."

Sydney frowned, some inner voice telling her to tread carefully. "What do you mean, you have to stay away from the other children? You don't mean all the time, do you?"

"Well, pretty much. Dr. Turner said it was for my own

good 'cause I catch every bug that goes around." She paused, then lowered her voice to a whisper, as if she and Sydney were conspirators. "But, I think they're afraid I'll get the other children sick."

Sydney didn't know what to say. The thought of this beautiful child kept in isolation was too cruel to consider. "But certainly . . ." She must have misunderstood. "You go to school with the other children, don't you? And live in a dormitory?"

"Uh-uh." Callie shook her head. "I have my own room and private teachers." She grinned. "They say I'm special."

Sydney's thoughts spun out of control. Just how sick was the girl? And was she contagious? "You are special, Callie." Sydney squeezed the child's hands. "But I have a hard time understanding why you weren't allowed to play with the other children."

"It's okay," Callie said, as if reading Sydney's mind. "I wasn't alone all the time. Danny used to come and see me almost every day."

This sounded more normal, except Danny had claimed no one told him or Callie they were related. So why would the children's guardians single him out to visit her? "Why did the doctors let Danny come to see you?"

Callie's cheeks flushed with obvious discomfort. "Well, they didn't exactly let him."

"What do you mean?" Sydney had a feeling she wouldn't like this. "I thought you said he came to see you."

Callie kept her eyes locked on the floor. "He sneaked in after lights-out, using the maintenance shafts. They run all through the buildings."

Now this didn't surprise Sydney. Danny was turning out to be infinitely resourceful, and in her estimation, headed for Juvenile Hall. Between breaking into computer systems and climbing through maintenance shafts, he'd probably get there before his thirteenth birthday.

"Don't be mad, Sydney."

Sydney reached over and tucked a strand of pale hair behind the child's ear. "I'm not mad." And she wasn't. Not really. "In fact, I'm glad you had company."

Callie brightened. "You are?"

"Sure." Callie's simplicity was infectious, a single bright spot in what had otherwise been a very dark day.

"Danny and I used to stay up for hours talking," she said, chattering away in the way of seven-year-olds. "Sometimes he'd read to me. He taught me chess and started showing me tai chi."

Sydney glanced at Danny, still asleep on the couch, and her heart softened toward him. Okay, so the boy meant well, at least as far as his sister was concerned.

"We didn't have a lot of time, and I don't know much yet." Callie had wiggled around until her backside rested against one of Sydney's legs. "But Danny says it will help me get better. He says there's healing power in the moves."

Sydney couldn't help but smile. Callie obviously adored her big brother every bit as much as he did her. Whatever else happened, these children belonged together.

"Danny and I practice every morning," Callie continued. "Even Anna helped me some."

Anna again. Just the mention of that name brought Sydney out of her bemusement at Callie's chatter. Anna's presence hovered over them like a particularly unpleasant ghost. "Did you like Anna, Callie?"

Callie shrugged. "She was okay." She hesitated. "You know, before."

"You mean before she helped you run away?"

"Uh-huh." Again she hesitated, this time glancing at her brother. "I didn't tell Danny 'cause I didn't want him to feel bad."

"Did she hurt you?"

Callie shook her head, and Sydney released her breath. "No. I just didn't like her. She wasn't very nice."

Sydney considered asking more questions, but decided it was best to drop the subject. She didn't trust her own motives when it came to Anna Kelsey. Besides, whatever else the woman was, she'd died helping these children.

The silence spun out between them again, more comfortably this time. Callie moved back to the window, while Sydney continued to wonder about the girl's illness. She supposed it could be as simple or as complicated as a weak immune system. However, that didn't make sense when you considered Callie had been out of her controlled environment for several days and seemed fine. If she was overly susceptible to infection, she probably would have caught something by now. The problem was, without tests, Sydney couldn't draw any definitive conclusions.

"Are you coming with us?" Callie asked without turning from the window. "To help find our father?"

Sydney kept her eyes on the rapidly fading day. "I don't know." She paused, choosing her words carefully. "I'm not certain that going off on our own to find your father is the best thing." Then, as much to herself as to Callie, she added, "Maybe it would be better to call the authorities and let them find out what's going on." Or Charles with his extensive network of connections.

Callie looked at her with eyes that were big and blue, and suddenly a lot older than her seven years. "You're mad at him, aren't you?"

The question surprised her, and Sydney considered pretending she didn't understand. But what would be the point? They both knew Callie meant Ethan.

So, was Sydney mad at him?

It wasn't a word she'd have used, but she guessed it applied. Or it had as recently as last night. She'd been angry at Ethan, deeply angry and hurt. Their son had died, she'd needed her husband, and he hadn't been there for her. She'd never allowed herself to look past that simple equation. But here, with the spring sunshine highlighting the tight features of the man she'd once loved, she knew she could no longer leave it at that.

She needed to know why he'd left her. *They* needed to tie up the ends of their unsettled marriage and forgive each other. None of which would be possible if she walked away.

"No, Callie, I'm not mad," she said. "Not anymore. But my staying isn't just about Ethan."

She couldn't leave these children, either. She'd sensed their need from the moment she'd met them, and if she turned them over to the police, she'd never learn the truth. The authorities would whisk them away, returning them to that school, and she'd never know whether they'd been ripped from their parents' arms, or were orphans as their guardians claimed. Nor would she learn why Callie got sick, or why these two children who obviously loved each other had been kept apart.

Callie didn't look convinced.

Sydney reclaimed the girl's hands and forced a smile. "It's about the best way to help you and your brother."

Callie tilted her head, a myriad of emotions playing across her small features. Doubt, fear, hope, they all flickered on her face. Finally she said, "We need you."

The simplicity of the statement was Sydney's undoing. Closing her eyes, she squeezed the child's hands. "I know."

CHAPTER THIRTEEN

Ethan wanted to hit something. Hard.

For three long years he'd told himself he was finished with the Agency and its waltz with death, all the while dreaming of hunting down Ramirez and watching him die. Ethan wanted to close his hands around the other man's throat and feel the life drain away beneath his fingers.

Then a few short hours ago, Ramirez had been within his grasp. Ethan had almost lost it, risking everything for the sake of his revenge. They'd barely escaped. And now Ramirez was still close, so close Ethan could sense him, feel his presence like a foul wind against his skin. But he couldn't do a damn thing about it. Not with Sydney and two runaway orphans depending on him for their lives.

Ethan closed his eyes and fought the need to pummel his fist against the nearest hardwood surface. If he started, he wouldn't stop. He'd drive himself until he drew blood and shattered the bones of his hand, until he collapsed, pain screaming through him and blotting out all thought, all memory.

What good would he be to any of them then?

He forced himself to breathe deeply, slowly, then fell into the rhythm of tai chi. He needed to forget Ramirez, get his anger under control, and concentrate on the lives in his care. His body moved from one position to the next, smoothly, seamlessly, but his thoughts remained with his son. And the man who'd killed him.

Hate circled within him like a living thing, a force threatening to consume him. He pulled back, blocking out everything but the steady flow of movements, his breathing, and the beat of his heart. Over and over he performed the ritual, as the need to hunt pulled at him, tore at the ties that held him to this place and the three people he'd left sleeping inside.

He couldn't say how long he repeated the movements, but exhaustion finally dulled his senses. He could still feel the need for revenge within him, buried beneath a lifetime of discipline, but for now, he had it under control. Only then did he dare bring his arms up in a wide, final sweep and press his palms together in front of his chest. As he dropped his hands to his sides, he caught Sydney watching him from the window.

She was so pale. Like she'd been the day of Nicky's funeral.

The memory stung, but he couldn't escape it. Not with Sydney so close. Nicky had died in mid-April, during a heat wave that had made the day feel more like August, when the dry, lifeless heat of the Texas summer would be at its height. Even beneath the live oaks that shaded his final resting place, it had felt like an oven.

The day crystalized in Ethan's mind.

He and Sydney had ridden to the cemetery in a black limousine. Her parents had wanted to accompany their daughter, but Ethan had consigned them to the second car, and Sydney hadn't objected. She hadn't even spoken, even as she stood, her hand placid in his, listening to the ragged voice of the young minister attempting to offer comfort as they buried their five-year-old son.

Around them, the world seemed unnaturally bright. Vivid. Like something not quite real. The sky had a celestial quality, its very blueness a slap, a mockery of the day's purpose. As was the smell of fresh mown grass and the hum of a distant lawnmower. Insects chattered. A toddler squirmed and whined and was taken off by a flustered adult. Sydney's mother, standing on the other side of her daughter, sniffed, wiped her eyes, and clung to her husband's arm. The hole in the earth appeared cavernous, the earth a rich brown. The roses on Nicky's casket a deep bloodred.

And Sydney.

Her face bleached of color. Her hair pulled severely away from her face. Her swollen eyes hidden behind dark glasses. A part of her had died with Nicky, and Ethan sensed her willingness to crawl into that coffin with their son. He saw himself burying her in the plot next to the boy and slipped an unsteady arm around her shoulders.

He couldn't allow that.

At least, that's what he'd told himself, how he'd justified his actions later that day. In truth, he'd simply been helpless in the face of her grief and desperate for something he could do to make her whole again.

He'd made his decision as he watched the small casket descend into the ground. Sydney had choked back a sob, then let go as her mother turned and folded her into maternal arms. Ethan had stepped back, knowing what he had to do. He couldn't allow his wife to follow their son. He would do whatever it took to keep her safe, to give her a chance at life.

Now he saw that he'd chosen the easy way out. She'd managed to go on living these last three years, pulling herself and her life together, while he'd wallowed in his guilt, telling himself it was all for her. Instead, he should have told her the truth and gone after Ramirez.

She moved away from the window and stepped outside. As she walked toward him, he had the urge to walk away—from her, from those two kids, and from the memories both evoked. But, he held his ground, and she stopped a few feet away.

"Were you able to sleep?" he asked.

"A few hours." Her voice was cool, polite. "You?"

"I had some things to take care of. What about the kids?"

"Callie's awake, but Danny's still sleeping." Sydney folded her arms and glanced back toward the empty parking lot. "Where's your truck?"

He reminded himself to tread carefully. Beneath her civility was a brittle edge he couldn't quite read. "I parked it in town behind an auto-body shop. It will be a while before anyone questions what it's doing there." Then, before she could ask any more questions, he added, "I rented a car. It's in back."

"Wasn't that risky?" she said. "I mean, can't they trace your credit card or something?"

"I used a different name. I have several, courtesy of the Agency." And a couple they knew nothing about. It was another precaution he and his team had taken, like their desert hideaway. They'd acquired identification, credit cards, and passports that not even the Agency could trace, at least not right away. "We have at least forty-eight hours before anyone picks up anything unusual, maybe longer."

"But someone in town could have recognized you from the news report." She seemed more curious than concerned, and he figured she probably wished someone *had* spotted him and called the police.

"I had to chance it. The truck was too visible, if someone saw us drive away from your condo . . ." He let the comment trail off. She could fill in the blanks herself. He bent to pick up his jacket and slipped it on, suppressing a wince at the sudden needle of pain.

She noticed anyway. "Are you bleeding again?"

Funny, he'd forgotten the injury while going through his routine. He supposed he had his anger at Ramirez to thank for that. The bullet's trail on his arm was nothing in comparison. "It's just sore."

"That's not surprising. You need to get some rest, Ethan." She'd switched to her best doctor voice. "And you need to give that arm time to heal."

"I *need* to keep limber."

She looked ready to argue, but evidently thought better of it. Her politeness was beginning to unnerve him, as was his own. They were dancing around each other, both avoiding more pressing questions, like what to do with those two kids.

After they'd seen the news report earlier and listened to Danny's story, they'd reached an impasse. Sydney wasn't the type of woman who dealt well with uncertainty, but the morning's events had depleted her. Ethan had seen it before. When someone whose life fell within traditional boundaries was suddenly forced into dangerous circumstances, they could only take so much before their minds shut down. That was the case with Sydney. Too much had happened too quickly for her to make any rational choices. She was out of her element, and she wasn't the only one. The children were strung out as well. He'd hoped a few hours' sleep would do all of them a lot of good and help Sydney see things clearly.

"So, what now?" she said, finally braving the question on both their minds. "What do we do about Danny and Callie?"

"We find Timothy Mulligan."

"We're not even sure he's Danny's father. What if he's wrong, what if—"

"That's why we need to talk to Mulligan. Look,"—he rubbed a weary hand over his face—"I don't like this any more than you do, but at the very least, we need to find out what's going on at that school. And Mulligan is the place to start."

"I'm not sure about this, Ethan."

"It's the only choice we have."

"That's not true, we could—"

"What? Turn them over to the authorities? You want to do that, Sydney?" He'd known she would question his decision about Mulligan and was prepared to convince her, even if it meant playing on her maternal instincts. "After what Danny told us a few hours ago about that place they came from? Do you want to take a chance they'll end up missing like their friends?"

She shook her head. "We don't know—"

"That's right, we don't."

He knew her instinct to help those kids was battling her reluctance to trust him. He couldn't blame her, and if he could leave her out of this without risking her life, he would. But Ramirez was still out there, and Ethan couldn't rely on the assassin's interest in Danny and Callie to keep him from going after Sydney.

Although it made him feel like a heel, he played his last card. "And don't forget, Anna died delivering them to me."

Sydney's eyes locked on his, irritated at his manipulation attempt. But there was also the recognition that he was right. "So what do you suggest?"

"We wait until full dark," he said, "then head to Illinois. It's about eight hundred miles. If we drive straight through, we can make it before noon tomorrow." He broke off, one more secret nudging at him. "But there's something else you need to know," he said and lowered himself to a log at the edge of the trees. "Sit down. It's not just Ramirez I'm worried about."

She stared at him without moving.

"Come on,"—he nodded toward the log—"sit."

She did finally, keeping her distance, as if getting too close would hurt. And maybe it would.

Meanwhile, he searched for the words to explain, though he knew of no easy way to tell her he'd been lying to her since they'd met. He picked up a twig from the dirt, snapped it in two, and tossed it down. "When we were together, I didn't tell you the truth about what I did for the Agency."

She went very still. "Go on."

God, how he hated this. "I didn't work in DI." The DI, or Directorate of Intelligence, was the analytical arm of the CIA. "And I wasn't an analyst." He paused, bracing for her reaction. "I was an operation officer for SCTC, the Strategic Counter-Terrorism Center."

"Operations?"

He kept going, afraid if he stopped he wouldn't get it all out. "Not many people know about SCTC, even within the Agency." He shifted on the log, leaning forward to rest his arms on his knees. "It's a highly classified division, fashioned after the old Counter-Terrorism Center but with more anonymity and clout. But like its predecessor, the SCTC draws its people from all the other directorates. Intelligence, operations, science and technology." He checked his stream of words, searching her face for a reaction, and realized he hadn't answered her single-word question.

"Yeah," he said, "I was in Operations." The clandestine intelligence-gathering division of the Agency most people thought comprised the whole of the CIA. But Sydney knew it was only a part of a much larger organization.

"My team specialized in finding and bringing in fugitives," he said. "And sometimes we conducted rescue missions, but mostly we pursued international renegades, the kind of people who operate outside the mainstream: terrorists, revolutionaries, whoever the-powers-that-be determined was a threat."

Again he stopped, waiting, hoping she'd say something, anything. But she didn't oblige him. They may as well have been talking about the weather for all the reaction he got. Except her hands, which she'd wadded into tight fists.

He kept talking because he didn't know what else to do. "Officially, my team was called the Strategic Rescue and Retrieval Unit." They'd been so damn cocky, and he'd been the worst of all. "We referred to ourselves as Hunters."

This time when he finished speaking, he let his words settle between them. Now it was up to her to go or stay, trust him or not. At least now, she knew the kind of man she'd married.

"So, everything you told me about the Agency, about your job there . . ." Her voice broke, then hardened. "Was a lie."

He wished he could deny it. "Yes."

She turned away, her body a study of rigid lines. He reached out to touch her but changed his mind, thinking she might shatter at the contact.

When she spoke again, he heard the first stirring of anger in her voice. "How long?"

"From the beginning." He'd joined the Agency after Desert Storm, two years before they'd met. "I was recruited into SCTC straight out of training."

She looked back at him, understanding flickering in her eyes, the recognition of a hundred untruths, a thousand incidents which he'd explained with lies.

"I couldn't tell you— No, that's not true."

"By all means, Ethan, don't lie to me now."

He ignored her sarcasm. "I was discouraged from telling you, but the final decision was mine." And he could have walked away, resigned, or asked for a transfer to one of the other divisions. But he hadn't wanted to quit. He'd loved the work, reveled in his own skill. "I thought it was better that you didn't know."

"Better for whom?" she snapped. "And who gave you the right to make that decision for me?" She met his gaze with accusing eyes, then pushed to her feet. "You always were so sure you knew what was best for everyone else."

He followed her. "I was protecting you, Sydney, both you and Nicky." And he'd failed miserably. Would she have been better off knowing the truth? Would Nicky still be alive? They were questions he'd asked himself a million times in the desert.

"Is that supposed to make me feel better? My God, Ethan, you lied to me for six years."

They fell into silence again, facing each other from a distance that had nothing to do with the space between them. Finally, she sighed and looked away, the anger draining from her features, revealing a deep exhaustion.

"What about now?" she asked. "Are you still in Operations?"

"I left the Agency three years ago."

She made the connection instantly. "When Nicky died."

He hesitated. They were skidding close to the one truth he couldn't reveal without destroying her. "Yes."

"So you walked out on the Agency as well as me."

He flattened the impulse to tell her the rest. "I'm not proud of leaving you."

She seemed to have no answer for that, and time strung out between them, brittle and seemingly endless. She was the first to drop her gaze, and only then could he breathe. It took a few minutes, but she regained control, her anger focusing her thoughts like nothing else could.

"So, why are you telling me this now?"

"Because I want you to understand the kind of people we're dealing with." And because he needed her to understand he was her best shot at protection. "Ramirez was," *careful, Decker,* "one of us."

"A Hunter?"

Again he ignored her sarcasm. "Officially he was part of my unit, but in reality he reported directly to the SCTC director, a man by the name of Avery Cox. Or he used to. I don't know who pays Ramirez now. I doubt it's the Agency, but their fingerprints are all over this. The shooter on your balcony, Danny and Callie . . . Anna."

"You think the Agency is involved?"

"If not the Agency, then some of its people."

"But isn't there someone you can call?" A bit of fear had crept back into her voice. "Some way to find out?"

He had considered it, calling Cox, but decided it was too risky. "Not until I have a better idea who's involved. For now, you have to trust me, Sydney. There—"

She raised a hand to cut him off. "Don't start that. You've just admitted you lied to me for six years. I don't have to do anything, especially trust you."

It was the wrong thing to say. "Okay, I guess I deserve that. But you do have to make a decision, and we're about out of time. Are you coming with me to find Timothy Mulligan?"

She frowned, glanced away, then looked back at him. "I want to call Charles, he's my—"

"No." Ethan's response was automatic and abrupt.

Anger flashed in her eyes again. "What do you mean, 'no'? He can help us."

"He can only hurt us. Even if the Agency's not involved, every police officer in the state is looking for me. They think I'm a cop killer. That means they're pulling out all the stops. They'll be everywhere, setting up roadblocks and tapping phones, yours, this"—he about choked on the name—"Charles, and anyone else the authorities think you might contact."

She didn't budge, except to lift her chin. "That's a chance I'm willing to take."

"Well, I'm not." His temper snapped, and he moved back to put some distance between them. When he spoke again, it took an effort to keep his tone neutral. "You make a call, and I mean to *anybody*, and they've got us.

Then the chances of my making it to a jail cell in one piece are zero to none."

That, at least, seemed to get her attention. "You're exaggerating. If I tell them—"

"You'll never get the chance. Two of their own are dead. Someone has got to pay, and at the moment, I'm their prime target."

She stared at him for long moments, and he could almost see the battle waging within her. But he had his own battles to fight, and his patience was gone.

"Go or stay, Sydney. The choice is yours. But if you stay, you play by my rules."

"Is this a game, then?"

"The deadliest. Your life is the prize, and those kids . . ." He glanced back at the lodge. "They're nothing but pawns."

"You bastard." Her fist clenched, and for a moment, he thought she'd hit him. He'd almost welcome it.

"Yeah," he said. "And I play to win."

He watched her work through it: her anger and the desire to tell him to go to hell, her fear for Danny and Callie, and her acceptance of an intolerable situation. He buried his guilt over manipulating her once more. After all, he'd just given her a chance to survive.

"It looks like I don't have any choice," she said finally. "We'll do it your way."

CHAPTER FOURTEEN

The next thirteen hours passed in a blur.

Ethan had rented a black late-model Ford Explorer and stocked it with camping gear: sleeping bags and a tent, a cooler filled with bottled water and sandwich meat, and a variety of gadgets to make the outdoors more hospitable. She supposed anyone inspecting the vehicle would think the contents perfect for a family camping trip.

Or, for a group of fugitives.

They started out a little after eight and drove straight through from the lake to Illinois, stopping only for gas, an occasional bathroom break, and at a drugstore to pick up a few things for Callie.

She'd started coughing, and Sydney was worried she might be coming down with something. Although Danny claimed his sister got carsick, and Callie insisted she was fine, Sydney wasn't buying it. She remembered their earlier conversation and worried that the girl was sicker than she appeared. So at Sydney's insistence, they stopped and picked up cough syrup and children's aspirin. After taking both, Callie drifted off to sleep.

Danny, on the other hand, remained stubbornly awake, refusing to lie down and give into the exhaustion tugging at him. Occasionally Sydney would turn to see him dozing with his head against the window. Then, as if sensing her, he'd open his eyes, straighten in his seat, and pick up his Game Boy. So she stopped checking on him.

Like Danny, she remained awake, her thoughts refusing to shut down as the car streamed along the nearly deserted highway. Within the vehicle's warm interior, they seemed in a world of their own, protected and isolated from the darkness beyond the glass. The steady hum of the engine and the soft green light of the dashboard lulled her with a sense of normalcy and the feeling that nothing of the past twenty-four hours could touch her here.

Once, when Nicky had been four, the three of them had taken a road trip to San Antonio. Ethan had wanted to show Nicky the Alamo. They'd left on a Friday evening and driven for five hours, Nicky asleep in the backseat. She remembered her feeling of contentment. There had been a rightness to their being together, a sense of belonging to her husband and son.

She could almost imagine the same thing now.

If she threw her thoughts out of focus just a bit, she could pretend they were a family—the four of them. The boy fighting sleep with his head against the window, the little girl stretched out on the seat beside him, and the man, father and lover, protector and provider.

A set of headlights pierced her fantasy, lighting the car's interior and Ethan's face. Sydney blinked and turned away, embarrassed and angry at her self-indulgent daydreaming. The approaching car passed and the darkness ebbed in, but her view of the man behind the wheel remained intact.

A man who was no longer her husband, whose hard features bore little resemblance to the man who'd once given her a son. A man she'd pretended was someone else for too many years.

Their trip to San Antonio had been their only family vacation. She'd blamed herself and her busy practice, but she saw now that it hadn't been her fault. More times than she could count she'd arranged for them to get away together. It had been Ethan who'd never had the time, who'd spent more days and nights away than at home. Ethan who'd always had some business to take care of that no one else could handle.

Strange that she should remember all his excuses now. Odder still that she'd closed her eyes to it during the years of their marriage. If there was blame to accept, it was that she'd let him lie to her and accepted everything at face value—when she should have known better. He wasn't the type of man to be satisfied as an analyst, or stay in the background while others fought on the front lines.

Ethan had always been a patriot. In Sydney's world, he'd been something of a novelty. It had been more chic in her circles to slam the country and its government than to support it. On the other hand, Ethan had grown up in a military family. He'd spent seven years in the service, three of them in Special Forces. His father was career Army and his brother had died in Desert Storm. The instinct to serve was born, bred, and trained into him.

How could she fault him for that? Or remain angry when he'd lied in the name of that which came as naturally to him as the beat of his heart: the need to protect. And how could she keep her own defenses in place when he still had the power to weaken her with nothing more than a touch or a smile?

It was midmorning when they pulled into River Ridge State Park, south of Champaign, Illinois. Both children came fully awake as Ethan parked in front of a low building near the entrance. Danny scooted forward to see through the front windshield, and Callie stared wide-eyed and curious out the side window.

"Why are we stopping?" Danny asked.

Ethan shut off the engine. "We're getting a cabin."

"Is that a good idea?" Sydney said.

"No one will look for us here, and we need to rest before we decide on our next step."

"I want to keep going," Danny said.

"Be my guest." Ethan gestured toward the north end of the park. "Champaign is about fifty miles that way."

Danny opened his mouth to protest, but Sydney placed a hand on his arm. "He's right, Danny. We're all tired."

The boy crossed his arms and shoved back into his seat.

Ethan tossed him a quick frown, then climbed out of the car and entered the building. He returned a few minutes later carrying maps, a parking permit for the dashboard, and a key on a large wooden ring.

"We picked the right time of year," he said. "The place is almost empty, and we got an isolated site back in the woods." He glanced at Danny, who remained sullen, staring out the window.

When they pulled into a clearing a few minutes later, Sydney wished again that things were different. The setting reminded her of something out of a child's picturebook. A modest log cabin sat among towering pines that covered the ground with soft needles. A porch stretched across the front, and a tire swing hung from a nearby oak.

No one spoke as the four of them got out of the vehicle, and Sydney suspected the place had charmed even Ethan. It was the ideal vacation spot for the ideal family. Too bad neither fit their situation.

"It's like a fairy tale," Callie said.

Sydney smiled, pleased that the girl's thoughts had mirrored her own. "Which one? Hopefully not 'Hansel and Gretel' or 'Little Red Riding Hood.' "

Callie giggled. "No. I think maybe 'Snow White' would be better."

"Then I guess we'd better watch out for the evil stepmother." Sydney squeezed Callie's hand.

Danny rolled his eyes and wandered off to the tire swing, his backpack slung across one shoulder.

"How are you feeling?" Sydney asked, placing a hand on Callie's forehead. "You feel cooler."

"I'm fine."

Sydney smiled, relieved.

"Let's get inside." Ethan started for the cabin. "I need a couple hours' sleep, then I'll head in to Champaign and talk to Mulligan."

"Alone?" Sydney asked, following.

"It's the best way." Ethan unlocked the door but turned to her before entering. "We can't all just show up on the man's doorstep."

"I agree," she said. "But I don't think you're the one who should approach him."

"What about me?" Danny asked. Startled, Sydney turned to see the boy standing behind her. "I'm going," he said.

"Not this time," Ethan answered, without even looking at him. "You'll be safe here while—"

"I'm going," Danny repeated. "And you can't stop me."

Ethan turned and leveled a hard stare at the boy. "Don't count on it, kid."

Danny climbed the short steps and faced Ethan with an angry glare. "He's—"

Sydney stepped between them. "Stop it, Ethan. You're not helping the situation." Then she turned to Danny. "For once I agree with him. We can't just show up on Dr. Mulligan's doorstep."

Danny shifted his anger to her. "He'll want to see me."

"Maybe, but we have to do this right."

"You can't keep me here. I want—"

"The four of us haven't come all this way for nothing," she said, cutting him off. "We're here because we believe Dr. Mulligan may be your and Callie's father."

"He *is* my father."

"You can't be sure of that." She hated to deflate his hopes, but he had to face the possibility that this was a wild-goose chase. "Not until we talk to him."

Danny clamped his mouth shut, his jaw working.

"Even if Timothy Mulligan is your father, he won't recognize you," she continued more gently. "You don't remember living anywhere but the Haven, which means you were a baby when they took you from your parents. So if you just show up, claiming to be this man's son, he'll think it's some kind of bad joke."

Danny's frown deepened, but she could tell she was getting through to him. He wasn't stupid.

"You've waited this long," she said. "Just give it a few more hours. If Dr. Mulligan turns out to be your father, we'll know it soon." *And hopefully, he'll want you back.* She couldn't say that, however, not to this boy who desperately wanted to find his family.

Although still obviously unhappy, Danny didn't have an immediate reply, so she shifted her attention to Ethan. "But I think I should be the one to talk to Mulligan."

"Forget it." Ethan went inside, leaving her standing with the children on the porch.

It took her a minute to push down her annoyance. She'd had it with Ethan's heavy-handedness. She wasn't used to taking orders without question and refused to take a backseat and let him make all the decisions without her input. If they were going to help these children, they were going to do it together.

To Danny and Callie she said, "Give us a few minutes, will you?"

Danny frowned but led Callie back over to the tire swing.

Sydney followed Ethan into the cabin. It was sparsely furnished with a pair of bunk beds, a dresser, and a chair. All the pieces appeared handcrafted from some light wood, making the room warm and appealing. Ethan had stowed his duffel under one of the bunks and stretched out on the unmade mattress.

"I want to talk about this," she said.

He folded his hands under his head and closed his eyes. "I don't."

Again, she had to tamp down a rush of irritation. Giving in to her temper would get her nowhere. "You're the one who told me every cop in the Midwest is looking for you," she said.

"They're looking for you, too."

"But my picture hasn't been plastered all over the news." She crossed her arms and stood her ground. She was right about this, but it was like talking to a dead man for all the response she got. In exasperation, she tossed her hands in the air. "Okay, so you go traipsing off to campus and someone spots you. What then?"

He opened his eyes.

"I'll tell you what happens. You'll be arrested and charged with murder." He was at least listening to her now, so she pushed her advantage while she could. "And I'll be left alone to deal with these children."

"And what if someone recognizes you?"

"It's a long shot, but so what if they do? I'll tell them what happened and that will be the end of it." After a moment's pause she added, "You asked me to trust you, Ethan. Now I'm asking you to trust me. I can do this, and Mulligan is much more likely to talk to me than you."

He pushed himself to a sitting position. "You're forgetting about Ramirez."

"You said you lost him."

"I did."

"Then he's not a problem. But if you're wrong, then

I'm in more danger here than in Champaign." She settled her hands on her hips. "In fact, the children and I are sitting ducks here."

He studied her, considering, then nodded. "You're right."

Her legs about gave out beneath her. Not only was he listening, he'd actually heard her.

He didn't seem to notice. "The only other question is whether someone else is watching Mulligan and waiting for Danny or Callie to show."

She slipped into the room's only chair, because she wasn't at all sure her legs would continue to support her. "Someone from the Agency?"

"Or whoever runs the Haven."

"You think they know Danny hacked into their computer system and will head here?"

"I'm not ruling anything out." He ran a hand through his already disheveled hair. "But if they do, you have a better chance of getting in and out without anyone noticing you."

He reached under the bed and pulled out his duffel, and she had to wonder if he'd planned for her to go to Champaign all along. "Let's see if Anna has anything in here to help you become someone else." He removed a leather bag and dumped its contents on the bed.

A few minutes later, Sydney *felt* like someone else. The changes were minor but effective, turning back the years and making her into a student. The jeans worked, according to Ethan, but she'd replaced her Ellen Tracy top with one of Ethan's T-shirts, and her leather jacket with his denim one. In Anna's bag, he'd found a pair of wire-rimmed glasses. From her own overnight case, Sydney applied a bit more makeup than usual, making her eyes appear owlish behind the frames.

Ethan backed up and surveyed their handiwork. "It

won't fool anyone who looks too closely, but hopefully that won't happen."

Her doubts must have shown on her face.

"The change doesn't have to be drastic," he said. "People see what they expect. Nothing more and nothing less. Now do you know what to do if you get into trouble?"

She dug out her cell phone, which he'd programmed with Anna's number. "Press the speed dial, let it ring, then hang up."

"And I'll know to get the kids out of here."

"How are you going to do that without a car?"

"Don't worry about me, there are plenty of vehicles in this park."

She didn't want to think about that too closely and slipped the phone into Anna's well-used bag, which she'd carry instead of her own Coach purse.

"And you won't use the cell phone for any other reason," he insisted for about the tenth time.

"Ethan, I know what to do."

"Okay, I just . . ."

"I know." His protective instincts were in overdrive. "But I'll be fine."

He looked her over again, but this time she suspected his examination had very little to do with the disguise. A flush of heat brushed her cheeks, and she backed up a step. Then he did the most unexpected thing, he closed the distance between them and kissed her. Just one, quick, hard kiss that rattled her thoughts and returned her to when easy displays of affection had been commonplace between them. And she wondered how she'd ever taken them, or him, for granted.

He released her too soon, two words fluttering against her lips. "Be careful."

CHAPTER FIFTEEN

On the way to Champaign, Sydney replayed Ethan's kiss in her mind a dozen times. Though it really hadn't been much of one, not romantic in the least. More like a good luck send-off or an affectionate peck for a sister, friend, or the woman you'd been married to for six years. But they weren't married any longer and she wasn't going to start thinking like they were.

So why had he kissed her?

Everything he'd done in the last twenty-four hours had been calculated, like a finely planned mission. Yet for an instant she'd sensed his surprise at the kiss as well. He'd recovered quickly, but for a few brief seconds she'd felt something more from him. After all, she'd lived with and loved this man for years, she should know when a kiss meant something.

Sure.

Just like she should have known what her husband did for a living, or when he was lying to her.

In the end she decided he'd kissed her for one reason only: to distract her and keep her mind off the upcoming meeting with Timothy Mulligan. Ethan knew she'd obsess about the kiss for the entire fifty-mile drive and forget to worry about a particular physics professor and his relationship to two runaways.

And in that, Ethan had succeeded.

* * *

The University of Illinois was large and sprawling, with an attractive mix of old and new buildings and generous stretches of green space in between. The sights took her back to her own college days, when life had been so much simpler. She'd had one goal back then, one vision: getting her medical degree. Who would have guessed she'd end up being stalked by an assassin while trying to locate the parents of a couple of runaways?

As she made her way across campus, she reviewed the cover story she and Ethan had devised. She would approach Dr. Mulligan as a doctoral candidate in sociology, doing her dissertation on missing children and the effects on their families. She'd tell him that her faculty adviser—a name she'd looked up in the university catalog—had suggested Mulligan might be willing to give her an interview.

It was a plausible story, especially at such a large university. The chances were slim that Dr. Mulligan, a senior faculty member of the physics department, would know any of the sociology faculty, and an even slimmer possibility that he'd know their Ph.D. candidates.

She located his office without too much trouble, a surprisingly tidy cubbyhole in the Loomis Laboratory of Physics. It was empty. Finding someone who could tell her anything about his whereabouts was a little more difficult. After several inquiries, she found a secretary who pulled up his schedule and sent Sydney to a first-floor classroom.

It ended up being an auditorium, seating at least two hundred students in tiered rows. In front, on a low stage, a man in pressed jeans and a crisp white shirt lectured in a monotone. His voice implied he was teaching elementary material, while one glance around the room told a different story. At least half the students were completely lost.

The wardrobe might be different, but the man and his

classroom brought back unpleasant memories of her own years as an undergraduate. For her the class had been organic chemistry, junior year. With two hundred primarily premed students, the course had been used to weed out the potential medical-school applicants. Day one, the professor, who'd seemed older than God at the time, had informed his class that only one-third would pass.

"Look to the student on your right, then to the student on your left," he'd said. "Only one of you will finish this course."

Unfortunately for most of the students, finishing wasn't their only concern. While the object of the department seemed to be to thin out the ranks of the curriculum, each of the premed students needed an A to get into medical school.

She wondered what major Dr. Mulligan's physics class was meant to thin. There couldn't be that many physics majors, could there? Engineering maybe?

Turning her thoughts away from her automatic dislike of the man, she considered him as Danny's father. He was tall, probably six four, and somewhat awkward with his height, even gangly. He wasn't heavy, but soft-looking, as though he'd never done a day's worth of physical labor in his life, or even participated in a sport. His coloring was unremarkable: brown hair, medium complexion. She couldn't see his eye color from a distance, but it probably didn't matter. Nothing about the man told her one way or the other whether he was Danny and Callie's father.

One conclusion she did come to was that she needed to change her strategy for getting information from him. He wasn't the type to care one whit about helping a graduate student from another department. So if she took that approach with him, she'd be lucky if he'd give her the time of day. Timothy Mulligan appeared rather impressed with himself. It would take someone with equally impressive credentials to get his attention.

She probably should have kept the leather jacket and designer top and considered returning to the car and making the switch. But if she did, she might lose her chance to talk to Mulligan.

Finally, he completed his lecture.

Sydney waited for the class to clear before making her way toward the front. A few students clustered around Mulligan, asking questions. He answered in a blunt, no-nonsense way, paying little attention to whether they followed his explanation or not. She had to wonder if he delighted in being obtuse, or whether he really didn't fathom his audience's lack of understanding.

Then, obviously, he decided he'd dispensed enough wisdom for one day. "That's it for now," he said, gathering his books.

"But, Dr. Mulligan—"

He started toward the edge of the dais, brushing past his students as if they were annoying insects. "You know my office hours. Make an appointment with my secretary if you have more questions."

Sydney waited for him at the bottom of the steps. "Excuse me, Dr. Mulligan, do you have a minute?"

He barely glanced at her, much less slowed his pace. "My office hours are posted on my door."

She made no move to follow him. "I'm not a student," she said, adding a trace of annoyance to her voice. "I'm Dr. Sydney Branning." She used her maiden name, just in case he'd been following the news. Though he looked like a man who never much lifted his head out of the sand—or maybe that would be the laboratory. "I'm on staff at Covenant Medical Center."

He paused, not stopping exactly, but turned and gave her a second look. "Well, come on, then." He gestured for her to join him, as if he hadn't just been incredibly rude. "I only have a few minutes."

She fell into step beside him but waited for him to speak.

"You look too young to be a doctor. What's your specialty?"

She supposed that was a compliment, in a backhanded sort of way. Particularly since she *had* dressed to look like a student. "Pediatrics."

"Are you new?" he asked. "I don't remember seeing you on campus before."

Ethan had told her to keep as much to the truth as possible. "I just came up from Texas."

"That explains the drawl." He threw her another glance, only this one took in more than a potential colleague, and she expected he was taking in the jeans and oversized jacket. "You're pretty far from the medical center, Doctor."

Since she wasn't at all sure where the medical center was located, she ignored his comment. "I would have called first, but I suddenly had a few hours free and decided to take the chance you'd have time for me."

He shrugged. "Well, you're here now. What do you need?"

"I'm doing research on missing children and the effects of their disappearance on their families. I was told you might be willing to add your insight."

"I don't know how."

"I apologize if this brings up bad memories, but I need to ask you about your son's disappearance."

He came to an abrupt stop. "My son?"

"I'm sorry, Dr. Mulligan. I know this must be a painful subject, but—"

"Painful? Hardly." He frowned. "In fact, I don't know what you're talking about."

Confused, Sydney stumbled forward. "I know it's been a long time, but—"

"I don't know where you got your information, Dr. Branning, but you've made a mistake." He took a step back. "Now, if you'll excuse me, I have things to do."

This time she hurried after him. The children's future was at stake, and suddenly she knew she had the right man. "Please, Dr. Mulligan, hear me out. You did your undergraduate work at MIT, then went on to Caltech, where you received your Ph.D. in 1991." When she looked up at him, she saw he was angry.

"Obviously you know a great deal about me, except for the most pertinent fact." His earlier frown turned to distaste. "My son didn't disappear, Doctor, because I don't have a son. And never have."

Sydney just stared at him, stunned.

"I don't even like children," he said in an offhand manner. "They're a nuisance."

She opened her mouth to respond, but nothing came out.

"I suggest the next time, you do your research a little more carefully." Dismissing her without another word, he walked away.

Sydney stood frozen in place. Then an idea struck and she went after him. "Dr. Mulligan, please . . ."

"Dr. Branning—" He shook his head and kept walking.

"One more question." She grabbed his arm, bringing him to a halt, and braced herself for his reaction—which no matter what, wouldn't be good.

"Have you ever donated to a sperm bank?"

CHAPTER SIXTEEN

Danny dreamed of hands.

Large, groping hands, reaching for him in the darkness. He scrambled backward across his bed, crablike, falling as he reached the edge and . . .

Found himself in a maintenance shaft.

It was like those at the Haven. Aluminum all around. Shiny. Cold. Airless.

He shivered.

Then he saw the light where the shaft dumped into a room. Instinctively, he backed away, coming up hard against a wall. Only, it hadn't been there a moment earlier.

He turned, panic gripping him as he searched for a way out.

Suddenly, the shaft tilted, its walls narrowing and forcing him down toward a light. But he couldn't go there. Not to that room. He knew the horrors that lay within those walls and wouldn't look.

But he had no choice. The aluminum walls tightened around him. They were alive, squeezing him forward, pushing him to the edge until . . .

Below him, Sean lay on a stark white bed. Tubes sprouted from his arms, his legs, his chest, and with each labored breath, they pulsed a deep, bloodred. He coughed, the tubes ballooning to the point of bursting before returning to their original size. Another cough, and they expanded again.

Danny tried to back away, but the walls held him. He didn't want to be here, didn't want to see. There was nothing he could do, no way to help his friend.

But cracked lips moved, forming syllables that pulled Danny forward, made him strain to hear. Pleading words. Then Sean opened his eyes and looked up. Danny felt a scream struggle to escape as those eyes, all black, searched and found him hiding behind the metal grate. Not Sean . . .

No!

Danny jerked awake, caught in a tangled blanket, heart pounding and a silent scream echoing in his head.

The dream. Again.

He didn't move, afraid it would reclaim him and drag him back down. It was always like this, gripping him even after he awoke. Then, as his racing heart slowed, the images usually faded. Only, this time they stayed with him, and he remembered every detail, especially those black eyes and the face behind them. A face that hadn't invaded the dream before.

Adam's.

Fear for his friend settled in Danny's stomach. Adam was the oldest of the boys, almost thirteen, and the only one who knew about Danny's plan to find his family. They'd made a pact. Adam would stay and watch out for the little ones, and Danny would find his father, then bring help. Now he was afraid if he ever did get back, it would be too late.

Adam would already be gone.

Scared to go back to sleep, Danny sat up and looked around the silent cabin. Callie was still asleep in the lower bunk, but Ethan had gone out.

After Sydney left, they'd all lain down to get some rest.

Callie hadn't been feeling well, though she tried to hide it. Danny was worried about her and hoped he hadn't made a mistake taking her with him when he ran away. Then he remembered his dream, shivered, and his doubts fled. He wasn't going to let Callie end up like that. No matter what.

He found Ethan on the porch, a park map spread out in front of him. From the position of the sun, Danny figured Sydney had been gone for hours. He sat on the steps. "Isn't it time she was back?"

Ethan's idea of a response was to scowl.

In Danny's opinion, Ethan was worse than the Keepers. They at least pretended to be nice while telling their lies. Ethan didn't even do that. He didn't fake anything, least of all that he wanted Danny or his sister anywhere near him.

If it weren't for Callie, Danny would be long gone.

"What are you looking for?" he asked, more to irritate Ethan than anything else.

"Nothing."

"So why are you studying the map?"

"I'm not . . ." Ethan sighed and glanced up for the first time. "I'm making sure I understand the area."

Anna had done the same thing. "Our position and the location of the nearest cities or towns. Roads and where they lead. That sort of thing?"

"Yeah." Ethan laughed abruptly and went back to his task. "That sort of thing."

Encouraged, Danny went on. "It's always a good idea to know where you are, what's around you, and the best exit points." He waited for a response. When he didn't get one, he added, "That's what Anna said."

"She would know."

Danny remained quiet, for about five seconds. "What time is it?"

"Give it a rest, Danny."

"I just want to know what time it is."

Ethan looked up. "Sydney will be back soon."

Would she? Danny wasn't so sure. "I should have gone with her."

Ethan ignored him.

Danny picked up a stick and poked at the dirt beneath his feet. A smile would probably crack Ethan's face. The only time he'd come close was right before Sydney left for town. Callie had picked a handful of wildflowers from the woods behind the cabin. He'd almost smiled then. She had that effect on people. Even Anna had softened around her. Not that Callie's sweetness did her any good. She was still sick all the time.

As for Sydney, he didn't know what to think of her. She was almost too nice. Some of the Keepers had been like that, and in the end they'd been liars, too. Danny had learned not to trust any of them. At least if Ethan decided to turn them over to the authorities, he'd just do it. He wouldn't lie about it first. Danny wasn't so sure about Sydney.

She sure was taking a long time.

He should have hid in the back of the Explorer or something. That would have been the safest thing to do. Instead, he was stuck here waiting.

The sound of an approaching engine brought his head up as the black SUV pulled into the clearing. Danny sprang off the porch, but waited as Sydney shut off the engine and took her time getting out of the car. Behind him, the screen door slammed, and he glanced back and saw Callie on the porch. He smiled at her, then turned back toward Sydney, stopping when he saw the expression on her face.

"Did you see my father?" he asked, suddenly afraid of the answer.

She frowned. "Danny."

"Well, did you?" He took another step toward her. "Did you talk to him?"

She folded her arms. "I talked to Timothy Mulligan."

Yes! He knew it. "Did you tell him Callie and I were here? When can we—"

"Danny." She shook her head. "I didn't tell him about you."

"Why not?"

A large hand settled on his shoulder. Ethan had come up behind him. Danny jerked away from the man's touch, keeping his eyes on Sydney. "Why didn't you tell him we were here?"

"I'm sorry . . ."

His stomach churned. "You're lying."

"Timothy Mulligan doesn't have any children."

"No." *Liar.* He backed away, his heart pounding, his head ready to explode. *Why was she doing this?*

"I'm so sorry."

"Why are you lying to me?" It came out as a scream.

He continued to back away, looking at Ethan and Callie, then turned back to Sydney. She was a liar, just like all the rest, just like the Keepers. And Anna. He hated Sydney. He hated them all. His eyes stung, and he felt sick. Turning, he fled toward the woods, one word repeating in his head.

Liar. Liar. Liar.

Ethan stepped forward, stopping Sydney from following the boy. "Let him go. You can't help him now."

Tears gathered in her eyes and she looked ready to bolt. Instead, she went to Callie and took her hands. "I'm sorry, sweetie."

"It's not your fault," Callie said, with a sadness that twisted Ethan's heart.

"I know." Sydney glanced toward the tree where Danny had retreated. "But I wish I could make it right."

"What's he like?"

"He's not a very nice man."

Callie bit her lip, but her eyes remained dry. "Don't worry about Danny, I'll take care of him."

Sydney touched the girl's cheek, a gesture Ethan had seen a million times when their son was alive. He closed his eyes briefly at the sudden ache the memory produced. He and Sydney had lost so much. Not only their son, but all the small things that had defined them as a family.

"It's okay," Callie said, the child comforting the adult. "You tried." Then she walked over to her brother.

"Are you all right?" Ethan asked, taking his jacket from Sydney and tossing it over the porch railing.

"I don't know." Her eyes remained on the two children. "I'd hoped . . ." She brought her gaze back to him. "It wasn't a pleasant experience. Mulligan's a jerk. I'm almost glad he didn't claim them."

He reached for her, but she stepped back. Who could blame her, considering he'd kissed her the last time she'd let him near? It had been the craziest thing, and if he'd thought about it for half a second beforehand, he never would have done it. But it had just happened.

"Let's go inside," she said. "I have something to tell you."

Once in the cabin, she dropped into the rough-hewn wooden chair. Ethan stayed near the door, giving her the space she needed. Though it was hard, when what he wanted to do was fold her into his arms. He hadn't thought about much else since she'd left. One brief kiss, and his mind had ventured down roads where it didn't belong. It wasn't the smartest move he'd ever made, especially now when he needed all his concentration to keep them alive.

"How was Callie? Any more coughing?"

"Yeah, I gave her more of the cough syrup and a couple more aspirin."

"I'm worried about her."

"Kids get sick."

"I guess." Though she didn't look convinced, sitting with her elbows propped on the chair arm, her head resting on her hand. "This will sound strange, but I don't think Danny is entirely wrong about Timothy Mulligan."

"You think Mulligan was lying?"

"Not exactly." She massaged her temples and told him about her conversation with Mulligan. When she mentioned asking him about donating to a sperm bank, Ethan realized she was on to something.

"The most damning thing," she said, "is that he acted like he'd been caught with his hand in a cookie jar."

"It would explain a lot. Or at least why his name is in Danny's files at the Haven."

"There's more, although the rest of this is even more speculative." Again she rubbed at her temples. "Have you ever heard of James Cooley?"

"Didn't he start one of the first Internet companies, then sold it for a mint? A real eccentric."

"That's him." Sydney dug an aspirin bottle from her purse. "He's worth millions, maybe billions." She stood and crossed to the dresser, then rummaged through the cooler Ethan had brought in from the Explorer and pulled out a bottle of water. "No one really knows how much money he made, and I don't even know if he's still alive." She swallowed the aspirin, then returned to the chair.

Ethan moved up behind her and slipped his hands beneath her hair. She stiffened, then relaxed as he began to work the tension from her neck. No wonder she had a headache. She felt tight enough to snap. As he kneaded first one and then another muscle, she let her head drop forward with a sigh.

"God," she said. "You always did have the best hands."

Ethan smiled to himself. How often had they performed this ritual after one of her grueling days? It had started while she was in med school and continued through her pregnancy to the days when she'd had her own practice. She would come home exhausted, and he'd start on her neck, working his way to her extremities until she was putty in his hands. Then they'd make love for hours, until neither of them could move.

"I miss it," he said softly. "I miss you."

She tensed immediately, her barriers slamming back into place as she pulled away from him. "Yes, well, leaving was your choice." Her voice was hard.

As if he needed reminding of how much he'd hurt her. "Sydney . . ."

"Let's get back to James Cooley." She left the chair and moved to stand with her back against the dresser. "Shall we?"

It wasn't what he wanted, but he had little choice but to accept whatever parameters she set for their relationship. From now on, he'd keep his hands to himself. "If that's the way you want it."

"It is." She met his gaze for a moment, a spark of defiance in her eyes, but something else as well. Loneliness? Longing? He couldn't be sure which. Then she went on, as if he hadn't just put his hands on her, reminding them both of things better left in the past. "In the early eighties, Cooley started a sperm bank which only accepted donations from highly intelligent men. They were also very selective about whom they impregnated. The women had to be stable and married, with an IQ of over 140."

"Kind of narrows it down a bit, don't you think?"

"The idea was to create a more intelligent gene pool."

"And you think Timothy Mulligan made a donation?"

"Cooley's people searched for the right kind of donors, and Mulligan would have been a good candidate. High IQ."

There was a certain logic to the idea. "Nice theory, but that's all it is."

"I know, but it makes sense and explains how Mulligan's name got into Danny's file. Plus, both the timing and location are right. Mulligan did his doctoral work at Caltech in the mid-eighties. Also, he's so arrogant he might like the idea of creating more minds like his own. Especially if he doesn't have to raise them himself."

Ethan thought about it and walked to the window to check on the kids. They were no longer on the swing, but Danny's backpack rested against the porch support. They couldn't have gone far. Making a quick visual sweep of the area, he breathed easier when he saw them sitting on a boulder near the woods.

He'd told Sydney the truth earlier. No one had followed them from Texas. Not many people could track him when he wanted to get lost, and he'd been particularly vigilant on the drive north. He'd used cash for everything, switched license plates three times, and picked the less-traveled roads where a tail would be easy to spot. He'd even doubled back once, just to make sure. So he wasn't expecting Ramirez, or whoever was after these children, to show up anytime soon. But he wasn't taking any chances.

Callie spotted him and waved.

Absently, he raised a hand in response. If Sydney was right, where did that leave these kids?

"Okay, let's assume you're onto something," he said, watching as Callie led her brother back to the tire swing and got him to push her. "And Timothy Mulligan was a sperm donor. It doesn't explain how Danny and Callie landed in a facility off the coast of Washington State." *Or why.* "And it doesn't shed any light on Danny's story about kids disappearing."

"I know." She sounded frustrated. "But it's a start."

He turned away from the window. "We can check the facility's records and . . ." He stopped abruptly, suddenly uneasy when she avoided his gaze. "What is it?"

"We can't do this alone, Ethan. We need help."

"Are you saying you want to turn them over, and let social services send them back to that island?"

"Of course not. I know there's something wrong here. I have no proof, but I believe those children are products of in vitro fertilization and that Timothy Mulligan may be their biological father." She let out a short disgusted laugh. "Though I'm convinced he doesn't have a clue." Then she dismissed the statement with a wave, as if irrelevant. "But whoever their mother was, she's either dead or has deserted them. I want to know which and why."

"So what do you suggest?"

"I want to call my friend Charles in Dallas."

"We've been over this . . ."

"Hear me out," she insisted. "Charles has connections. He can access information about James Cooley and the Haven that you and I can't touch."

"Don't be so sure about that."

She crossed her arms. "Is this a male ego thing? Because if it is—"

"It has nothing to do with ego." Though he'd like to wring this Charles's neck.

"Good, because besides helping us with information, Charles can let my parents know I'm okay. They're probably worried sick."

"It's too risky."

"They won't call the authorities, Ethan."

"Not on you." He thought of the last time he'd seen his mother-in-law, at Nicky's funeral, and how she'd looked at him over her grieving daughter's shoulder. *She'd* known who to blame for her grandson's death. "They'd turn me over in a minute."

"They wouldn't do that."

"Look, Sydney, I'm really sorry about your folks. And you might be right that this Charles could help us."

"But?"

"If we contact them, especially if they start digging into things, they'll be at risk." And he couldn't put anyone else in danger; too many people had died already. "Someone wants this island kept quiet, and they're not going to take it very well that we're poking around."

She remained stubbornly quiet for a couple of seconds, then her entire body seemed to deflate. "You're right, the less they know the better."

"And the less they'll worry."

"That, too." She pushed away from the dresser. "So what do we do?"

"We head for Chicago. I'll drop you and the kids off at a library where you can get on the Internet and do some research on the Haven and Cooley. Danny says he's good with computers, so let him prove it."

"What about you?"

"I have a few contacts of my own." She didn't know about the network of connections he'd built over half a lifetime of service to the Agency, nor about the type of debts owed and collected by men who lived their lives on the fringes of society.

"And if that doesn't work?"

"One step at a time, Sydney." If necessary, he'd stow her and the children somewhere safe while he went to that island. But he wasn't about to mention that now. He needed a lot more information before even considering it. "Meanwhile, we shouldn't stay here any longer. So let's head out."

Ethan turned back to the window and knew immediately something was wrong. The tire swing was empty, as was the boulder. And the porch.

Danny's backpack was gone.

CHAPTER SEVENTEEN

Ethan rushed outside with Sydney right behind him. Danny and Callie were nowhere in sight.

"Where did they go?" Sydney turned, searching the clearing and surrounding trees.

"They've run off." Ethan ran a hand through his hair, cursing the movement and the offending arm. "They must have heard us talking and decided they'd be better off on their own."

"That's crazy." She kept looking, as if Danny and Callie would suddenly reappear. "They're only children."

"Tell that to Danny."

"He thinks I'm lying." She let out a short, humorless laugh. "Why not? Every other adult in his life has lied to him. The Keepers. Anna. Everyone." Sydney tossed up her hands. "Why wouldn't I lie as well?"

Turning to Ethan, her voice took on a pleading tone. "We have to find them. It will be dark in a few hours, and we can't leave them alone in these woods."

"Take it easy, Sydney. They'll head for the highway but can't have gotten far." He snagged his denim jacket from the porch and started for the trees. "I'll catch up to them before they reach it."

Sydney followed. "Why the highway?"

"They'll go to Mulligan," Ethan said, while looking for the spot where they'd entered the woods. "Danny's smart and he pays attention. Last night he watched road signs and asked to see the map." Which made sense, considering their conversation while they'd waited for Sydney. Anna hadn't just sprung these kids, she'd taught them something about being on the run. Who would have ever guessed?

"He knows where we are," Ethan assured her, "and how to get to Champaign."

"It's fifty miles, and even if they make it, Mulligan doesn't want them."

"Danny's not thinking that far ahead."

"Go on." She dug the keys out of her pocket and started toward the Explorer. "I'll take the car."

"No." Ethan turned quickly, but she was already halfway across the clearing. "Sydney, stay here. It's safer. Ramirez—"

"Screw Ramirez." She climbed behind the wheel. "We need to find those children."

"Shit." Ethan headed back across the clearing. "Sydney, wait."

It was too late.

Before he could reach her, she'd started the engine and thrown it in gear. "Look in the woods," she yelled out the window. "I'll watch for them on the highway." The back tires spit dirt as she tore off down the road.

Ethan had no choice but to let her go. He had to find those kids, then he'd go after Sydney and make her see reason. She was too damn obstinate for her own good, and sooner or later it would get her in trouble. Eventually Ramirez would surface, then she'd need more than stubbornness to survive.

Spotting where Danny had entered the trees was easy enough. For all his bravado and smarts, he wasn't very good at hiding his trail. Not, Ethan guessed, that the kid was even trying. He was an angry and frightened boy, a child, and he was heading for the safety of a man he believed was his father.

It was the most basic of instincts to return home, to seek the familiar, family, and friends. Sooner or later even the most experienced fugitives made that mistake. Even Anna. She'd come back to the desert, to their team's emergency rendezvous point, knowing if anyone was left alive she'd find them there. She'd been right, she'd found Ethan, but she'd found Ramirez as well.

Likewise, Danny would head for Mulligan, but the place the boy thought of as home didn't exist. That in itself wasn't a serious problem. Mulligan would be merely an unpleasant surprise for Danny, as long as nothing or no one else was waiting for him in Champaign.

Ethan continued along Danny's path.

Bent and broken branches, small footprints in soft mud—it was as simple to read as any road map. They were moving fast, running most likely, heading away from the park road and deeper into the woods. Danny was smart and had studied the maps. He knew the highway curved around the park, and if he went far enough in the right direction, he'd eventually find it.

Ethan couldn't fault the boy's basic strategy. If he could reach the highway, someone would pick them up. What Danny probably didn't realize was that most adults, after offering a ride to kids too young to be on their own, would head straight for the cops. Then Danny's search for their father would be over. The authorities would send them straight back to that island off the Washington coast, a place Ethan had begun to have more and more misgivings about.

As for a driver who'd pick up a couple of strays and not head for the nearest police station, it wasn't a scenario Ethan liked to dwell on. The world was full of kooks, but Danny was a smart kid and resourceful as hell, he'd—

Ethan stopped.

Next to Danny and Callie's small muddy footprints was a third set of tracks.

Sydney sped down the dirt road.

The car bumped and jerked, finding every rut and hole in an attempt to yank the steering wheel from her grasp. She held on, trees whipping past, their low-hanging branches slapping at the roof.

She couldn't believe she'd been so stupid.

She never should have let Danny go off on his own. The time between his finding out about Mulligan and when he'd decided the adults in his life were lying again had been critical. She should have talked to him, convinced him she was telling the truth, and reassured him she would help him and his sister. Instead, she and Ethan had spent those precious moments theorizing about James Cooley and sperm banks.

She hit a pothole and let up on the gas. But only for a moment. Just long enough to get the vehicle under control.

What had she been thinking? She and Ethan couldn't solve these children's problems on their own. They had no right even to try. If they'd called the authorities yesterday, none of this would have happened. Danny and Callie would be safe with people who knew how to care for them instead of alone in the woods or on an interstate, hitching a ride.

Just the thought terrified her. Anything could happen to children alone. Didn't she and Ethan, of all people, know that?

She scanned the woods, hoping to spot a couple of small figures scrambling through the underbrush. Instead, she almost missed a sharp turn in the road, and at the last minute swerved to avoid driving into a ditch.

Focus, she told herself. Just get to the highway and watch for Danny and Callie there. Let Ethan cover the woods. He knew what he was doing, and chances were, he'd catch up to them first anyway. If not, well, then they'd head to Champaign. Danny had proved his resourcefulness more than once. He'd find a way to get to Mulligan, and when he did, she and Ethan would be waiting.

The ranger station passed in a blur. And as she hit the paved road, she pressed a little harder on the accelerator. Until she spotted the stone entrance gate.

At first she didn't pay any attention to the car turning into the park, or even the second one behind it. It wasn't until she noticed the blue-and-white color scheme as the vehicle spun across her path, that she let up on the gas pedal and slammed on the brakes.

The Explorer screeched to a halt.

The other car pulled up alongside her, and men jumped out of both. Police officers. Guns aimed at her.

Confused, she reached for the door handle.

"Hands in the air," one of the officers hollered.

Sydney froze.

"Right now, Dr. Decker."

They knew her name. Slowly, Sydney raised her hands. "What's going on here? How do you—"

An officer jerked open her door, while the other kept his gun trained on her like she was some kind of dangerous criminal or something. "Okay, take it slow, Doc. No sudden movements. Get out of the vehicle."

For a second she just stared at him, Ethan's warnings racing through her head. Someone must have recognized him. Or her. He was suspected of murdering two police officers, and they would come after him with a vengeance. But she didn't have time to explain his innocence now. "I'm alone, and I need your help."

"Just get out of the car, ma'am."

"No, you don't understand—"

The officer with the gun flicked his wrist, reminding her of the weapon in his hand. As if she could forget. "Now."

"Okay." She climbed out, but didn't even try to keep the impatience out of her voice. "Look, we don't have time for this. I need your help to find a couple of missing children."

"You're under arrest."

Someone was following them.

Danny caught Callie's arm and pulled her behind a bush. "Did you hear that?" he whispered, knowing his sister's ears were better than his.

She nodded, her eyes wide. "But it's stopped now."

They waited another couple of moments, the sudden silence creeping up Danny's spine. Someone was back there, out of sight but watching them.

"Maybe it's Ethan or Sydney," Callie said.

"They wouldn't have stopped. Let's go," he said, afraid to move but more afraid to stay. Sooner or later, whoever was out there would come for them. "The road can't be far."

Callie didn't need prodding.

As soon as they started, the sense of someone or some thing behind them returned. They half walked, half ran on the uneven ground. At one point Callie stumbled, and Danny caught her.

"Don't look back," he said.

Together, they broke into a loping run.

Not looking was easier said than done, Danny soon

realized. Maybe it wasn't a man at all. It could be a bear. Or something worse. He risked a glance over his shoulder and saw movement, but it was gone so quickly he didn't know whether he'd really seen it or his imagination was playing tricks on him.

He picked up the pace, and Callie stayed with him.

She was a pretty brave kid, for a girl. Any other seven-year-old would be bellyaching about going too fast. Not Callie. Not his little sister.

Around them, the woods closed in, growing denser and harder to navigate. Plus, whoever or whatever was following them was no longer moving quietly. Danny could hear it even as he ran, something heavy pushing its way through the underbrush.

They should have headed for the park road instead of cutting through the woods to the highway. At least then they could have made a dash for the ranger station or circled back to the cabin for help. Now it was too late. If they turned back, whatever was behind them would grab them for sure. So he kept on, helping Callie when she needed it and watching for a break in the trees.

Suddenly he slipped, his feet going out from beneath him on a muddy slope. He grabbed at a nearby bush, barely avoiding sliding into the creek. Callie grabbed his hand and helped him up.

"This is it," he said. "We're almost there." On the map the creek and highway had been almost on top of each other, a blue ribbon and narrow black line, crisscrossing each other for the length of the park, until the ribbon became a lake. "The road is just a little way past the creek."

Getting across was the problem. It wasn't very deep, he could see the bottom, but it was running fast and cold. He looked up and down the bank for the shallowest point to cross. Suddenly, a commotion disturbed the silent woods behind them. Danny turned as a blur struck the standing figure of a man and sent him to the ground.

Ethan?

Danny wasn't sticking around to find out. "Come on. We've got to do it."

He took Callie's hand and started down the slippery bank, wading into the icy water and splashing across. Then a quick run through the last of the trees, and they burst onto a grassy embankment leading up to the highway. Neither of them stopped until they reached the edge of the asphalt.

Callie, breathing hard, watched the woods. "They're back there."

Danny couldn't see anything but looked for somewhere to hide. Nothing. They were in the open, on a two-lane country highway. Other than a black truck parked on the curve of the road, the highway was empty.

Callie seemed to read his mind. "The driver won't help us."

Danny didn't know what to do next. He tried to think what Anna would say, but his mind went blank. Then a car topped the horizon, coming in their direction. Danny took Callie's hand, heading across the road to flag it down, and then froze as the black truck started toward them.

CHAPTER EIGHTEEN

A man's tracks.

Ethan guessed they were a size ten. Fresh. And heading deeper into the park in Danny and Callie's wake.

He didn't like this. The extra set of tracks was no coincidence. Whoever was after those kids had to have extensive resources. He reassessed the precautions he'd taken on the drive from Texas and came to the same conclusion he had earlier. No one had followed them from Dallas. So someone had known they'd head for Mulligan and had followed Sydney back from Champaign.

The question was who?

Ramirez? No, this wasn't his style. This was someone else's game, and it had to be connected to the Haven. Anna had told him there was a line she wouldn't cross. When he'd found her body, he'd assumed that line had something to do with Ramirez. He'd been wrong. Anna had been helping Danny and Callie run away, and now whoever was behind that place had caught up to them.

Instead of the Glock, Ethan pulled out his knife: a Buck folder with a three-and-a-quarter-inch blade and a one-arm bandit opener. His older brother Doug had given it to Ethan for his sixteenth birthday. A coward's weapon, their father would have said. But he'd never been a military brat in a small southern town, where boys regularly carried more than knives and liked to use them on the more scrupulous.

"Don't let anyone know you have it," Doug had said. "And only use it as a last resort."

Doug had taken a lethal bullet in Iraq a few years later, and the knife had become more than a weapon. It had become his legacy to Ethan. He'd carried it ever since, through his years in the service and as an Agency officer. It had saved his life more than once because, like now, sometimes a gun was just too loud and clumsy.

Snapping it open, he held it low and crept forward, avoiding the mud and using the foliage to shield his movements.

He heard them first, a startled yelp, muffled but distinct, then he saw them, poised at the edge of the fast running stream. Danny had slipped, and Callie was helping him up, both seemingly unaware of the stranger skulking behind them.

Ethan flipped the knife, thumb and forefinger catching the blade, then launched it at the other man. It found its mark, burrowing into the man's back just below his right shoulder. He grunted and arched forward, staggered, but managed to keep his feet, and started to turn. He was too slow. Ethan was on him, grabbing the man's shooting arm and sending his gun skittering across the forest floor, snapping an elbow into his chin. The man went down, howling as the knife struck earth, then rolled onto his stomach.

Ethan snagged his collar, lifting the half-unconscious man to see his face. A trickle of blood dripped from his mouth. "The only reason you're alive, you son of a bitch, is because I need answers." He gave the man a shake, extracting a groan. "Who are you working for? And why the hell are you following those kids?"

"Fuck you."

Ethan gripped the knife handle, and the man keened. "What was that?" Ethan said, and glanced toward the creek for Danny and Callie.

They were gone. "What the . . ." He'd expected his appearance on the scene to stop them, or slow them down at the very least. Except he'd forgotten: they were running from him. "Goddamn it."

He yanked his knife from the man's back, wiped off the blood, and dropped it into his pocket. Then he drew the Glock and brought it down on the back of the man's head. "Stick around, we're not done yet."

Leaving the unconscious man, Ethan raced across the leaf-slick ground, slowing only for the stream's muddy seams and moss-covered rocks. On the other side, he picked up speed through the last patch of trees and hit the highway just as a green junker pulled away from the curb. Danny and Callie were in the front seat.

Danny was looking out the back window, then caught Ethan's eye as the car passed. The boy was scared. Ethan spun and saw a jacked-up black Ford truck bearing down on them. He put it together in an instant. The driver must have been waiting for the man in the woods.

Ethan stepped into the road, taking a double-handed shooter's stance as the Ford charged toward him. He aimed for the driver's head, blocking out everything but the dark mass behind the windshield, counting down. Five, four, three . . .

The truck screeched to a halt, but idled, as if deciding whether to attempt the run.

"Come on, you bastard," Ethan said. "Let's play chicken."

The driver revved his engine, and Ethan's finger itched against the trigger.

Suddenly, a siren rent the air.

It came from behind him, racing toward them on the two-lane highway. The truck's driver rammed his engine in reverse, spinning around by the side of the road, and sped off in the other direction. Ethan reached the tree line just as a county cruiser streaked by, tires squealed as it took the curve that led to the park entrance.

He went cold inside. Sydney?

Through the back window, Danny saw Ethan dart into the road between them and the black truck. Feet planted wide, he took aim at the truck as it hurtled toward him.

Guilt tightened Danny's chest. He'd never seen anything like it, except maybe in the movies. Ethan was risking his life for him and Callie as they ran away.

Their car went over a hill, and he lost sight of both truck and man. He turned back around, feeling sick to his stomach. Callie took his hand, and he squeezed hers reassuringly. She knew how close they'd come. If it hadn't been for her, they'd still be back on that road, or inside that truck on their way back to Haven Island. When he'd frozen at the sight of the truck, she'd snapped him out of it, urging him to flag down the car.

"You kids in trouble?" asked the old man behind the wheel.

Danny forced a smile. "No, sir. We just need a ride."

The man was nice enough, but really old and skinny. Deep lines carved up his face, and his hair was yellowish white and greasy looking. "Don't think I've seen you two around," he said. "You live in Riverbend?"

"No, sir. We're from Champaign."

"Nice town that, with the university and all."

"Yes, sir."

"You sure are a long way from home." He gave them a long sideways glance. "How did you say you happen to be all the way down here on your own?"

Danny made up a story. "We were with a group from our school, and they accidentally left without us."

The man kept on with the questions, and with each new one, Danny came up with another on-the-spot answer. He was spinning tales so fast, he figured it would only be a matter of time before the old guy caught on and took them to the nearest police station. Fortunately Danny saw their chance to escape at the first stoplight in town.

"Hey, Callie, look," he said. "There's Dad." He pointed across the street to a man standing next to a red minivan. "See, over there, in the gas station?"

"Oh, yeah. He must be looking for us." She didn't sound very convincing, but at least she hadn't totally blown it.

"We'll get out here, mister." Danny already had the door half open. "That's our father."

"Well, hold on there a minute, son," the old man said. "I'll drive ya across the street. I wouldn't mind having a word or two with your dad."

"That's not necessary, sir." Danny pulled Callie from the car. "Thanks for the ride." He slammed the door, and with a tight grip on Callie, waved and hollered as he ran toward the gas station.

Danny was afraid the old man would follow them. The light had turned green, and he sat in the middle of the intersection, as if trying to make up his mind. Then a horn blasted behind him, and he moved on.

From now on, Danny thought, he needed to be more careful.

No way he'd risk asking another adult for a ride. They were all too nosy, asking questions about stuff that wasn't any of their business. So unless he and Callie wanted a quick trip to the local police station, he'd have to find some other way to get to Champaign.

A bus lumbered past, and he thought about finding the station. He had a few dollars but no idea what bus fare cost. If he tried to buy a couple of tickets and didn't have enough money, he'd look pretty dumb. Then he'd have more adults asking questions.

He thought about calling his father, but knew he didn't

dare. Sydney's warning about showing up on Timothy Mulligan's doorstep had made sense, though Danny hadn't wanted to admit it. A phone call would be worse. What were the chances he'd drop everything and drive fifty miles to pick up a couple of kids claiming to be his children? Besides, who knew what lies Sydney had told him?

Danny began to worry that he'd never find a way to Champaign. Then he spotted an oversized gray pickup with University of Illinois, Forestry Department, printed on the side. The back was filled with small trees, stacked bags, shovels and other tools he didn't recognize, but with plenty of room for him and Callie to hide. He knew there was no guarantee the driver was on his way to Champaign, but it was worth a shot.

A few minutes later, the truck pulled out of the parking lot and headed west with Danny and Callie in the back. Then it turned right onto an interstate, and Danny relaxed.

They'd gotten lucky.

He'd been in such a hurry to get away from Ethan and Sydney, he hadn't even taken a few minutes to think things through. He knew better. In the weeks before they'd run from the Haven, Anna had taught him the importance of planning. She'd plotted every step of their escape, including how to deal with the unexpected. Evidently, the lesson hadn't stuck. Because he'd run from the park with only one thought in mind: He would find his father and show them all.

The question of *how* hadn't occurred to him. He'd just been so mad. When he'd heard Sydney and Ethan talking about asking someone in Dallas for help, he'd lost it. He couldn't wait. He and Callie had to get as far away as possible. In his hurry, he'd almost blown it. And if Ethan hadn't stopped that truck from following them . . .

A sudden slip of cold air reached beneath the rim of the truck bed, and Danny shivered. He glanced at his sister. She looked really pale, sitting huddled against a stack of fertilizer bags, her arms folded tightly around her knees.

What a jerk he was.

He hadn't even noticed how cold it had gotten, and all Callie had on was a sweater and a thin cotton shirt. On top of that, he knew she wasn't feeling too well. She'd been trying to hide it, but she'd picked up a cough somewhere.

"Here." Danny unzipped his jacket and took it off. "Put this on."

"But what about you?"

"I'm not cold. Besides,"—he opened his backpack and pulled out his one other shirt—"I have this."

"That won't keep you warm." She pushed the jacket back at him.

She could be so stubborn sometimes. "Look, Callie, you're sick again." He kept his voice low, but it came out mean anyway. Her eyes clouded, and he immediately regretted snapping at her. "I'm sorry. I didn't mean it."

"I'm not sick." Then, as if to punctuate the lie, she suppressed a cough and looked ready to cry.

He didn't know what to do. Callie was the only girl he knew who never cried. Boy, he couldn't believe how badly he'd messed up. He could have at least thought to grab her jacket and backpack from the Explorer.

"I'm sorry," he said again. "Come on, put the jacket on and you'll feel better." He said it nicer this time, but he hated reminding her she was sick.

She slipped on the jacket and zipped it up to her neck. "Okay?" she said, as if asking him if he was still angry at her.

"It's gonna be all right," he said, feeling more guilty than ever. "If we stay together, we'll be fine." He put his arm around her shoulders and pulled her close. "Better?"

She nodded. "How long will it take to get there?"

"Not long. We turned onto the highway a while back."

Except, he couldn't be sure *which* highway. But it seemed right. They'd left Riverbend heading west, then turned right and accelerated. He pictured the map in his head. One inch to the left of Riverbend was the main highway, then just a couple of finger lengths north to Champaign. If he could catch sight of a road sign, he'd know for sure if they were on the right road. But he couldn't risk looking out, or the driver might see him.

"It's only a few miles up the road," he said, stretching the truth a bit.

Callie rested her head against his arm, and he thought she'd fallen asleep until she said, "Was it the Keepers in the woods today?"

"I don't know how they could have found us so quick." He'd given the question some thought and hadn't come up with an answer. "Maybe it was just some nutcase."

"What about that truck?" Her eyes were wide, questioning.

Had the truck really been after them? Or had they been spooked and let their imaginations run away with them? The danger had seemed real at the time, and Ethan had been concerned enough to block it from following them. Danny just didn't know. "It doesn't matter, we're safe now. Go to sleep."

She looked about to say something else. Instead, she closed her eyes and finally drifted off.

Danny watched her, thinking that if anything happened to her, he'd never forgive himself. If only he'd thought of that before taking off from the cabin. Shivering, he settled closer to her for warmth. At least they were headed in the right direction.

He hoped.

CHAPTER NINETEEN

Ethan backtracked through the woods.

The man he'd left unconscious was gone, leaving a trail a first-year Cub Scout could follow. But Ethan didn't have time for that now. The cops were headed straight for Sydney. He wanted to run full out toward the park road, but forced himself to a steady, even pace. He couldn't help her if he broke an ankle or ran into the kids' stalker and got himself shot in the process.

Finally within sight of the entrance, Ethan fell back behind a giant sycamore, then eased around it to see what was happening.

From the direction of the road, blue lights flashed.

Keeping low, he moved toward the road until he had a clear view of the scene. Three county patrol cars surrounded the Explorer and Sydney. A sheriff's department deputy held a weapon on her, an older man Ethan assumed was the sheriff faced her, and a third man stood beside one of the cruisers.

Ethan had to get her out of there.

She was hopelessly naive when it came to dealing with law enforcement officials. She thought all she had to do was tell them the truth and they'd believe her. It was seldom that easy. Whether she knew it or not, she needed help.

He checked his clip, then crept closer.

"Did you find anything?" the sheriff called over his shoulder.

"Just this." A fourth man withdrew from the back of the Explorer and held up a bright purple backpack. He came around to the front of the truck and handed it to the sheriff. "Looks like it belongs to a kid."

Four men, not three. "Damn."

Ethan dropped to his belly and crawled forward on the leafy ground to a position behind a fallen log.

"What do you think, Dr. Decker?" said the sheriff. "Look familiar?"

Ethan peered above the decaying wood, calculating the distance from the edge of the brush to the cluster of cars and men. He figured there was a good twenty-five feet of open space surrounding them.

The sheriff held the backpack.

"It's Callie's," Sydney said. "I told you, I'm looking for her and her brother." Her voice was nervous, but impatient as well. They hadn't totally intimidated her. "You know how children are, they got mad and ran off. I need to find them."

"Where's your husband?"

She crossed her arms. "I don't have a husband."

"Your ex-husband, then."

Ethan considered killing them. Four quick shots. They wouldn't know what hit them, and in less than sixty seconds he and Sydney would be on their way in the Explorer.

And he'd be a cop killer just like they claimed.

But Sydney was too close to the sheriff for comfort, even if Ethan could bring himself to gun down innocent men.

"I don't know where Ethan is," she said.

The deputy with the gun waved it at Sydney. "You don't know? Or you don't want to tell us?"

Ethan aimed at the hotshot. If he so much as blinked, he'd be the first to die.

"Take it easy, Kenny," the sheriff said. "And put away that gun."

"But, Sheriff—"

"Does she look dangerous to you?" the sheriff snapped. "Besides, what do you think she's gonna do? There are four of us here. Put it away."

Hotshot Kenny holstered his gun with obvious reluctance.

Ethan eased back on the trigger. If he couldn't kill them, he needed to get closer. He scooted sideways to the edge of the log, then waited.

"Look," Sydney said. "We're wasting time. Danny and Callie are probably already out on the highway, trying to catch a ride."

"We just came from there." The sheriff looped his thumbs through his belt. "There weren't any kids hitchhiking on that road."

Ethan saw his chance.

In a low crouch, he darted from the log to a thick blackberry bush. It was the last cover between him and the county rat pack, but there was still too much open space.

"Maybe they're still in the woods," Sydney said, "or have already caught a ride." She spoke slowly, like the sheriff was too dense to get it on his own. "Either way, we have to find them. They're only twelve and seven."

All Ethan needed was one man, close enough to grab. With the Glock pointed at his throat, the others would hand over Sydney without a fuss. After all, they thought Ethan was a cop killer.

The sheriff caught Sydney's sarcasm and frowned. "Don't you worry. If there are kids out there, we'll find them." He returned Callie's pack to his deputy. "Now, are you gonna tell me where to find your ex-husband, or not?"

"I told you the truth, I don't know where he is."

"Have it your way." The sheriff took her arm and started toward one of the patrol cars.

Ethan tensed and lifted the Glock to his shoulder, ready to make a dash for the fourth man, the quiet one, leaning against the cruiser.

"Since you don't seem ready to answer our questions here," the sheriff said, "I guess we need to take you in." When she resisted, he said, "Do I have to put cuffs on you, Dr. Decker?"

She stared at him, obviously stunned, then let him lead her to the car.

"Kenny, escort Dr. Decker to town."

Ethan lowered his weapon, another idea forming. He liked these odds better. With Sydney out of the way, he could disable the others, then grab the Explorer and go after her. And nobody had to get shot.

The deputy opened the back door of his cruiser and helped Sydney in.

"Hal and I will go check out the cabin," said the sheriff. "And Larry," he motioned toward the fourth man, "stay with her vehicle."

The officers climbed into their cars. The deputy with Sydney turned around and steered toward the highway, while the other two drove deeper into the park.

Ethan spared about two seconds' thought for his duffel bag back at the cabin. He hated losing it, and the contents alone would incriminate him, but he couldn't worry about that now. He had to go after Sydney, and to do that, he needed the Explorer. Everything else could wait.

He stepped out from behind the bush, ducked behind the cruiser, and waited for the count of three. The deputy lounged against the car's bumper, humming a snippet of "Let It Be." Ethan rose, circled the hood, and brought the Glock up to the man's temple. "Be very still."

The deputy's face bleached of color. "Don't shoot, I got a wife."

"Get rid of the weapon."

"Please, mister . . ." He inched his hand toward the holster at his waist.

"Don't be a dead hero. Just drop it on the ground."

With shaking hands, the man obeyed.

"That's good. Now your car keys and cuffs."

"What?"

"Would you rather be dead?"

The deputy handed over his keys, then awkwardly removed the cuffs from his belt. "Now what?"

"Snap them on one wrist, then put your hands behind your back." Ethan gave the man room and himself space in case he tried anything.

He didn't, and Ethan secured the cuffs.

Grabbing the man's arm, he pulled him toward the back of the cruiser, opened the trunk, and shoved him inside. As he shut the lid, he said, "Congratulations, you'll live."

Sydney had never been more humiliated.

She didn't understand why the sheriff and his men were treating her this way. She wasn't a criminal. On the news they were calling her a kidnap victim.

And what about Callie and Danny?

If Ethan didn't find them in the woods, they were out on this road somewhere alone. She felt like a broken record trying to get the police to realize the seriousness of the situation, but they obviously weren't listening to her. All they seemed to care about was finding Ethan.

"Deputy, we have to look for those children." She

scooted forward, lacing her fingers into the metal grille. "They could be in danger."

"We'll find them, don't you worry." He tossed her a look. "That, and snare us a cop killer."

"Ethan didn't kill those police officers."

"I thought you didn't know where he was."

"I don't. But I know he didn't kill those men. I saw it all, there was another man on the balcony."

"Yeah, right." He laughed abruptly. "And that's why you ran." Unfastening his seat belt, he leaned over, opened the glove compartment, and pulled out a candy bar. "Yep, missy, we know all about it, and you're in trouble now. Your best bet is to come clean and cut a deal with the prosecutor." He threw her another glance. "Meanwhile, put on your seat belt."

She started to protest but changed her mind. It would be a waste of breath. This man had already decided she was lying.

"You know, Dr. Decker." The deputy looked at her in the rearview mirror. "It'll go a lot easier on you if you tell us where to find your ex."

"I told you the truth, I don't know where he is." There seemed no point denying Ethan had been with her earlier. "We split up to look for the children."

"Well, I guess . . ." Suddenly, his eyes widened. "What the hell—"

Something slammed into them from the rear.

The cruiser lurched forward and fishtailed. Fighting the steering wheel, the deputy kept them on the road. "Is he stupid or something, running into a cop?" He made a grab for the radio receiver.

Sydney swivelled and saw a jacked-up black truck behind them. "He's coming at us again."

The second blow snapped her forward, bruising her against the seat belt. The patrol car swerved, tires screeching as they skidded into a spin. Earth and sky whipped by in a three-hundred-sixty-degree blur, her stomach churning in fear and dizziness. They hit the shoulder of the road, nose first over the embankment, hurtling toward a grassy riverbank.

Sydney choked back a scream as the young man in the driver's seat wrenched the steering wheel hard to the left and punched the accelerator. The engine roared. The tires slipped, then caught and spit gravel, dragging them around and back up toward the road and the bridge spanning the river.

Terror froze in her throat when a concrete bridge support appeared through the front windshield. They struck pavement with the shriek of metal against metal as they scraped the railing and crossed the bridge in a flash of movement.

"Son of a bitch." The deputy's hands trembled as he made another grab for the radio. "He did that on purpose. He's trying to run us off the road."

Sydney couldn't argue—even if she'd had the voice to do so. She looked out the back; she couldn't help herself.

Could Ramirez have found them?

The truck rammed them again, sending a sharp finger of pain up her neck and throwing the deputy forward, cracking his chin against the steering wheel. Blood oozed from the gash. He appeared stunned, lifting a hand to his face and staring at his blood-streaked fingers.

"Are you okay?" Sydney asked, panic gripping her. If he passed out, they were both dead. She was trapped in the backseat of a vehicle, a metal grid between her and door locks, while some lunatic used his truck like a battering ram.

"Yeah." The deputy's earlier bravado had vanished, and he suddenly sounded young and frightened.

Then he pulled himself together. "Hang on, Dr. Decker.

I'm going to try and outrun him." He floored the gas pedal and the cruiser seemed to leap forward.

It was a valiant effort, but too late. The cruiser was no match for its pursuer. Out the rear window, she watched the other vehicle shift to straddle the lanes. Like a fighter getting into position. He came at them hard, and Sydney got the impression he was done toying with them.

The fourth strike sent them spinning. Time stopped. Trees and asphalt whirled and flipped. The sharp tang of blood filled her mouth, and the smell of gasoline bit her nostrils. Then she heard a scream, her own, just before everything went blank.

Ethan resisted the urge to floor the accelerator.

All he needed was to draw more attention to himself. In a short while, every cop in the county would have his description, plus that of the Explorer. If he passed another patrol car heading for the park, his chances of going unnoticed were close to zip. But if he was speeding? Well, that would be the endgame.

Although logic told him Sydney was safe for a few hours, his instincts screamed she needed help now. Fortunately the road was empty, giving him time to make plans. He hadn't gotten beyond the question of how to extract her from the sheriff's office, when he spotted the vehicles ahead: a county cruiser, followed by a black Ford truck. Just like the one that had gone after the kids.

Ethan punched the accelerator.

The pickup hugged the cruiser's bumper, while the patrol car swayed and swerved. Then the truck picked up speed, ramming the cruiser's left rear bumper and sending it spinning. Once. Twice. It made two full three-hundred-and-sixty-degree turns, before a rear tire caught on the soft shoulder and the car tumbled over the embankment. The truck slowed, as if admiring its handiwork, then sped off as Ethan came up behind him.

Ethan abandoned the Explorer almost before it came to a full stop, fear seizing him.

Not again.

He couldn't lose Sydney. He'd lost too much already. Nicky. His marriage. His work. He wouldn't let it happen, wouldn't allow her to die like this.

As he scrambled down the incline, the scene took on a surrealistic feel. Everything slowed, his forward motion stymied by invisible hands. Blood pounded in his ears. The vehicle sprawled on its back like a dying insect, tires hissing and spinning in the eerie quiet. And the certainty that once more, like with Nicky, Ethan would be too late.

Reality returned with a jolt, as he slid to his knees beside the cruiser and pain ricocheted up his injured arm. Inside, Sydney hung upside down in the backseat, unconscious, her seat belt anchoring her in place. In front, the deputy lay crumpled amid broken glass, blood covering his face.

Circling the car, Ethan kicked out the side rear window and shimmied into the cramped quarters on his back. "Sydney, can you hear me?"

She moaned and stirred.

"Sydney?" He brushed the hair from her face, looking for outward signs of injury. A fine trickle of blood wet her lips and a lump swelled on her forehead, but the pulse point in her neck throbbed steadily. Thank God.

"Come on, sweetheart," he said. "I need your help to get you out of this thing."

Her eyelids fluttered, and she mumbled something incoherent.

"That's right, Syd. Fight it." He found the seat-belt clasp. "I'm going to release this. Are you ready?"

She nodded, only partially with him.

They didn't have a lot of time. If the deputy had managed

to radio for help before ending up in this ditch, the cops would be crawling all over this place any minute.

Ethan had to get Sydney out of here. Now.

Bracing her, he ignored the scream of protest from his arm and unfastened her seat belt. She came down in a heap, but he broke her fall, protecting her head and neck.

She groaned and opened her eyes, her expression confused and frightened. "What—"

"It's okay, Sydney. I'm getting you out of here." Flipping over, he backed out through the window, drawing her with him. Once he had her in the open, he carried her away from the wreck and laid her on the soft grass.

"Sydney?"

She blinked. "Ethan?" She half smiled, her eyelids fluttering, then closing.

"I've got to go back for the deputy," he said. "Will you be okay for a minute?"

She nodded, drifting back into unconsciousness.

Ethan returned to the cruiser.

The deputy proved both easier and harder to free. Easier because Ethan could simply grab him under his arms and pull. Harder because the man weighed a good hundred pounds more than Sydney.

After getting him out of the vehicle, Ethan checked for life-threatening injuries. A couple of cuts on the man's forehead and chin bled freely but weren't critical. As for internal injuries, Ethan didn't have a clue. He'd done all he could for the man, taken all the time he dared.

He carried Sydney to the Explorer, settling her in front and lowering the seat to its full stretched-out position. Then he strapped her in and covered her with his jacket, started for the driver's door, and stopped.

"Damn it," he said, looking back at the wreck of a cruiser and the man lying beside it.

He couldn't just leave an injured man and hope help

would show up. From the back of the Explorer he got a blanket, carried it to the deputy, and covered him. Then Ethan scooted back into the front seat of the cruiser and grabbed the radio transmitter.

As he pressed the transmit button, he said, "There's been a car accident on Highway 120, north of River Ridge Park. The officer is injured and will need an ambulance."

Ethan released the button, not waiting for the reply.

Back outside, he said to the unconscious deputy, "They're coming. You're gonna be okay."

Conscience clear, Ethan returned to the Explorer and headed north, hoping he hadn't just made a big mistake.

CHAPTER TWENTY

Danny came awake with a start.

The truck had stopped. Rubbing his eyes, he wondered how long he'd been asleep. The last thing he recalled was curling up beside Callie to keep warm. He began to sit up, then remembered he had to keep low so the driver wouldn't spot him out the back window.

"Callie," he whispered. "Wake up." He gave her a gentle nudge. "We're off the highway." Only, since he'd been sleeping, he didn't know for sure when they'd gotten off or which way they'd gone.

The truck started moving again.

"Callie." He shook her a little harder. "We're here." It sounded like a town, with traffic on all sides. He wanted to peek over the sides of the truck but didn't dare. "I think we're in Champaign."

Callie's eyes opened wide. "What—"

"Shhh." He pressed a finger to her lips.

"Are we there?"

He nodded, excited. "I think so." Where else could they be? "Get ready. We're gonna have to get out of the truck really quick."

But the next time they stopped, Danny didn't think it was such a good idea to climb out. It sounded like they were on a busy street, and he wasn't sure they could get away before the light changed. He wasn't going to be stupid enough to risk Callie getting hurt on top of everything else. So they waited, stopping and starting several more times, while watching traffic lights pass overhead.

He was beginning to get nervous, afraid the driver was just passing through town, when they turned. The sound of traffic faded, which only made Danny more certain he'd made another mistake by stowing away in this truck. He visualized the map, trying to remember the area around Champaign, but couldn't. He hadn't really paid attention to anything except how to get here.

By the time the truck stopped and the driver shut off the engine, it felt like they'd been riding forever.

Wherever they were, they needed to make a run for it. If the driver caught them, it would be all over.

"Come on," Danny said. "We've got to go now." Grabbing his backpack, he scrambled between the burlap-wrapped roots toward the rear of the truck bed.

Doors opened and shut, and voices drifted back to him.

Keeping low, Danny swung himself over the tailgate and reached back to give Callie a hand. "Hurry."

"Hey, you kids."

Too late. They'd been spotted.

"Come on, Callie." Danny half pulled, half lifted her

out of the truck, no longer worrying about staying out of sight.

"What are you doing back there?"

The voice was closer now, and Danny saw two men coming straight at them. The first and nearest man was huge, with a scraggly beard and a gray-streaked ponytail, while the second was younger and looked a lot faster.

Danny grabbed Callie's hand. "Run."

They raced away toward the parking lot exit and a small empty street. It was deserted. Warehouses and empty fields stretched side by side for several blocks, but in the distance was a busy road.

"Wait," came the command from behind them. "Come back here."

"Don't look," Danny said. "Keep running."

They headed toward the intersection.

Even as he ran, Danny realized he wasn't scared. Not really. Not like earlier today in the woods. Compared to that, this was a piece of cake. He didn't think the men from the truck would catch them. The big man sounded out of breath as he called out for them to stop, and another glance over his shoulder convinced Danny that the younger man wasn't even trying. If he did decide to grab them, it still might not end their search for their father. The men might even turn him and Callie over to Timothy Mulligan, if Danny was convincing enough.

As he'd hoped, the men only followed for a block or two. But Danny kept running when he reached the intersection, looking for some place where they could blend in—just in case the men called the police. He could hear Anna's voice in his head.

"It's always best to hide in plain sight. As long as you look like you belong."

First, they went into a convenience store, but the lady

behind the counter watched them like they were going to steal something. Next they tried a Wal-Mart a few blocks down the street. It was a good choice, crowded, with lots of other kids. Danny figured they could stay there all day and no one would know the difference. Sooner or later, though, they'd have to leave, and he wanted to get as far away from the truck and the men driving it as possible.

After that they spent time in a grocery store, tagging behind a woman with a baby, hoping people would think she was their mother. They even followed her out to the parking lot, then slipped away between the cars and headed back out to the street. For a few minutes they stood with a group at a bus stop, while Danny thought about what to do next. Then the bus came, and he and Callie started walking again.

It had become a game, pretending to belong where they didn't, and they were getting pretty good at it. Too bad it was getting dark. Then Danny's stomach growled, reminding him that they hadn't eaten in hours.

Meanwhile, cars choked the road, four deep, moving along at a stop-and-go pace. Now that they were well away from the men and their truck, Danny realized no one even noticed them. He'd spotted several signs on businesses, claiming Champaign as their home. So at least they were in the right town.

"I'm cold," Callie said. "Let's go inside." She pointed down the road, and Danny's mood lightened when he saw the mall sign.

"Good eyes," he said. "Let's go. We can get something to eat and warm up."

They nearly ran the few blocks.

They'd only been in a mall once before, and that had been with Anna. She'd taken them right after they'd fled the island, claiming they needed different clothes to blend in. It had only taken a couple of days on the outside for Danny to see she was right. They would have looked like a couple of freaks in their Haven clothes of dark wools, crisp white shirts, and blazers.

For two kids who'd never even been in a store, that first mall with Anna had been overwhelming. They'd both wanted to leave right away and didn't know what to make of so many people in one place. But after they'd gotten over their initial wariness, they'd both agreed it was about the neatest place they'd ever seen.

Anna had told them there were malls all over the country. Danny hadn't really believed her. But here they were, halfway across the country, and Anna had been telling them the truth.

This mall wasn't as big as the one in Seattle, but it was still pretty awesome. He couldn't imagine what anybody needed with so many stores, but he was glad they did. Plus, there were lots of other kids around, some with grown-ups and some without. Everyone was minding their own business. Even more than when they'd been on the street, Danny felt like he and Callie were invisible. No one here would come running up to them and ask what they were doing alone.

At the food court, they ordered slices of pizza and Cokes. It had become their favorite food since leaving the Haven. The girl behind the counter, a teenager with spiky pink-and-purple hair and a nose ring, took their money and served them without even a smile, much less any questions.

Danny carried their tray to a corner table, where they ate in silence. Callie was particularly quiet, watching everyone around them with wide eyes. He wondered how she was feeling, but was afraid to ask. She hadn't started coughing again, but she looked pale. Despite worrying about his sister, the food worked wonders, making him feel better as soon as he started eating. After all, they were in the same town where their father lived.

They were home. If Callie was sick, their dad would get her better.

While they ate, he watched a store named Aladdin's Video Arcade. It was brighter and noisier than the other stores, with a steady stream of kids coming and going. From where he sat, the store looked filled with games of some kind.

What could it hurt to check it out?

Besides, he wasn't ready to leave the mall. Mainly because he didn't know where to go when they did. Although he had his father's address, he had no idea how to find it. Not without asking an adult—a mistake he didn't plan on repeating.

"Let's go look in that store," he said to Callie as they finished their pizza. "It looks like fun."

Callie frowned. "You go. I'll wait here."

"I can't leave you alone." After all, she was only seven. "Come on, it'll be great."

"But . . ."

"What's wrong?"

"There are only boys over there. And, well, older kids."

She was mostly right. "There," he said, spotting a skinny girl hanging on to one of the older boys. "You won't be the only one."

"She's a teenager," Callie said, as if it were a disease.

"It'll be okay. You're with me." Danny picked up their trays and carried them to a trash can like he'd seen everyone else doing. When he got back to her, he said, "Come on, it will be fun. You'll see."

Callie eyed the store warily, but finally agreed. Maybe she wasn't ready to go back outside, either.

Inside, the arcade was even neater than Danny had hoped. The store was packed with video games of all types. Some you sat in, while a screen flashed in front of you like you were driving a race car or flying a plane. Others involved tossing disks or rolling balls. Most, though, were standing video games, some of which were bigger variations of the ones he had on his Game Boy.

The kids, most of whom Danny had to admit were older, played by themselves or in twos or threes. Danny was drawn to an animated group surrounding two boys who were only a couple of years older than he. Each boy had his own control, and they were obviously playing against each other.

Danny was mesmerized.

The game was Street Fighter. It was a bigger, more elaborate version than he had on his Game Boy, but it was basically the same. Except, it was so much cooler than his version. Not only were there more controls and better graphics, but everything moved faster as well.

He watched the two boys carefully, paying particular attention to the extra buttons and their uses. One of the kids was definitely better than the other, and everyone kept calling him Gerard. When he made his final move that destroyed his opponent, the group let out a loud cheer. He was obviously the favorite, and everyone pummeled him on the back and shoulders, declaring him the best.

"He isn't so good." Callie's soft little-girl voice cut through the ruckus. "My brother can do better than that."

"Callie." Danny looked at his sister with disbelief as the space around them went very quiet. This guy was twice his size. Did she want to get him killed?

"Well, you can," she insisted.

Gerard pushed his way through the group to Danny. "You think you can beat me, kid?"

"Uh . . ." Danny glanced at Callie, wondering why she'd picked this exact moment to brag about him. Looking back to Gerard, who towered over him, Danny shrugged. "Don't know. Probably not."

Gerard laughed and so did his friends. "Well, your little sister thinks you can."

Danny shrugged again, thinking he was gonna strangle her if they got out of this.

Gerard held up an odd-looking coin, then slapped it on the game top. "You afraid to try?"

Danny pulled some change from his pocket. "I don't have any of those."

The boys standing around laughed louder.

"Tell you what," Gerard said in a condescending tone. "You go on over to that machine and buy yourself some tokens. I'll wait here."

Danny hesitated, and Callie elbowed him in the side. "Go get the tokens, Danny."

He threw her another frown but headed over to the machine. Tokens were twenty-five cents apiece or five for a dollar. He couldn't believe Callie had gotten him into this. Like they had a dollar to spare for Danny to make a fool of himself.

When he returned, Gerard said, "I'll even let you go first." There was a general snicker from the onlookers.

"That's okay," Danny said. "You go ahead."

"No way, man. You're the newcomer. You go first." He took one of Danny's tokens and slipped it into the slot. "Rules are, loser pays for the next game."

Danny warily stepped up to the machine.

It took most of the first game for him to get the feel of the controls. But by the last move or so, he'd gotten the hang of it and no longer even noticed the other boys behind him. He lost, of course, but not as badly as he'd expected.

Slipping another token in the slot, he looked at the older boy. "Ready to go again?"

Gerard gave him a small smile and nodded.

By the time Danny had used up his five tokens, he was making Gerard work to win, and the kids watching were treating him like one of their own. They cheered him on when he did something right and moaned when he missed a move.

The last game was close, but several of the boys slapped him on the back and wished him better luck next time. Even Gerard seemed impressed and followed Danny and Callie back out into the mall. "You're not bad," he said. "Do you live around here?"

Danny's earlier wariness returned. "Not really."

"So, where are you from?"

Danny didn't know exactly how to answer. "Uh, we're from Seattle."

"Cool. You here with your parents?"

"Yeah, they're—"

"We're looking for our dad," Callie said at the same time. "We were stolen."

Danny shot her a worried glance. What was with her tonight? Talking to strangers and all? She had no idea how Gerard would take the news that they were runaways. He might call the police or tell his parents.

Gerard, however, seemed fascinated. "Really? Awesome."

"Look," Danny said, giving Callie a don't-say-another-word glare. "Do you know where Henning Street is?"

Gerard glanced back and forth between them, then shook his head. "Nope. But hey, my big brother would know."

"Your brother?" Danny backed up. "No thanks. We better—"

"It's okay. Really. He's cool. He delivers pizza for Domino's and knows his way around. And if he doesn't know, he's got a map."

"That's okay," Danny said. The more people who knew about him and Callie, the bigger their chances of getting caught. "I don't want to bother him."

"I bet he'll even give you a ride."

"He can drive?" Callie asked, and then immediately

went quiet again as Danny threw her another poisonous look.

"Well, like, duh. How else is he gonna deliver pizzas? He's seventeen." Gerard grinned as if just the fact of having a seventeen-year-old brother made him special. "Come on. Domino's is right outside the mall."

It was Callie who made the decision, agreeing before Danny could come up with an excuse. Before he knew it, they were leaving the mall and heading for the pizza place.

Gerard's brother was okay. He was about to make a delivery and agreed to drop them off afterward. He didn't even ask any questions. Thirty minutes later, as it started to drizzle, they turned onto Henning Street. About halfway down the block, blue lights flashed and a crowd had gathered.

The older boy stopped the car. "Wonder what's going on."

Danny's stomach knotted, and one look at Callie told him she was thinking the same thing. "We can get out here," he said.

"Are you sure? I mean it's raining and whatever's going on, it don't look too good."

"It's okay," Danny assured him. "We're staying right over there." He pointed toward the second house on the block.

"Sure, okay." Gerard's brother pulled into the driveway, while most of his attention was on the activity down the block.

"Thanks for the ride," Danny said as he and Callie climbed out of the car and closed the door behind them.

They waited until Gerard's brother had left before starting slowly down the street. Despite the cold rain, neither of them seemed in a particular hurry to find out exactly what was happening. Danny watched the addresses, hoping to find the right one before they reached the crowd on the sidewalk. But as they drew closer, he knew that the house with the police cars and people swarming over the front lawn was their father's. And that something bad had happened.

Suddenly, he picked up his pace.

"No, wait." Callie grabbed his arm.

"We have to see what's happened. Maybe we can help."

"We can't."

He stopped and looked at her. They'd run halfway across the country to get here, and now she was holding him back. "That's his house."

"That's why we can't go over there. They're waiting for us," she said. "They know we're coming."

"Who? The Keepers?"

"I'm not sure. All I know is that it's not safe. Come on." She backed into the shadows of a nearby hedge. "We can watch from here."

Danny glanced from her to the beckoning house.

"Please, Danny." She had his arm again, tugging him toward the bushes. He wanted to pull free and race across the street, but he'd learned to trust her instincts. She might be just a kid, but she knew things.

With a sigh, he let her draw him out of sight.

CHAPTER TWENTY-ONE

Sydney couldn't stop shivering.

"You okay?" Ethan asked from the driver's seat.

She nodded, but it wasn't true. No matter how tight she pulled his jacket around her, she couldn't get warm. She was in shock and possibly had a mild concussion.

"I need to stay awake," she said, as much to herself as to Ethan.

"Just hold on a little longer." He reached across and squeezed her hand. "We're almost to town."

"What about the children?"

"We'll find them after we take care of you."

The drive seemed to take forever, though she knew it couldn't have been more than a few minutes. At one point she glanced at the clock on the dash. She'd gotten back to the park with the news about Mulligan less than two hours ago. It felt like days.

Ethan talked continuously. She didn't think she'd ever heard him say so much in the entire six years they'd been married. It was a shame she couldn't follow him, except the children's names, which popped up again and again in his stream of words.

She held on to both, the sound of his voice and those names.

When they stopped, she couldn't figure out where they were. He said something about no one finding her. But he'd found her, hadn't he? Maybe it had all been a dream. Because suddenly he was gone, and she was alone.

Then darkness rescued her.

When she awoke, he was back, wrapping her hands around something warm. "Drink this." He brought a cup to her lips. The liquid scalded her mouth and jarred her to full consciousness.

"Are you trying to drown me?"

He laughed softly, and she thought she heard relief in his voice. "No, I'm just trying to get you warm. Can you handle this now?" He indicated the hot coffee.

She took a sip on her own.

"Good. When you get done with that, there's some food here." He lifted a bag from the floor next to her. "And some aspirin. I need to go out again."

The idea panicked her. "Where are you going?"

"I have to find another car. Every cop in the county is hunting for this Explorer. We won't make it through town unless we get rid of it."

She noticed for the first time that he'd parked inside a building. From the looks of it, a warehouse. "Where are we?"

"Somewhere safe, but we can't stay here long." He pulled a sandwich from the fast-food bag and handed it to her. "Besides, we need to find Danny and Callie."

"Do you think they got out of the park?"

"Yes, but . . ."

"Tell me."

"There was someone else in the woods today."

Her stomach tightened. "The sheriff's office?"

"My guess is it was someone from the Haven, but Danny and Callie got away. They hitched a ride with an old guy in a beat-up green junker. They're okay."

Sydney wished she hadn't asked, or at least that Ethan hadn't chosen this particular time to start telling the truth. But how could she fault him for being honest when it was the one thing she'd claimed she wanted?

"We'll find them," he said.

And she believed him. "What about the deputy? The one driving the car? Was he—"

"He's fine," Ethan assured her. "A couple of days in the local hospital, giving the nurses hell, and I'm sure he'll be good as new."

She studied his face, searching for some sign of guile. When she found none, she relaxed somewhat. "Go on," she said. "Find us transportation to Champaign."

He gave her a half smile, surprised maybe, and left.

Sydney managed to stay awake, finishing the coffee and sandwich, while refusing to think of all the terrible things that could happen to children on their own. It would only cripple her ability to help Ethan find Danny and Callie.

She felt better after eating, except for the pounding in her head. So she swallowed some aspirin and took a look at herself in the rearview mirror. Her lip was swollen and a lump had formed on her forehead. She touched the bump and winced.

She recalled the black truck ramming them—was it two or three times? The deputy had radioed for help, but she couldn't remember if he'd gotten through. He'd been frightened and bleeding. It was all so hazy. She prodded her memory, trying to reenact the last seconds of the accident. She remembered spinning and Ethan pulling her out of the cruiser. Other than that, she saw only darkness.

When Ethan finally returned, he was carrying a bulging brown paper bag. "Are you feeling better?" he asked.

"Yes." This time it was true. "What's in the bag?"

He smiled, although it looked forced. "My disguise."

He dumped out a pile of clothing onto the seat. "And you need to turn back into Dr. Decker."

Fifteen minutes later, she'd changed into her own blouse and leather jacket and wiped the extra makeup off her eyes. Ethan had exchanged his jeans for khaki slacks and a navy alligator sweater over a pale blue oxford shirt. Then he'd slicked back his hair and slipped on a pair of wire-rimmed glasses.

"The cops are on the lookout for a couple of campers in an Explorer," he said. "So we've just become university faculty on our way back to Champaign."

"What about the Explorer?" she asked.

"We'll have to risk it for a little longer. There's a country club about five miles from here. We'll pick up a different vehicle there."

"You're going to steal it."

"Yes."

"Is that the only way?"

"My duffel bag is back at the cabin, along with all my identification and most of my cash."

She supposed she should refuse, or at least think of some other way to get to Champaign, but she couldn't. Funny how all other considerations—like breaking the law—went out the window when a child's safety was at stake.

"Okay," she said, "tell me what to do."

With a bittersweet smile, Ethan reached over and brushed the back of his fingers along her cheek. She couldn't breathe. The gesture was so like Ethan, the other Ethan, the one who'd stolen her heart all those years ago. Then his eyes clouded again, and he touched first her lip, then the bump on her head.

"They're going to pay for this, Sydney."

"It's okay." She could hardly get the words past the lump in her throat. She couldn't let this happen, couldn't let him affect her like this.

"No, it's not." He pulled away, and her lungs once again filled with air.

If she allowed it, he'd draw her in with his gentle caresses and fierce protectiveness. And she'd be no better off than she'd been before he left. At the moment, however, she couldn't remember exactly why that was such a bad thing.

A few minutes later, they left the shelter of the warehouse. It had begun to rain, a steady late-spring shower that chilled the air. They rode in silence, Ethan keeping an eye on the rearview mirror as he'd done in Dallas. Finally he turned onto a country road that wound through a golf course. Several minutes later, a long, low building came into sight.

"We're going in a side door and out the front," he said, and drove past the main entrance to park in a rear lot marked EMPLOYEES ONLY. "As long as you act like you belong, no one will question you."

Sydney nodded, her heart hammering in her chest.

They climbed out of the Explorer, and Ethan took her arm. No one even noticed as they pushed through the door to the building, then made their way to the lobby. Just before they went out the front door, he slipped his arm around her waist and said, "Hold your hand to your forehead, you've just taken a nasty spill.

"Can I get some help here?" he called as the door closed behind them. "My wife fell and hit her head."

A valet hustled over to them. "Should I call nine-one-one?"

"No, I'll take her to the emergency room myself. Here . . ." He handed Sydney over to the flustered young man. "Watch her while I'll get my car."

He reached behind the valet stand and claimed a set of keys, executing the move so deftly that no one blinked, then darted out to the parking lot. Even Sydney almost believed him, while wondering how he'd know which car belonged to the keys. She touched the knot on her head and leaned into the man at her side, hoping to keep his mind on her rather than on Ethan.

Lights flashed and a horn beeped, and she watched Ethan jog toward a car in the first row. Sydney almost laughed aloud. He'd pressed the unlock button on the keychain remote to locate the car. It was too simple, and a little scary. But in less than a minute, he pulled under the portico in a white four-door Volvo and jumped out to help the valet settle his injured wife into the front seat. And as they drove away from the country club, Sydney couldn't believe how easy it was to become a felon.

Marco had never cared much for small towns.

They made him feel conspicuous. Cities were melting pots, where you'd be hard-pressed to stand out. But in towns like Champaign, his accent always seemed a bit heavier, his Latin features more pronounced. As far as he was concerned, middle America was best left to those who'd settled it centuries earlier.

It started to drizzle, and Marco pulled up his collar. The rain didn't deter him any more than the twenty or so other people gathered on the sidewalk outside the house.

Three patrol cars sat in front of the two-story frame structure, their strobing blue lights catching and reflecting off damp surfaces. At the foot of the front steps, a uniformed officer blocked any attempts by the curious to venture inside. On the porch, an older woman in a heavy sweater spoke with a plainclothes detective.

Marco circled the back of the crowd, scanning for familiar faces. Decker? His lovely ex-wife, Sydney? The *niños*? Or maybe the man who'd led Marco to this dead-end street?

He recognized no one.

An ambulance arrived, threading its way through the milling neighbors. As it stopped in front of the house, a paramedic leapt from the back carrying a collapsed gurney. The driver joined him, and together they hurried up the walkway.

Marco moved around behind the ambulance and approached the uniform guarding the front steps.

"Sorry, you can't—"

Marco pulled out a slim leather identification wallet and flashed his badge. "Special Agent Ramirez. FBI." Using his own name was risky, but he liked the idea of concealing a lie within a truth.

The officer instantly turned solicitous. "Of course, sir, go ahead in."

Once inside, Marco followed the sounds of activity to the back of the house and a small kitchen. The medical examiner was finishing her inspection of a body stretched out on the faded linoleum, while the paramedics stood by to transport the victim to the morgue.

As Marco stepped into the room, a man in a dark suit and overcoat stopped him. "Hey, you can't come in here."

Marco flashed the FBI badge. "Agent Ramirez."

The detective frowned. "What's the Bureau's interest here, Agent?"

"I'm not here to step on any toes, Detective." Marco smiled, but not too warmly, as he returned the identification to his inside pocket. Relations between local and federal agencies were often shaky. If he was too friendly or accommodating, the cops would wonder why. "I just want to look around."

"What for?"

"There are some similarities between this case and another I'm working on at the University of Chicago." He glanced past the detective's shoulder to the body on the floor. "I'm here to see if there's any connection."

The detective's scowl deepened, but Marco knew he wouldn't deny him access. Not without good reason. If it came to a showdown over jurisdiction, the feds usually won. The detective wouldn't risk that.

"Feel free to call the Chicago office and check it out," Marco offered, knowing he had hours before the detective would get around to making the call—if ever.

"Yeah, I'll do that." He stepped back, away from Marco. "Meanwhile, don't get in the way. This is my crime scene."

"No problem. But I do need to examine the body before it's taken away." He had no interest in the corpse and already knew what he'd find, but if he failed to make at least a cursory inspection, it would seem suspicious.

The detective nodded his grudging consent.

Marco slipped on a pair of latex gloves, moved to the body, and squatted down. "Single gunshot to the head," he said. "Looks like a .45."

"Tell us something we don't know, Agent." The detective sounded disgusted, which was fine with Marco. He wanted the man to dismiss him as useless.

Marco stood and glanced around the room. "No signs of a struggle. How did the perp get in?"

The detective nodded toward the body. "He opened the door."

"Sounds like they knew each other."

The detective rolled his eyes and walked away, going back to confer with one of the other cops.

Marco pretended to scrutinize the room, then seeing that the detective had lost interest in him, he backed out of the kitchen to size up the floor plan of the small house.

An entrance foyer, with a staircase leading to the second story, gave way to a hallway leading to the kitchen. To the right of the foyer were a living room and a dining room, and opposite it, a book-lined office. If answers existed, they would be in there.

He stepped inside the room and partially closed the door behind him, figuring he had several minutes before the cops finished with the corpse and found their way in here. With any luck, Marco would be in and out before that happened.

He sat behind the dead man's desk and took inventory. It was meticulously neat, which surprised him. The computer was state-of-the-art, which didn't. He flipped on the system unit, and while waiting for it to boot, looked through the desk drawers. They confirmed his first impression of a man who lived an orderly life. He had neatly stored pencils and pens in the top drawer; backup supplies—paper, staples, rubber bands, stamps—in the left drawers; neatly labeled files in the deep drawer on the right.

Dr. Timothy Mulligan was no absentminded professor.

A hurried glance through the files revealed an organized system for bills and tax records, but two things were noticeably missing. He found nothing concerning Mulligan's position at the university, no student records, graded papers, or course outlines. Second, and more interesting to Marco, was the lack of legal documents or important records of any kind.

Where did the man keep his mortgage and insurance papers? What about his will or car title? Someone as organized as Mulligan must have kept such documents together. And with them he might also have records that would help Marco find out about the man's connection to Decker or those *niños*.

Forgetting the computer, Marco searched the drawers and came up with two identical keys on a small ring. His first thought was that they went to the desk, but a quick check dispelled that idea. Then he considered a safety deposit box, but the keys were too small and flimsy for bank issue. Frowning, he realized they could be to anything, or nothing. But that didn't fit with the image Marco had formed of Timothy Mulligan. He was a meticulous man, who wouldn't keep keys in his desk drawer unless they served a purpose.

Marco scanned the room.

The built-in cabinets didn't lock, nor did he find anything of interest inside. There were French doors leading out to a side porch, but he didn't even need to try them to know the keys wouldn't fit. Next he checked out the closet, which, like the desk, was fastidiously neat with storage shelves from top to bottom.

He found what he was searching for on the floor.

Mulligan hadn't been worried about hiding his papers, he'd just been cautious. The box was made of lead, large enough to hold legal-sized documents, and could be bought in any hardware store for the purpose of protecting its contents from fire.

Marco smiled, pleased that he'd read Mulligan correctly.

Squatting down, he tried one of the keys. It fit. Inside, he found all the papers he'd expected to find in Mulligan's desk: mortgage and loan agreements, car title, Mulligan's university contract, and, at the bottom, a single unmarked envelope. As he reached for it, voices came toward the room.

Quickly, he slipped the envelope into his inside jacket pocket and closed the box. Locking it, he pulled it out of the closet and stood just as the detective stepped into the room.

"What the hell are you doing?"

"I found these." Marco dangled the keys from a finger. "And wondered what they opened." With that, he set the box on the desk. "Looks like I saved you and your men some work."

"You have no jurisdiction here, Agent, and you may have contaminated the crime scene."

"Don't worry, Detective, you won't find any of my prints on anything." Marco pulled off the gloves with a snap and shoved them into his pocket. "By the way, you might want to have your computer experts check out Dr. Mulligan's files."

"I know my job."

"Good for you. Then tell me, did Dr. Mulligan have a silver coin beneath his tongue? Something Spanish?"

"How did you—?"

Because they want it to look like I killed him. But instead of saying it, Marco left the detective sputtering with anger and stepped out into the damp night. No doubt the man would now make that call to the FBI field office in Chicago, only to find out they'd never heard of Marco Ramirez. They knew him only as the Spaniard.

Pausing on Mulligan's front porch, Marco checked out the remaining bystanders. The rain and lack of further excitement had driven most back to the comfort of their homes, but a few determined sightseers lingered.

Then he spotted the *niños*.

They stood in the shadows of a large ficus hedge across the street. Marco looked harder at the lingering crowd and deeper into the shadows surrounding the children. They were alone.

Well, now, wasn't this a coincidence? Just when he thought he'd lost his only connection to them, they show up on Mulligan's doorstep.

Marco descended the front steps.

It was dark by the time they arrived in Champaign.

The rain had slowed to a drizzle, and Sydney hoped the children had taken shelter. They weren't dressed for this kind of weather. Callie didn't even have her jacket, and Danny was so stubborn and disillusioned with adults, he'd never ask for help. Plus, she was worried about Callie's cough.

Ethan stopped at a gas station and got directions to Mulligan's house. She knew he was concerned about the children as well, but she guessed his fear had more to do with the man or men who'd followed them through the woods.

As they turned onto Henning Street and saw the blue lights flashing, an all-too-familiar fear knotted her stomach. "Ethan?"

"I know." His voice echoed her feelings.

She reached for the door handle before they came to a full stop, but Ethan grabbed her arm. "Wait. We can't jump to conclusions."

She couldn't take her eyes off the policemen and the small crowd milling about the house. It was happening again, just like before.

"No." It was as if Ethan had read her mind. "This is nothing like the day Nicky died."

Stunned, she looked at him. He must be remembering the same thing. The ambulance and police cars. The bystanders. It would be worse for him, though. He'd been the one who'd found Nicky and dealt with the first rush of emergency workers, police, and onlookers. By the time she'd arrived, he'd been able to shield her from much of it. In the aftermath of his desertion, she'd forgotten that. He'd been so good, so strong in those first hours—hours when she'd wanted to curl up and die.

"Okay. What do we do?"

"Just follow my lead."

They got out of the car and walked arm in arm up to the small group of people standing outside the house.

Ethan's ability to remain calm no longer amazed her as he put on his best smile, the one she remembered from when their lives had been normal. "What's going on?" he asked a man standing on the fringe of the crowd.

"Haven't a clue. I just got here myself." The man gestured toward the end of the street. "I live down the block and saw the lights when I pulled into my driveway. Thought I'd come have a look."

"Mrs. Jennings called the police," a teenager in front

of them said over his shoulder. "She lives next door." He nodded toward the front porch. "She found the body."

"Who lives here?" Sydney asked, surprised that she could even speak, much less ask a coherent question. Evidently lying got easier with practice.

"Dr. Mulligan. He's a physics professor over at the U."

"Oh, that's right." Ethan took up the slack for her. "I remember meeting him a couple of months ago."

He stopped speaking as two paramedics pulling a gurney exited the house. The body was covered with a white sheet.

Sydney didn't think she could get any colder, but she'd been wrong. Thankfully, Ethan slipped an arm around her shoulders, pulled her tight against his side, and stepped away from the other people.

"Is it—?" She couldn't bring herself to look too closely or even finish the question.

"It's an adult, Sydney."

"Thank God." *Not a child.* She felt instantly contrite. How could she be thankful that a man was dead?

"It's okay," Ethan said, again reading her mind. Then he went very still. "Son of a bitch."

Sydney followed his gaze to a man stepping out onto the porch. He was tall and smartly dressed in an expensive overcoat. She couldn't tell much else about him, except that he was dark.

"Who is it?" She could hardly get the question out because she was afraid she knew the answer.

"Ramirez."

CHAPTER TWENTY-TWO

Ethan went cold inside.

Ramirez descended the front steps of Mulligan's house, and Ethan felt the hate and need for revenge stir within him again. Only this time, he couldn't afford to give into either.

"Ethan?"

He kept his eyes on Ramirez. "Go back to the car, Sydney."

"No."

"Do it." He spoke softly, but with undertones of violence, the violence of a man stalking his son's killer.

"The children."

He saw them, half hidden beside a six-foot hedge across the street. "I'll get them."

Ethan worked his way around the last of the gawkers, his eyes never leaving the assassin, then stepped behind the ambulance. Pulling out the Glock, he checked the clip and held it against his leg, trailing Ramirez through the vehicle's front windshield.

He reached the front sidewalk and turned toward Danny and Callie, though no casual observer would notice or think twice about the well-dressed man walking away from the scene. Ethan waited until he'd reached the shadows of the next yard before leaving the shelter of the emergency van to follow Ramirez.

Fortunately, all Ramirez's attention seemed focused on

the kids. Otherwise he might have noticed Ethan, stealing between parked cars and skirting the lawn to come up from behind, where he pressed the Glock to the small of the assassin's back.

Ramirez stiffened and stopped in his tracks.

"You're slipping," Ethan said, conscious of the weapon in his hand, his desire to use it, and the need for restraint. "Allowing an enemy to come up behind you."

"But then," Ramirez said, "you are not just *any* enemy, *amigo*. Are you?"

Ethan's grip tightened on the Glock. "Nor am I your friend."

"Ah, but once . . ."

"Let's take a walk."

Ramirez tilted his head, as if considering Ethan's command. "I think not. You will not kill me in front of the *niños*." The kids stood not more than a dozen strides away, watching with wide eyes. "But if I start walking into the night," he shrugged, "who knows?"

"Wait." Sydney pushed past them and swept Callie into her arms. Then she turned to the boy, removed her jacket, and draped it over his shoulders.

Ramirez made a tsking sound. "Such a lovely woman. It would be a shame to make her watch as well. I have a feeling she would not understand the kind of man she married."

"If she knew the truth, she'd pull the trigger herself."

"Would she?"

"Oh, yeah. But at the moment, *I* have no intention of killing you. I want something else from you."

"Really? What do I have that could possibly interest you?"

"Information. Tell me what I want to know, and you're free to go."

"And how can I be sure of that?"

"You'll just have to trust me, as I did you." Ethan

glanced at Sydney, fussing over the kids. "Sydney, get them out of here."

She straightened. "Come with us."

"Let's go somewhere a little more private," Ethan said to Ramirez. "Where's your car?"

"You ask a lot, *amigo*."

"You're wrong, you know. If necessary, I'll kill you right where you stand." And to hell with the consequences. "Kids or no kids."

"Ethan?" Sydney sounded desperate and frightened.

"We're just going to have a conversation." He nudged Ramirez with the gun. "Right, *amigo*?"

"It would seem I have no choice," Ramirez agreed.

"You got that right. Sydney, take the car and wait for me where we stopped earlier."

She looked ready to object. Then Callie started coughing, and Sydney's attention shifted. The girl sounded bad as she buried her head against Sydney's side. "Okay," she said, her concern for Callie winning out. "We'll wait for you." She grabbed two small hands. "Hurry, please."

As she headed for the Volvo, Ethan patted Ramirez's sides for weapons, then reached beneath his overcoat and removed a Beretta .22 caliber automatic from its holster. "I'll take this."

"Evidently the trust is not mutual."

"Hardly." Ethan slid the Beretta into his left pocket, the Glock into the right. "Now lead on, and don't try anything. I really would like to pull this trigger."

They moved off together, Ramirez hunched against the rain and Ethan following behind and slightly to the side, with the weapon inside his pocket trained on the assassin. A block over from Mulligan's house, they stopped beside a black BMW.

"Still favoring the flashy imports, I see." Ethan scanned the street. "It's one of the reasons you're not worth shit at running a tail." When he spotted no curious eyes, he nodded toward the backseat. "Get in."

They settled into the vehicle's chilly interior, with the rich smell of expensive leather surrounding them. Ethan put his back to the door and brought out the Glock, keeping it clearly visible and aimed at the other man.

"What now?" Ramirez asked.

"You," Ethan flicked the weapon at him, "need to start talking."

"About?"

"Don't play games with me, Ramirez. I'd still rather shoot you than look at you. Why are you here?"

Ramirez tilted his head. "I want the same thing as you. Information."

"Is that why you killed Anna, because you wanted information?"

"Now who is playing games?" Ramirez snorted and looked away. "That was old business."

Ethan fought the tremor of anger. "And Mulligan? Was he old business as well?"

"I had no business with Mulligan." His voice was flat, noncommital. "You know this, or you would have already pulled that trigger."

Ethan kept silent, waiting.

"Why would I kill the man?" Ramirez asked, annoyance in his voice. "He was nothing to me."

"What about Dallas?"

"I was there, if that is what you are asking."

"It's not."

"Then you must be referring to the gentleman outside your wife's apartment." Ramirez folded his arms. "If I had been on that balcony, she would be dead. Again, you are asking questions when you already know the answers."

Ethan ignored Ramirez's impatience. "Then tell me something I don't know. How did you track us from Texas to Illinois?"

"Not you." Ramirez reached for his jacket.

Ethan raised the Glock. "Easy."

Ramirez opened his palms wide.

"Left hand only," Ethan warned.

Ramirez grinned, opened his coat with two fingers, and removed a white business card from an inside pocket. He offered it to Ethan.

"Just tell me."

"I found this in the Kelsey woman's bag." He held up the card, flipping it from one side to the other. It was blank, except for a series of numbers printed in black ink. "It took me a while to figure out exactly what the numbers meant. A bank account, a password of some kind . . ."

"The point?"

"It is a telephone number." He slid the card back into his coat. "Timothy Mulligan's telephone number."

It was no surprise that Anna had access to information about Mulligan. Danny would have told her the same story he'd told Ethan and Sydney. But it did surprise him that she'd taken the trouble to find and keep Mulligan's number. Maybe she *had* planned to contact him as she'd promised Danny.

"After that," Ramirez said, "it was a simple matter to locate this Mulligan."

"And kill him?"

Ramirez laughed abruptly and shook his head. "He was dead when I got here, though they will say it was my work. Like they are claiming those two police officers are yours."

Even if Ramirez was telling the truth, it didn't tell Ethan jack about his interest in Danny and Callie, or why he'd bothered to find Mulligan. "So what's your stake in all this? If you didn't kill Mulligan, what are you doing here?"

"I told you, I want answers." He brushed nonexistent lint from his sleeve. "And I thought Anna Kelsey, those *niños*, or maybe this Mulligan could provide them."

"What kind of answers?"

Ramirez met his gaze then, his eyes cold. And hard. Reminding Ethan that an assassin lived behind the cool civility and manners. "There is a connection here, between this man Mulligan, those *niños* . . ." He hesitated, his lips curving upward, but not in anything resembling a smile. "And your orders to kill me three years ago."

It felt like a sucker punch, straight to the gut.

"So," Ramirez said, "this is something else you did not already know."

A part of Ethan wanted to stop this conversation right now. The raid on Ramirez's cabin was something he'd like to forget, a time and place he'd rather not revisit. But he knew he could no longer run from his past. "Go on."

Ramirez didn't say anything right away. And for several long moments, the only sound was the rain, which had picked up, beating steadily against the roof.

"My last target for the Agency was a man by the name of George Taleb," Ramirez said, finally. "About four weeks before you and your team tried to kill me."

Ethan kept his expression carefully blank. The events of that night three years ago were something he'd carry with him forever, a sin he'd never redeem. But he couldn't believe Ramirez was innocent in that, or in the deaths that followed.

"It was a straightforward hit, nothing difficult." Ramirez turned to the window, where rivulets of water streaked the glass. He traced one with his finger. "The man—"

"Just give me the highlights."

Ramirez faced him. "The highlights, you say? Well, I would not like to bore you with too many details." Hate brimmed in his eyes. "After the Agency ordered my termination, I wanted to know why. So I investigated, starting with Taleb. Only I found nothing. The man did not exist, no driver's license, no birth certificate, no employment or school records. Nothing."

"One of ours?"

"Possibly, though it did not explain why *I* had become a target." He focused again on the damp night beyond the window. "So I kept searching. Then six months ago, my sources led me to that island." His voice took on an edge of anger. "For three years I have been hunting for answers, and that is what I found. Taleb was running from an island of children."

"And you killed him."

He dismissed the statement with a flick of his wrist. "The Agency ordered it." He focused again on Ethan. "Then they sent you. I got too close to something when Taleb died, something they did not want me to know."

"What?"

"That is the question. An old man, looking to live out his life in peace? A bunch of *niños* on an island. You tell me, *amigo*."

"And you believe the Agency ordered your death."

"Not only mine." Ramirez's eyes took on a deadly glint, not lost on Ethan. The old business between them was not finished, despite this momentary truce. "The child you killed that night in my cabin . . ."

Ethan flinched.

"She, too, was running from Haven Island."

CHAPTER TWENTY-THREE

Sydney waited for Ethan.

She'd driven the children back to the convenience store where she and Ethan had stopped earlier. For a while, she'd occupied her thoughts with Callie. The cough she'd been fighting for the last couple of days had fully developed, accompanied by a low-grade fever. And for the first time, she'd complained of a sore throat and headache. Sydney had done what she could without knowing exactly what she was treating. Because of their conversation at Laurel Lodge, she feared the girl's symptoms were more than those of a simple flu or cold. Plus, Sydney couldn't rid herself of the nagging fear that something else was going on here, something connected to the children's island home. She was beginning to think Callie belonged in a hospital.

Meanwhile, Sydney dried off both children and turned up the car's heater to warm them. Then she bought them prewrapped sandwiches and hot chocolate. Once she'd gotten some food into Callie's stomach, she gave her more Liquid Tylenol and another dose of over-the-counter cough syrup. Finally, both children drifted off to sleep, Callie with her head on Sydney's lap and Danny stretched out in the backseat.

Only then did Sydney allow her thoughts to slide back to Ethan and the man he'd held at gunpoint in front of Timothy Mulligan's house: Marco Ramirez.

Just the name made her shiver, despite the heater at full blast. She didn't want to die, but neither did she want to be responsible for someone else's death. It went against her oath as a doctor and her conscience as a human being. Ethan had said he only wanted to talk to Ramirez, but she had no way of knowing whether that was the truth. In her heart she knew Ethan would do anything and everything in his power to protect her. Even kill. And there was always the chance that something could go wrong and Ethan would end up on the wrong side of that equation.

But when Ethan finally showed up, slipping into the car without a fuss, she couldn't bring herself to ask about Ramirez. Ethan's presence filled the car, and relief blocked her throat.

"Is everyone okay?" he said.

She shook off her paralysis. "Danny and I are fine, but Callie's sick."

Ethan smiled sadly at the sleeping child and brushed a strand of hair from her cheek. "Yeah, I know."

The gesture caught at Sydney's heart. How had she forgotten all these things about him, his courage and protective nature? His gentleness? It took effort to speak normally. "She's better now, but I'm worried about her."

"What about you, Danny?" Ethan glanced in the backseat. "Are you sure you're okay?"

"Yeah," came the muffled reply.

"No sore throat or coughing?"

He didn't answer, and Sydney shifted to look at him. "Are you getting sick, Danny?"

He still didn't respond, or even move. Not right away. Then he pushed to a sitting position, his eyes brimming with tears. "I'm really sorry."

Sydney ached for him. "Oh, Danny."

"Everyone makes mistakes," Ethan said.

Danny lowered his head, tears dripping down his cheeks.

Ethan reached back and gently lifted Danny's chin. "It's okay." His voice was firm but kind, the voice he'd used when he'd had one of his talks with Nicky about some boyish mischief. "I know why you ran, I even understand it."

"You do?"

"Yeah, I do." Ethan withdrew his hand.

"But Callie, she's so sick."

"You didn't make her sick, and we're going to take care of her. Besides . . ." He shot Danny a grin. "Didn't I tell you Sydney was the best kid doctor in all of Texas?"

A ghost of a smile brightened the boy's face.

"There's nothing to worry about," Ethan assured him. "A little rest and some of Sydney's magic, and Callie will be fine."

Danny sniffed and swiped at his eyes. "So, you're not mad?"

"No, I'm not mad, but we *do* have to get one thing straight." Ethan grew serious again, and Danny mirrored his expression. "I'm not Anna, or anything like her. And I'm certainly nothing like those folks you call the Keepers." He paused, searching Danny's face. "I'm not going to let you and your sister down. I'm in this to the end."

Danny didn't respond immediately, and Sydney held her breath. Finally, he said, "You'll help us find out what happened to our parents?"

"*And* why your friend Sean disappeared." Again Ethan waited for the boy to digest his words. "So promise me you won't run off again."

Danny hesitated a bit more, then nodded. "Okay."

Sydney let out her breath. Ethan had succeeded in getting Danny to trust an adult again, when she hadn't been sure it was possible.

"Okay, then, let's get out of here." Ethan reached for the door handle but stopped at Danny's next question.

"Is that man dead?"

"Ramirez?" Ethan looked back at him. "No, I didn't kill him. Though I admit I wanted to. He's a pretty bad man."

"What about my . . . Timothy Mulligan. Did Ramirez . . ."

Ethan shook his head thoughtfully. "No, I don't think so."

Surprised, Sydney started to ask a question but decided against it. There would be time later. Right now she wanted to put some distance between these children and whoever had killed Timothy Mulligan. And she wanted to get Callie into bed. "Shouldn't we get going?" she said.

Ethan agreed, and they switched places so he could take the wheel. And as they navigated the damp streets of Champaign, Sydney considered how easily Ethan had handled Danny. No, that wasn't quite right. Ethan hadn't "handled" the boy, he'd been sincere and straighforward, and in the process gotten Danny to trust him. Quite a feat considering everything he and his sister had been through. But then, Ethan had always had a keen sense of how to deal with people. He'd been a wonderful father, patient and capable of delivering an explanation without losing his authority. He'd probably been that way with the men under his command as well.

Sydney stared out the rain-streaked windows as they pulled onto the highway, leaving behind the lights of Champaign.

She'd been wrong to let her grief and anger blind her to all the good in her marriage, in Ethan. There had been so much that had been wonderful about their years together. Yet she'd chosen to remember only how it ended.

Now, riding in a stolen car with two runaways and an assassin on their tail, she had to wonder if she'd waited too long to see things clearly.

They headed north, toward Chicago.

Ethan wanted to get as far from Champaign as possible, but one look at Callie and he knew he needed to find a place for the night. And soon. Despite what he'd told Danny, he was worried about the girl. If she didn't get better soon, they'd need access to medical facilities. Chicago was as good a place as any and better than most. And it was always easier to disappear in a big city.

It was near midnight when he decided to stop. He picked a chain motel, one a family on vacation would choose. Callie was still asleep, and he carried her into the room while Sydney got Danny inside.

After that, he let Sydney tend them. She took to it naturally, as she'd done with their son, while Ethan felt as far removed from parenthood as one could get. A few hours ago he'd ached to rip the life from another man.

The thought brought a bitter smile to his lips.

He was hardly what you'd call father material. Though he'd loved Nicky unconditionally, it had always been Sydney who'd nurtured their son, given the boy a loving home. As a father, Ethan had been a bust, traipsing around the globe tending to other people's problems, leaving his own family alone and vulnerable. He'd told himself he was creating a safer world for them, but that had been the biggest lie of all. Nothing he'd done in those years had ever changed anything, except to tear his family apart and ensure that Sydney no longer had a child of her own to mother.

So he left Danny and Callie to her and stepped outside. The rain had continued, chilling the air and stealing the stars from the sky. After three years in the desert, he couldn't get enough of the rain. Or the coolness. Crossing the small patio to the pool area, he took up watch at an umbrella-covered table with a clear view of the room.

His encounter with Ramirez had left him unsettled. The assassin had done Ethan's leg work and confirmed his suspicion about several things, including his growing certainty of the Agency's involvement. Even the surprise connection between Haven Island and his team's attempt to bring in Ramirez had only confirmed what Ethan had already guessed. Something was happening on that island, something the Agency had killed to keep secret. The only remaining questions were what and who was involved.

Ethan supposed he should be grateful to Ramirez for filling in the blanks, but gratitude wasn't something he could offer the man who'd killed his son. Instead, hate simmered within him, distant now, like a fading bruise or bout of sickness almost past. As was his fear that Ramirez would come after Sydney.

"What now?" he'd asked Ramirez before leaving him in the chilly interior of his car. "Is Sydney safe?"

Ramirez waved off the question with a flick of his wrist. "She is of no interest to me."

"If you're lying—"

"I told you what I want. Answers. And if your woman or those *niños* had them, you would not have come looking for Mulligan." He met Ethan's stare with hard, unflinching eyes. "My answers and yours, *amigo*, are on that island."

Reality sucked, but Ramirez had been right.

Sydney came outside, making him forget Ramirez. Her slender silhouette hovered in the doorway, looking too young and fragile, though Ethan knew neither was true. Only a strong woman could have held herself together these last forty-eight hours, and Sydney had done more than that. She'd stood up and fought back.

"How's Callie?" he asked as she crossed the terrace to join him.

"Sleeping. But she's a pretty sick little girl." Sydney settled in the chair opposite his. "She's also very stubborn."

"Like her brother."

"She woke up just long enough to tell me she wasn't really sick, just a little tired."

Ethan smiled to himself. What a pair they were, angelic Callie and her fierce big brother. They were the type of kids who'd drive their parents nuts one day, and make them incredibly proud the next.

"I'm worried about her, Ethan." Sydney leaned forward. "Yesterday Callie told me the doctors at the Haven keep her away from the other children because she has a weak immune system. Even if this started out as a simple cold or flu bug, it may develop into something much more serious." Her face tightened. "But without tests or equipment, I just don't know."

"What do you want to do?" It was her call, she was the doctor.

With a sigh, she settled back in the chair. "I'm not sure yet. I'll keep an eye on her tonight, and if she's not better in the morning, we need to take her to a hospital."

It was a risk. At the very least, they'd open themselves to questions and scrutiny they weren't prepared to answer. Someone could recognize him, or all of them if the media had gotten word of Sydney's arrest at the park. But he wouldn't risk Callie's life by denying her medical treatment.

"If you decide she needs a hospital," he said, "we'll take her." He'd just have to find some way to protect her in the process.

Sydney smiled tightly, obviously relieved. "All right."

He fell back on his silence, but after a few moments he realized she was still looking at him. "What is it?"

"I haven't thanked you for coming after me today and pulling me out of that car."

It surprised him that she'd think he'd do anything else, or feel the need to thank him. "You shouldn't have been in that situation to begin with." The park and car accident seemed long ago, much longer than the reality. "I shouldn't have let it happen."

Her soft laugh sounded sad. "Who made you responsible for the world, Ethan?"

Not the world, not any longer. "I'm supposed to be keeping you safe."

"And I haven't made it easy."

He chuckled. "Well, there is that."

For a moment, she met his gaze, then turned away. Quickly. A little too quickly, he thought. They were both fighting it so hard, this attraction, the chemistry that had brought them together nine years ago and still simmered.

"Don't be so hard on yourself," he said, referring to more than her willingness to accept blame. "You've done okay under very difficult circumstances."

"Maybe, but before tonight, when . . . when Mulligan was killed, none of this seemed real. Or at least, I didn't want to believe it was real."

"And now?"

"I'm scared." She shivered and pulled her jacket closed. "More than that, I'm angry. A man is dead tonight because I talked to him."

"You can't blame yourself."

"I don't, not really. Mulligan died because he's linked to the children, and someone doesn't want us to find out how." She paused, frowning, then added, "But even knowing that, I can't shake the feeling I'm responsible. If I hadn't sought him out, he might still be alive."

It was the kind of guilt Ethan understood, but he couldn't let her accept it. He moved to the chair next to hers and grasped her hands. "Sydney, you've been drawn into this against your will. If anyone is at fault—"

She pressed two fingers to his lips. "Stop. Don't say it."

Ethan went very still, unable to breathe.

"I won't listen to you blame yourself," she said, her hand on his cheek now, cupping his face. "You do that too much."

Her touch almost undid him. She had such small hands, with long tapered fingers that were adept and competent, yet capable of such tenderness. The feel of them against his face was like a cool breeze against his scorched skin. He wanted to wrap his own around them and absorb their comfort, but he resisted, letting her set the pace.

Whatever happened next, it had to be her choice.

Slowly, she leaned closer and kissed him. A soft brushing of lips that lingered, tantalized, and mixed with the gentle scent of her. Still, he restrained himself, fighting the need to drag her into his arms.

She broke the kiss, taking the last of his breath with her, and rested her forehead against his. "I told myself I wasn't going to do that, that I didn't even want to do it." She sighed, then lifted her head to look at him. "But I'm done lying to myself."

Her words shattered the last of his restraint, and he framed her face with his hands. "That's the one thing I never lied about, not even to myself." This time, he controlled the kiss, drawing her in and opening her mouth with his. Wanting her. Needing her to dissolve the years, the hate, the anguish over losing their son. He'd been a fool to leave her. In time, this woman had the power to heal him, to fill all the dry places within him and make them bloom again. Now time was the one thing they didn't have.

"Sydney . . ." He pulled away. "God, I can't believe I'm going to say this, but—"

"I know." She barely breathed the words. "This isn't the right time."

"There's Danny and Callie, and that damn island, we—"

Again she pressed her fingers to his lips. "It's okay. I understand."

He turned his face into her hand, kissed her palm, and felt her tremble.

"Sooner or later we need to settle this, Ethan. There are things that must be said, questions I need answered. Promise me you won't leave again until we have time to talk." She pulled her hand from his face and sat straighter. "I can deal with anything if I know the truth."

"You have my word, Sydney."

"Okay." She took a deep breath, but it was several minutes before either of them spoke again. Then she said, "Tell me about your conversation with Ramirez."

He did, both sorry and grateful for the change of subject, hesitating only when he got to his team's mission to bring in the assassin, and how they'd failed. But he went ahead, knowing he risked losing her for good, and told her about the child who'd died in the raid on Ramirez's cabin.

Sydney glanced back at the room where Danny and Callie slept, her expression grim, fearful. "So Ramirez believes the Agency sent you to silence him about the Haven."

"Yes, but there's a hole in his theory." Or was there? "I wasn't ordered to terminate Ramirez," Ethan said. "That's not what my team was about, we didn't do ghost work. I was told he'd gone renegade and to bring him in. Nothing more." He shoved his hands through his hair, the memory of that hellish night haunting him still. "And we knew nothing about the girl.

"I don't know what happened." Though he had his suspicions, devised and churned over during the desert nights. "My team surrounded the cabin, taking up position before moving in. Then the word came down the line that Ramirez was getting away." He remembered the dark, moonless sky and the smell of the damp earth. The voices, a child's among them. Then the sharp staccato of gunfire. And her screams.

"Someone fired, and before I could stop it, all hell broke loose." He stopped speaking as the memories crowded in around him. So much blood. Who knew one small body could spill so much of it? "At the time, I thought it was an accident. Now, I'm not so sure."

He met Sydney's gaze, afraid of what he'd see in her eyes. Disgust? Loathing? Instead, he saw sympathy. "And Ramirez blames you?"

"It was my team."

"But Ethan—"

"Maybe he was supposed to die." And the girl with him. "One of my team sold us out." Ethan didn't want to believe it, but he couldn't ignore the evidence. They hadn't been a bunch of raw recruits who'd open fire in a panic or without provocation. "One of them must have had different orders." Orders Ethan would have refused.

Anna? They'd had their differences, but Ethan had a hard time picturing her as an Agency plant. Except somehow she'd survived, been protected, when the rest of Ethan's team had paid with their lives. For that reason alone he couldn't dismiss her as a candidate. There was another possibility, however, one that made a lot more sense.

"I had an extra man that night." He settled back in his chair. "He'd been assigned to me temporarily a couple of months earlier, supposedly to gain field experience. But he could have been placed on my team for any number of reasons, including sabotaging our mission." Unfortunately, there was only one way to be sure. "I have to go to Haven Island."

"No."

"It's the only way."

"What about our plans? We were going to do research on the Internet. You were going to check out your informants on the streets. What about James Cooley? And I can call Charles—"

"And make him a target as well? Is that what you want?" When she didn't respond, he went on, "The answers are on that island. Anna knew it, Ramirez knows it." He took her hand again. "And now, so do I."

"Anna brought Danny and Callie to you."

"For protection only." Even though she hadn't been willing to go along with whatever the Keepers were doing. That had been the line she wouldn't cross. "She may have even planned to locate Mulligan, but she was running from that island, not trying to expose it."

He watched Sydney struggle with the idea, trying to accept that this was the only way. "Okay, but I'm going with you. We'll find someplace safe—"

"No, I want you and the children out of this." He squeezed her fingers, trying to reassure her. "I have contacts, people who will help. Tomorrow I'll make some calls and arrange protection for the three of you."

She'd opened her mouth to argue, when the door behind them flew open.

"Ethan!"

He sprang to his feet, his hand already on the Glock.

"It's Callie." Danny sounded scared. "Come quick."

CHAPTER TWENTY-FOUR

The drive to West Metro Hospital was the longest fifteen minutes of Ethan's life. In the backseat, Sydney cradled Callie in her arms and pressed cold compresses to her forehead and cheeks. Danny hovered beside them, an ice bucket of tepid water on his lap, refreshing washcloths and passing them to Sydney.

Back at the motel, Danny's frantic call for help had sent Ethan and Sydney racing for the room, where Callie had thrashed on the bed, mumbling incoherently.

"She's burning up," Sydney had said as she felt Callie's forehead. "We need to get her to a hospital. Danny, fill a bucket with cool water and grab a handful of those washcloths. Ethan, get her into the car. I'm going to check with the front desk for the nearest emergency room." Sydney's voice had been strong and steady, and neither of them had questioned her orders. Minutes later, they'd been on their way.

Ethan glanced at the backseat. "How is she?"

"She'll be fine," Sydney answered. "Just get us to the hospital in one piece."

Ethan refocused on the road, resisting the urge to push the stodgy Volvo to its limit. He couldn't risk getting stopped for speeding. By now even the Chicago cops would be on the lookout for him, and if he were arrested, he wouldn't give Sydney and the kids more than a few hours before whoever killed Mulligan picked them up.

But damn if Ethan wasn't tempted to take the chance and push the speed limit anyway.

And where had all these other cars come from?

It was two in the morning. These drivers should all be home in bed, instead of getting in his way, the slowest seeking him out.

Finally, they reached a large sprawling hospital on the outskirts of Chicago. The parking lot alone took up an entire block, but Ethan pulled straight to the emergency room door, threw the car in park, and was out of the vehicle before the engine stopped rumbling.

"Let me have her." He lifted Callie from Sydney's arms and carried her inside, Danny and Sydney right behind him.

Sydney went straight to the triage desk. "I'm Dr. Branning," she said, using her maiden name. "I have a seven-year-old girl here. Her fever is spiking and she's delirious."

The woman took one look at Callie's pale, sweaty face and hurried from behind the counter. "This way," she said and led them through swinging doors into the heart of the treatment center. "Dianne," she called as they swept past the nurses' station, "bed one, stat."

She hustled them into a glass-fronted room close to the desk, and the second nurse rushed in, pushing past Ethan as he placed Callie on the bed. "Okay, what do we have here?" Without waiting for an answer, she briskly started her exam.

"High fever, delirium." The triage nurse glanced at Sydney. "Mom's a doctor."

Sydney didn't bother to correct her. "She's had a cough for the last couple of days. Tonight she started complaining about a sore throat and headache. I've been giving her Liquid Tylenol, but her fever spiked about twenty to twenty-five minutes ago."

"Get Dr. White in here and someone to start an IV and

help with a rectal temp." She lifted Callie's eyelids, then probed her neck. "And I need a cooling blanket."

The first nurse left, and the second said, "You gentlemen want to step out into the hall, so we can tend this young lady."

Beneath Ethan's hand, Danny tensed. Ethan squeezed his shoulder. "Come on. Let's get out of their way."

They backed out of the room as another woman in royal blue scrubs went in and snapped the curtain closed around the bed.

"Have a seat." Ethan motioned toward the row of plastic chairs along the wall and sank into one himself. As he did, an impossibly young man, looking tired and harried, strode toward them, nodding as he passed and entered Callie's room.

Ethan felt less than useless. It wasn't something he was used to, or liked. He had a feeling Danny didn't care for it either. "Tell me how you and Callie got to Champaign."

Danny looked at him like he was nuts.

"It will help pass the time."

So Danny told him about the hours between when they'd run from the park and arrived at Mulligan's house. He spoke in short, abrupt sentences, taking all of about five minutes to tell his story. Even with Danny's unimaginative narrative, Ethan found it pretty amazing. The kid's ingenuity never ceased to amaze him. Once he'd finished, though, they returned to their antiseptic silence.

After a few minutes, Ethan could no longer sit. He managed to refrain from pacing, but just barely. Patience was an attribute he'd once possessed in abundance. It was one of the abilities that had set him apart, first in Special Ops, then in the Agency. He'd waited out targets while half buried in the muck of a forest and stretched out beneath layers of hot desert sand. He'd perfected the art of stillness that often meant the difference between life and death. But never had his patience been so sorely tested as it was in that sterile hospital corridor, waiting for word about a little girl he'd known less than a week.

When Sydney finally joined them, Danny leapt to his feet. "Is Callie—"

"She's holding her own." Sydney gave him a tight smile. "Her fever is down, but it was up to one-oh-five." Ethan took her arm and drew her into a chair between them. "That's too high for a simple flu bug. So they're running some tests to find out what kind of infection she's fighting."

"But she *will* be okay?" Danny said, his voice shaky.

Sydney brushed a strand of hair from his forehead. "As soon as we know what's causing the fever, we can fix it."

Danny didn't seem convinced. Then one of the nurses stepped out of the room, and all three looked up.

"It's going to be a while," she said kindly. "So if you want to go get some coffee or something, now would be a good time. Plus, there's some paperwork you need to fill out up front."

Ethan stood. "Thank you. I'll take care of it." Once she was out of earshot, he said, "I want to have a look around."

"Do you think they can find us here?" Danny said, voicing the question Ethan saw in Sydney's eyes as well.

"It's probably nothing." Just the sense that he should be doing something. He slipped his hands in his pockets. "Stay here with Sydney and your sister." An unnecessary command, since he suspected it would take force to get Danny more than a few feet from Callie's side.

Ethan started down the hall, dropping his shoulders and keeping his head lowered. A posture that might raise suspicion elsewhere, it worked in a hospital, where life and death balanced on a razor's edge. He looked like one more worried relative.

He bought a cup of coffee from a vending machine and stepped into the waiting room. While sipping the hot liquid, he slid his gaze over the room's occupants. It was the standard mix of broken bones and swollen jaws—the results of late-night fun or fear.

No one looked suspicious.

He wandered out the sliding doors, where he'd left the Volvo earlier. The damp air slithered beneath his skin, chilling him. All was quiet. If he were going to slip into a hospital unnoticed in the middle of the night, it wouldn't be through the main doors of the emergency room. Where would he enter? A service door or loading dock? Somewhere away from the regular flow of hospital traffic.

Maybe he was being overly cautious, paranoid even. But he couldn't shake the feeling he'd exposed Sydney and the kids by bringing them here.

As he reentered the emergency room, he sensed a heightened level of activity. Those in the waiting room felt it, too, sitting straighter and more alert, even though nothing obvious had changed. A dozen or so people still waited their turn, the television still chattered nonsensically from the corner, and the triage nurse still sat behind her desk. She smiled at him as he approached and opened her mouth to speak—no doubt to ask for insurance information or a credit card. He walked by without stopping, his hand already inside his jacket, unsnapping the safety strap on his shoulder holster.

He slowed as he approached the inner doors, all his senses on alert. He wasn't wrong. In the few minutes he'd spent looking around, something had changed. An older couple pushed out through the doors, and Ethan stepped in behind them, slipping into the closest room. He flattened himself against the wall and cracked the door to watch the commotion around the nurses' station.

He recognized Cox immediately.

He hadn't changed much, a bit heavier and less hair maybe, but he still favored the custom-made suits. He was a deceptively small, squirrelish man, whom people often underestimated. It was a mistake they only made once. He was sharp, well informed, and well connected. And he understood how to make the system work for him. He'd scraped his way to power within the Agency, and more than one rival had broken his own career trying to bring Cox down. Within the Agency, Cox was one of the most dangerous men Ethan knew.

The man beside him was different but equally deadly. John Morrow. Seeing him with Cox answered Ethan's questions about the betrayal within his team three years ago. Morrow had been the temporary member of his team, firing the first shot that sent everything spinning out of control.

Beside Cox and Morrow, four guns in suits had taken up positions in the hallway. Sydney stood with her hand on Danny's shoulder.

"What's this all about?" she demanded.

"Let's not kid each other, Dr. Decker. You know perfectly well what this is about. You kidnapped a very sick child." Cox handed her a piece of paper from the desk. "All area hospitals were notified that she would probably turn up in one of them."

"Kidnapped!" Danny said.

"Hush, Danny." Sydney read the paper, then tossed it down. "This is ridiculous." She looked up, first at Cox then at the ER doctor standing off to the side. "Why not ask one of these children for the truth?"

"Sydney's helping us find our parents," Danny said.

Cox ignored him. "Where's your husband, Dr. Decker?"

"Even if we knew," Danny said, more snarl than answer, "we wouldn't tell you."

Cox frowned. "What an unpleasant child. Reminds me of his friend Adam."

Danny lunged forward. "What'd you do to Adam?"

Morrow caught his arm and jerked him back. "Your friend had a similar attitude problem, which needed adjusting."

Danny yanked furiously at Morrow's hold.

Sydney took his hand and drew him away, wrapping her arms protectively around his shoulders."We don't know where Ethan went," she said.

"You expect me to believe that?"

Before she could answer, two orderlies wheeled Callie's bed out of the room.

Sydney moved toward them. "You can't—"

Morrow grabbed her arm. "Get the boy," he snapped, and one of the other men took hold of Danny.

"Wait just a minute . . ." The ER doctor stepped forward.

"This woman is under arrest," Cox said. "Do you need to see my identification again?"

"No, I know who you are, but that doesn't give you the right to take the girl. She's very sick."

"Her personal physician is familiar with her condition and medical history. He'll take care of her."

"But where—"

"Don't waste your breath, Dr. White," Sydney said. "These children are prisoners."

"I think you're confused, Dr. Decker." Cox smiled indulgently. "You're the one under arrest. These children are simply going home. Now, it's time for us to leave. Thank you, Dr. White, for informing us of Callie's location."

Ethan faded back into the room until the hospital hush had reclaimed the hallway beyond the door. Then he inched it open and stepped out. The ER doctor looked up from the desk, his eyes widening. Ethan lifted the Glock, pressing the barrel to his lips. Fear tightened the other man's features but he kept silent.

From down the hall came a soft ding.

Ethan followed the sound, stopping and checking the corner just as the doors slid shut on the service elevator. A few moments later, he knew Cox's destination. The basement.

He took the stairs and ended up outside the morgue. Backing into the shadows of a nearby hallway, he assessed the situation. The loading dock doors stood open, while Cox's people lifted Callie into a large white van. Another man held Danny's arm, but it was Morrow's gun that kept Sydney in place.

Ethan weighed his options. He could take Cox and probably Morrow, but the other four were a crapshoot. Once bullets started flying, Sydney and the kids could as easily get in their way as anyone else. He couldn't risk it.

"Decker? I know you can hear me," Cox said, as the rear door closed behind Callie. "Come on out where we can talk." Cox motioned toward Morrow, who raised his gun to Sydney's head. "Your wife is nothing to me. And I *will* kill her."

Ethan ignored the fear sickening his stomach, but it wasn't as easy to deny the rush of anger following right on its heels. He couldn't afford either. Not if he wanted to get Sydney out of this alive.

He stepped into the light, hands and gun pointed skyward. "I'm here."

"I knew you'd be reasonable." Cox shifted closer to Sydney, claiming her arm. "Morrow, take his gun."

"What do you want?" Ethan said as Morrow relieved him of his weapons.

Cox laughed abruptly. "You haven't changed, Ethan. Still all business."

"Let Sydney and the kids go, they're no threat to you."

"Can't do that. I'm taking these children back to their rightful guardian."

"You mean warden," Sydney said.

"Not at all. These children are cared for and educated. I'm sure you noticed how bright they are."

"I don't give a damn what you're doing on that island," Ethan said. "Just let me take Sydney and the kids out of here, and you'll never hear from us again."

Cox tsked. "If only I could believe that, Ethan."

"Believe it."

"But I know you too well. You'd make some kind of mission out of this, and these children are far too valuable. Besides, there's something I want from you." Cox paused. "Ramirez.

"I want you to finish the job you botched three years ago." For the first time, a shade of anger tinged Cox's voice. "That shouldn't be too difficult, I wouldn't think."

Ethan crossed his arms. "And if I agree?"

"Then I'll let her live."

"And if I don't, I suppose—"

"Don't fuck with me, Ethan." Sydney winced as Cox gripped her arm. "Don't forget who taught you all those delay tactics. Just say yes or no."

Ethan raised his hands. "I'll bring in Ramirez." And when he got his hands on Cox, he'd make him pay for every second of discomfort he was causing Sydney.

"I thought you would." Cox released her. "So, I put together a few things you'll need." He withdrew a key from his pocket and tossed it to Ethan. "You'll find cash and your duffel bag of tricks in locker one-nine-two at Union Station."

"What about the kids?"

"They're going home, where they—"

"No!" Danny sprang forward, kicking Cox and jumping from the van.

Ethan swung around, circling and catching Morrow's forearm with his own. Then he grabbed Morrow's wrist, twisted, and brought a leg up hard against the man's side. Morrow grunted, resisted, and released the weapon that went skating across the concrete.

Danny slowed, looking back.

"Run!" Sydney yelled.

"Get out of here," Ethan echoed, grabbing the Glock, and spun around.

Cox held a small Colt to Sydney's head. "Are you quite done?"

"You son of a bitch." Anger clawed at Ethan's gut.

"Put it down, Ethan." Cox's hands shook, from anger or pain Ethan couldn't say. Danny had landed a foot in the center of his chest. "And get that kid," Cox yelled at the others.

Morrow staggered to his feet, snatched the Glock from Ethan's hand, and stumbled after the weapon Ethan had kicked away. Glancing in the direction Danny had run, Morrow saw the boy had gotten away.

"Let's get one thing straight, Decker." All pretense of camaraderie had vanished from Cox's voice. "I want Ramirez, and *you* will bring him to me."

"Fuck you."

Cox drew Sydney close to his side. "Don't tempt me, Ethan."

He memorized every detail of Cox's face, every angle and plane. "If anything happens to her—"

"Spare me the threats. You have one week to bring me Ramirez. That's all the protection I can offer your wife."

Ethan hoped Sydney could read the apology in his eyes. "Where?"

"The island, of course." Cox shoved Sydney into the van. "I expect you know where it is. We'll be waiting. Oh, and I want the boy back as well."

CHAPTER TWENTY-FIVE

Ethan found Danny in a video arcade.

He'd gotten the idea from the boy's brief account of his and Callie's exploits in Champaign. The kid was smart, resourceful, and gutsy as hell. He'd head for a public place.

With a large suburban mall sitting not more than a mile from the hospital, Ethan's first stop should have been a no-brainer. Except it didn't open for hours. So he went to the motel, in case Danny found his way back there. He hadn't, and Ethan left a note before returning to the hospital. Circling the area, he was looking for places where a frightened boy might hide. He didn't have any luck. As he'd expected, Danny had gone to ground and would only emerge with the sun and the crowds.

When the city finally awakened, Ethan had more options: a busy gas station and minimart, a Wal-Mart that opened at seven, and a nearby field where a group of kids gathered for softball tryouts. Danny didn't show, but Ethan hoped it was only a matter of waiting until the shopping center opened.

Fortunately, he'd guessed right.

For a few minutes he watched the kid beat a video game into submission. A couple of older boys flanked him, urging him on. He played with a fever, completely focused on the mechanical device. He was good, he was angry, and Ethan could guess at the enemy Danny battled in his mind.

"You play a hell of a game," Ethan said.

Danny spun around, relief softening his features. Until he saw Ethan was alone, then he visibly deflated.

Ethan stepped forward. "You okay?"

Danny nodded, wrapping himself once again in a hard shell.

"Hey, man," one of the other boys said, "you got two more free games."

"You can have them," Danny said without looking back.

Ethan gestured toward the storefront. "Come on, let's get out of here." He handed Danny a bulging fast-food bag and led him to a bench outside the noisy arcade. "Not a bad spot to hide." Ethan stretched his arms across the bench back. "Especially on a Saturday morning." There were kids everywhere. "And we have quick access to the highway. Anna taught you well."

"Yeah, right," Danny snorted, and dug into the meal.

Ethan let the silence settle and watched Danny polish off two breakfast sandwiches, a pile of disk-shaped hash browns, orange juice, and a carton of milk. He consumed food like a typical boy, like Nicky had, never quite getting enough. At first glance, Ethan realized, everything about Danny was pretty normal. Yet nothing could be further from the truth. Anyone taking the time to really look would see the anguish haunting his eyes, aging him beyond his years. Danny's Keepers had stolen his youth, stripped him of family and a normal childhood.

Someone, Ethan vowed, was going to pay for that.

When Danny had finished eating, he balled up the bag and tossed it into a nearby trash container. He returned to the bench, slouching on the hard wooden surface briefly. Then, as if he couldn't help himself, he sprang forward, his arms balanced on his bent legs, his body lined with tension.

Ethan reached out, hesitated, then placed a hand on his shoulder. "We'll get Callie back."

Danny took a deep, steadying breath. "I didn't want to leave her alone with them."

Ethan remembered the way Sydney had looked at him as Cox pushed her into the van. "I know."

"Those men knew we'd take her to a hospital." Danny glanced up, his eyes bright with anger. "That's how they found us."

"Yeah." And it weighed on him. By taking them to the hospital, Ethan had put Callie, her brother, and Sydney in harm's way. It had been a mistake. Yet he knew that with Callie burning up and delirious, he'd do the same thing all over again.

Checkmate.

"They sent a fax to all the hospitals in Chicago," Danny said. "It described Callie and even what was wrong with her."

Ethan had guessed as much from the conversation he'd overheard between Sydney and Cox, and the implications had been scurrying through his thoughts ever since.

"They made Callie sick, didn't they?" Danny said.

The boy's insight no longer surprised Ethan. "Either that, or she was sick before you left the island, and the Keepers knew it." It was the point he kept coming back to, and one slightly more palatable than the alternative.

But Danny had made up his mind. "No, she was fine. Then she went to see Dr. Turner, the day we ran away. *He* made her sick."

Ethan didn't want to believe it. He'd known some monsters in his life, and this was right up there with the worst of them. In the end, though, he had to respect the boy's instincts, at least about this. He'd lived on that island for twelve years, interacted with the adults in charge, and seen his friends disappear in the middle of the night. He knew more than he realized, and the knowledge was beginning to surface.

"Did this Turner give Callie anything that day?" Ethan asked. "A shot or pill or something?"

"He's always giving her something." Bitterness edged Danny's voice. "But I thought it was to help her get better."

"What about the other kids who disappeared? Could the Keepers have made them sick as well?"

"I guess."

"What about you?" Ethan leaned forward, forcing Danny to look him in the eye. "Ever go see Turner and end up in bed the next day?"

Danny frowned, the answer in his dark, troubled eyes.

Ethan sat back, scrubbing a hand over his face.

What the hell was going on here? Sydney believed the children were products of in vitro fertilization, but that didn't account for the disappearances, or Cox silencing anyone who got too close to that island. No, the Keepers were purposely making these kids sick, *that* was a secret worth killing over. But why? Was it something special about them? Or were they just convenient guinea pigs? Children born and bred for the purpose of experimentation? Orphans with no relatives who'd miss them?

Just the idea stirred an anger and loathing Ethan couldn't afford. If he was going to bring those bastards down, he needed to remain objective and calm. Under the circumstances, that wasn't going to be easy.

"Are we going to the Haven?" Danny asked.

"They want me to bring in Ramirez." Ethan paused. "And you."

"Figures. What are we gonna do?"

"Well, that depends." Ethan suppressed a grin. A few

years from now, and Avery Cox would have a formidable enemy in this young man. "Are you as good with computers as you claim?"

"Yeah, I'm pretty good."

Ethan believed him. "What do you need to hack into the island's system?"

Danny looked at him, a tentative smile creeping across his face. "A computer with an internal modem. A high-end laptop should do it."

"Okay, let's go shopping." Ethan stood and slipped his hands into his pockets. "Then, I think we should go pay a visit to our favorite island."

Paul wished he'd fled the island days ago.

His best chance would have been right after the children disappeared, before Cox and that nasty piece of work Morrow had shown up. Paul could have gotten away clean, taking everything he needed with him.

Now he had to pick and choose.

Slipping another CD into the drive, he issued the command to download his personal files. Fifteen years of research, and he had to decide in fifteen minutes what was most important, what he required for survival. A half hour from now, the ferry that ran twice weekly between the island and Anacortes would be leaving. And Paul intended to be on it.

Although he'd considered running many times, the news of Timothy Mulligan's death had sealed his decision. A few days ago the item would have been just another violent episode reported by the media. The name would have meant nothing to him. Or if it had touched a memory, he probably would have dismissed it as unimportant. It was surprising that he'd even heard the coverage. The Seattle paper should have buried it on page five, or not reported it at all. He suspected that its proximity to the manhunt for Ethan Decker was the only reason Mulligan's murder had made the national news.

Once Paul had heard it, however, he knew what he had to do. If his name wasn't already near the top of Cox's termination list, it would be soon. He had to make a run for it.

He'd finished deleting his files and emptying out his safe when his last hope of escape died.

"Going somewhere, Doctor?"

Startled, Paul looked up to see his death standing in the doorway. "Morrow, you surprised me."

"A particular talent of mine." Morrow moved into the room, a shark circling its prey. "Shall I repeat my question?"

"Your question?" Paul's hands trembled as he closed his briefcase.

"Are you going somewhere?"

"No." Paul stood, steadying himself on the hard leather case. "I mean, yes. To my apartment. Is that a problem?" He tried adding a note of indignance to his voice but failed miserably.

Morrow glanced at the briefcase but walked over to the windows. With his back to Paul, he said, "A little early to call it quits for the day, don't you think?"

"I . . . I'm not feeling well."

"Really?" Morrow turned, his smile sickening. "What's in the briefcase?"

"Just . . . you know, work."

Morrow's eyes narrowed. "You wouldn't lie to me, Doctor, would you?"

"No, of course not. I—" Before Paul could finish his sentence, Morrow started toward him.

Instinctively, he backed up.

As Morrow reached for the case, Paul gathered his courage. "That's personal property. You have no right to go through it."

It was a token protest at best, and Morrow obviously knew it. He flipped open the briefcase and stared at the contents while Paul held his breath.

"Yes," Morrow said finally. "I can see where you might need this in your apartment." He picked up a bundle of bills and riffled through it.

Suddenly, Paul resigned himself to the inevitable. What was the point of resisting fate, when he'd most likely sealed his the day he'd accepted Cox's proposition—fifteen years ago? Sooner or later, Cox would kill him. And Paul no longer had the energy to fight it.

"What do you want, Morrow?" he asked, surprised at the steadiness of his own voice.

Morrow looked at him, a flicker of unease on his face. Then his predatory smile returned. "Oh, I expect we'll get to what I want sooner or later."

He slipped the cash into his pocket and picked up the jewel case of CDs. He looked them over, then dropped them back into the briefcase. Claiming the rest of the money, he stashed it in his pockets along with the first bundle. "But for now, Doctor, I have something else for you. Something you lost."

It took Paul a few seconds to realize what Morrow meant. "The children?"

"Just the girl, and for my money, she ain't gonna make it. But what do I know? My men have taken her to the infirmary."

Anger rose up to replace Paul's surprise. "Why wasn't I notified when you found them?"

Morrow arched an eyebrow, obviously amused. "I guess I must have forgot to call you from the plane."

"If she dies because of your incompetence . . ." Paul pushed past Morrow and headed toward the hospital wing. By the time he arrived, his staff had already begun treating Callie. They'd put her in the isolation ward, in the room next to Adam, one of two equipped with critical-care equipment.

Paul used the intercom. "How is she, Dr. Bateman?"

"Her fever's under control for now. Other than that, we don't know yet."

"Can you be more specific, Doctor?"

"Not now."

Paul stabbed the button again, angry at Bateman's dismissal. The man had become entirely too bold in his attitudes and actions.

Then Morrow stepped through the doorway. "It's hell finding good help nowadays."

"What are you still doing here?" Paul dropped his hand from the intercom. "You've done your job and delivered the girl, you can leave now."

"I thought I'd stick around for a while."

"That's totally unnecessary." *And unacceptable.*

"You're losing it, Doc." Morrow moved to Adam's window. "How long has the boy got?"

Paul took a steadying breath. He couldn't let Morrow push him like this, the man was unstable and unpredictable. "I'm surprised he's lasted this long." Adam had developed viral pneumonia, and despite the respirator, was failing.

"He's a fighter."

"Well, he's not going to win this battle."

Morrow eyed him, again amused. "I guess he should have given you your information right up front, hey Doc?"

Irritated, Paul resisted commenting. "Is there something else you need?"

"In fact, there is." Morrow moved away from the window. "There's going to be some changes around here."

"What are you talking about?"

"Cox will be arriving in a couple of days to oversee

a change of staff." Morrow smiled, a predator on the loose. "Meanwhile, I'll be here to make sure things run smoothly."

Paul felt the walls close in around him, and his legs felt suddenly unsteady.

"Oh, and one other thing," Morrow said. "We have a guest."

"A guest?" The concept didn't register.

"Yes, we found the girl with Ethan Decker's wife."

Paul suddenly realized what Morrow was saying. "And you brought her here? Won't he come looking for her?"

"That's what I'm counting on."

It was twenty-one hundred miles from Chicago to Seattle, a comfortable five-day drive, four if you pushed it. They made it in three and a half and even that wasn't fast enough for Danny. Not with his sister waiting at the other end, sick or in danger of disappearing like so many of his friends.

Danny had to give Ethan credit, he did his best to keep Danny's mind occupied. Before leaving Chicago, they'd bought an IBM laptop. Then they'd gotten rid of the Volvo and paid cash for a used pickup, not unlike the one they'd left behind in Texas.

After that, days and nights blurred together and settled into a pattern. As they drove, Danny told Ethan everything he knew about the Haven: number of teachers, doctors, students, office personnel, and even the janitorial workers. Ethan grilled him about schedules, habits, and anything personal Danny could remember about the staff. He also wanted to know the physical layout of the island and its buildings. So they picked up a large sketch pad, and Danny drew as he talked, describing floor plans and island landmarks.

At night, after ten to twelve hours on the road, they'd

find a motel and spend an hour on tai chi before dinner. It was Danny's favorite part of each seemingly endless day. Ethan was better than the instructor at the Haven and knew variations of the traditional positions. He also explained how the moves, when executed with the emphasis on force, became the fighting forms of the martial arts.

After dinner, Danny would plug his computer into the phone jack and chip away at the Haven's systems. Someone had built a new firewall in front of the children's files, which had him stumped. He tried every back door he knew. Nothing worked. Whoever had constructed the new security knew his way around computers.

Danny kept at it, and though he couldn't get into the more sensitive files, he found other neat stuff: floor plans and diagrams, time sheets and personnel information. He'd even gotten into Dr. Turner's personal journal, which noted Callie's arrival and treatment in the hospital. But Danny couldn't find the answer to Ethan's most pressing question. Why had Dr. Turner made Callie sick to begin with?

They arrived in Seattle late in the afternoon of the fourth day, though it seemed like they'd been on the road much longer. Looking back, Danny realized that under different circumstances it wouldn't have been a bad trip. Ethan had turned out to be okay, for a grown-up. Danny had never spent time alone with someone like Ethan before, a man who taught him things and treated him like an equal. Danny liked it.

Then, everything changed.

CHAPTER TWENTY-SIX

Sydney waited for the children.

She knew it was too early. The sun had barely risen, casting a pearl gray light over the island. The children's Keepers were probably just now rousing them from sleep. It would take another thirty minutes or so before they emerged in the courtyard below.

Sydney had come to count on this small ritual. Every morning before dawn, she'd abandon her attempt at sleep and leave her bed to stand by the window. A short time later, the children would come outside. All twenty-two of them. Watching them practice tai chi gave her a measure of peace. And kept her sane.

She almost laughed aloud at the thought. Only four days. Yet it felt like as many months, and she was already concerned for her sanity.

She hadn't seen Callie since they'd first arrived. Avery Cox's men had immediately separated them—whisking Callie off on a stretcher and bringing Sydney to this locked room and leaving her without a word. Since then, her only human contact had been a solitary guard who brought her meals but refused to answer the simplest of questions.

Except for the lack of bars, the room may as well have been a prison cell. It was small and sparsely furnished with a narrow bed, desk, dresser, and closet-sized bathroom. Five short steps from one wall to the other, and five more back again. Pace it enough times and the walls closed in, and claustrophobia became an intimate. The window was her lifeline, standing between her and the need for padded surfaces. It's where she spent her days, long, seemingly endless hours, worrying about Callie and wondering when Ethan would show up. Because he *would* come and take them away from this wretched place, she knew.

Or die trying.

The thought coiled in her stomach. It wasn't what she wanted, his taking their rescue on himself. For once she wished he'd let someone else play the hero. She'd just found him again and had begun to understand what had happened to them, between them, when Nicky died. She couldn't lose Ethan now. Yet she knew nothing would keep him away, and a part of her, the selfish, frightened part, loved him for that.

To distract herself from her fears, she studied the surrounding structures and activity. What she could see of the facility consisted of a U-shaped building caging three sides of a grassy courtyard, with the open end facing the water and landing dock. For the first couple of days, the movement in the yard below didn't vary much. The staff went about their business, bustling from one place to the next on the sidewalks crisscrossing the green.

Sydney tried to guess each's occupation. The lab coats meant a doctor, or if her theory was correct, a scientist or research assistant. The younger men and women with the children were teachers or coaches. A middle-aged woman in a suit was an office worker or administrator. The small groups in white uniforms, always moving together, were kitchen or housecleaning staff. It all seemed so ordinary that if she didn't know better, she'd think this was a high-end boarding school.

Then, yesterday, the activity had changed drastically, reminding her that this place was far from normal. Over the course of the day, the staff had begun leaving the island, and by midafternoon the facility appeared deserted, but with an eerie air of expectation. Then several boatloads of men arrived, and she understood.

Avery Cox had replaced the staff with soldiers. If Ethan's chances of mounting a successful rescue had been difficult yesterday, today they'd become impossible.

Below her window, the children finally appeared in the courtyard. She hadn't been sure they would today, with the entire complex feeling different than it had twenty-four hours ago. But they assembled in three loose rows, and a young man she hadn't seen before positioned himself in front of them. The day seemed to hold its breath as they stretched.

Sydney looked for Callie—as she'd done every morning. Scanning the other windows, she hoped to catch sight of a small face pressed against the glass. She knew Callie would be watching the other children if possible, if she'd recovered and felt well enough, and if her Keepers allowed it.

A word from their instructor, and the small bodies flowed into the first tai chi position, drawing Sydney's attention back to the courtyard. The children moved with surprising grace. They certainly didn't look abused or mistreated in any way. Instead, they looked . . .

The door opened behind her, but she paid no attention. She'd given up asking questions or making demands of the man who brought her meals.

"They're lovely, aren't they?"

Surprised, she turned. A middle-aged man stood in the doorway.

"I'm Dr. Paul Turner." He stepped forward, hand extended. "Head of this facility." When she didn't accept his offered greeting, he moved aside to let the guard push a breakfast cart into the room. It had been set for two. "I thought you might enjoy some company for a change."

So this was the head Keeper, as Danny called him. She would have liked telling him off, but thought better of it. This might be her only chance to get information about Callie.

"Leave the tray," Turner said to the guard. "I'll let you know when we're finished."

The man hesitated.

"It's okay," Turner said without looking at him. "You can wait right outside." Pouring a cup of coffee, he offered it to Sydney. "I'm too old to jump out the window with her."

The guard snorted his reply and left, the lock falling into place with a loud click.

Sydney accepted the cup. "Where's Callie?"

"You'll be happy to hear she's feeling much better." He positioned the cart near the corner of the bed, then pulled the desk chair to the other side. "We moved her back to her own room last night, and I expect she's having breakfast even as we speak."

"I want to see her."

"I'm afraid that's not possible." He settled into the chair. "At least not right away."

Which meant, not ever. She looked down at the courtyard. "Why isn't she with the other children?"

"She's not quite up to exercise yet. Besides, she's not the best influence on the others right now." He lifted the stainless covers from the plates and grinned. "Belgian waffles. My favorite. I tell you, we have the best breakfast chef on—"

"Because she and Danny ran away?"

He shrugged, then motioned to the bed across from him. "I'm sorry we don't have another chair, but why not have a seat? Enjoy your breakfast. The waffles really are delicious."

The last thing Sydney wanted was food, but she forced

herself to remain civil. She needed information, and if she had to play nice to get it, so be it.

She moved to the bed, sat, and picked up her fork. "What about before she ran away? Callie said she had very little contact with the others."

"Children do say the strangest things." He took a large bite, closed his eyes, and sighed. "I do like a good meal."

She watched him, trying to figure him out. He was a tall, thin man—almost emaciated, hardly the type to be preoccupied, or even interested in food. It was all for show, a cover for his real purpose. He wanted something from her.

"Did you discover what was wrong with Callie?" She took a stab at eating, cutting the waffle into pieces and pushing them around her plate. "We left the hospital before the test results came back."

"Oh, it wasn't anything, just a touch of the flu."

"Don't insult me." She smiled to ease the sting of her words. "Her fever peaked at one-oh-five. A touch of the flu doesn't cause that kind of temperature spike unless there's a secondary infection."

"Well, she did develop a mild case of pneumonia, but we dealt with it. The medical doctors here are top-notch."

"Is that so?"

"One of the boys caught the same bug, and for a while we weren't sure *he* was going to make it, but Callie's fine. She's very resilient, you know."

"Really? Callie told me she gets sick quite often. Something about a weak immune system."

"Did she? How curious. As I said—"

"Children say the strangest things. Yes, I remember." Sydney took a bite, forcing herself to chew and then swallow. She sensed he wanted to talk even while evading her questions. So what was he doing here? Maybe she just hadn't hit the right topic or pushed the right buttons. So she'd try a more direct tack. "Was Timothy Mulligan the children's father?"

Turner coughed, thumped his chest, then grinned. "Do you really expect me to answer that?"

She suspected he wanted nothing more. "Why not?" She refilled her cup, then his. Two could play this game. If he wanted to make believe they were old friends having breakfast together, she could pretend with the best of them. "As you said, we're not going through the window, and Cox isn't going to let me off this island alive. So what's the harm?"

He frowned but didn't deny it.

"I'm right, aren't I? Mulligan was their biological father." She sipped at her coffee, keeping her eyes on him. "A sperm donor?"

"I'm impressed." It was as good as an admission. "Neither of the children look anything like him."

"It's the only thing that makes sense. Mulligan had no children, but his name is in Danny's file." She paused a minute to gauge his reaction. "You did know Danny found Mulligan's name, didn't you?"

He nodded, wariness creeping into his eyes. "Yes, I knew."

Something else struck her, something she hadn't considered before. "*You* sent Cox to Mulligan."

"I didn't expect them to kill him." Guilt tightened his features. "I just wanted the children back."

For a brief moment, she pitied him. He was pathetic, really. Then she buried her sympathy. She wouldn't allow herself to be sidetracked by Turner's convenient streak of conscience. Because of him, a man had died, and she, Ethan, or both could be next.

"So, what is this place?" Sydney leaned forward. "Are all these children products of in vitro fertilization, or just Danny and Callie?"

"In vitro is rather old news, don't you think?" Turner had regained his composure. "These children are so much more."

She had no doubt about that. Whatever was going on here, Avery Cox was willing to kill to keep it secret. "Clones?"

Turner laughed, a little too heartily. "Of course not." He wiped at his eyes. "What good are clones, when you can create perfect originals?"

She put down her cup and sat back. "You've lost me."

He paused, for effect no doubt. "Genetic engineering, Dr. Decker." He scooted forward in his chair, breakfast forgotten. "Just think of the possibilities. What if we possessed the technology to not only select healthy genes in human embryos, but to alter defective ones?" His eyes lit with excitement. "I tell you, it would change life as we know it. We could redesign the human race to be anything we wanted. Smarter. Stronger. Healthier."

She shook her head slowly. "Maybe, but we're years away from perfecting those techniques, decades. And the potential for disaster is . . ."

"*You* are years away at Braydon Labs."

"How do you—"

He cut her off with a wave of his hand. "I researched your background as soon as you arrived, and found out all about your work for Charles Braydon." He spoke like he and Charles were old friends.

"You know Charles?"

"Not personally, though I met him once, briefly, at a conference in Houston. A most interesting man, with a great deal of interest in genetic engineering."

"You know that from meeting him once?"

Turner laughed shortly. "Of course not. I keep up with current research, and Braydon's name surfaces quite frequently." He sat back in his chair, carefully folding his napkin. "Braydon Labs is only one of the research projects he sponsors or finances. There are others, without his name attached."

She knew Charles had various business interests but had assumed Braydon Labs was his only research facility. Not that it mattered. Neither she nor Paul Turner was here to talk about Charles or Braydon Labs. "What does any of this have to do with these children?"

"Everything." He smiled. "And nothing. The work at Braydon Labs is admirable, but it's child's play compared to what I've accomplished." He pushed away from the table and crossed to the window. "Just look at the results."

A chill slipped down her spine. She finally knew what he wanted from her—admiration and approval from someone who grasped what he'd achieved. Only now she was afraid to know. "What have you done?"

Obviously, it was the question he'd been waiting for. He returned to the chair across from her and leaned forward. "I've developed a means to successfully deliver gene packs to human embryos." He paused, his expression fervent and expectant. "Think of it. Hundreds, thousands of designer genes built into the genetic makeup of a one-cell embryo, resulting in a genetically enhanced child."

At first she didn't believe him, for no other reason than the implications stunned her. Her denial lasted only a few seconds, though, just long enough to register the near madness in his eyes. He wasn't talking about possibilities, he was boasting about successes.

Suddenly, Sydney couldn't breathe.

If Turner was telling the truth, it explained the Agency's involvement and willingness to kill in order to keep the children's existence a secret. She also understood why they couldn't allow her or Ethan to live, or Danny and Callie their freedom.

Those offenses, however, paled in comparison to what she suspected Turner had done in his laboratory to produce living, breathing children. "You took shortcuts, didn't you?" Even with a major breakthrough, it was the only explanation for the speed of his success. "You tested and experimented on human embryos from the start."

His expression turned smug. "Nothing great was ever accomplished without risk."

"Or without mistakes." The thought sickened her.

"We've had a few mishaps," Turner said, irritated, dismissing her objections. "Especially in the beginning. But without mistakes, you don't make progress."

Her anger boiled over. "Yours cost lives."

"And created them." He was on his feet again, moving to the window and gesturing toward the children below. "Look at those children, Dr. Decker, *look* at what I've created."

She knew the pitfalls of cutting corners when working with human DNA. The slightest error, miscalculation, or misinterpretation of data could result in the unthinkable. A stillbirth would be a merciful end versus the alternative, a child born chronically ill or deformed in any one of a thousand ways. "The end justifies the means, is that it?"

"In this case, yes."

"What kind of monster are you?"

He recoiled. "Monster?"

"You've disregarded every scientific and ethical code of decency, and those children are still paying for your arrogance." Remembering Danny's friend, who'd disappeared in the middle of the night, she added, "Like Sean paid."

"Sean?" Turner frowned, perplexed, then brightened. "Oh, yes, well, I'm afraid he didn't make it. All great advances require sacrifice."

"How noble of you, since Sean made the sacrifice, not you." She didn't even try to keep the fury from her voice. Otherwise, she might start screaming. She had to focus on the victims she knew about and the children still living under this man's thumb. Because if she thought about those who hadn't survived, who'd died before taking a breath, or been destroyed at Turner's command, she'd go mad. "What about George Taleb? Was he a mishap, too?"

"George?" Turner laughed abruptly. "Very good, Dr. Decker. How did you find out about George?" When she didn't answer, he waved the question aside. "Never mind, George was my assistant, and he did a very stupid thing. He stole one of our children with the intention of exposing my work to the media."

"So you had him killed?"

"Me? Oh, no." He shook his head. "That was Cox's doing. A rather brutal man, really. But none of that matters." Suddenly, he was at her side, dragging her to the window. "Have you ever seen a more beautiful set of children? You, of all people, should appreciate the work I've done here. These children have every advantage."

"Every advantage?" She pulled away from him and backed up. They *were* beautiful, but also lacking in fundamental ways. She thought of her son, and the life he'd had before he died. He'd been a happy child, filled with light and love. "You've denied these children their most basic rights. What about family? Freedom? They know nothing of either."

"Don't be absurd, they have a good home here. They're well cared for, educated, healthy."

"All except Callie with her weak immune system. Is she one of your mishaps?"

A slow smile crept across his face. "Callie's very special."

"So special that you've kept her and all these children locked up like rats in a cage?"

"Certainly what we've given them makes up for that?"

She leaned forward, pinning him with her gaze. "What could you possibly have given them that's more important than the opportunity to lead a normal life?"

"Health, Dr. Decker. I've given them perfect health."

CHAPTER TWENTY-SEVEN

Ethan left Danny in a hotel room.

He knew the kid hated staying behind, but he had things to do and couldn't take the boy with him. Danny was already in too deep, and Ethan wouldn't risk exposing him to further danger by dragging him around the seedier side of Seattle.

As they'd driven across the country, Ethan had listened to Danny's stories about the island and put together the kernel of a plan. It was high risk, but that wasn't surprising. Especially with Cox on the other side of the fence.

First Ethan needed a boat and had decided to get it in Seattle, where he was less likely to arouse suspicion. In a town the size of Anacortes, it would prove more difficult. One misstep and he'd have the local authorities breathing down his neck. Besides, he knew people in Seattle, men who owed him or who were simply afraid to deny him.

His best shot was Tony Rio, a small-time smuggler who also owned and operated a legitimate charter service.

Ethan found Rio Charter without any trouble. It was one of the few charter companies with an office at the marina on Lake Union. He strolled past the single-story wooden structure to a refreshment stand near the docks and bought a cold drink. Then he sat at one of the picnic tables where he could see the front of Rio's building.

He'd first met Tony Rio six years ago.

A group of terrorists had illegally entered the country. The FBI had apprehended and detained all but their leader, Aswad Ben Zafir. When a ten-day, nationwide search had failed to secure him, Cox dispatched Ethan and his team. It would have been a routine mission, except for one thing: Cox had sent Marco Ramirez with them.

They spent a week hunting down Zafir, finally cornering him in Seattle, where he'd arranged transportation out of the country. Rio, who ran guns north to the Canadian border and brought back drugs, was the conveyor. Although all he knew about Zafir was that he had a small cargo and lots of cash.

As Ethan's team closed in, Zafir took Rio hostage. It was a fatal mistake. Ethan would have taken the terrorist in alive if given a chance, but while Ethan tried talking him down, Ramirez put a single bullet between Zafir's eyes.

Simple. Clean. Finished.

And a direct violation of Ethan's orders. He'd been furious, even while realizing Ramirez had just accomplished their mission. He'd used Ethan's team to locate Zafir, then done the Agency's dirty work. That was the first and last time Ethan had worked with the assassin, and fortunately Cox had never pushed it again.

As for Rio, Ethan should have called the locals to confiscate his boat and charge him. Instead, he let Rio go.

He'd become a known commodity Ethan could control and use. Over the years, the decision had proved a good one. Tony Rio had built up the legitimate side of his business, while expanding his contacts in the underworld. Twice he'd warned Ethan of large amounts of explosives coming into the States. Both tips had led to arrests and convictions, and possibly prevented deaths.

Now Ethan needed one more favor.

Across the way, the office door opened and Rio walked out with a woman.

"Damn." Ethan needed Rio alone.

Rio escorted the woman to a red Honda parked on the road. They stood talking while she fumbled with her keys, then unlocked the door and climbed behind the wheel.

Ethan stood and tossed the drink cup into a nearby trash can, then started back toward the building. He kept his pace easy, studying the boats along the wharf. "Okay, Tony," he quietly urged, "let the lady go."

They chatted a few more minutes, then finally the woman started the engine and Rio backed away. As he turned back toward his building, Ethan ducked behind a white Chevy, the last car of the half dozen in front of the charter office.

Whistling softly, Rio headed for the row of cars, and Ethan figured it was his lucky day. If necessary he would have gotten to Rio inside, but it wasn't his first choice. He waited until Rio had reached a silver-gray Jeep Cherokee and unlocked its door. Then Ethan stood, crossed to the vehicle, and slipped into the passenger seat just as Rio inserted the key into the ignition.

"How you doing, Tony?"

Startled, Rio went for the door handle.

"Whoa." Ethan grabbed the man's arm and pressed the Glock to his side. "Take it easy."

Rio's whole body sagged with relief. "Goddamn it,

Decker, you scared the shit out of me. And what's with the gun?"

"Wave to your friend," Ethan said as the woman drove past, "and start the car."

"Okay, okay, put that gun away."

Ethan sat back but kept the Glock visible. "Let's get moving first."

Rio scowled, put the car in gear, and backed out of the parking space. As they pulled away from the building, his temper flared. "What the hell are you doing, Decker? Showing up at my place like this?"

"Settle down, Tony. I'm not one of your flunkies."

"Well, what do you expect? If anyone sees me with you—"

Ethan reached over and tapped the man on the arm with the Glock. "Just drive."

Rio clamped his mouth shut, for a full ten seconds, then said, "Where to?"

"Get on the highway."

Neither of them spoke as they left the marina and headed into downtown Seattle. Ethan wanted some distance between Rio and his home turf before having this conversation, but heavy traffic kept them moving at a snail's pace.

"I thought you were dead," Rio said as they stopped for a traffic light.

"Your mistake."

"So what do you want?" Rio looked at him, then back at the road as the light turned green.

"Not here." Ethan nodded toward the sign pointing out the highway entrance.

Rio steered into the turn lane, and they headed north.

Ethan breathed a little easier as the city fell behind them. The last thing he needed was an encounter with one of Rio's goons. "I need your help, Tony."

Rio threw him a quick glance.

"If you cooperate," Ethan continued, "I'll consider your debt paid in full. You won't see me again."

"Yeah, make me a promise I believe."

"Believe this one." Ethan smiled as if he wasn't about to cut the man's legs out from under him. "I need the *Sea Devil.*"

"What?" Rio turned to him, the car swerving, then straightening as he refocused on the road. "No fucking—"

"Take it easy, Rio." Ethan spoke slowly. "This isn't a negotiation." Rio's boat was fully loaded with top-of-the line navigational equipment and lots of storage compartments. Hidden storage compartments. The kind a smuggler used to run guns or drugs, and just what Ethan needed to take down Cox. "And you will give her to me."

"Just like that? A two-hundred-thousand-dollar boat, and you expect me to turn her over to you?" He slammed open fists against the steering wheel. "You're crazy."

"Crazy enough to get what I want." Ethan pressed the Glock to Rio's side. "Or make a couple of phone calls, which would shut you down in a matter of hours. My guess, you wouldn't even get out of the city, much less the country. As for the *Sea Devil*? Well, the cops would confiscate her and lock—"

"Okay, okay. I get it." Rio looked again at the gun. "Put that fucking thing away, will you?"

Ethan slipped the weapon under his jacket. He wanted Rio cooperative, not terrified. For several minutes Rio didn't say anything, and Ethan let him work through his anger. He almost felt sorry for the man, until he remembered Avery Cox holding a gun on Sydney.

"So, will I get her back?" Rio finally asked.

"If everything goes as planned, you can pick her up tomorrow night." Otherwise, Ethan would be dead and the *Sea Devil* destroyed or in Cox's hands.

"And if things don't go as planned, what am I supposed to do?" Some of Rio's earlier bravado had returned. "That boat's my livelihood."

"Your *illegal* livelihood. Besides, I bet the damn thing's insured."

Rio's grip on the steering wheel tightened. "Insurance doesn't cover all the special upgrades I've put into her."

"Get over it, Rio," Ethan said. "I've had a really bad week, and I need that boat tonight. Do as I say and you'll get it back in one piece."

Rio's jaw tightened. "Okay, what do you want?"

"I need a supply of C4 and a high-powered rifle."

"Jesus, Decker, you don't want much."

"Can you get it for me or not?"

Rio pressed his lips into a tight line, then nodded, obviously resigned to filling Ethan's needs. "The rifle's not a problem, but the explosives are tough. And expensive."

"Just get it and store it on the *Sea Devil.* Then prepare one of your charter boats for an overnight trip. You'll be making a pickup tomorrow night in Puget Sound."

"What the hell are you up to, Decker?"

Ethan didn't respond, Rio knew better than to ask too many questions.

"Never mind, forget I asked." He raised a hand in surrender. "Is that it?"

"You can bring one man with you, no more. So be sure it's someone who can pilot a boat."

"So what am I picking up?"

"Just passengers, including me. Then I'll tell you where to find the *Sea Devil.*"

"Where exactly are we going?"

"I'll tell you tonight, when you deliver the *Sea Devil.*"

"If I do this, then we're even, right?"

Ethan sat back and breathed a little easier. "Yeah, you do this, and we're even."

* * *

Tony Rio was as good as his word.

He and his boat showed up a few minutes before midnight at the designated rendezvous point: a deserted pier on the Duwamish River south of Seattle. Ethan waited for him in the shadows of a nearby abandoned warehouse, with Danny a couple of feet away, safely out of sight.

Ethan would have preferred leaving the boy behind in the motel until he'd checked out the *Sea Devil*, but he couldn't risk it. As soon as he had control of the craft, he needed to get out of Seattle. Just in case Rio changed his mind. So he made Danny promise to stay hidden inside the building and hoped the boy would follow orders for once.

Rio took his time showing off his boat, acting like a proud papa. He explained the navigational systems and controls, then took Ethan belowdecks to display the hidden storage hold which was the boat's special feature. Inside was stowed a Remington 700 and enough C4 to take out half the damn island.

Ethan had to admire the man's ability to deliver on such short notice, but the delay in getting under way was making him nervous. He trusted Rio to a point, as long as Rio thought Ethan's team might appear at any moment or a shooter had a bead on his forehead. Otherwise, Ethan wouldn't make it out of the area alive. Or if he did, it wouldn't be with the *Sea Devil*. So he behaved like a man with five guns at his back. The act was easy to pull off. He'd played the part so long that even now, it was as much a part of him as the Glock beneath his jacket.

Finally Rio finished his tour.

"And the arrangements for the pickup?" Ethan asked.

"I have one of my boats and her captain standing by. We can leave as soon as we know where we're going."

Ethan dropped a large padded envelope on the table. "This is half what I'll pay you for the weapon and explosives, plus the instructions for tomorrow night. You carry out your end of things, and you'll get the other half and the *Sea Devil.*" It was the bulk of Ethan's stash, but if his plan succeeded it would be worth every penny. And if he failed? Well, he'd be dead. "If you don't show, I'd make sure *all* your insurance premiums are paid up, if you know what I mean."

"Yeah, I get it." Rio picked up the envelope without looking inside. "We'll be there."

"Make sure you are."

CHAPTER TWENTY-EIGHT

After gathering Danny and his laptop, Ethan turned the *Sea Devil* north. They headed toward Anacortes, a town on Fidalgo Island and the jump-off point to the San Juan Islands. Normally the trip took six hours, but Ethan planned for at least eight. He was traveling unfamiliar waters in the dark and knew better than to push it.

As Ethan maneuvered away from the docks of the Duwamish River and toward Elliott Bay, Danny seemed unusually quiet. Ethan had expected a stream of questions about Rio, the boat, or their agenda in Anacortes. Normally the boy never shut up, and Ethan had become accustomed to the constant chatter. The unexpected silence worried him.

"Go below and get some rest," he said. "It's going to be a long night."

"I want to stay here." Danny stared out at the dark water, his expression grim.

"It'll be okay," Ethan said, taking a stab at what was bothering the boy. "We'll get Callie back."

For the first time since boarding the *Sea Devil*, Danny looked Ethan full in the eye. "I know you'll try."

Ethan curbed his automatic impulse to offer reassurance. Danny had a firm grip on reality and knew they were heading straight into the devil's lair, with little more than their wits and nerve to pull them through. It made no sense to try to convince him otherwise.

So Ethan left him alone.

They made the rest of the trip in silence—Danny nodding off occasionally but never giving in to sleep—and arrived in Anacortes midmorning. The sky had turned gray and overcast, reflecting both their moods. Ethan hoped the weather wouldn't deteriorate further as the day aged. A storm would complicate and jeopardize his plans.

He checked them into a beachside motel, and after securing the room's doors and windows, collapsed on the bed. "I need a couple of hours' sleep before making the final arrangements," he said. "You might try to get some, too."

Closing his eyes, he waited for the squeak of the other mattress. Danny lay down, but for some time tossed and turned, struggling with his demons. Ethan wished Sydney were here, she'd know how to ease Danny's mind, while Ethan merely waited for the boy's exhaustion to win out.

Finally the room quieted, and Ethan relaxed.

He'd never needed much sleep, not more than four or five hours at a stretch, but he wouldn't undertake a mission tired. Exhausted men made mistakes, and he'd need to be sharp this afternoon when he secured the final component of his plan.

Marco Ramirez.

Ethan was counting on Ramirez still being in Anacortes.

The assassin hadn't survived this long by being careless or stupid. "The island is heavily guarded," he'd told Ethan in Champaign. "Or I would already have my answers."

"Are you asking for my help?"

"Penetrating such a place is your specialty."

"Forget it, Ramirez. You and I are more likely to kill each other."

"Perhaps." Ramirez had shrugged. "But if you change your mind, I'll be around. Just don't wait too long, *amigo*. I am a patient man, but I grow tired of this game."

Now, less than a week later, the world had tipped upside down and Ethan planned to enlist Ramirez's help to raid Haven Island. All it had taken was Cox holding a gun on Sydney, and Ethan's hate for Ramirez had become secondary. Ethan would go in alone if necessary, but Ramirez would greatly increase the odds of success. If Ethan could find him, and he hadn't changed his mind.

Anacortes was a picturesque waterfront town, but even postcard towns had an underside. Ethan started with the bars closest to the water, where Ramirez would leave a trail if he wanted Ethan to find him.

An hour later he walked into Joe's Place, a clone of the other three bars Ethan had checked out first. It was dark, with the smell of stale beer and cigarettes permeating the room. A couple of men, tattoos running up both arms, circled the single pool table. An old woman, alone in a corner booth, nursed a drink. And a couple of regulars watched a basketball game on television.

Ethan took the stool farthest from the door and ordered

a beer. When the bartender brought it, Ethan pulled a roll of bills from his jacket pocket. "You Joe?"

"Yeah, so?"

Peeling off a hundred, Ethan laid it on the bar. "I'm looking for a friend."

The man snorted. "Aren't we all?"

"A good friend." Ethan withdrew a second hundred and dropped it on top of the first. "Latino, a little under six feet, big tipper."

Joe eyed the bills. "We get lots of Mexicans in here."

"This one's different." Ethan fiddled with the roll in his hand, flicking the corner of another hundred. "He keeps to himself." He saw the recognition in the bartender's eyes, and the sudden fear. "Doesn't drink much, just sits and watches."

Joe hesitated, then dragged his gaze from the money. "Sorry, don't know him, and I can't break no hundred. If you don't got nothin' smaller, the beer's on the house." Turning, he walked away.

Ethan sipped his beer, smiling to himself.

Old Joe was definitely uneasy, glancing back as he refilled drinks at the other end of the bar. So, Ramirez had not only been here but came in regularly enough to make the natives nervous. Ethan had found the assassin's calling card.

After dropping a couple of singles on the bar, Ethan headed for the door. "Thanks, Joe."

The man nodded, the relief on his face almost humorous. And premature. Whether he knew it or not, he *would* help his newest customer. It would just take some persuading. Too bad. Ethan would have preferred parting with the money.

Outside, he surveyed the neighborhood. Fortunately, it was the kind of area where everyone minded their own business. He headed down the street, then cut over a block and worked his way to the back of Joe's Place.

Like a lot of restaurants and bars, the rear entrance had no outside handle. It opened from the inside with a push bar. Not the easiest barrier to get through without the proper tools.

Ethan looked for an alternative entry point and found an open window into the men's room. He hoisted himself through and dropped to the dingy floor. The place was filthy. No wonder Joe wasn't worried about anyone getting in this way.

Ethan moved to the door and cracked it just enough to see the hallway beyond. The corridor was long and narrow, with the outside door at one end and the entrance to the bar at the other. Along one side was the storeroom, and opposite it were both rest rooms and a pay phone. Withdrawing his knife, he slipped out and sank into the shadows of the far corner.

Now all he had to do was wait. Unless he missed his guess, Joe would be heading this way real soon.

It was one of Ramirez's favorite ploys. He'd stake out a likely location and give the locals a number, asking them to call if anything interesting happened. He didn't bribe or even threaten them, but his presence was enough to scare them into cooperating, giving him eyes and ears in a variety of places.

Ethan figured Joe's was no different.

It had been about fifteen minutes since Ethan had left by the front door. Anytime now he expected the bartender to head for the john. He'd think he was fooling everyone by waiting and using the pay phone instead of the one behind the bar.

Sure enough, Ethan didn't have long to wait before Joe showed, heading straight for the phone without noticing Ethan in the far corner. Joe picked up the receiver, dropped a quarter into the coin slot, and punched in a couple of numbers. Three strides, and Ethan reached over the bartender's shoulder and pushed the disconnect button.

"Hey—" Joe half turned.

Ethan slammed him face first against the wall, pressing the unopened knife against his spine. "Hello, Joe. Remember me?"

One of the pool players stepped into the doorway, cue in hand. "What's going on here?"

"Just a friendly chat." Ethan shifted to reveal the Glock under his arm. "So why don't you let us get back to it?"

Raising his hands, the pool player backed up. "Hey man, I ain't got no argument with you."

"Let's keep it that way," Ethan said.

"Sure thing." The man disappeared, and a couple of seconds later the slam of the front door reached the dim hallway.

"Looks like your customers have decided to give us some privacy," Ethan said.

"He'll call the cops."

"He didn't look much like the good-citizen type to me."

A sheen of sweat broke out on Joe's forehead. "What do you want?"

"Like I said, I'm looking for a friend of mine."

"I told you I don't—"

Ethan snapped open the blade and lifted it to Joe's cheek. "Want to try that again?"

"He'll kill me if I tell you."

"Looks like you're in a tough spot."

Joe licked his lips. "I don't know nothing about him. He's been in every night for the last week. He has a beer or two, but doesn't drink them, then leaves. That's all I know."

"Who were you calling?"

"Please." Joe tried to turn, but Ethan held him against the wall.

"Come on, Joe." Ethan could smell the man's fear. "Let's not drag this out."

"He told me you'd come looking for him, said to call when you came in."

Ethan loosened his grip just a bit. "Give me the number."

The man fumbled in his shirt pocket and pulled out a business card. Ethan snatched it and saw the number scrawled on the back. "Are you sure you're not trying to pull something on me, Joe?"

"That's what he gave me, I swear."

"Then I'll save you the trouble of making that call."

"Look, don't tell where you got that number. He'll kill me if he finds out."

"I don't think so." Ethan stepped back, releasing his grip on the man's neck. "As you said, he's expecting me. Now, why don't you stay here and count to fifty, and I'll be on my way."

Joe didn't move as Ethan lowered the knife and backed toward the exit. Once outside, he closed the blade and dropped it into his pocket. A few blocks over, he pulled out Anna's cell phone and punched in the number on the back of the card.

Ramirez picked up on the third ring. *"Sí?"*

"I hear you're expecting me."

Soft laughter rippled across the line. "You are so predictable, *amigo*."

"Hey, I found you without breaking a sweat. What does that make you?"

"I wanted you to find me."

"Look," Ethan said. "I don't have time for a pissing contest. You said you wanted on that island, well so do I."

"What changed your mind?"

"Cox grabbed Sydney and the girl."

"And you want them back."

"I want to expose him and that gulag he's running." Ethan switched the phone to his other ear and glanced around. No one seemed to have any interest in him. "And yeah, I want Sydney and the girl freed."

"What about the boy?"

"He's out of it."

"So, now you want my help. How quickly things change."

Ethan gritted his teeth, then forced himself to say, "Cox promised to release Sydney if I delivered you. So, I thought you might oblige me by giving yourself up."

Ramirez laughed again. "He means to kill us all, you know."

"He won't be the first to try."

Ramirez let the silence stretch for a few long moments. "Okay, when and where?"

"Come to the marina tonight at midnight. Look for the *Sea Devil.*"

"I will be there."

"Don't be late." Ethan disconnected and slipped the phone into his jacket pocket.

The last piece was in place.

When Danny woke, Ethan was gone.

For the second time in two days, he'd left Danny alone in a crummy motel room, and he hated it. It gave him too much time to think. As they'd headed west from Chicago, he'd thought only about getting Callie away from the Keepers. Then in Seattle, reality had dug a hole in his stomach. He was going back to Haven Island, and he was scared.

He abandoned his attempt to work on the computer

and went to the window. Looking out at the bleak northwest weather, he remembered the hawk in the desert. If he had a choice, that's where he'd be right now, with the hot sun beating down on his head and the horizon stretching forever in all directions. Here, the damp air chilled him, and the sea threatened to confine him.

He didn't want to go back to the Haven.

He wasn't proud of it, but his fear had grown as they'd gotten closer to Anacortes. He kept telling himself that Callie and the others needed him, were depending on him to bring help. Even Ethan trusted him. He couldn't let them down, but if the Keepers caught him . . . He shuddered at the thought.

He didn't want to be the next kid to disappear.

By the time Ethan returned, it was late afternoon.

"Everything's set," he said. "If things go right tonight, you and Callie will be back together before the sun comes up."

After that, they didn't talk much. Ethan seemed withdrawn, pulling into himself as he prepared for the night ahead. Danny wanted to ask about their plans, how Ethan intended to get on the island and rescue Callie and Sydney, but something held him back. He suspected his reluctance had something to do with not wanting to admit he was scared.

In order to keep a low profile, they ate in the room, picking up fast food and bringing it back. Afterward, Ethan handed him an overstuffed envelope.

"What is it?" Danny turned the envelope over, examining the tight seal.

"In case I don't come back."

Danny looked at him, confused.

"If I'm not back within eight hours, I want you to run. Find a way to the Canadian border. It's not far, fifty, maybe sixty miles. Go to Vancouver. You'll find everything you need in that envelope: money and an introductory letter to a friend of mine. We served together in Special Ops, he'll take care of you."

Danny dropped the envelope and backed up. "No."

"Take it, Danny."

"I'm going with you." Despite his fear, it had never occurred to him that Ethan would leave him behind. Not after all they'd been through and all the planning over the last five days. He was part of this.

"It's too dangerous," Ethan said.

Danny's eyes smarted. "And staying here is safer?"

Ethan put the envelope on the desk, moved over to the bed, and started packing his duffel bag.

"She's *my* sister."

Ethan glanced back over his shoulder. "And I'll bring her to you."

"You need me."

"No. I don't."

That stung, and Danny fought the tears.

"What I needed was information." Ethan pointed to the sketch pad. "Which you gave me."

"That's not the same. I know the island and the buildings better than anyone."

Ethan picked up the envelope. "Take it."

Danny stared at it as if it had teeth. Then, very slowly, he took it. He'd learned a lot over the last week from Ethan, but mostly patience.

Ethan studied him for a moment, then nodded. "Okay. Eight hours, and if I'm not back—"

"Yeah, I got it." Danny plopped down on the bed and grabbed his Game Boy. "I'm out of here."

CHAPTER TWENTY-NINE

Ethan set out at ten.

The night was damp and dark, the streetlamps reflecting off pools of silent water. The storm had never materialized, but a light mist had moved in from the Sound, chilling the already cool air. The streets were empty, with all sensible people indoors, tucked in their beds or in front of warm fires.

For Ethan, however, the weather worked.

He took the long way to the docks, circling back on his own path several times, watching and listening. Overconfidence wasn't a mistake he intended to make. Not tonight. Not with so many innocent lives at stake.

He considered his last glimpse of Danny, still hacking away at the Haven's computer system. Ethan hadn't expected the boy to agree so easily to staying behind. A week ago, it would have been a battle. Danny had come a long way since the day Anna had left him and Callie on Ethan's doorstep. He'd begun looking at Ethan the way Nicky once had, with trust, but Ethan wasn't sure that was such a good thing. He'd never wanted the responsibility for another child's life, yet here he was with the fate of a whole island of kids in his hands. And he'd be damned, or dead, before he let them down, before he allowed the trust in Danny's eyes to fade again.

When Ethan got to the docks, he carefully inspected the *Sea Devil* to make sure everything was in order.

He didn't expect any problems, but this was Cox's turf, within an hour's boat ride from the island. Ethan couldn't be too careful.

As soon as he was sure nothing had been tampered with, he readied the engines and made one last check of the navigation charts. Then he went down into the cabin to wait.

For his plan to work, he needed Ramirez's help. Ethan hated the idea, but not as much as he hated the thought of Sydney in Cox's hands. He'd do whatever it took to get her off that island, even cut a deal with the devil. Or Marco Ramirez. That is, if he showed. And if he didn't, well then Ethan would have to go with his backup plan, a slightly modified and riskier version of the original.

He didn't have long to wait.

The boat swayed gently against its mooring. Footsteps, barely audible, moved overhead. Then Ramirez appeared in the hatchway.

Ethan greeted him with the Glock. "I wasn't sure you'd show."

Unruffled, Ramirez descended the remaining steps. "You do not need the weapon, *amigo*."

"Forgive me if I don't take your word for that. Now, lose the hardware." Ethan flicked the muzzle of the Glock at the assassin, reminding him of his precarious position. "Slowly."

"If I wanted you dead"—Ramirez removed the Beretta from his jacket and placed it on the floor—"I could have killed you many times."

"You could have tried." Ethan gestured toward the Beretta. "Nudge it this way, and the one on your ankle, too."

Ramirez arched an eyebrow and smiled, a slow, caustic smile. "Oh, I think I would have done more than try."

"The ankle."

"Oh, yes." Ramirez bent, unbuckled the holster, and slid it over next to the Beretta. "Satisfied?"

"Anything else?"

The assassin opened his jacket. "You are welcome to search."

"Turn around and put your hands on the bulkhead."

Ramirez grudgingly obeyed, and Ethan patted him down. When he was sure the assassin was clean he backed away, picked up the discarded weapons, and placed them in a cabinet behind him. "Okay, sit."

Ramirez complied. "So, we are going to Haven Island."

"You said you wanted answers."

"As do you. But, if we are to work together," he nodded toward the gun in Ethan's hand, "you must trust me."

Trust Ramirez? Hardly. But for the time being, their interests ran along the same path. After Ramirez had his answers, it would be a different story. Ethan returned the Glock to its holster.

"Since we are displaying trust." Ramirez slid a hand inside his jacket. "I have some information for you."

"Easy." Ethan reached reflexively for his weapon but stopped before drawing it.

Ramirez made no comment, opened his coat, and retrieved a manila envelope from an inside pocket. "I was not idle while waiting for you." He pulled out a sheaf of paper and handed it to Ethan. "I found this in Mulligan's home."

Ethan studied the document. It was a receipt from Cooley Cryobank and Laboratories, San Francisco, California, made out to Timothy Frederick Mulligan, dated 1983. Sydney was right. Mulligan had been a sperm donor and, if the Haven's records could be believed, probably Danny and Callie's biological father.

Then Ramirez handed him a five-by-seven glossy. "Do you recognize this man?"

"Should I?"

"It is James Cooley, founder of this Cooley Cryobank. He looked familiar to me, so . . ." Ramirez showed Ethan a second photograph, this one computer generated. "I had the original aged twenty years."

Ethan studied both pictures and waited for an explanation.

Ramirez tapped the edge of the second picture. "That is George Taleb."

Ethan leaned back, another detail falling into place: the link between Cooley and the island. He and George Taleb were the same man, now dead. It didn't tell them how or why Cooley got tied up with the Agency, why he ran, or what they were doing to those children, but it was one more piece in the puzzle.

"There's more," Ethan said, and explained what little he knew about the children, how they tended to disappear, and his belief the doctors were using them as guinea pigs.

Ramirez grew quiet, his mask of civility eroding. "Cox will not make it off that island alive."

The same thought had crossed Ethan's mind, but he couldn't afford to indulge it. "Our first priority is Sydney and the kids, then getting proof to shut down Cox's operation. Understand?"

"I will keep my part of the bargain."

"See that you do. After that, Cox is yours." Unless he harmed Sydney, then Ramirez would have to get in line behind Ethan.

"So, how will we accomplish this great task?" Ramirez asked.

"I have a plan," Ethan said, offering the devil his deal. "Check beneath the bench where you're sitting, and you'll find a hidden compartment."

Ramirez glanced down, surprised.

"Go ahead," Ethan said. "Move it aside, the latch is all but invisible unless you know where to look."

Ramirez followed Ethan's instructions, releasing the locking mechanism to reveal a storage space beneath the floor: a space big enough for a man.

"Smuggling along the U.S. and Canadian borders is a fact of life," Ethan said. "It's simply a matter of knowing the right people."

Ramirez squatted down and pulled out the Remington 700. "You have some very unsavory friends."

"We all have our sources."

Ramirez grinned like a kid in a candy store and stroked the rifle barrel. "A fine weapon."

"It's not loaded." Ethan nodded back toward the compartment. "In the duffel bag you'll find ammunition, a supply of C4, blasting caps, and a transmitter."

"We are going to war, yes?"

"When we get close to the island, you're going into that hole."

Ramirez looked back at the small space.

"Don't worry," Ethan said, "you'll fit. As soon as we put in at the island, Cox's people will take me ashore. They won't be too happy that I came alone and will search the boat. But they won't find you."

"If you are wrong?"

"Then we're both dead."

Ramirez snorted in disgust. "I do not like this part of the plan."

"You got a better idea?"

When Ramirez didn't reply, Ethan said, "Look, I know Cox. He'll expect me to try something, but he won't expect me to come through the front door."

For eight years Cox had used and directed Ethan's team. He knew Ethan's standard operational strategies, his skill at slipping into secure areas without detection. That's why he had to do the unexpected. "Cox will blanket the island with men watching all the back doors, shallow beaches, rugged shorelines, the least hospitable places to land a boat or receive a diver." Ethan had thought about this on the long drive west, analyzed it from every conceivable angle, and knew this plan was their best shot. "That's where he'll expect me to come ashore."

Ramirez didn't look convinced.

"Plus we have one other advantage." Even before the disastrous raid three years earlier, bad blood had existed between Ethan and Ramirez. "No one, especially Avery Cox, will ever suspect us of working together."

Ramirez's eyes sparked. "About this, you are right."

Tension crowded between them, a reminder that theirs was a temporary truce. The past had not been forgotten. Old hatreds crouched in the wings, ready to pounce.

"Once they take me off the boat," Ethan said, breaking the silence, "it's your turn. First I'll need a diversion, that's where the C4 comes in. Then I want you to even the odds." He motioned toward the Remington in the assassin's hands. "That's what your friend's for."

Ramirez laughed abruptly.

Ethan pulled out Danny's map, giving a rough overview of the island's layout, and explained his strategy. Ramirez listened attentively until Ethan had finished. "And do we have a way off that rock?"

"Well now, that's my insurance policy." Ethan smiled tightly. "If anything happens to me, you'll be stuck. Unless you want to try getting out on the *Sea Devil*, which might prove difficult under the circumstances. So I suggest you make sure I stay alive by taking care of the resistance outside the facility. Meanwhile, I'll get Sydney and the girl and enough proof to shut Cox down for good."

"And then?"

Ethan pointed to a position on the map, behind the main building. "We'll meet here, and all get off the island together."

Ramirez's eyes had gone cold and hard. "It is a crazy plan."

"Just up your alley."

"And yours, *amigo*."

"We're not friends." Ethan rolled up the drawings, secured them with a rubber band, and dropped them into the hold next to the bag of explosives. "If I had any other choice, I'd drop you where you stand."

"We are in agreement then."

"Looks that way." Ethan gestured toward the hatchway. "I want you topside where I can keep an eye on you until we get close to the island."

"So much for trust." But Ramirez climbed the stairs.

On deck Ethan turned his attention to the boat, releasing the ropes and pushing away from the dock. He took the wheel, slid the throttle into reverse, and eased the boat out of her slip.

"There's one other thing you need to know," he said as he maneuvered toward open water.

Ramirez glanced back at him briefly, as if uninterested.

"My team wasn't ordered to terminate you," Ethan said. "I was told to bring you in alive. And, I didn't know about the girl."

Ramirez's eyes remained fixed on the dark water.

They left the marina behind, but Ethan kept the speed down. Despite the charts and expensive electronic equipment, he was unfamiliar with these waters.

When he finally spoke, Ramirez's voice was deadly calm. "Cox wanted his secret dead with me no matter the cost. No price was too high, they sacrificed you, your team, and then . . ." He paused. "And then your son."

Ethan felt the deck shift beneath him. "What are you saying?"

"I do not kill children." Ramirez met Ethan's gaze and held it. "Not even yours."

"And I'm supposed to believe that?"

"Believe what you want."

Ethan gripped the wheel to steady himself. It was a lie. Ramirez was covering his ass. "What about the letter?" And the coin beneath Nicky's tongue? "The one telling me Sydney was next on your hit list?"

"I sent it," Ramirez admitted. "It was *my* insurance policy to keep you from coming after me."

"Bullshit."

Ramirez shrugged and looked away.

"Why didn't you contact me?" Ethan asked. "If you didn't kill Nicky, why not just tell me?"

The assassin turned, and even in the dim light, Ethan could see his anger. "Would you have believed me?"

No, Ethan wouldn't have believed him. There was too much history between them, too much blood. Ethan had led a team after the man and ended up killing a child instead. In return, Ramirez had assassinated Ethan's team, one by one. Nicky was the last to die, a more fitting revenge than Ethan's own death.

An eye for an eye. One child's life for another.

Ramirez was right. If he'd made contact three years ago and claimed innocence, Ethan would have killed the assassin with his bare hands. Gladly.

Ethan turned back to navigating the boat, a fresh wave of rage rising within him. All these years he'd blamed Ramirez for his son's death, when it had been the Agency's doing, Cox's warped strategy to maneuver Ethan into killing Ramirez. And it had almost worked.

Ethan jammed the throttle forward.

CHAPTER THIRTY

Suddenly, the boat lurched and picked up speed, lifting the bow from the water. Hiding in a cramped storage hold, Danny and a stack of life preservers went sliding, hitting the side of the compartment with a thunk. Although he knew Ethan couldn't have heard him over the whine of the engines, Danny remained perfectly still for several minutes. When no sound of footsteps came from the hatchway, he breathed a little easier and shoved the spongy preservers off him.

After Ethan had left the motel room, Danny had waited five minutes before following. Then he'd raced through the wet streets, taking a shortcut to the marina across yards and over fences. But his fear of arriving too late had been for nothing. He'd had plenty of time before Ethan showed up, and he should have used it to find a bigger place to stow away.

For about the tenth time since climbing into the dark, musty space at the front of the cabin, he tried to straighten his legs and failed. Chances were he could climb out without being seen. Navigating the channels in the Sound would keep Ethan busy, and he wasn't likely to return to the cabin anytime soon. But Danny didn't want to risk it.

He had to time this just right.

If he came out of hiding too soon, Ethan would turn around and head back to Anacortes. On the other hand, if Danny waited until they reached the island, it would be too late. He'd heard Ethan's plans and knew things would get confusing on the island. Ethan needed his help, so the best time to show himself was when they stopped to let Ramirez into the smuggler's hold—which was about the neatest thing Danny had ever heard.

Meanwhile, he made himself as comfortable as possible, using one life preserver as a pillow and the others for warmth. Despite the cramped quarters and adrenaline pumping through him, he must have dozed off, because the next thing he knew, the boat slowed and came to a stop. A few minutes later, he heard the approaching footsteps as the two men returned to the cabin.

It was now or never.

Taking a deep breath, Danny lifted the lid of his hiding place and stood. Startled, both men spun around, Ethan leading with a gun.

"Wait." Danny raised his hands defensively. "It's me."

Ethan lowered his weapon, his fierce expression shifting to anger. "What the hell are you doing here? I told you to stay put."

Danny glanced from Ethan to the dark man beside him, then back. "Callie's my sister."

"Damn it." Ethan turned away, dragged a hand through his hair, then came back at Danny. "What the hell did you think you were doing? This isn't a game we're playing here, Danny. People are going to get hurt, and I don't want you to be one of them."

"I . . ." Words failed him, Ethan's anger smarting more than he'd expected. "I wanted to help."

For a moment no one spoke, and Danny fought the sudden sting behind his eyes. Ethan couldn't take him back, could he? It was too late.

Ramirez broke the tense silence. "Your plan will work better with the boy, Decker. You turn him over as a sign of good faith."

"And get him killed in the process?" Ethan turned his anger on the other man. "We're bringing a war to that island."

"And to the other children, no?" Ramirez motioned toward Danny. "The boy has a right to be here, they are his family."

The silence descended again, and Danny watched Ethan struggle with his choices.

"So are you going to take me back?" he asked, afraid of the answer.

Ethan looked at him. "You know I can't."

Ethan eased the throttle forward. To his right, Danny sat in the copilot's chair, his spine stiff.

Ethan tamped down his guilt.

He'd had no choice but to bring the boy. If they turned back, Ethan would have to cancel the mission for the night. That would mean another day in Anacortes, which they couldn't afford. With each passing hour, the risk of someone connected to the Haven discovering their presence grew exponentially. He had to catch Cox by surprise, and that meant hitting that island tonight.

Ethan glanced at Danny.

Besides, the boy was determined to help free his sister, and who was Ethan to fault him? As much as he hated to admit it, Danny had earned the right to be here. That didn't mean Ethan had to like it.

"What's in the backpack?" Ethan asked.

"Nothing much." Danny seemed surprised by the question. "The usual stuff, clothes, my Game Boy."

"Not the laptop?"

"I left it in the motel room."

"Good, we don't want them knowing we've been inside their computers. Now I want you to take this." Ethan pulled out his knife. "Just in case."

Danny's eyes brightened. "But won't you need it?"

"They'll search me for sure, but they might not look at you as closely. Get out the first-aid kit from under the console, and I'll tape the knife to your rib cage. Maybe we'll get lucky."

Danny found the white tape, then pulled up his shirt. Ethan used two long strips to secure the knife. "This is only a precaution. Use it only if we get separated and it's absolutely necessary." Ethan echoed his brother's words, spoken half a lifetime ago. "Don't tell anyone you have it."

Danny nodded.

"This is important, Danny. If the Keepers discover you have this, it's gone."

"I understand."

"Once we dock, follow my lead and do exactly what I tell you." They were drawing close, the protected cove of the southern shore emerging from the dark mass of the island. Ethan slowed the boat. "And don't be surprised by anything I say or do. Remember we're here—"

The glare of a spotlight cut off his words, and a disembodied voice rumbled through a bullhorn. "Bayliner motor yacht, this is a private island and you're in private waters. Turn about."

Ethan flipped his own microphone switch, sending his voice back across the water. "Haven Island, this is Ethan Decker. I'm expected."

The voice went silent for several minutes, but the light continued to track them as they moved toward the landing. Ethan could almost feel the hairs of a high-powered rifle scope following them as well.

Finally, the voice returned. "Put in."

Ethan maneuvered the boat toward its berth where Morrow waited with four armed men. A little closer, and Ethan could see they were obviously mercenaries, hard-looking and mean, men without conscience or allegiances. Ethan hadn't liked the idea of going up against Agency officers, righteous men following orders. Mercenaries would make what he and Ramirez intended easier.

He tossed out his lines, and Morrow directed two of his hired thugs to catch and tie them off.

Once the boat was secure, Morrow stepped forward. "You're early."

"Yeah, well, I aim to please."

Morrow scanned the deck. "Did you forget something?"

Ethan reached inside the hatchway, where he'd told Danny to wait, and grabbed him by his jacket collar. "I brought the kid."

"Hey—," Danny started as Ethan pulled him out into the open.

"Shut up, boy. No one wants to hear it." Ethan shoved Danny forward. "So, Morrow, why don't you run along and tell your boss I'm here?"

Morrow scowled, obviously unhappy with the reminder that he wasn't calling the shots. Stepping back brusquely, he motioned with his gun. "Off the boat."

Ethan gave Danny another shove, then followed him up onto the dock. With a gesture toward the large building set back from the shoreline, he said, "You first, gentlemen."

"Search him," Morrow said.

Ethan held out his arms, while one of Morrow's lackeys patted him down, relieving him of the Glock and Anna's .38. "Is this necessary?"

Morrow nodded toward Danny. "Check the kid's backpack."

Ethan tsked as the man rummaged through Danny's pack. "Better be careful, John, Mr. Cox wouldn't like it if you damaged one of his precious children."

"Shut up, Decker."

"Nothing here," the mercenary reported.

"Fine." Morrow looked back at Ethan and grinned. "Search the boat."

CHAPTER THIRTY-ONE

Something woke him.

Sitting upright, Paul listened. He heard a voice speaking through a bullhorn—though he couldn't make out the words—and the low putt of an approaching engine. Curious, he slipped from bed and made his way toward the front room of his private bungalow. Edging up to the window, he scrutinized the activity near the water.

Despite the late hour, lights blazed, highlighting the landing and searching the black waters of the inlet. The newly arrived boat lolled against its moorings. Morrow, flanked by several of his thugs, stood on the docks, talking to the craft's captain.

Paul hurried back to the bedroom.

Several days ago, he'd found Danny's electronic trail, threading its way through the Haven's system. After setting up firewalls to prevent him from accessing the children's records, Paul had let the boy roam. This time, however, he hadn't made the mistake of mentioning it to Cox. It had soon become obvious that Danny was gathering information about the island, maybe to pass on to someone planning a rescue attempt. Paul had experienced a rush of hope, because succeed or fail, a raid on the island might give him one last chance to escape.

Without turning on the lights, he rummaged along the top shelf of his closet. He'd hidden his clothes behind a stack of extra blankets, hoping the cleaning crew wouldn't find them. His hands closed on the soft bundle, and he breathed a sigh of relief. Quickly, he pulled on the dark clothes: black slacks and turtleneck, a heavy sweater, boots, and gloves.

Next, he retrieved the soft overnight bag from beneath his bed. He'd packed it the day Danny and Callie had disappeared and he had been tempted to pull it out more than once. Something had always stopped him; now he was out of time. If he failed to get away tonight, they would kill him for sure. Whether they caught him fleeing, or because Cox no longer needed him, dead was dead. Running was no longer a risk, or a choice.

Bag in hand, he went to the bathroom and lifted the lid off the toilet tank. Inside was a handgun—he didn't even remember what kind—stored in a plastic bag and taped to the side. He'd bought it years ago, never expecting to need it. Or so he'd told himself. Although some part of him must have known that he'd eventually have to run.

He slipped the gun into his pocket, then returned to the living room and took up his position near the window.

Now the real test, getting away from the bungalow.

Since Morrow had shown up with Callie and Sydney Decker, Cox's men had kept Paul under constant watch. They escorted him to and from his office and assigned a guard to stand outside his door. Morrow had said it was for his safety, but Paul knew better.

Movement brought Paul's attention back to the docks. Morrow and a couple of his men led two people from the boat toward the front entrance; one of them was Danny. Paul hadn't expected that: He'd thought the boy would stay behind. Two other of Morrow's soldiers boarded the boat. But whatever was about to happen, Paul was ready. All he needed was a distraction, just a few seconds to slip out the door.

Marco felt the boat rock as the two men boarded her.

They descended into the cabin, opening cabinets, drawers, storage compartments, and dumping the contents. On his back beneath them, Marco aimed the Beretta upward. If they found the latch to the smuggler's hold and opened it, he'd make them pay. That is, if they didn't riddle the deck with bullets first.

They took their time, banging around the cabin like a team of gorillas. Marco waited patiently, eager to put a bullet between a pair of dull eyes. He could imagine the first man's surprise as he faced his death. Killing the second man would be a contest of speed, a question of who wanted to live more.

Suddenly they left, cursing vividly about Morrow's heritage as they deserted the cabin, the boat swaying again as they scurried off her. Marco frowned. He'd actually warmed to the idea of taking on the two clowns. It would have screwed up Decker's carefully orchestrated plan, but it might have been worth it.

Tentatively, he pressed the release lever to shift the couch overhead. Then he waited: twenty seconds for the sound of returning feet.

Nothing.

He lifted the lid off his hiding place and shimmied out, staying close to the floor and clear of the portholes. He tucked the handguns into their holsters, slung the bag of explosives over his shoulder, and claimed the Remington from the hold. It was a nice piece, and he took a moment to stroke the walnut stock. He would enjoy using it. Too bad he didn't have time to get off a round or two before all hell broke loose.

Keeping low, he went topside and inched his way to the railing. He spotted only one man patrolling the area, which didn't mean there weren't others lurking about. From the waterfront, the land sloped upward across a wide expanse of open space to a building complex, backed by a wall of trees. And smack in the middle of the front yard was a landing pad, complete with helicopter.

Marco smiled.

Decker had identified several permanent fixtures for his little light show, but Marco thought he might improvise a bit. He'd start with the other two boats. They'd provide a nice prelude for things to come, while drawing Cox's men into the open.

He waited until the solitary guard had passed the *Sea Devil*, then Marco eased over the side. Slipping from shadow to shadow, he crossed to the nearest boat and flattened himself on the rough wooden dock beside it. He secured a lump of C4 to the hull just above the waterline, attaching a receiver with an electric blasting cap so he could trigger the explosion remotely. Again he had to wait for the guard to move off, then he repeated the procedure on the second boat.

Taking out the guard was the next step.

The man didn't even see it coming. He stopped to light a cigarette, bending away from the breeze that lifted off the water. Marco jumped him from behind, snapping his neck with one quick twist, and lowered the body silently into the inky water.

Marco set the third charge on the gas pump at the far end of the landing, one of Decker's targets. Then Marco darted ashore, skirting the tree line as he worked his way toward the helicopter pad and watched for more of Cox's men.

Where were they?

Once Decker had shown up, Cox should have pulled

them in from whatever remote corners of the island they patrolled. As if in answer to his question, a half dozen men carrying Uzis exited the woods. They scattered to various sentry positions around the building: two to flank the building's entrance, another couple to the docks, a fifth to the helicopter pad, and the last inside.

Things were beginning to get interesting.

Marco circled behind the landing pad, used the chopper to cover his approach, and dispensed with the guard in the same manner as the one on the docks. He dragged the body into the woods, then returned to set the fourth charge.

That left only Decker's main objective: a small concrete bunker near the main building. Marco gave the other men a wide berth as he edged his way toward his objective. He had to admit, the structure with its power wires sprouting like weeds from its roof would make a spectacular finale.

After setting the last charge, it was only a matter of timing. He returned to the woods and took up his position on a small rise overlooking the facility and its small marina. He placed the transmitter within easy reach and set his sights on one of the men outside the facility's double glass doors. When the fireworks started, he'd be the first to die.

CHAPTER THIRTY-TWO

Ethan paid careful attention as Morrow's men escorted him and Danny through the facility. He mentally checked off corridors and offices from Danny's drawings and descriptions. The boy had an eye for detail and hadn't missed much. Ethan guessed they were headed for a conference room buried deep within the building.

A few minutes later, Morrow confirmed Ethan's hunch.

Ethan sized up the room. "Not bad. One door and no windows." He'd have used this location himself if his and Morrow's positions had been reversed. "Is it soundproof?"

"Sit." Morrow indicated a chair against the far wall. "You, too, kid. Cox is on his way."

Ethan dropped into the chair. "You didn't have to wake him, did you?"

Morrow scowled and walked out, leaving behind two of his men. But Ethan doubted Cox's lapdog had gone farther than the other side of the door. He would stay close, keeping an eye on his prize.

Ethan scrutinized the guards. They didn't look too bright, but then, brains weren't a job requirement for mercenaries. Hopefully the two tearing the *Sea Devil* apart weren't the exception. Because if they found Ramirez, this charade would end real quick.

Everything hung on the smuggler's hold.

The irony of that didn't escape him. There was something almost humorous about men like him and Ramirez relying on a criminal device for survival.

Glancing at Danny, he gave the kid a tight smile. The boy was holding up well, which wasn't surprising. He'd proved himself more than once over the last week.

Cox walked into the room. "Well, this is a twist." He barely glanced at the boy before settling his gaze on Ethan. "I expected more finesse from you."

"Sorry, I'm fresh out."

Cox frowned. "Where's Ramirez?"

"Do you think I'm stupid enough to bring him with me?"

"Don't play games with me, Decker."

"No games." Ethan held up his hands, palms out. "You have the kid and I have Ramirez. He's all yours, once Sydney and I are safely off this rock."

Cox turned to Morrow. "Bring her."

Morrow looked ready to object. "What about the boy?"

"Leave him for now."

As Morrow left, Ethan stretched out in the expensive leather chair. "I have to congratulate you, Avery, I didn't know you were so devious."

Cox ignored him.

"Putting Morrow on my team to kill Ramirez was a good move." Ethan nodded his approval. "Too bad it didn't work, it would have saved us all a lot of trouble. Instead the kid dies, and you end up with the Agency's top assassin on a rampage. Talk about bad luck."

"You don't know what you're talking about."

"Don't I? George Taleb, or should I say James Cooley, runs from the island with one of your precious children. But you can't allow them to get away. They know too much. So you send in Ramirez, but he doesn't take care of the kid."

"I misjudged you, Ethan." Cox settled into a conference chair and folded his hands. "You have quite an imagination."

"How long have you been looking for Ramirez without success? Three years? So you decide to pull me back into the game to do your dirty work. Not bad. A bit inconvenient for me, but a good strategy on your part."

"You talk too much."

"Funny, I said that same thing to Ramirez not more than," he glanced at his watch, "a couple of hours ago."

The door opened, and Morrow shoved Sydney into the room.

Relief flooded her eyes when she spotted Ethan, then she saw Danny. "Oh, no."

"Kill her," Cox said flatly.

All color fled her face. "What—"

"Sorry about this, Doc." Morrow grabbed her arm, pulling her back and pressing a gun to her head.

"If you shoot her . . ." Ethan put ice in his voice and called Cox's bluff. "You'll never get Ramirez."

Cox seemed to consider. "Maybe I should kill the boy instead." He drew a pocket Colt from his jacket and pointed it at Danny.

Next to Ethan, Danny flinched.

"No," Sydney pleaded. "Ethan, do something."

"You won't hurt him, either. He's worth too much alive."

Cox studied Ethan a moment, then lowered his gun. "You're right." His eyes hardened, his smile turning deadly. "Morrow, take out her kneecaps, one at a time."

Morrow grinned and took aim.

"Wait." Ethan lifted his hands. "You've made your point." Hopefully he'd bought Ramirez enough time.

"Where is he?" Cox asked.

"On the boat."

Cox looked at Morrow, who shook his head. "We searched it."

"He's there," Ethan assured them. "Your goons didn't look hard enough."

"Take a couple of men and make sure." Cox grabbed Sydney's arm and dragged her into the chair next to his. "I can handle Dr. Decker and her errant husband."

Morrow left, and Ethan looked at Sydney. She was pale, but her eyes betrayed her anger. Good. Because no matter how things went with Ramirez and the boat, she'd need her anger to get through the next few hours.

"You know what I still haven't figured out?" Ethan said. Cox looked bored. "I thought you had all the answers."

"How did you get Anna to go along with the children's escape, when she knew Ramirez was hunting her?"

Cox laughed. "You never were as smart as you thought you were, Decker." He relaxed in his chair, his expression smug. "I had nothing to do with Anna's decision to run with the kids. She came up with that brilliant idea all by herself. Pretty stupid of her, don't you think?"

Ethan struggled to keep his anger in check. Like Ethan, Anna had been recruited, trained, and used by Cox. He owed her more than a flippant account of the mistake that had killed her.

"Opportunity knocked, I acted." Cox waved a dismissive hand toward Danny. "Because you're right, that boy and his sister are far too valuable to run free, even to bring down Marco Ramirez."

Ethan scooted forward in his chair. "Why, so you can use them like lab rats?"

Cox ignored the question. "As you said, it would have

been more expedient if you'd just gone after Ramirez when he killed your son."

Ethan froze.

Across the room, the last bit of color drained from Sydney's face.

"Oh, I see." Cox turned to her. "You didn't know."

Ethan gripped the chair arms. "Cox."

"You know, Dr. Decker." Cox radiated charm, taking Sydney's hand and patting it. "I believe honesty is always the best policy in a marriage, don't you?"

Sydney, obviously dazed, looked at Ethan.

"You see," Cox continued, "your son's death wasn't an accident." He shot Ethan a satisfied smile. "Someone murdered him."

Her eyes begged Ethan to deny it.

"There was a certain logic to it," Cox said. "Your husband . . . Excuse me, your ex-husband, killed a child under Marco Ramirez's protection. So in Marco's mind, it was fair retribution to take your son."

Sydney seemed to sink into herself.

Ethan lunged to his feet, but the guards snapped to attention, weapons drawn, and stopped him cold. "You son of a bitch."

Cox smiled.

The next instant, an explosion wiped it from his face.

CHAPTER THIRTY-THREE

The building trembled, jarring Sydney back from hell.

The men in the room came alive as well: Cox jumping to his feet and dragging her with him; the two guards scanning the walls and ceilings as if they'd fall; Danny gripping the arms of his chair.

And Ethan. Immobile. And unsurprised.

"Check that out," Cox ordered one of the guards. "And you," he said to the other, "don't take your eyes off—"

A second blast rumbled, followed by brief popping sounds.

"You." Cox turned on Ethan, waving his gun. "This is your doing."

Ethan didn't move, his expression deadly calm.

When the third explosion rocked the building, the lights flickered and died. Silence filled the room.

It took Sydney a mere second to react. This could be her only chance. Cox had a vicelike grip on her upper arm, and before she could second-guess herself, she drove her fist down into his crotch.

Grunting in pain, he released her.

Reeling backward, she collided with a chair and grabbed at the table. Darkness blinded her. Her eyes should have adjusted by now. Why couldn't she see anything? Shapes at least. There was only sound, echoing through the inky blackness with terrible clarity: bodies slamming against bodies, muffled grunts and curses, furniture breaking.

Fear gripped her.

She backed farther, heart racing and hands trembling as she attempted to get her footing. Her fear wasn't just for herself, however. It was for Danny. And for Ethan, in the center of the maelstrom.

Then a shot. The crack ripping through the darkness and ringing in her ears. A door slammed. Then silence.

"Ethan?" she whispered, afraid he wouldn't answer.

"I'm here."

Relief coursed through her.

The lights blinked on, dimmer, as the backup power system kicked in. Ethan crouched beside one of the guards, stripping him of weapons and ammunition. The man was unconscious or dead. Sydney didn't want to know which.

"Danny?" she said, looking for the boy.

He crawled out from beneath the table, his face pale and eyes wide. "Here."

"Thank God." Sydney wrapped her arms around him before he could object.

Ethan stood and slung the guard's automatic weapon over his shoulder. "Are you both okay?"

Sydney nodded, though she doubted she'd ever be truly okay again. At least, not for a very long time.

"Ramirez hit the island's power station," Ethan said, moving toward the door.

"He's here?" Surprise and shreds of her earlier anger surfaced. "He's causing these explosions?"

"It was the only way," Ethan answered, but his concentration was elsewhere. Holding a handgun as though it were an extension of his arm, he edged through the door, pivoting first one way then another. "Come on," he said, gesturing for them to follow.

"Where's Cox?" Danny asked.

"Probably out regrouping." Ethan ushered them through the door. "We need to get out of here while we can."

Another explosion rippled through the walls, followed by the distant cracks of gunfire.

"Where's Callie's room?" Ethan asked.

"This way." Danny started forward, but Ethan grabbed his arm.

"Stay behind me."

They hurried through the empty corridors to the enclosed breezeway, which connected the facility's two main buildings: administration in one, and the school, hospital, and dormitories in the other. Except for the occasional blurts of gunfire outside, it was too quiet.

"Upstairs," Danny said as they entered the far building. "The steps are over there."

Silence drenched the second floor as it had the first.

Sydney strained to hear something, anything other than the soft pad of their feet. The abnormal stillness unnerved her, testing the grip she had on her fear. She wanted to shout. Or scream. Everything about this place felt wrong.

Ethan must have sensed something as well, because he slowed, checking around each corner before proceeding. Sydney kept close, one hand on his back while the other clutched Danny's. The building seemed deserted, but she knew that wasn't true. Two dozen children lived in this facility, and Cox wouldn't leave them unguarded.

Finally they reached what Sydney guessed was the hall leading to the dormitories. Ethan inched around the turn but jerked back, pressing himself against the wall.

"Guards," he mouthed and motioned for her and Danny to stay back.

"There's another way," Danny said in a whisper. "Come on."

"Wait—" Ethan didn't speak the word, but Sydney

clearly read it on his lips. It was too late. Danny had already slipped his hand from hers and started back the way they'd come. She and Ethan had to hurry to catch up.

Danny led them to a door several corridors away. "These are all classrooms."

"How will we get to Callie?" Sydney asked.

The boy just smiled as Ethan checked out the room before waving them inside. Danny went directly to a desk near the wall, clambered on top, and removed the mesh cover from a maintenance shaft.

Of course, Sydney thought.

"These run all through the building," Danny said. "It's how I used to get into Callie's room without the Keepers finding out."

Ethan stepped up to have a look. "I'm not crazy about the idea, but I don't want to get into a firefight on a floor full of kids, either." He readjusted the automatic weapon he'd taken off the guard and holstered the handgun, then gave Danny a boost. "Wait here, Sydney. We'll be back with the girl."

"No way." Without waiting for Ethan's response, she climbed into the opening behind him. "I'm coming."

Ethan mumbled something incoherent, but Sydney ignored him. He'd gotten her into this, he wasn't leaving her behind now.

As they crawled through the network of heavy, industrial aluminum, the last hour closed in on Sydney. In the aftermath of the explosion, she'd nearly forgotten Cox's claim.

Nicky murdered? Was it possible? Had Ethan known?

The idea churned her stomach, nauseating her. Of course he'd known. And he'd kept it from her.

Another blast, and the shaft bucked and groaned, straining against its supports. Sydney froze, fearing the structure would collapse around them, trapping them in an aluminum coffin. No one would ever find them, or know about the wrongs visited on the children of this place.

The tremor passed, and the cold alloy beneath them stabilized. Sydney closed her eyes, fighting back tears of relief.

"Damn it," Ethan said. "It feels like he's trying to blow up the whole place."

The comment fanned her anger. "Are you sure he's not?" She wiped dust from her eyes, smearing it across her cheeks.

Ethan glanced back at her, but in the dim light she couldn't make out his expression. It didn't matter. Even if she could see his face, she couldn't trust what it told her.

Stop it. She couldn't do this now, not when Callie's life hung in the balance.

"Let's go," she said. "You're going to lose Danny."

The boy had scrambled ahead of them, smaller, more nimble, and more accustomed to traveling through aluminum tunnels.

Ethan hesitated, then continued on.

A few yards farther, and Danny popped the grate ahead of them and clambered out of the shaft. "Hey, Callie."

Ethan and Sydney followed him into a small room identical to the one Sydney had occupied. Callie was fully dressed and hugging her brother. "I knew you'd come."

"You're not sick anymore," he said, looking a bit embarrassed by his sister's show of affection.

"I'm all better."

"Hey, sweetie." Sydney wrapped the little girl in her arms. "You feeling okay?" She pressed a hand to Callie's forehead. "No fever or anything?"

"I'm fine."

"We were worried about you," Danny said.

"Let's have the reunion later." Ethan stood near the

door, the gun once again in his hand, listening. "We need to get out of here."

"What about the others?" Callie looked from Ethan to Sydney. "We can't leave them."

"She's right," Sydney said. "We have to take all the children with us."

"Forget it," Ethan said. "We can't even get to them."

"We can go through the maintenance shafts again," Danny suggested.

"Then what?" Ethan asked. "How are we supposed to get them past those guards?" He positioned a chair under the vent. "Let's go. If the four of us make it out alive, we'll send back help."

Callie settled on the bed with crossed arms, resembling her stubborn older brother. "I'm not going unless everyone goes."

Sydney sat next to her. "I'm with Callie."

"Danny . . ."

He backed up. "I'm not going, either."

"This is nuts."

"Do we really have time to argue about it, Ethan?" Sydney asked. "You won't change our minds. So, let's just go get the rest of the children and be done with it."

Ethan glanced from one of them to another, his frustration obvious. "You three are crazy, you know that?"

"But we're right," Danny said. "We can't leave them."

"Okay, where are they?"

"The girls' dormitory is at the end of the hall," Danny volunteered. "The boys' is on the next corridor over."

Ethan just looked at them, and Sydney winced. Of course there would be separate dormitories. It would make their escape more difficult.

To Ethan's credit, he simply shook his head and gestured toward the chair. "Danny, you lead."

Both children climbed into the shaft, with Ethan and Sydney behind them. They emerged cramped and dirty a few minutes later into a large room with a dozen frightened girls in pajamas, the youngest about Callie's age, the oldest Danny's.

"It's okay," Sydney said. "We're here to help."

They shied away from her, closing in around Danny and Callie instead with a buzz of questions.

Ethan pulled Sydney aside. "There's no way we're getting these kids back through that shaft. We have—"

Suddenly, gunfire erupted outside the room.

"Quick." Ethan spun toward the door. "Take cover."

The children froze.

"Hide!" Danny yelled, and they scattered behind beds and into closets.

Sydney crouched beside a desk, and Ethan pressed his back to the wall beside the door, both hands gripping his handgun.

More shots, and the door crashed open. Two men burst in. Back to back, one guarding their retreat from the hallway, while the second swept the room with his weapon. Ethan swung around, grabbing the first man's arm, yanking him off balance and firing twice in quick succession, dropping the man in the hall, then the other at close range.

Sydney suppressed her gasp of horror as the bodies tumbled to the floor, and Ethan flattened himself against the wall again. All she could think of was the children, who'd just watched two men shot to death.

Silence.

Then, a distinctly Latin voice, "*Amigo,* is that you causing such havoc?"

A moment later, Marco Ramirez stepped through the doorway.

CHAPTER THIRTY-FOUR

Ethan lowered his gun. He never thought he'd welcome the sight of Ramirez. "You're lucky I didn't kill you."

"You are still alive, too, I see. A shame."

"How bad is it out there?"

The assassin shrugged. "There are a few guns looking for me. And you. When they do not find us outside, they will come here."

"Then we better get going." Ethan slipped the dead guard's .44 Magnum into his holster. "Danny, get everyone together."

One at a time, starting with Callie and Danny, a group of frightened little girls crept out from the shadows and corners of the room.

"Have them put on some warm clothes," Ethan said. "Quick."

Ramirez looked stunned. "What is this?"

"What does it look like? We're taking them with us."

"This was not part of our bargain."

"It is now. That is, if you want off this island before Cox's reinforcements arrive." Ethan turned to Danny. "Where's the boys' dorm?"

"It's just down the hall."

"You promised me answers," Ramirez said.

"These kids are your answers."

"Ethan." Sydney stepped forward, giving Ramirez a

wide berth. "He's right. We can't leave without proof of what's going on here."

Right now, all he cared about was getting everyone out of here alive. "We're leaving."

"Cox will try to gather records." She acted as if Ethan hadn't spoken. "Notes, laboratory findings, whatever he can put his hands on. He'll download what he needs and destroy the rest. We have to stop him."

"It's suicide, Sydney."

She turned to Danny. "Where would Cox get access to those files?"

"Dr. Turner's office," Danny answered. "It's in the administration building. I can take you."

"Wait a minute—," Ethan started.

"No, you go with the others and I'll catch up. Ethan, tell me where to meet you."

"Have you lost your mind?"

"I will go with her," Ramirez offered.

Ethan turned on the assassin. "Like hell."

"I don't want him anywhere near me," Sydney said, without even glancing at Ramirez. "Now, tell me where to meet you."

Ethan felt like the only sane person in the room, but he knew he was wasting his breath trying to change Sydney's mind. "Okay, look. We can't all go traipsing around this facility. I'll take you to Turner's office and—"

"I'm going with you," Danny insisted. "I know the Haven's computer system better than anyone."

The boy was right. Besides, he was every bit as stubborn as Sydney and not likely to back down. "Okay, you're with us. Ramirez, take the girls and get the boys from down the hall."

Holding up his hands, Ramirez backed away.

"I'll get your proof," Ethan said. "I give you my word. Just get these kids to safety."

The assassin scanned the small faces, and Ethan understood his reservations. Setting explosives and facing an army of mercenaries was one thing, being responsible for young lives was something else entirely. Something neither of them had succeeded at before.

"There's a boat waiting to pick us up on the north side of the island. It belongs to Tony Rio, and since he owes you his life, he should be very accommodating."

"I'll go with you." Callie stepped forward and took Ramirez's hand. He stiffened. "I know the back way out of the building." She lifted soft blue eyes to the assassin. "And the quickest way through the woods."

Ramirez looked ready to bolt.

"It's okay," she said. "Danny and I did it the last time we ran away." She smiled, and Ramirez visibly folded.

"Okay, listen," Ethan said. "There's no landing dock on the north shore, just a small cove. The boat will be waiting in deep water, so you'll have to signal before they send a dinghy ashore." Ethan glanced at Callie, then refocused on the other man. "Lift your weapon over your head with both hands."

Ramirez nodded his understanding, and Callie turned to gather the others. Then Ramirez took over, barking orders like a drill sergeant. "You children, stay together and behind me."

"Ramirez," Ethan said as they headed for the door. The assassin stopped. Ethan moved in close, where only Ramirez could hear. "You better be on that beach when we get there."

"Do not worry about that, *amigo*. You and I have unfinished business."

Once they'd gone, Ethan checked the Uzi. It wasn't a weapon he'd normally have chosen, but considering the resistance they might encounter, he was grateful for the added firepower. "Okay, Danny, which way?"

The boy led them back down the stairs and across to

the administration building. From outside came the occasional burst of an automatic weapon or a small rumble as one of Ramirez's fires reached another source of fuel. Inside, everything remained quiet, but Ethan knew that wouldn't last. They were running out of time, with only minutes before what remained of Cox's forces decided to search the building.

Not surprisingly, the door to Turner's outer office was locked.

Ethan pressed a hand to his lips, then gestured for Sydney and Danny to stand back. One hard kick, and the door splintered open. Inside, Cox's man went for his weapon and died, spraying bullets as lead from Ethan's Uzi caught him in the chest. Ethan crossed to the inner office, slamming through the door as Cox leapt from his chair and fumbled for the Colt in his pocket.

He was too slow.

Ethan pinned him against the far wall. "You son of a bitch, I ought to kill you right now."

"But you won't." Even with Ethan's hands around his throat, Cox was arrogant as hell. "You don't have the balls."

Ethan tightened his grip.

"Don't," Sydney said. "Let the authorities take care of him."

Yeah, right. Men like Cox somehow always managed to slip through the legal system's fingers, but Ethan let him live. For now. "Danny, find me something to tie him up with."

Sydney settled in front of the computer. "Looks like he already started the download, medical records, the children's files. It's going to save us time."

Danny helped Ethan bind and gag Cox, using cords from the blinds and towels from Turner's private bathroom, then went to help Sydney.

Ethan took a position at the door. "How long will this take?"

"Just a few . . ."

He glanced back at her. "What is it?"

Danny looked confused, but Sydney obviously understood what she was seeing. She keyed in more commands. "I'll tell you later. Just give me a few minutes."

Turning his attention back to the silent hallway, Ethan knew they were about out of time. It had been several minutes since he'd heard anything from outside, and his recent exchange of gunfire with Cox's guard would call attention to the building. "Come on, Sydney, hurry."

She didn't answer, the clicking of the keyboard echoing through the room. Finally, she pushed away from the desk. "That's it. Let's get out of here."

"Have you got it?" Ethan asked.

"You bet." She held up a CD, gave him a half smile, then slipped it into her pocket. "Oh, one more thing." She turned, walked over to Cox, and slapped him across the face. Then, she joined Danny and Ethan at the door. "Okay, let's go."

As they left Cox's office, Ethan recognized the sound of running boots pounding against tile. "Get us out of here," he said to Danny. "Fast."

The boy took off, threading his way deeper into the building with Ethan and Sydney right behind him. Finally they reached a large storage area filled with boxes and crates. It was the loading dock, and the back door out of the building.

Ethan had to admit: The boy was good.

Outside, the cool damp air hit him, along with a greater sense of foreboding. Their pursuers weren't far behind. He could almost feel them breathing down his neck. The temptation to face them was great, the need to turn the game around almost overwhelming.

Gripping Sydney's arm, he followed Danny into the woods. They hadn't gone far when Ethan slowed, sensing something ahead. "Danny, wait."

He half turned at Ethan's command, then fell back as someone stepped into their path. A man held a boy in a choke hold, a .38 automatic pointed at the kid's head.

Danny stepped toward them. "Adam?"

"Danny, no." Ethan aimed the Uzi at the pair, knowing damn well he couldn't use it. "Whoever you are, let the boy go."

"I'm a doctor here, Dr. Paul Turner, and I need your help." He shifted his hold on Adam, tightening it and using his body as a shield. "I don't want to hurt him."

"You're not doing a great job of convincing me of that."

"I just want off this island." Turner's hands visibly shook. "Is that too much to ask?"

"Drop that weapon and we'll talk."

"Put down yours first."

Ethan might risk a head shot with the Glock or even the .44 under his arm, but not the Uzi. "I'm putting it down." He positioned himself in front of Danny and Sydney and held out the weapon, slowly laying it on the ground. "There. Now let the boy go."

"Do I have your word you'll get me off this island?"

"No promises until you put down that gun." Ethan sensed Danny behind him, then felt the hard butt of a knife pressing against his spine.

"I'll kill him." Turner yanked the boy closer. "I swear."

Ethan believed him. The man was too rattled to think clearly and realize that with Adam dead, he'd have no leverage.

"You win." Ethan raised his left hand, counting on the darkness to conceal the other behind him, and accepted the open blade from Danny. "Keep the gun. But you can't walk through the woods holding Adam like that."

Turner hesitated, his eyes darting toward the complex as distant shouts reached them. Cox's men had obviously regrouped.

"We don't have a lot of time." Ethan looked directly at the boy in Turner's grasp, hoping Danny and Callie weren't the only gutsy kids on this island. "If they catch us, we're all dead."

Adam's eyes remained steady, resolved, as he gave Ethan a single nod of understanding. The voices drew closer, and Turner became more agitated. "Are you—"

Adam rammed his elbow into Turner's gut. He grunted, his hold loosening. Adam dove forward, and Ethan hurled the knife, both finding their target at the same instant. The boy hitting the ground, the knife burying itself in Turner's throat.

Sydney and Danny were at Adam's side, helping him up, before Turner's body hit the ground. Ethan retrieved his knife and turned to the others. "You okay, Adam?"

He nodded. "Thanks."

"No problem. Come on, let's get out of here."

Ethan grabbed the Uzi, and they started up again, running this time, the shouts chasing them. They wouldn't make it, Ethan realized, not this way. He slowed. "Danny, go on ahead and get Sydney and Adam to the boat."

"Where are you—"

The others stopped, too, and Ethan waved them on. "I'll be right behind you. Go on."

He thought the boy would argue, but for once he seemed ready to follow orders. He punched Adam lightly in the shoulder. "Let's go."

"Hey," Ethan said. Danny looked back at him, and Ethan tossed him the knife. "Good job."

Danny grinned. "We'll wait for you on the beach."

Ethan turned back, fading into the thick woods. No longer the hunted, now *he* was the hunter. And the men on the trail had just become his prey.

He slipped into the shadows of a nearby tangle of wild rhododendrons. Crouching low, he watched. Two men appeared from the trees, their forms little more than dark silhouettes in the night. They moved cautiously. Too many of their comrades had died tonight for them to ignore the danger. Nor could they have missed Turner's body a ways back.

Ethan waited for them to pass.

He took the first from behind, bringing the butt of the Uzi down on his skull. The lead man turned, and Ethan kicked the weapon from his hand then swung around, driving an elbow into the man's temple, dropping him where he stood.

With both men sprawled on the forest floor, Ethan squatted and turned their faces to see their features. He'd expected—had hoped for—Morrow, but didn't have time to waste on disappointment when he recognized neither man.

He needed to move.

Surging to his feet, he followed in Danny's wake. Maybe Morrow was already dead, caught by Ramirez's deadly rifle.

A few minutes later, he broke through the trees onto the rocky beach. In the cove, two boats waited. The charter Rio had promised and beyond it, the *Sea Devil*.

"Damn, Rio."

He'd gone after his precious boat on his own before Ethan had given him the all clear. Fortunately, several hundred yards to his right, the dinghy stood ready for its last launch, Ramirez at its helm eager to shove off. Danny and Sydney stood side by side at the edge of the water, watching the woods. Waiting for him.

Yet, something was wrong.

Ethan started forward, scanning the surroundings. Nothing. Except a premonition of disaster pricking his spine. A gut feeling he'd learned never to ignore. Then a dark form emerged from the trees.

And time slipped out of synch. Slowing.

"No!" The word tore from Ethan's lungs, a long echoing single syllable. He stumbled over the rocks, his legs heavy, leading with the Uzi, firing.

Too far.

Ramirez swung around, a man in slow motion. First toward Ethan, then the other. His mouth opened. A warning. And dove forward, a dark explosion bursting from his chest as he knocked Danny to the sand.

Time shifted into motion, returning.

And the sound of Ethan's scream ripped through the night, punctuated by the staccato of automatic-weapon fire as he emptied the Uzi into John Morrow.

Too late.

CHAPTER THIRTY-FIVE

Strong, unfamiliar hands helped Sydney into the waiting boat, then hauled up the body of Marco Ramirez. Ethan clambered aboard last, and after exchanging a few quick words with him, the two strangers quickly descended into the dinghy and pushed off.

"They're heading back to the *Sea Devil*," Ethan said, nodding toward the second craft anchored outside the cove. "They don't want to be around if anyone comes after us."

Sydney's stomach tightened, a sensation she'd grown all too familiar with these last days. "And will they?"

"That depends on if Cox was on top of the food chain or . . ." He broke off, suddenly focusing on her, as if seeing her for the first time. "Forget them. What about you, Syd?" Lifting a hand, he brushed a strand of hair from her cheek. "Did Cox or any of his thugs hurt you?"

She fought the sting of tears, Ethan's concern threatening her control in ways nothing else could. "No, they didn't touch me."

"Are you sure?"

"Yes." She stepped back, away from his touch and the temptation to seek reassurance in his arms. Later. When this was done, they'd have time for comfort, and maybe more. "Shouldn't we be leaving?"

He hesitated, glanced around, then nodded. "Yeah. Check on the kids, while I get us out of here." He turned away, stopped, and looked back at her one last time before starting toward the bridge. "Danny, you're with me."

A few minutes later the engines rumbled to life and the deck tilted as the boat started to move. Then she went below, where the children had overwhelmed the cabin, covering every available surface, crowding together, little ones held by the older ones. In the absence of parents or adults who cared, they'd created their own family, and it about broke Sydney's heart.

With Callie's help, she tended them. Except for a few scratches and bruises, they'd come away from Haven Island unscathed. At least physically. She didn't know about their emotional state. These children had lived all their lives on that island and knew nothing else. Some of them would adjust and take to the outside world as eagerly as Danny and Callie. Others wouldn't.

For now, Callie circulated among them, calming them with just a touch or a word. So much power for one so young. She seemed to have the gift of a born healer, which was ironic, considering what Sydney knew about the girl.

She wondered what would become of Callie and her courageous brother. Or Adam, the oldest and obvious leader, who sat with the younger children gathered around him, telling them about his escape as if it were a tale from a child's adventure book. What about the others, who knew nothing about what men had made of them?

Everything inside her ached for these children, for the lives that had been stolen from them. They may have escaped the island, but their nightmare had just begun.

When Danny came down, Sydney went topside. The cool air washed over her, but did little to ease her mind. She joined Ethan on the bridge, trying not to look at the canvas-covered body strapped to the deck. In the end, Marco Ramirez had exchanged his life for Danny's. She couldn't reconcile that with what Cox had told her about Nicky's death. No, not his death, his murder.

"How are things below?" Ethan asked.

She wrapped her arms around her waist. "Okay."

Noticing, Ethan took off his jacket and draped it over her shoulders. She knew better than to protest and slipped her arms into the sleeves, the lingering scent of the man doing more to warm her than the jacket. "Thank you."

"I radioed ahead to the local authorities," he said. "And told them we're transporting a couple dozen kids who've been held captive."

"I suppose that's for the best." Although she hated the idea of these children being shuffled into yet another system. Once the world found out about them, they'd end up caged again.

"The sheriff's department will meet us when we dock." He fell silent, while the steady whoosh of water against the hull infused the night with a false serenity.

After a few minutes, he asked, "Did Adam explain how he ended up in the woods with Turner?"

She eased into the seat beside Ethan. "He was in the infirmary, after a bout with the same flu as Callie. A male nurse was watching him, but when things started blowing up, the man went to investigate." She pressed her lips together and shrugged. "Adam took off but ran into Turner in the woods."

"He was lucky," Ethan said. "If not for Turner, Adam might not have found us."

Maybe. But she wished he and Danny had been spared the sight of Ethan's knife in Turner's throat.

Shivering, she pulled Ethan's jacket tighter around her and scanned the dark waters. The second boat was no longer in sight. She couldn't blame them. Not after what she'd seen in those files. These children were more valuable than she'd realized. And more dangerous.

"Turner was experimenting on them," Ethan said. "Wasn't he?"

"He was testing them." She explained that Turner had developed a means to alter the genetic makeup of human embryos to create healthier children. Then she filled in the gaps from the files. "Each child was engineered for a particular immunity, either biological or viral."

"You mean, they don't get sick?"

"They're only resistant to whatever illness or disease they've been designed to withstand. Except for Callie, she's the culmination of Turner's research, and supposedly immune to multiple forms of biological and viral infections."

Ethan glanced at her. "Why isn't that a good thing?"

The same question had tormented Sydney since Turner had first told her about his accomplishments. Ultimately, she believed genetic research had the potential to help mankind immeasurably. "It was Turner's methods that were wrong." Horribly wrong. She'd downloaded files filled with her worst fears about his activities. He'd documented cases, hundreds, maybe thousands of failed trials. She hadn't had time to read them, but certain key words had leapt out at her: stillborn, deformed, defective.

"He took shortcuts and made mistakes," she said. "And in order to confirm his results, he infected the children to see what would happen." She shuddered at the thought of Danny's missing friends. "Sometimes, it killed them."

Ethan's grip tightened on the wheel. "And you got all that on disk?"

"I got enough, and we have the children."

She returned to her thoughts, to her fears for the children and the topic she and Ethan had studiously avoided. Nicky. Sooner or later they'd have to talk about what had happened to their son.

"Sydney?" Ethan said, his voice concerned. "Are you okay?"

She nodded, an automatic reaction at best. How could any of them be okay? "Ethan . . ." She faltered, questioning her timing, then pushed on. "I don't blame you for Nicky."

He tensed, then seemed to deflate as he let out his breath. "I wish you hadn't found out that way."

"Me, too." Although she doubted there was any good way to find out that your son had been murdered. "Would you have ever told me?"

He considered. "I don't know."

She knew, even if he didn't. He wouldn't have told her, he would have kept his secret, letting it rip him apart inside before sharing the burden with her. Because that's what he did. He protected.

Her heart softened toward him.

Ethan was a compelling mix of strengths and flaws. He'd walked unarmed into a viper's nest to rescue a child, but he'd also killed without hesitation. Or remorse.

She knew the latter, at least, should appall her. It was a

side of him she'd never seen, and it went against everything she believed. Despite that, she couldn't despise him or even condemn his actions. He'd done what he'd thought was right, what was necessary, and saved their lives in the process.

"Sydney?"

She realized she'd been staring, felt her cheeks heat, and looked away quickly. "Sorry."

"Don't be." Ethan reached over and found her hand, buried within the too-long sleeves of his jacket. Without taking his eyes off the channel, he drew her hand to his lips and kissed her fingers. "Tell me, Syd, where do you and I go from here?"

The question didn't surprise her. She'd asked herself the same thing while locked away on that island, while wishing for one last glimpse of the man who'd been her husband. And that hadn't been the first time. From the morning he'd burst into her condo, they'd danced around each other, pretending they no longer felt the pull of attraction. It had been a lie.

She'd never stopped loving him, wanting him.

Yet so much had happened, and it wasn't over yet. "I don't know," she admitted. "Until these children are settled, it won't feel finished. Or safe." She slipped her hand from his to brush it against his cheek. "Ask me again later, when everything is . . . over. Will you? Please?"

He turned his face into her palm and kissed her gently, his gaze catching and holding hers. "Try and stop me."

She smiled, his promise warming her, before she turned away.

After that, Sydney couldn't say how long it took them, but they finally reached the mainland under a sky tinged with the first blush of morning. The authorities had directed Ethan to a small, private dock away from the main marina at Anacortes. Two vehicles waited at the end of the pier, a van and a dark sedan. Sydney returned

Ethan's jacket, concealing the holstered gun under his arm. Danny had come topside and jumped out as Ethan maneuvered the boat into a slip, caught the lines, and tied them off.

"Wait here." Ethan dropped onto the dock. "I want to talk to these people first."

Sydney scrambled off the boat after him. "I'm coming." Whatever became of these children, she was part of it.

"I'll watch the other kids," Danny volunteered, and she thanked him with a smile.

She hurried to catch up with Ethan, who suddenly slowed, his right hand sliding beneath his jacket as five men got out of the vehicles. Two hung back, while the other three started toward them, one leading, the other two following, bodyguards in suits.

The leader looked vaguely familiar, but out of context, like . . . She stopped cold. "Charles?"

In a blur of motion, Ethan drew his gun. As did the others, the bodyguards behind Charles and the one near the car, a rifle materializing on its hood. All three weapons aimed at her and Ethan.

Fear raked its way down her spine. "Charles?" She took a step toward him. "What's going on?"

He ignored her and spoke to Ethan. "Put down the weapon."

Ethan held his place, his gun pointed at Charles's head. "I don't think so."

"You're outnumbered, three to one."

"Ever see what a .44 Magnum does to a man's skull?" Ethan's eyes were hard, cold. "At close range?"

Charles flinched, licked his lips. "You pull that trigger, and Sydney dies."

"Looks like a stalemate to me. So, who pulls the trigger first?"

"No one has to die." Charles sounded desperate. "My

name is Charles Braydon, and I'm here to make a deal. You give me what I want, and the two of you walk free."

Suddenly, she remembered her conversation with Paul Turner, and it all came together, locking into place. "You son of a bitch," she said. "You know all about Haven Island and what they did there, don't you? You're behind it."

CHAPTER THIRTY-SIX

Ethan had no doubt.

Charles Braydon had his dirty little fingers all over the Haven. Which answered Ethan's question about Cox's position on the food chain. "What do you want?"

"You have something that belongs to me." Braydon crossed his arms, trying to steady his nerves. Not an easy task for a man with a gun to his head. "A disk."

"You'll have to be a little more specific."

Braydon frowned. "My people on Haven Island tell me you downloaded some files, some very sensitive files. I want them."

"We don't have your disk," Sydney claimed. "I destroyed it."

"Who are you kidding? I know you better than that, Sydney." His smile resembled a sneer. "You may be outraged by Turner's methods, but you're fascinated by his science."

"Not enough to use children as guinea pigs," she shot back.

"Hey." Ethan flicked the muzzle of his gun, recapturing Braydon's attention. "What happens if we give you this disk?"

At his side, Sydney gasped.

"The two of you walk away," Braydon said.

"With the kids."

"Sorry, just you and the little woman."

"Forget it," Sydney said. "You're not getting your hands on those children."

"They're already mine. It's just a question of whether I have to kill you to get to them." Braydon obviously thought he held all the cards.

Except Ethan still had the man's head in his sights and wouldn't mind pulling the trigger. "Why would you let us go?"

"Why not? Without the disk, you have no proof. Everything on Haven Island was destroyed within an hour after your departure. Besides, who would believe you? You're wanted for the murder of two police officers, and Sydney's wanted as an accessory." Satisfaction sparked in his eyes. "Just give me the disk and you can be in Canada before noon."

Ethan weighed his options. He could kill Braydon in a heartbeat, and maybe survive long enough to take out one or both gunmen on the dock. The guy with the rifle was another story. Ethan suspected he was the man's prime target, and if the shooter was any good at all, Ethan would be dead before Braydon's body hit the ground. Sydney's chances, either way, were close to nil.

He needed time, which the disk would buy him, and a whole lot of luck. "Give it to him, Sydney."

"What?"

"Do it."

With trembling hands, she pulled the disk from her pocket and handed it to Braydon. "You really are a bastard."

He smiled tightly as he took the disk, his eyes never leaving Ethan. "I'm sure you won't mind if I check this out." He lifted a hand, and a young man, a boy really, no more than eighteen, scurried toward them. Instead of a gun like his three companions, he carried a lap-top. Braydon handed over the disk. "This will only take a minute."

The boy squatted, then opened and started his computer.

"You know, Sydney," said Braydon, "it's really too bad the way things worked out." Evidently feeling more confident, he risked a glance in her direction. "I'd grown quite fond of you."

"Go to hell."

"Cox worked for you," Ethan said, reclaiming Braydon's attention. "Didn't he."

"In a manner of speaking," Braydon admitted. "I kept the funds flowing for his organization. Otherwise, his project would have died an unremarkable death." He paused, a smirk of a smile playing across his features once again. "Such a funny little man. I expect he's dead by now." He glanced at his watch. "Yes, I'm sure of it."

"I left him alive."

"Did you?" Braydon shrugged. "Unfortunately, he never understood the children's true value. He was only interested in the money."

Sydney laughed abruptly. "And you weren't?"

Braydon frowned. "My dear, money is simply a means to an end. A woman with your background should understand that."

"Power?" Ethan offered.

Braydon grinned, obviously pleased that Ethan had caught on. "Now that's something worth striving for, don't you think?"

Ethan suspected this asshole didn't really want to know what he thought. Men like Charles Braydon seldom did.

"And," Braydon continued, "the unique genetic makeup of Haven's children creates an extraordinary route to power."

"You plan to sell them?"

"Don't be naive. Whoever owns the genetics to create children like Callie commands more than a new science, they control biological warfare as well."

"What? Are you insane?" Sydney's anger came alive beside him, and Ethan threw out an arm to keep her from doing something stupid. Like charging the other man.

"I don't think insane's the right word," Ethan said. At least not clinically. Evil hit closer to the mark.

Braydon chuckled. "No, indeed. I'll create an entire army with Callie's immunities. A small, invisible army that will defeat its enemies without firing a single gunshot or suffering casualties of its own."

In theory, Ethan admitted, it sounded appealing, but the reality was far less noble. It involved manufacturing soldiers, engineering lives. In the end, too many would suffer. Only men like Braydon would benefit, and children like Callie would pay the price.

"And Sydney?" Ethan tempted fate and his own control with the question. "How does she fit into all this?"

Braydon shrugged. "I arranged for her employment at Braydon Labs in case you surfaced. I never trusted Cox to contain the situation with you and Ramirez, and I knew as long as the two of you were free, we were exposed."

Ethan suppressed his anger. Charles Braydon manipulated lives, played on people's emotions for his own ends, and it took every ounce of Ethan's willpower to keep from squeezing the trigger and ridding the world of Braydon's miserable presence.

"It was only later that I came to realize her benefit to my long-term ambitions," Braydon said, obviously ignorant of Ethan's tenuous control. "She comes from a good family, and it would have looked good, very liberated, to have married a woman doctor."

"Mr. Braydon?" said the kid with the computer.

Braydon looked down at the nervous teenager. "Well?"

"It's all here."

"Good. Go on and take the disk. I still have some negotiations to finish."

The boy shut down the laptop and stood, throwing Ethan an anxious glance. Then he hurried away, climbing into the van with the man who'd held the rifle.

"You're very trusting to let that disk out of your sight," Ethan said. And arrogant to let the rifle go. His and Sydney's chances had just doubled.

"My people are loyal."

"Are you sure about that?" Ethan estimated the distance to the two men, who still had their sights fixed on Sydney.

"Very sure . . ."

But Ethan was no longer listening. He was out of time. No matter what Braydon claimed, he couldn't allow them to walk away. Ethan had one chance, and if either of Braydon's men were too fast or too accurate, Sydney was dead.

He waited as the van with the kid and the disk started up, moved, braced himself . . .

Suddenly, from behind him, came a pop and a rush of air.

"Get down." Ethan lunged forward as a tree exploded near the departing van and Braydon's men pivoted toward the blast. He rammed an elbow into Braydon's jaw, then dropped and rolled, the .44 spitting bullets as the hired guns swung back around.

He winged the first man, sending his gun skittering across the wooden planks. The second got off a round, bits of wood erupting from the dock as Ethan scrambled behind a piling and pressed his back against the stout, fifteen inches of lumber. Another bullet ripped a sliver near his head.

"Shit." He grabbed Ramirez's Beretta from the holster on his ankle.

Braydon sprawled on the dock, woozy but still conscious. If he had a gun—which seemed damn likely—Ethan was in trouble. But so far, the fallen man had made no move to defend himself. Farther back near the boat, Sydney had taken cover behind a large wooden bait-and-tackle box. Ethan couldn't tell if she'd been hit, but he saw no blood. As for the kids, there was no sign of them—thankfully.

With one eye on Braydon, Ethan turned and eased to a standing position, keeping his body close to the piling. Another bullet struck the boards beneath his feet. They were trying to flush him out, and he needed to move before one of them grew impatient and went after Sydney. If Ethan could get to her, then to the boat . . .

He darted out, firing both guns, and backed away. The wounded man took the bait, letting his anger rule his head, and came from behind a stack of crates with a roar.

Ethan leapt sideways as a bullet whistled past his ear, and his shots found their target. The man doubled, gripping his torn belly where the lead had found flesh.

The second gunman, more cautious than his dying comrade, held back. Ethan kept the Beretta aimed his way and took another couple of backward steps toward the boat. "No one else has to die here," he said. "You've got the disk, just let us get on the boat and go."

Braydon staggered to his feet.

Ethan swung the .44 toward him. "Don't."

Braydon lifted his hands in a gesture of surrender, then, "Kill the son of a bitch."

The remaining gunman lunged forward, taking advantage of the split second Ethan had paid to Braydon.

Ethan sensed rather than saw it, the play he'd have made in the man's place. A belly dive to the deck with a two-fisted hold on his weapon. Only he was a split second too slow. Ethan wheeled sideways, making himself a smaller target, and put a bullet between the man's eyes.

As the final shot echoed and died, Ethan turned back to Braydon, the Beretta still trained on the fallen men. "Sydney, are you hurt?"

Behind him, he heard her climb to her feet. "No. Are they—"

"Here." Ethan handed her the Beretta and motioned toward Braydon. "Aim straight for his heart. If he so much as twitches, pull the trigger."

Sydney took the gun, and Ethan crossed to the downed men, kicking their weapons out of reach. No question about the first. From his forehead glared a third eye, a round black hole, as blank and lifeless as the other two. Ethan moved to the second man, squatted down, and checked the pulse point at his throat. Dead as well.

He turned on Braydon then, the rage he'd kept in check since climbing off the boat rising to the surface.

Braydon held up his hands, palms out. "I'm unarmed."

"I don't give a damn." Ethan rammed his gun against the man's temple. "If there weren't a bunch of kids on that boat watching every move we make, you'd be as dead as your friends."

"Looks like a draw." Though Braydon didn't sound as confident as his words.

"Not quite, because now I'm the only one with a gun." And he was damn tempted to use it.

"Ethan?" From behind him, Sydney's voice stayed his hand.

He backed away and relieved her of the Beretta. "Get some rope," he said. "And tell Danny to start up the boat."

"This isn't over," Braydon said, once she was out of earshot. "My people will be after you within the hour."

"I'm really good at this game, Braydon. Didn't Cox tell you that part?" Ethan lowered his voice, his words meant for Braydon's ears only. "So, I wouldn't sleep too soundly if I were you." He paused to let his words sink in. Cox had accused Ramirez of killing Nicky, but the assassin had claimed he didn't do it. Ethan believed him. "There's still the matter of my son's murder to settle, and the way I figure it, *you* know more about that than anyone."

Braydon forced a smile Ethan didn't buy. "I'm looking forward to the encounter."

Sydney returned with the rope. Ethan took it, again handing her the Beretta. "Watch him," he said, and slipped the .44 into his shoulder holster.

As he did, Braydon's hand darted beneath his jacket, and a flicker of sunlight caught on steel. Ethan dove in front of Sydney, closing his hand around hers, his finger finding and squeezing the Beretta's trigger.

Braydon staggered, his single shot gone wild, his eyes and mouth wide. One hand went to his chest, touched the gaping hole, and came away bloody. He looked down at it, surprised, confused, then at Ethan.

Braydon's stunned expression gave way to fury. "You . . ." He raised the gun.

Ethan fired again, claiming a father's vengeance. "That's for Nicky."

Braydon tumbled backward off the dock, the heavy splash of water breaking the sudden quiet. Ethan followed him to the edge, one arm keeping Sydney back. Braydon's body floated, rolled, spread-eagled in the troubled waters of Puget Sound.

"You knew," Sydney said, her voice sharp, accusing. "You knew he had a gun."

Ethan looked at her, unflinching. "I wasn't sure."

"But you didn't search him, didn't even look . . ." She broke off, closed her eyes briefly, and seemed to gather herself.

"Sydney?" *He killed our son.* But he couldn't say it. Not aloud.

She opened her eyes, her gaze searching his, as if she could read his thoughts. Finally she spoke, steadier now and resigned somehow. "I'm sorry, that was uncalled for. There's no way you could have known he'd have a gun."

"Yeah," he said, acknowledging her acceptance of the lie. "He took me by surprise."

Together, they boarded the boat. Danny had the engines running, and Adam threw off the ropes when Ethan took the wheel. A few minutes later, the small cove fell away behind them.

Sydney joined him on the bridge. "Where are we going?"

"Canada. I have an old Army buddy living north of Vancouver. He'll help us."

"And the children?"

"We'll find homes for them where they'll be safe." Though in truth, they would never be safe, not with their unique genetic makeup. It would make them prime targets for any fortune hunter who happened to find out about them. And the burden of that settled on Ethan's shoulders.

"This isn't over," he said. "Charles may be dead, but that disk is still out there. And those kids are still . . . what they are."

"I know." Sydney pulled another disk from her pocket.

Ethan glanced at her. "Is that what I think it is?"

"I made two copies." She slid the disk into his jacket pocket, letting her hand linger for just a second longer than necessary. "I'd planned on taking it to CNN. I thought it would help us get on with our lives if the world knew what Turner had done to these children. But now . . ."

"Now?" He held his breath, afraid to hope.

"Now I think the fewer people who know about them, the better."

He couldn't allow her to make that sacrifice, not without fully understanding the implications. "You need to think about this, Sydney. That disk is your ticket home. Without it—"

"I can't go home, Ethan. Not even with the information on that disk. Not after all this."

"You'll be giving away your life."

"Should I forfeit the children's lives instead?"

No, he should have known she'd never do that. "It won't be easy."

She met his smile. "I'm not sure 'easy' is what I want anymore." Then she turned toward Danny and Callie as they clambered up the three steps to the bridge.

"Everything settled below?" Ethan asked, as Sydney helped Callie into the copilot's seat.

"Adam's got it under control," Danny answered.

"He's real good with the little ones," Callie added.

Ethan fought a grin. Callie was one of the little ones. "You know, you guys did real good back there. You probably saved our lives."

Danny beamed.

"Whose idea was the flare?" It had supplied just the split second of distraction Ethan had needed.

"Danny's," Callie answered. "But Adam fired it."

"Not bad, but he's going to need some target practice."

"No kidding." Danny rolled his eyes. "He was aiming for the van."

Ethan laughed abruptly. He must be crazy. The freedom and lives of twenty-five kids and his ex-wife depended on him. A smart man would disappear, something Ethan knew all about. But he wasn't going anywhere. Not this time.

"You know, Syd, there are no guarantees." He looked over at her, standing with a protective arm around Callie's shoulders. "But with a little luck, we might have a chance."

"A chance," she said, "is all anyone can ask."

Read on for a sneak peek
at Patricia Lewin's new
riveting novel of suspense

OUT OF REACH

Coming soon from Ballantine Books

PROLOGUE

The new kid was finally crying.

Softly, into his pillow, while the rest of the mansion slept. But Ryan, standing outside the door, heard, and a touch of sadness squeezed his throat. This one had held out longer than most. He'd been here two days, with no sign of breaking. Ryan had to admire that.

Shifting the tray to one hand, he unlocked the door.

The crying stopped.

Some of the kids broke right away, the soft ones, sobbing nonstop for their parents. Others took longer. The street kids, the fighters, they got angry, hiding their fear with hateful words. The really strong ones, the leaders, said very little, telling Ryan and the rest to go fuck themselves without uttering a word. This boy, pretending to sleep as Ryan crossed the room, was one of those, refusing even to eat.

But his defiance had finally begun to crumble.

The tears were Ryan's cue to offer comfort. One child to another in a scary adult world. Though Ryan wasn't much of a kid anymore. Sixteen on his last birthday, he'd long outgrown any usefulness other than tending the new arrivals.

"I thought you'd be hungry," he said and set the tray on the night stand.

At first there was no response. Then the kid's survival instincts kicked in as the smell of fresh bread and hot chicken soup teased his empty stomach. He swiped a fist across his eyes, then rolled over.

"I'm not supposed to bring up food after hours." Ryan sat on the edge of the bed. "But it won't hurt this once."

The boy pushed up against the headboard. "Who are you?"

Ryan felt the squeeze of sadness again. "My name's Ryan." He hesitated, then broke one of his own rules. "What's yours?"

"You don't know?"

Usually it was better that way, easier, not knowing anything about the kids he cared for. Not even their names. "They don't tell me much around here." The truth, but something more, a common bond between them.

The kid looked doubtful, or maybe he was just figuring the downside to sharing his name. Finally he said, "Cody Sanders," then, "Where am I? And what is this place?"

"Just a house, or I guess you'd call it a mansion." The rest, that Ryan didn't know the exact location of the estate, he'd keep to himself.

Cody hesitated, then asked, "Where is he?"

"Trader?" Though Ryan knew exactly who Cody meant. "Don't worry, he's not here right now."

"What does he want from me?" As usual, once the questions started, they tumbled out one after the other and begged for answers Ryan didn't have, or wasn't willing to share.

"Look," Ryan shoved off the bed, "I better get going." It was easier than staying. "I just brought you the tray."

Cody looked at the food, obviously hungry, but made no move toward it. "Help me get out of here."

"I can't." Ryan started for the door. He could no more leave than Cody. Nor did he want to. He was safe here.

"Are you afraid of him?"

Ryan couldn't deny it. Trader was the scariest man he knew, and Ryan hadn't survived this long by defying him. "Eat your soup, it's good."

"You could help me if you wanted."

"It's just not possible, okay? There's no place to go. We're in the middle of nowhere." There were guards. And the dogs.

"So you're a prisoner, too."

That touched off a spark of anger. "This is my home." In a few days Cody Donovan would be gone, but Ryan would still be here. "I live here."

Cody studied him for a minute, as if evaluating Ryan's claim, then said, "I *will* get out of here."

Ryan didn't answer. What was the point? The kid wasn't going anywhere until Trader came for him. Sooner or later he'd figure that out for himself.

CHAPTER ONE

He was big. Two, two hundred twenty pounds at least. Visibly strong. And young. No question his body had made the journey to manhood, but the stupid grin on his face said his mind was stuck in adolescence.

He'd taken an aggressive stance, feet planted wide, arms flexed. "You're going down, bitch."

Erin backed up. "Whatever you're trying to prove, this isn't the way."

"I'm not the one with something to prove." He edged toward her.

She put more distance between them, reaching for the calm that would get her through this. Instead she found something else, something darker.

"Where do you think you're going?" he asked, a smirk in his voice and on his face.

He was right. She had little maneuvering room. Though she doubted more space would make a difference. If she ran, he'd be on her in seconds, and it would be over. Her best bet was to stand her ground.

"Look—" she started.

He made a sudden grab for her, and she barely escaped his big hands, ducking and rolling. Back on her feet, she pivoted to face him again.

"You're quicker than you look," he said.

"And you're clumsier." The reply escaped before she could check herself, and he obviously didn't like it.

"Enough of this shit." He came at her again, fast and straight this time.

Erin blocked him, her foot outside his, ankle to ankle. The heel of her right hand slamming against the underside of his chin, her left striking his bicep, then delivering a stunning blow to the side of his neck and forcing his head sideways into his shoulder.

At another time, the shock on his face might have been comical, but today, she wasn't laughing.

She seized his elbow, twisted, and he landed on his back. Hard. But she kept him rolling onto his stomach and jammed her knee against his kidney, his arm wrenched behind him, bent at the wrist. Her free hand shoved his head to the floor, and he frantically slapped the mat in surrender.

The class applauded.

Erin held him a few seconds longer, then let go, releasing his arm and backing away.

"Good job, Erin." Bill Jensen, head martial arts instructor at the CIA's Farm, stepped away from his trainees and extended a hand to the man on the floor. "Sorry, Cassidy. It's the price you pay for being the biggest s.o.b. in the class."

The younger man ignored the offered assistance and sprang to his feet. "No problem." He rotated and massaged his shoulder. "I like getting roughed up by a woman half my size."

"Life sucks sometimes," Erin said, as she retrieved her towel from a corner of the mat. "Especially in the Company." She was still edgy. More than she should be, more than would be healthy if this had been real. Maybe that was the problem. This had all been a game, and she didn't like games.

"Okay," Bill said to the others. "Do I have to interpret these results for the rest of you?"

"I want some of what she's got," said a short, compactly built young woman in front.

"They don't hand out balls to wimps, Sheila" goaded a man behind her.

She turned a brief, cold stare on him. "You should know."

The class whooped, congratulating her while offering condolences to her target.

"Okay, joke if you want," Bill said. "Just don't miss the point. Which is . . . " He looked from one student to another.

"Size don't mean shit," said Sheila. "The big ones just make more noise when they fall. And the small ones . . . ," she threw another quick glance at the man behind her, ". . . they squeak."

Another burst of approving laughter, and again Bill cut it short. "That's right. You can be strong as an ox, and this little lady," he gestured toward Erin, "will use that strength against you. Any questions?"

"I've got one," said another woman. "What happens when she comes up against someone who's just as good, *and* he outweighs her by a hundred pounds?"

Before Bill could answer, Erin said, "No matter how good you are, there is always someone better. And in this business you're bound to run into that person sooner or later."

"So what do you do? Hope for the best?"

"You get good." Erin paused, letting her eyes drift from one face to the other. They were young and brash, the best of the best in their respective fields. Or else they wouldn't be here. The CIA recruitment criteria was very tough. Every one of them was used to winning. "Then it comes down to heart, and the will to survive." Not win. Survive.

"It becomes a chess match," Bill offered. "You fight with your head as well as your—"

"More than that," Erin interrupted. "It's a question of which of you is willing to pull out all the stops." She looked pointedly at the guy she'd taken down. "And who gets meaner, quicker."

For a moment, no one spoke.

Then, "Okay, thanks, Erin," Bill said, indicating the end of the session.

Dismissed, Erin started toward the locker rooms, but before she'd gone more than a few steps, Bill fell in beside her.

"Sooner or later, one of your gorillas is going to wipe the floor with me," she said.

"Sounds familiar."

She threw him a sideways glance. "That was an accident."

"So you've always claimed."

Four years ago, as a career trainee in Bill's class, she'd

put him down in a demo similar to the one she'd just given for his current class. It never would have happened if he'd taken time to read her student file, which revealed her years of martial arts training. "So this is your way of getting even. You're *hoping* one of your recruits can take me."

"I'm not holding my breath, but it wouldn't exactly break my heart."

"Easy for you to say. You'd be watching from the sidelines."

"As you said, life in the Company sucks."

They'd reached the women's locker room, but as she reached for the handle, he said, "Wait up a minute, Erin. We need to talk."

She stopped, aware of the sudden shift in his voice. "Okay."

He hesitated, briefly. "You were a little rough on him. Cassidy, I mean. You put him down pretty hard."

"Please." She rolled her eyes. "He was looking to hurt me."

"He was playing a part."

"And I wasn't?" She folded her arms, not believing he was serious about this.

"Sometimes you play the part too well."

She frowned, surprised. He meant it. He was actually worried that she'd hurt one of his handpicked testosterone junkies. "This isn't a game, Bill, those recruits—"

"This isn't about them, it's about you."

"What are you talking about? The only reason I do this is to give them a taste of what they're up against. If—"

"Look," he interrupted. "I know you're not crazy about working in the States. You're angry, and it shows. Hell, Cassidy really pissed you off out there."

"Give me a break. You know better than that."

"I'm worried about you," he said. "You don't belong at Georgetown babysitting a bunch of foreign students."

It was a guess, but he wasn't that far off. "What do

you want from me, Bill? You want me to play nice with your students?"

"Either go back overseas, or—"

"You know that's not an option."

"Then get your anger under control. Talk to someone, see a counselor or a—"

"Or what? A shrink?"

He rubbed a hand down his face, looking distinctly uncomfortable. "All I'm saying, Erin, is—"

"I know exactly what you're saying." She stepped forward, into his space. He was the one making her angry. "And you're out of line. I come here for one reason only, to show those recruits just how nasty the real world can get. So if you want someone to coddle them, get yourself another demo-queen."

She spun around, grabbed the locker room door and slammed it open. Inside, she collapsed against the lockers, the adrenaline pumping through her system in angry waves. Balling her fists, she barely kept herself from pounding the cold metal behind her.

Damn it. Damn him.

Except for her supervisor, Bill was the only one of her colleagues who knew about Janie and Claire. Now, he was using it against her. He wanted her to see a shrink, for God's sake. There was no way. That was her sister Claire's territory, and Erin wasn't about to trespass.

Since age twelve, when Erin had watched the adults in her life flounder in the wake of Claire's disappearance, she'd sworn she would never be a victim. No one would ever have that power over her. And she'd trained all her life to keep that promise.

Of course, Bill was right. She was miserable at Georgetown.

She'd joined the CIA because it fit her, because working undercover suited her temperament and her training, and because no one would expect that of Claire Baker's big sister.

Then, a year ago fate had twisted her life.

Her mother's illness had been sudden and unexpected. Cancer. During a routine cleaning, Elizabeth Baker's dentist had found a spot in her mouth and suggested she have it checked out. Six months later, after two rounds of radiation and another of chemotherapy, she was dead.

Erin blamed the doctors and their radical treatment of a woman who'd felt fine until they'd started treating her. She also blamed her mother for her three-pack-a-day habit and the vodka that had gotten her through the nights. And Erin had blamed herself. While her mother had been dying, she'd been overseas running agents for the U.S. Government, but more to the point, if not for her, Elizabeth never would have started with the cigarettes and the alcohol to begin with.

Erin sighed, the mistakes of her past a burden she couldn't ignore any more than she could walk away from the responsibilities of her present.

Standing, she headed for the showers, stripping off the Farm-issued sweats as she went.

She'd returned to the States for the funeral and never left again. With her mother gone, there was Janie to care for. And Claire. Always Claire.

Now Erin was stuck.

The CIA didn't know what to do with her, so they'd placed her at Georgetown while they tried to figure it out. She taught Ethics and International Relations to twenty-year-olds, while keeping her eyes open for potentially violent anti-American sentiments among the student population. And she worked the embassy circuit, attending parties two or three times a week.

Meanwhile, her bosses seemed to have forgotten her.

So, yeah, she was angry. But, as she'd told Cassidy, sometimes life sucked.

* * *

Thirty minutes later, Erin pulled into her driveway.

It was a small, two-story house in Arlington, one of the suburban neighborhoods servicing the D.C. area. She'd never pictured herself as a home owner, but with her mother's death, everything in her life had changed. Even this. Janie needed a place to be a child, a family area where she could grow up.

As Erin pushed through the back door, Janie looked up from the kitchen table and grinned. "Come see what I made, Aunt Erin."

Erin's mood lifted. No matter how frustrated she'd become with her job, she loved having this little girl in her life. Closing the door, she went to see Janie's latest creation.

"You like it?" Janie asked, eyes wide. "It's for Mommy. I want her to know what my new school looks like."

"It's great."

Janie's talent was unmistakable. Even Erin, who had no experience with children, could see the child had a special gift. She'd used colored pencils to draw her school, an older, three-story brick monstrosity, flag in front, children's drawings in the window. On the sidewalk in front of the building walked a little girl with curly blond hair, two women at her side.

"It's the first day of school," Janie explained. "Remember? When you went with us?"

"I do." Janie's eye for detail translated into a realism Erin found difficult to believe came from seven-year-old hands.

Just then, Marta entered the kitchen.

"Erin likes my drawing, Marta." Janie had returned to her colored pencils, adding flowers along the edge of the building.

"Of course she does, dear," Marta said. "Are you done drawing?"

"Almost," Janie said, picking up a pencil and adding touches of yellow to the trees.

"Well then," Marta said, "put it away. You need to get cleaned up before going out."

"O . . . kay." The word came out in two long syllables as Janie carefully put away her pencils and slid her drawing into her pad. Then she scurried out of the room, bouncing up the stairs to her bedroom.

Erin smiled at the other woman. "You're so good with her."

"And you're not?"

Erin shrugged. "Not like you."

"You are her mother's sister. Her blood. You give her time, and you give her love. It is all she needs."

"You make it sound so easy."

"Easy? No. Simple? Yes."

Erin didn't know how to answer that, what to say. For ten months she'd been worried that she wasn't enough for Janie, that she needed someone else. A real mother. And here Marta was telling her none of that mattered.

Erin pushed off the stool, deciding it was best to leave this conversation while she could. Then she spotted the newspaper on the counter, and the headline stopped her.

48 HOURS AND COUNTING. CODY SANDERS STILL MISSING. POLICE AND FBI NOT GIVING UP.

A wave of nausea rolled through her. She'd heard those exact words herself, standing next to her mother, thirteen years ago. "We're not giving up, Mrs. Baker."

But of course, they'd had to. Eventually.

As for this little boy, this Cody Sanders . . . Forty-eight hours. Too long. By now there was a good chance the boy was dead.

"Why do you torture yourself?" Marta asked.

Erin looked up, saw the concern on Marta's face. "Should I avoid the news because it's unpleasant?"

Marta snorted. "You're not kidding anyone, Erin. It's

time to stop blaming yourself for what happened to Claire."

"Who should I blame then? I was supposed to be watching her." Erin wrapped her arms around her waist.

"You were twelve years old. A child."

"Old enough—"

"No." Marta moved from behind the counter, planting two round fists on her hips. "Now you listen to me, Erin Elizabeth. I loved your mother dearly. She was more of a sister to me than my own. But I never, *never*, agreed with how she left you to watch Claire while she worked."

"She didn't have a choice."

"There are always choices." Marta tossed her hands into the air. "Your mother just refused to consider hers. And watching the two of you afterwards, the way you blamed yourself and each other . . . Well, it hurt my heart."

"It hurt all of us." Erin went cold inside, rigid. "Claire most of all."

For a moment Marta seemed at a loss for words. When she finally spoke, she kept her voice low. "It's over now. Done. The monster who took your sister is in jail."

"And what about Claire?"

"Claire is exactly where she needs to be. You have seen to that. And someday, she will be well. You've done what you can."

Erin knew she couldn't win this argument. So she lied. "You're right. I'm sorry. And I'll try to remember that."

Marta eyed her, possibly detecting the truth. But she evidently decided to let it go. "Okay, then. Now go get ready before Janie goes crazy waiting for her pizza."

Erin headed upstairs. Despite what Marta said, Erin knew she'd been at fault. She'd lost Claire that summer day thirteen years ago. And they'd all been paying for that mistake every since.